anna's journey

gerald miller

WORD ASSOCIATION PUBLISHERS
www.wordassociation.com
1.800.827.7903

ISBN: 978-1-63385-180-1
Library of Congress Control Number: 2016919481

Published by
Word Association Publishers
205 Fifth Avenue
Tarentum, Pennsylvania 15084

www.wordassociation.com
1.800.827.7903

On this journey through life,
one person's castle is another's prison.

Best Wish Leon!

Gerald Miller

chapter ....
.... one

Beams of morning sunlight crept into the bedroom through the cracks in the curtain. Once the intrusion was complete, the piercing rays of light bounced off the glass of the many photographs residing on Anna's walls. The pictures almost seemed to come to life as the sun lit them up on queue. Shadows danced around the room, gently revealing the remnants of elegance. Pieces of heavy, solid wood furniture with bear claw legs sat perfectly positioned on the large antique area rugs. Handcrafted woodwork done in oak complemented the beautiful stucco designs on the towering ceiling. The house was becoming more and more like a museum as the years passed by.

Pain had long since become a regular caller, and this day would be no different. Anna cussed under her breath as she forced herself out of bed to face another day. It was difficult for her to believe that eighty-four years had gone by. Even though celebrating birthdays had long since become a thing of the past, Father Time was taking his toll. Once she snatched her housecoat from the brass hook, located on the inside of the closet door, she made her way downstairs to brew a cup of tea. She rested her slender, frail fingers on the thick wood banister as she slowly made her way down the stairwell. She reached up to straighten a picture of her deceased mother and nearly lost her footing. Grabbing onto the railing with both hands saved her from losing her balance. An almost sinister smile found her lips when saying to herself aloud, "It's not time yet, Anna."

As the old woman neared the bottom of the steps, the ringing of the doorbell greeted her. Her first reaction was to ignore it; after all, she had not had her morning tea yet. She soon realized it was not an option because of the persistence of the person ringing the buzzer. She made a halfhearted attempt at fixing her flowing silver hair as she clutched the flannel housecoat close to her body while peeking out the peephole. The expression on her face softened when she saw that her unexpected caller was the boy who lived down the street. Robby, as his friends like to call him, was not only the newspaper delivery boy, but he also raked leaves and took on any other chores that might need done. Anna saw a great deal of promise in the boy's entrepreneurial attitude, considering he was only ten years old. The old woman's heart smiled each time she would pay him for some chore that needed done. A sparkle would find his eyes when she placed a couple of crisp dollar bills in the palm of his hand.

"Well, Robert, what brings you to my door this fine fall morning?" Anna said.

He looked down at the ground before saying, "I'm sorry to bother you, Miss Wilson, but it's time for me to collect for the newspaper again."

Anna gave him a stern look, declaring, "Young man, how many times do I have to tell to you, never apologize for asking for your due. After all, you must be rewarded for the fine job you do delivering my newspaper every day."

The old woman paid Robert and gave him two shiny quarters as a tip, but noticed he was in no hurry to scurry off. She hesitated in the doorway as he stared at his shoes, shuffling several fallen leaves back and forth in nervous anticipation. After what must have seemed like a great deal of time to the youngster, Anna finally made her inquiry.

"Is there something on your mind, Robert?"

He took his time replying, and finally said, "Miss Wilson, I was just wondering if you have any extra chores that need to be done around the house? I'd be willing to do anything to help out … errands that need run, yard work, and such."

Once he got started, he spoke so fast, she could not keep up. Laughing, she said, "Slow down, Robert. I think I understand what you're trying to say. You'd like to earn some extra money, right?"

"Yes, ma'am," he said, excitedly. "Halloween is coming up in a few weeks, and there is a really cool costume at the department store I want to buy. My mother said I could get it if I could earn half the money myself."

"Well, young man, it just happens that I have a project to tackle in my basement storage area, but it's going to be a great deal of hard work," Anna said.

"I promise I'll work real hard!"

"There are two conditions," Anna said. "First, you must get your mother's permission, and second, you must give me your word that your studies at school will not suffer."

"Okay, Miss Wilson, thanks! You won't be sorry!"

"Now, don't forget, your homework must be done every night, whether you're working or not."

"Yes, Miss Wilson!" Robby said as he raced off the porch.

Anna watched the boy as he ran down the street and resumed his newspaper route. Her heart smiled because she was able to bring such excitement to Robert's life. There was no doubt in her mind that he was one of the good ones. Having taught English at Highland Park Elementary School for twenty-five years and five years at Erie Middle School, she prided herself on the ability to judge a young child's character.

A veil of loneliness fell over Anna as she closed the front door. As she entered the sitting room, she paused for a moment to look at the photographs hanging on the walls. The picture of her younger brother Nathan immediately caught her eye. She recalled how the two of them would play school when they were children: Anna as the teacher and Nathan as the student. She missed those days.

Letting her memories slip away again, Anna went into to the kitchen to make a pot of tea. The morning was her favorite part of the day. Like the sunrise, it signified the dawn of a new day.

She placed the pot of freshly brewed tea on an antique serving tray and carried it into the sitting room, where she placed it on the table in front of the sofa. The only noise in the room was the occasional tapping of the spoon against the sides of the delicate rose-colored cup. Anna felt restless this morning, and she longed to be at peace. Oftentimes, she felt as though there was some sort of strange movie playing repeatedly in her head. Unfortunately, the feature film showed the trials and tribulations of those closest to her.

Nathan was a bright light in Anna's life when he was born. She was almost seven years old when her mother brought him home from the hospital. Little Nathan's arrival to the house far exceeded any Christmas morning that Anna had experienced. The bright clean blankets that cuddled him symbolized purity, and the tiny man symbolized goodness. She eagerly took on any responsibilities concerning his care. She adored Nathan as a youngster, but he began getting into trouble at school and showing outward signs of cruelty to others. Despite how much she loved and adored him, she couldn't help but feel that something terrible was going to happen. No one believed Anna, though, about the changes in Nathan, not her parents or her sister, Elizabeth, but Anna knew that something bad was coming.

It was nearly two months after Nathan's thirteenth birthday that Anna's worst fear became a reality. On that fateful day, the family attended early morning mass at Saint Matthew's Church, several miles away. After the family returned home and everyone changed their clothes and had brunch, Nathan went outside to play with some of the neighborhood children. Anna spent a few hours escaping in the pages of one of her favorite novels, and Elizabeth was in her bed thumbing through a stack of glamour magazines. Her mother, Ruth, fired up the oven to do her Sunday baking as her father, John, worked on one of his projects out back in the garage. By all appearances, it was a Sunday like any other, but that all changed when Nathan returned home.

When Anna took a break from reading her book to go downstairs to make a snack, she overheard a commotion from the top of the stairs. Apparently, her mother had heard Nathan come in the front door and intercepted him as he tried to go up the stairs. Frightened by his appearance, she screamed, "Oh my God, Nathan, what happened to you?"

Nathan shot back angrily, "Nothing happened!"

Refusing to back down, Ruth Wilson said, "Don't tell me nothing! Your face and arms are all scratched up!" She continued to press him. "Who did this to you?"

Nathan ignored his mother's request for an explanation about his condition.

As soon as Anna's mother saw her standing at the top of the stairs, she motioned toward the back of the house and frantically ordered, "Go out back and tell your father I need him right away!"

Anna immediately hurried down the steps and ran out to the garage. She could not help but look at Nathan as she hurried by him. Seeing her younger brother's demeanor as he stood there, dirty and scratched, gave her cause for concern. What bothered her was the fact that he displayed no emotion whatsoever.

John Wilson heard her approaching and said, "What's wrong?"

"Something has happened to Nathan!" she said. "Mother needs you right away!"

As Anna's father raced into the house, she followed him, her mind racing. The fact that Nathan refused to explain what happened when confronted by her mother troubled her the most. Instead of joining the others amidst all the confusion, though, she decided to remain out of sight.

"Nathan, tell your mother and I who did this to you right now."

Refusing to divulge much information, Nathan said, "It was an accident."

In a stern voice, his father declared, "Don't tell me it was just an accident! Was it that Kelly boy who lives down the street?"

Sticking to his original story, Nathan replied, "No. I told you it was an accident, and nobody else was there."

His mother chimed in, demanding an explanation. "Explain to us exactly how you managed to get so dirty, with scratch marks on your face and arms, accidently."

Appearing to give in to her demands, Nathan said, "Okay, I was walking along the tree line and tripped over a dead branch and into a thick patch of briar bushes. The sharp thorns scratched me as I tried to get away from them. When I was finally able to break free, I lost my footing and fell into the dirt."

Anna carefully inched her way nearer to the archway joining the kitchen and dining area when her parent's voices suddenly lowered. For what seemed to be a long time, they mumbled to one another about how to handle the situation. She knew it was wrong to eavesdrop, but she was convinced that she had no choice in the matter at this point. Once the sounds of their voices were distinguishable, she slowly backed further into the kitchen. The interaction resumed and, of course, her father took the lead.

"How many times have you been told not to play near the woods?"

Cowering to his father's authority, Nathan said, "Yes, sir, it won't happen again."

Thinking he had the situation under control, his father said, "Well, maybe the scratches you picked up will serve as a reminder of how foolish you've been." He went on to add, "One more thing, Nathan; you're not to leave our property for the next two weeks except for school and church activities."

The youngster objected by saying, "That's not fair!"

With fire in his voice, his father replied, "Not only is it fair, young man, I think it's lenient considering the danger you placed yourself in! Now you'll go upstairs with your mother so she can clean up the wounds you've incurred!"

Anna quickly made herself busy in the kitchen so her father would not discover that she had been eavesdropping. He rushed by her without a word as he stormed out the back door to the garage. Young Anna sensed that her father was much more troubled over the incident than he was letting on. She thought that he might not totally believe Nathan's tale of having an accident. Curiosity got the better of her, so she decided that since it was such a fine day, she would take a walk to the park and investigate for herself. After snatching a book from the shelf, she went to the bottom of the stairs and announced that she was embarking on a walk before dinner. The chances that her preoccupied mother heard her plans to go to the park were fifty-fifty, at best, but she did the right thing by mentioning it to her mother. The park was a common gathering place for young people. Other than the occasional underage drinking, there was little crime to speak of in the neighborhood. Their tightly knit community was off the beaten path, which was the way the local residents preferred it.

The afternoon sun shone brightly in the sky as a light breeze drifted over the trees from the south. Beautiful beds of mums proudly exhibited their various splashes of colors under the protection of towering oak trees. The elms, maples, and oaks were in the midst of putting on their own panoramic show as the leaves changed from green to different shades of red and yellow. Anna loved the outdoors and gave the inhabitants of nature the respect they deserved. As she walked toward the location where the playground and picnic area were located, it became obvious that she was the only person there. Off in the distance there was a man with what appeared to be his young son, tossing a baseball, and in the other direction, there were two eager Cocker Spaniels jockeying for position as their female master tossed a bright green Frisbee far into the field. As the earlier events raced through her mind, she glanced down at the book and burst out laughing when she realized it was one of the books from her Nancy Drew Collection.

Anna casually walked over to the tree line, quickly surveying the areas in both directions. She hoped to discover the exact scene her brother had described to her parents. To her dismay, there were no briar bushes or thorny shrubs anywhere near the edge of the trees. This troubling fact stimulated her interest further, prompting her to walk along the tree line for closer investigation. After walking close to three hundred feet in one direction, she turned around and made her way back to the original starting point. On the journey back, she began to think herself silly for the manner in which she was handling the entire affair. The irony of choosing a book by Nancy Drew was steadily sinking in. After all, who was she to be secretly checking the validity of Nathan's story?

As Anna neared the bench on the return walk, the thought crossed her mind that it would be best just to pick up the book, put the strange thoughts out of her mind, and walk back home. After all, what would she do if she discovered he was not telling the truth? Instead of wrapping up her fact-finding expedition, she decided to finish inspecting the area in the other direction. The first hundred feet or so were undisturbed, but then she spotted something very unusual. An area several feet wide showed freshly made slide marks from about five or six feet into the grass, all the way to the tree line. The first thing that really caught her attention was the weeds in that particular area were very low. There was not a single shrub, let alone a jagger bush, anywhere in sight. She searched the details in her mind about what Nathan had reported to her parents. Convinced that she had all the details straight in her head, she began to check out the area a little closer.

After walking along the tree line for about two hundred feet, Anna concluded there were no other areas that had been recently disturbed. As she slowly made her way back to the location where the grass and mud had been freshly disturbed, she began to entertain various scenarios about what had really happened. Nathan was more than capable of distorting the truth. What puzzled her were the torn clothes and the scratches on his face and arms, which made no sense. She went close to the tree line where the disturbances in the underbrush were. Initially, she noticed a smudged print about the same size as Nathans. Then she suddenly saw something else, which immediately caught her attention. There appeared to be an additional set of smaller footprints in the soft soil. Her mind went blank as she quickly backed away from the edge of the towering oaks.

Anna decided to walk back to the nearby bench to sort out what she had just seen. Just as she turned to make her way to the park bench, she noticed something yellow lying on the ground. When reaching down to grab it, she felt an unexplainable chill come over her. After clearing away the fresh dirt, it became obvious the she was holding a yellow butterfly-shaped barrette containing a clump of torn blond hair. There was a small piece of torn pink material hanging from a broken branch. In the proximity of the trees, the grass was disturbed in a way that suggested that there had been some sort of struggle.

Once back at the bench, young Anna plopped down next to the Nancy Drew book to make some sense of the bizarre information she had just uncovered. Question after question paraded through her mind as to what really occurred here just hours earlier. A small part of her was starting to wish that she had not given in to her intuitive nature. More questions about what Nathan was capable of flashed through her mind. She had long ago known of the presence of dark energies inside Nathan, but did not know the extent of the evil that lurked within him.

She remained sitting on the bench for nearly an hour. While closing her eyes, a feeling of numbness settled over her like a dense emotional fog. The young woman could not seem to quiet the overwhelming thoughts of horror racing through her head. After slowly removing the small yellow barrette, along with the torn piece of fabric, from her pocket, she placed them between her index finger and thumb, gently rubbing them together. The movement of the sun reminded her that almost two hours had gone by since she came to the park. It was soon going to be time for dinner, and she definitely did not want to be late. After stuffing the barrette and piece of torn material into her pocket, she picked up the Nancy Drew book and started walking home.

≈ℰ ≈ℰ

When Anna arrived home, her mother was coming out of the kitchen carrying a stack of clean plates. "Where have you been, young lady?" she asked.

Anna casually responded by saying, "I went over the park to read awhile."

Her mother snapped back, "You should have told me where you were going."

Anna said, "When you were upstairs with Nathan, I told you I was leaving."

Ruth Wilson's focus immediately shifted to Nathan's situation. "Oh, poor Nathan was nearly killed, and I truly pray those scratches don't leave any scars on his face. He's such a handsome young man."

Wanting more information about what Nathan said, Anna inquired, "Mother, what *exactly* happened to him?"

"Anna, it was terrible!" her mother said. "Apparently, when your brother was in the park, he tripped over a dead tree branch. Your father and I told him to be careful, but you know how adventuresome that boy can be."

Anna asked, "How did he manage to get all scratched up?"

Her mother replied, "When the poor thing lost his footing, he got all tangled up in a patch of briar bushes. The nasty plants scratched him up terribly when he tried to free himself. I have a good mind to report the incident to the Parks Department. They should really do a better job at keeping that area safe."

Not letting on what she knew, Anna said, "I agree, Mother, the park should be safer."

Ruth Wilson, wanting to shield her son from any further reminders of the experience, said, "Try not to bring it up while we're eating dinner. Nathan has been through enough today. Now, Anna, I need you to wash your hands and help me finish putting dinner on the table."

Anna's mind was racing, but she managed to remain silent while assisting her mother in the kitchen. Elizabeth made a casual entrance into the dining area and, as usual, offered no help. Anna had long ago gotten used to her behavior and paid it no mind. Elizabeth made no secret of the fact that her goal was to marry well to ensure a comfortable future. When they would have those rare girl talks, Elizabeth would always manage to mention that each of them had a healthy inheritance coming someday, but she was not going to take any chances. There was no question in Anna's mind when it came to her vocation. She would be a molder of young minds. Teaching had been a dream for as long as she could remember, and that dream was coming closer to realization every day. Even though her father was restricting her choice of colleges to the Pittsburgh area, she was determined to take advantage of the resources permitted her.

The aroma of steaming hot vegetables, sweet browned dinner rolls, and freshly prepared roast beef danced in the air as the Wilson family settled in for the evening meal. As everyone sat down to say grace, it was obvious to Anna that the festive appearance of the meal was not going to match the atmosphere of dinner. She could sense the varying degrees of tension radiating from everyone seated at the table. Though she was no stranger to the usual family dynamics, what she was feeling this night was somehow different. Her father was very preoccupied, and Anna knew that he was troubled over the situation with Nathan. He was never talkative during dinner, but he always directed some polite conversation to each member of the family. Her mother tried her hardest to lighten the mood with only limited success. If Elizabeth felt the tension in the air, it did not seem to have an effect on her. Anna was almost relieved when the deafening silence turned into an outbreak of bickering between her siblings.

"Pass me the rolls, Elizabeth," Nathan said rather forcefully.

Angered by his tone, Elizabeth barked back, "Say please, you little toad!"

Reaching out to his mother for assistance, Nathan said, "Mother, tell this cow to pass me the dinner rolls."

Frustrated by their behavior, she snapped, "Now that's quite enough from the both of you. We don't call each other names, especially at the dinner table!"

Anna looked on in amazement, not because Nathan and Elizabeth were arguing, but because her father never uttered a single word. In fact, he never even took his eyes off his plate. He displayed no outward emotion as he finished the meal before him.

Production at the family factory was stronger than ever, ruling out the possibility of it being the problem. After dinner was over, Anna assisted her mother with clearing the table while Nathan and Elizabeth took pot shots at each other as they walked up the stairs. After finishing in the dining room, they went into the kitchen to continue cleaning up. Anna went way out on a limb by bringing up the subject of leaving home to attend college.

"Mother, why can't I go away to school?" Anna asked.

Trying not to engage in a conversation about the subject, her mother replied, "Your father and I feel it's best for you to attend college here in Pittsburgh."

Demonstrating her determination, Anna came back with, "It's nineteen thirty three, and a lot of girls my age are going away to college, and some of them don't even have scholarships."

Her mother's protective side came out, and she said, "I'm sure that's true, but, unfortunately, a lot of those young girls will fall victim to the bad things of this world." She continued, "When I went to school, I stayed at home with your grandparents, and I've had a very fulfilling life. Besides, you'll be able to focus more on your studies while living here."

Trying a different approach, Anna said, "Mother, sometimes I feel as though life is passing me by; there are so many things I want to see and learn in the world."

Her mother refused to budge on the matter, saying, "Don't worry, young lady, there will be time enough to explore the world once you've completed college."

Realizing the conversation was an exercise in futility; Anna put an end to her inquiries and finished her chores in the kitchen. When she was finished, she decided to go up to her bedroom for some quiet time and to reflect on the events of the day. As she walked by the sitting room, where her father was sipping on his evening glass of bourbon and enjoying a fine cigar, she paused to tell him she was going upstairs. He removed the billowing cigar from his lips and placed the amber colored beverage on the coaster resting on the table. The thought entered her mind to pour out the discoveries she had made earlier in the day concerning Nathan, but instead, she decided to hold off for a more opportune time. Suddenly, she felt very compelled to make sure that her father knew that she loved him very much. Outward displays of affection were not in abundance in their home.

Anna bent down and kissed her father on the cheek, whispering, "I love you, Father."

He looked up at her with a surprised look on his face. It was as though he wanted to ask her what was wrong. Of course, he thought better of it, and rebounded with the appropriate response. "I love you, too, Annie."

The fact that her father called her Annie when telling her he loved her nearly knocked her over. Anna's father had not referred to her as Annie since she was nine years old. Trying not to let on how taken aback she was by her father's behavior, she decided to retreat upstairs to the emotional safety of a good book. As she slowly climbed the stairs, the sound of the front door bell stopped her in her tracks. She could see her father rise up from his chair and begin walking toward the door. Her mother placed the dishtowel on the kitchen counter and headed for the front of the house. When she turned her attention to the top of the stairs, she spotted Elizabeth standing there. Nathan was the only member of the family who had not appeared to see what was going on. Even though she had no idea who was standing on the other side of the door, she knew it was going to be darkness calling.

Anna recognized the tall, slender man as Mr. Johnson. He and his family lived several streets down. By all outward appearances, they seemed to be friendly people. On occasion, she would cross paths with him, his wife, and young daughter while walking in the park. Anna could tell right away that he was not stopping by to demonstrate his social graces. She could tell by his body language that something was terribly wrong. He reached out to hand her father some papers from a large stack he clutched under his arm and nervously dropped them to the floor. When Anna rushed down to assist them in picking up the scattered papers, she overheard him tell her father that his daughter had disappeared earlier that day in the park. Every breath of air seemed to leave her body when she viewed the photograph of the missing young girl in the flyer. As she leaned against the wall, the image of the smiling young girl of nine, with her beautiful blond hair, became a permanent part of her memory.

Mr. Johnson's eyes were red and swollen, and he had a look of desperation on his face. His head hung low as the tears began to roll down his cheeks. The upset man proceeded to explain the situation to Anna's father.

"Earlier today," Mr. Johnson said, "my wife and I went out for a few hours for lunch and a little shopping. We left Carolyn at the house with the same sitter we always use. The sitter permitted her to go over to the park to ride her bicycle. Since she turned nine, we let her have a little more freedom! When we returned home and she still was not back, I went over to the park and searched every inch of it. The second I got back to the house, I called the police to report my daughter's disappearance. My wife is hysterical, and I was not about to sit around waiting for the authorities. I'm so scared; Carolyn is all we have!"

Anna knew all too well that her father was not the kind of man to lose control in any situation, but it was obvious that this news had shaken him. After several long moments hung in the air, her father offered to help find the missing girl.

"What can we do to help?" her father asked.

Visibly nervous, Mr. Johnson said, "Please pass these flyers along to anyone you come in contact with, and ask your children if they have seen her."

Anna's father said, "Of course we will, but there must be more I can do."

Touched by his concern, Mr. Johnson said, "If you can spare some time to join the men searching around the park, it would be greatly appreciated."

Anna's father quickly snatched his coat while Anna finished picking up the flyers that had fallen on the floor. As her father hurried out the door, he paused and instructed Anna to show the missing girl's picture to Elizabeth and Nathan. She immediately took the picture of young Carolyn up the stairs and showed it to Elizabeth first, because she was standing at the top of the landing. She glanced down at the picture and slowly nodded her head. Anna then knocked on Nathan's bedroom door. Initially, there was no response, but when she tapped on the door again, he answered.

"What?" Nathan asked.

Frustrated, Anna said, "Nathan, I need you to open the door so you can look at this photograph."

Still refusing to open the door, he answered, "What photograph?"

Her irritation was growing, and she yelled, "Open this door now or I'll let father handle it!"

Not wanting to press his luck, Nathan gave in, and said, "Okay, let me see the stupid thing."

Anna inquired, "Did you see this girl while you were over at the park today? Her father was just here passing out these flyers because she is missing. Father just left for the park to join in the search."

Nathan snatched the picture of Carolyn from Anna's hand and briefly looked it over before tossing it back at her. She could not help but steal a closer look at the scratches on his face and arms. Once she had seen the injuries up close, she knew for sure the barbs of a briar bush did not cause them.

He snapped at her. "No! I did not see her or anybody else while I was at the park today! Now leave me alone for the rest of the night!"

The cold stare Nathan directed her way as he closed his bedroom door sent chills down her spine. As their eyes met, Anna had the distinct feeling that he knew she had discovered what he had done. It was like the darkness she had sensed living inside him had finally given birth to the monster she saw before her. No longer could she give him the benefit of the doubt by thinking of him as a spoiled boy. It was painfully clear that the realm of darkness had embraced him as its son, and he had consummated the evil adoption earlier that day by taking Carolyn's life. Even though there was no doubt in her mind concerning his guilt, she was not quite sure what she was going to do with the evidence she uncovered earlier in the day. She could no longer tolerate the restrictive feeling any longer.

As Anna was buttoning her coat to leave, her mother asked her where she was going.

In a determined voice, she said, "Mother, I have to go over there to see what's going on."

"Anna, it's getting late, and I don't think your father would approve," her mother cautioned.

Walking out the door, Anna said, "Sorry, Mother, but I'm going!"

Walking toward the cluster of lights near the wooded area gave Anna a feeling of exhilaration. She could not be sure if it was the cold night air or her assertiveness with her mother. Whatever the reason, she embraced the feeling it generated.

The closer Anna got to the dozen or so people holding flashlights, the better her view of the overall scene became. She recognized many of the people as neighbors, and several were members of her church. The courage she so easily drew upon with her mother faltered for a moment when she saw her father standing next to a police rescue vehicle. It was too late to turn back because she had already gone beyond the point of no return. If her father saw fit to punish her, she would gladly accept it. She could not believe her eyes when she saw the volunteers standing around in the very spot where she saw the suspicious skid marks on the grass earlier that day. The spot where Anna discovered the evidence had well-meaning searchers trampling over it. She could feel the excitement intensify when a black and white patrol cruiser pulled in next to the playground. The officers immediately began to usher the volunteers away from the area. Some of the men complied without question, while others hesitated and demanded an explanation. Eventually, the members of the search party backed away from the area without incident.

Anna spotted an official vehicle driving up the park access road. A pair of detectives wearing suits exited the car and made their way to the edge of the forested area, where spotlights lit up the tree line and into the park. Words of speculation passed between the lead detective and the uniformed officers on the scene. While the detectives began scouring the surrounding area for clues concerning Carolyn's disappearance, the other two police officers started pounding stakes in the ground and stretching crime scene tape to enclose the area. Anna was still under the impression they had no idea what had happened to the little girl. She was startled by the sudden touch of her father's hand on her back.

"Anna, what are you doing here?" he asked in a stern but low voice.

She jerked back. "Father, you nearly scared me to death!"

"Young lady, that doesn't answer my question," he said.

With her back against the wall, she had no choice but to share her findings with her father.

"I found something earlier that I think you should see," she said.

As Anna was getting ready to show her father what she believed was evidence of the young girl's demise, they quickly ended their conversation when they heard a commotion among the group of people standing around the scene. What they saw next dashed any hope of Carolyn's safe return. One of the men exited the forest carrying a black body bag containing what proved to be the little girl's body. They had found it necessary to fold the ends to compensate for her size. Sadness fell over everyone much like the mist that gently rested just above the trees. One of the detectives notified the coroner's office that a body was on its way. Onlookers and volunteers alike quietly froze in their tracks as the men from the coroner's office unloaded a gurney from the back of the vehicle. Earlier in the day, Anna suspected that there had been foul play, but nothing could have prepared her for the harsh reality of what was unfolding.

Terrible thoughts about Carolyn's last moments alive pulsated through her brain. Mere minutes before her life-smothering ordeal, the nine-year-old girl rode her bicycle through the park, enjoying carefree reflections about her childhood friends. Much like any child her age, she savored the special freedom of a Sunday afternoon with the knowledge that she would be returning to school on Monday morning. Inspired by the childhood fantasies and the gentle love of her parents, she felt secure in the safety of her protected world. Desperation and fear were the young girl's only companions as she screamed and clawed to hang on to her young life. Begging and pleading with her violator, she looked at him with horror in her eyes, wondering what she had done to deserve his wrath. Realizing she was completely alone, except for her deranged attacker, stripped her of any remaining hope of escaping death.

Anna desperately wanted to believe that the author of this tragedy was someone other than Nathan, but she knew that was not the case. The soft touch of her father's hands against her shoulders startled her. Even though it was such a dire situation, she could not help but feel a moment of emotional warmth with her father. When Anna began to weep, her father pulled her close to him and held her firmly in his arms. For a brief moment, time stood still. Nothing mattered but the love of a father for his daughter during her emotional time of need.

With tears rolling down her cheeks, Anna asked, "How could this have happened?"

Her father replied, "Only heaven knows the answer to that question."

Picking up where she left off before all the commotion, Anna said. "Father, I found something over by those trees earlier today."

Confused, her father inquired, "What are you talking about, Annie?"

She put her hand in her pocket and carefully removed the items she found. When Anna placed the yellow barrette and the piece of torn material in the palm of her father's hand, he sent a puzzled look her way. Before uttering a single word, he studied the items very carefully, placing special emphasis on the lock of blond hair lodged in the barrette.

"What are these Annie?" he asked.

"After the situation with Nathan today, I came here to read a book," she said. "To tell the truth, I was trying to find a little quiet time. When I got to the park, I walked along the edge of the trees, thinking I might come across the location where Nathan received his injuries. Not able to find the area he described, I made my way back to the park bench. As I walked by the trees, the items in your hand caught my attention, and I picked them up."

"What possessed you to pick them up, Anna?" he asked, somewhat shocked.

Anna hesitated, but said, "Father, I just had a strange feeling that they were significant.

"Annie, you know we have to turn these items over to the authorities," he explained. "They very well could be evidence in the Carolyn Johnson murder."

Anna's father lovingly placed his arm around her as they walked toward the outer edge of the yellow crime scene tape. While Anna's father tried to get the detective's attention, she saw the uniformed officers telling the volunteers to go back home. As the flash of a camera lit up the dark night, Anna heard a woman's heart wrenching screams in the background. When she looked in the direction of the coroner's vehicle, she saw Mr. and Mrs. Johnson standing next to the black body bag. Mr. Johnson embraced his emotionally distraught wife as she shrieked in terror. All the chattering of the onlookers suddenly came to a halt. The sound of the distraught mother screaming answered any questions as to who was lying lifeless in the body bag.

Mr. Wilson was finally able to get the attention of one of the detectives. He politely asked, "Detective, can I talk to you for a moment, please?"

Focused on the unfolding situation, the detective said, "Sir, if you haven't noticed, we are in the middle of an investigation. If you will just return to your home, our office will have a press release sometime tomorrow."

John Wilson pressed the detective. "No, you don't understand."

The detective cut him off and said, "Don't you realize that there are two hysterical parents over there wondering how in the hell their little girl ended up lifeless in a body bag? Let me do my job, or I swear I'll have one of the officers remove you from the area."

Wilson raised his voice and said, "Detective, my daughter Anna found some items that might have a bearing on your investigation. If you don't have time to accept the potential evidence from us, I'll drive down to police head-quarters and discuss the matter with them."

In a calmer voice this time, the detective said, "I apologize, sir, but you have no idea how many distracting inquires I've had to field from well-meaning citizens. What information do you have for me?"

With a better understanding of the situation, Anna's father said, "Earlier today, my daughter found these items near that group of trees. She thought they were out of place and picked them up, but I'm sure it would be better if she explained it to you herself."

The detective looked kindly on Anna and said, "Hello, Anna, my name is Detective Brooks, and I'm the lead inves-tigator on this case. Please forgive me for being so rude to you and your father. Cases involving young people are always very stressful."

Anna said, "I found some items that might help."

"Why don't you show me exactly where you found these items?" the detective said.

Brooks then tucked the items away in a clear evidence bag. He escorted Anna toward the area where she had found the evidence.

In the weeks that followed, the fanfare of that fateful day died down, but an underlying fear had grown in the people who resided near the park. All the potential leads pursued by the homicide detectives came up cold. The homicide division was taking a lot of heat from City Hall because they had no credible leads. The scratches on Nathan's body were healing quickly, but the scars inflicted on the Johnson family and the community would never heal. The contempt Nathan displayed toward Anna became impossible to escape. His dark glances were becoming a regular occurrence whenever the two crossed paths. Even though Anna and her father rarely discussed the chilling events of that terrible night, they shared a new kind of emotional warmth for each other.

Newspaper accounts of the tragedy were chilling, but that was to be expected. Anna tried to purge her mind of the first headline printed by the local paper: Young Girl's Murder Sends Shockwaves through a Sleepy Highland Park Community.

The Wilson household was having a difficult time surviving the influx of tension into their lives. Meal times were especially hard to endure because of the deafening silence that hung in the air. Anna could feel her father staring at her sometimes, but he could not seem to bring his thoughts to words. Darkness had taken up residence in their once happy home, and it had no plans on leaving any time soon.

Ruth Wilson desperately tried to bring back some sense of normalcy to the home with little to no results. Her father was spending more time than ever out back in the workshop. On more than one occasion, Anna saw her mother trying to coax him to come to bed. Elizabeth seemed oblivious to the whole situation, even questioning at one point what was wrong with everyone.

The troublesome cloud hanging over Anna's head had become harder to tolerate with each passing day. Nightmares and her brother's subtle taunting were what she had to look forward to each day.

Anna loved Saturday mornings, and there was something very special about this one. After all the family had gathered around the table, Anna's mother took it upon herself to say grace. For her mother to say the blessing was normal, but the content of her prayer was not. She made it a point to ask the Lord to bless all of them, no matter where they might be. As they passed around the heaping platter of freshly grilled pancakes, Anna's mind began to wonder what was really going on. When her father passed the plate of sausage links her way, he chose not to make eye contact. The fact that her father was quiet during breakfast was not at all strange, but her mother was a different story. There was never a time that Anna could remember when her mother was not the center of mealtime conversation. It was obvious that something was on her mind, because she was very reserved. Nathan was as quiet as a church mouse. He did not complain; he didn't even make his usual snide remarks about his sisters. The wonderful aroma of breakfast floating in the air could not hide the underlying tension that was building in the room.

Anna peeked over at Nathan as he nervously played with his food. For some reason, she knew the tension had something to do with him. Suddenly, Nathan dropped his knife and fork and stormed away from the table. As he scurried up the stairs, Anna's mother instinctively started to get up from her chair to pursue him. Anna's father immediately intervened by gently taking hold of her arm.

"Let him go, Ruth" he said.

"But John—" she said, trying to make her point, but was interrupted.

"We have already discussed this matter," he said," and nothing will change my mind."

As the tension heightened, Elizabeth and Anna stopped eating and focused on what was unfolding before them.

After a moment of silence, John said, "Your mother and I had planned to make an announcement following breakfast, but I don't see any reason to wait. Nathan has an opportunity to attend a very highly rated boarding school upstate. We will be driving him up there the end of next week, and I expect both of you girls to accompany us on the trip."

chapter two

A kaleidoscope of memories flipped through Anna's mind as she relaxed on an aging high-back wicker chair on the front porch. Steam billowed as she raised the cup of tea toward her lips. She slowly closed her eyes as she enjoyed a warm sip of tea. The old woman then gently placed the delicate china cup next to a plate of freshly baked oatmeal cookies. When noticing the strands of the faded white paint peeling from the legs of the table, she smiled. She then caught a glimpse of the washed floral design of the aging chair pad on which she was sitting. The once brilliant red threads that held it together were partially unraveled. Thoughts that she was not the only thing getting old around the house delivered her a bit of amusement.

The sun was shining brightly on the cool October morning as Anna watched the neighborhood come alive. Saturdays were inherently an exciting time during the fall season. The dog days of summer were behind them and the cold confines of winter were just around the corner. Local residents were pushing strollers over the crunching leaves loosely covering the sidewalks. Curious dogs of various shapes and sizes led people down the street. She chuckled as the frisky pooches tugged their owners from tree to tree on sniffing and peeing missions. The fact that she recognized so few of the owners really did not trouble her. It was merely another reminder that life was passing her by.

The sight of Robert coming toward the front porch brought a smile to Anna's face. She saw in him the spark of life that she felt slipping away so quickly. She smiled as she said, "Good morning, Robert, how are you on this fine day?"

The youngster eagerly replied, "I'm great, Miss Wilson."

"Would you care for some of these oatmeal cookies?" she asked, offering him the sweet treats.

"Yes, I love oatmeal cookies!" Robert said excitedly.

"Well, I hope you're ready to do some work today," Anna said.

Wanting to please her, Robert said, "I promise to work hard."

"Good. When you have finished your cookies, I'll show you where to put the empty boxes. Oh, by the way, Robert, you did ask your mother for permission to come over here?" she asked.

"Yes, just like you said," he replied.

Robert was not exactly honest with the old woman. He told her what he thought she wanted to hear, for several reasons. The real story was that his mother had gone to his aunt's house the prior night. The decision to go to her sister's was because Robert's father had come home drunk after work. Robert had learned to take care of himself when need be, and knew that it was best to stay out of his father's way when he had too much to drink. Robert's father was a good provider, and he was not physically abusive to the boy. He was even known to spend some time at little league games and attend after-school activities on occasion. The abuse, which rained down on their household, was mainly emotional. Fear, guilt, and shame had already found its way into the young boy's life. Was it wrong of him to be untruthful to Anna? Of course it was, but the alternative was not acceptable to him. The last thing he wanted to see was the pity in Anna's eyes. Often times he thought that if he pretended the terrible things going on at home were not really happening, they might go away. All he ever wanted was the stability and love he saw in other families. He never agreed to be the keeper of the family secret, but the responsibility had landed upon his shoulders just the same.

The young boy patiently followed Anna up the stairs to the second floor. Carrying a cardboard box in each hand, he nearly lost his balance while gazing up at the beautiful woodwork as he slowly followed the old woman to the second floor. Thoughts ran through his mind, wondering what it would be like to be rich. Maybe life would be better in his home if his family was rich like Miss Wilson. Maybe his father would not find it necessary to drink so much. Maybe his mother would not lock herself in her room and cry when his father screamed at her.

When they reached the second floor, Anna turned to Robert and said, "Okay, Robert, we are going to start working in this guest bedroom. Place those boxes on the floor and go back downstairs for the others."

Dutifully, Robert replied, "Yes, Miss Wilson."

"There is one more thing to remember, young man," Anna said.

"Yes, Miss Wilson?" Robert said respectfully.

Anna didn't want the boy to have an accident carrying the boxes, so she warned, "Take your time, and be careful going up and down the stairs."

Robert was tired of instructions at this point. "Okay, Miss Wilson," he said, as he ran out of the room.

Anna stood next to a stack of family memorabilia in the guest room as Robert raced out of the room and down the steps. She could not help but smile and shake her head. The sound of his feet racing up and down the steps as he retrieved the boxes brought the sound of life back into the old house. It had been nearly twenty years since anyone occupied the home other than Anna. The only roommates that shared the old woman's life were books and memories of the past.

When Robert finished with the boxes, he said, "Miss Wilson, this is the last of the boxes."

"Okay, Robert, I'll show you how we are going to do this," she said. "The first thing I want you to do is bring several boxes over from the walk-in closet and place them on the floor next to the bed. Once you do that, we can start the process of sorting through the items." Speaking to the young boy like a concerned grandmother, she warned, "Robert, if any of the boxes are too heavy, I expect you to ask me for help. I don't want to send you home damaged."

Trying to impress the old woman, Robert said proudly, "Miss Wilson, I'll ask for help if I need it, but you'll see that I'm very strong. At home, I lift heavy things for my mom all the time."

Anna smiled in admiration of Robert's youth as she watched him maneuver the boxes from the closet. The old woman almost intervened when she saw him struggling and straining. She knew it would crush his young ego, so she decided to let him have the opportunity to meet the challenge.

Anna started sorting through one of the cartons while Robert carried over the remaining boxes. She placed the items in three separate piles on the bed. In one pile were items she no longer wanted, but did not want to put in the trash. The items would find their way to the local branch of the Goodwill. The next items were the things she still cherished and would probably keep until she left this world. Pile number three consisted of the things she was ready to discard.

While Robert worked on his part of the project, Anna made her way downstairs to retrieve a stack of old newspapers from the dining room. The newspapers were going to be used to wrap the items before carefully placing them in the boxes. Even though Anna was parting company with certain things, she did not want them damaged. After all, someone else might enjoy them, as she had for so very long.

As she slowly made the ascent back up the stairs with the old newspapers in hand, memories of the past began to creep into her mind. Fate forced Anna to preside over every member of her family's death.

Loneliness stalked Anna throughout the old house. What once seemed to be a mansion to her as a child was now closing in on her with every passing day. Now, here she was, letting go of items that held memories from days gone by. She sadly realized that Robert was the closest thing to a friend that she had. His bright young face took her by surprise when nearing the top of the stairs.

"Let me carry those for you, Miss Wilson," he said.

Startled, she laughed nervously. "Robert, you just gave an old woman a real fright."

"I'm sorry, Miss Wilson," the young boy said. "I am just trying to help."

"It's okay, young man; let's get to it," she said.

The unlikely pair joined forces to sort through the boxes of memorabilia. There were piles of knickknacks, stacks of picture frames, and old toys scattered on the bed. Anna placed the lion's share of the old photographs in the "save" box. At first, Robert worked diligently, trying to keep up with Anna's sorting, but his focus shifted when he came across items that interested him. Anna could not help but smile when she saw him closely examining several of the items from Nathan's childhood.

Noticing that Robert had set aside a bust of an Indian chief that had colorful headdress feathers painted on it, as well as a cast iron Model T Ford savings bank containing several coins, Anna said, "Robert, it appears that some of these items are catching your fancy."

Excited, the youngster responded. "Yes, Miss Wilson, I just hate to see them go to waste."

Smiling, Anna said, "That would be a shame, wouldn't it?"

"Can I ask you a question?" Robert asked.

"Of course you can," Anna replied.

"Did you have a son who owned this stuff?" Robert inquired.

Thinking about what he asked for a moment, Anna said, "No, the young man who owned these items was my younger brother, Nathan. He lost his life in an automobile accident many years ago while in college."

Feeling bad for unknowingly bringing up a bad memory, Robert said, "I'm sorry, Miss Wilson."

Placing her hand over his, Anna said, "No need to be sorry, Robert. He died exactly the same way he lived."

Confused, Robert asked, "What does that mean?"

"It means that my brother Nathan was a violent person his entire life," Anna said. "As a young man, he committed some horrendous acts and, unfortunately, never had to pay for his actions. His behavior did not improve as he got older." Changing the subject, she said, "Good, now let's get back to the task before us. It's obvious that you would like to keep a few of these things, is that right, Robert?"

The young boy's eyes lit up. "I sure would!"

Anna smiled. "What I've decided to do is let you set aside several of the items that catch your eye, and when we finish today, you can take them home with you. Is that acceptable to you?"

Robert was delighted. "That would be great, Miss Wilson!"

They did not discuss Anna's brother any further. Even for his young age, Robert was perceptive enough to realize that it was not a fond memory in Anna's life. It was obvious that something bad had occurred between the two of them, but he was not about to delve further into that subject. He understood all too well about not wanting to share family secrets.

After working hard all morning, Anna said, "Robert, would you like to have lunch with me?"

Hungry from the work, Robert said, "Sure."

"I'll go downstairs and prepare us something to eat while you continue to pack the items we have sorted," Anna said. "Once our meal is ready, I'll call you down."

Anna smiled at Robert before leaving the room. She loved the warmth his presence brought to her home, and she made him feel very safe and secure.

Before resuming his duties, Robert scrutinized the treasures laid out in front of him. There were plenty of great items to choose from, and he was going to be darn sure he picked the very best items possible. His next thought was that he needed to keep the items out of his father's sight so that he would not break them during one of his drunken rages. He looked around the room and marveled at the majesty of Anna's beautiful home. The young man tried to imagine what it must have been like to live in such glorious surroundings.

It had been a while since Anna had entertained, and she wanted to do it right, even if her guest was pint sized. Humming a tune from long ago, she decided that a grilled cheese sandwich, a bowl of tomato soup, and several Toll House chocolate chip cookies would fit the bill. She didn't know any youngster who could turn that meal away.

As Anna approached Robert, announcing that it was time to eat, he asked, "What are we having?"

Anna replied, "You'll see, but I have a feeling you're going to enjoy it."

Hungry from the morning's work, Robert raced over to the table and gazed at the tasty offering she prepared.

Once they were both sitting at the table, Anna said, "I hope you like grilled cheese sandwiches and tomato soup."

"I love them!" Robert said. "My mom makes them for me all the time."

"Do you say grace at home when you eat?" Anna asked, not wanting to offend the young boy.

Not sure how to respond, Robert said, "Sometimes my mother and I do."

"Would you like to do the honors now?" Anna asked.

Unsure of himself, Robert said, "Okay, but I'm not real good at it."

Anna smiled and said, "I'm sure the Lord will understand."

Robert began, "Thank you, God, for this food, and thank you for Miss Anna. Amen."

Anna smiled and said, "Now that's what I like in a man: short, sweet, and compliments to the lady of the house."

As the unlikely duo sat at the table finishing their lunch, Anna caught herself watching Robert. Even though their time together was limited, she treasured it nonetheless.

Anna chuckled when she saw Robert's face pucker as he took a long drink of the unsweetened iced tea she served.

"Miss Wilson, there's something wrong with this iced tea," he said.

"I'm sorry, Robert, the bowl on the table with the spoon in it contains sugar and the other bowl has lemon wedges," Anna said.

"Just sugar, please."

"Help yourself, young man."

They had worked hard that morning, and Anna said, "I believe we are going to call it a day after lunch."

Robert, eager to make more money, said, "But we still have a lot of work to do."

Anna was tired, though, and said "Yes, but this old woman needs to be done for the day. My hope is that you will come back again next Saturday and help me finish."

Happy at the chance to work more, Robert said, "Sure I will, Miss Wilson."

When they finished with lunch, Anna bagged the remaining cookies for Robert, and then removed a crisp twenty-dollar bill from her wallet. As she walked him to the front porch, she sensed that he was a little dejected; however, when she handed him the crisp twenty, he perked up quickly. Anna was overjoyed when she saw the smile light up his young face and the twinkle in his eye.

Waving goodbye, Robert ran down the sidewalk, thanking Anna repeatedly. She slowly walked over to the chair on the front porch and watched the young man walk out of sight.

chapter ·············
············· three

Beautiful autumn weather greeted Anna on the following day. She enthusiastically decided to embark on a walk through the neighborhood. Morning dew glistened on the leaves of the trees and the blades of grass on the lawns. When the old woman neared the street where Robert lived, something alarming caught her eye. The sight of crime scene tape stretching across the doorway brought fear to her heart. Two men in dark suits carrying note pads were conversing on the front lawn. As she got closer to the house, the reality that something very terrible had occurred became more evident. Standing there stunned, she watched as an official looking vehicle came to a stop in front of the house. A young black woman exited the car with a manila folder in hand, heading toward the house.

Anna approached the woman and said, "Excuse me, can you tell me what happened here?"

Thinking she was a nosey neighbor, the woman asked, "Who might you be, ma'am?"

"I'm Anna Wilson," she said. "The young man who lives here does odd jobs around my house. I was taking my morning walk when I stumbled upon this situation."

"I'm Melissa Smith, from Social Services."

Concerned, Anna asked, "Is Robert okay?"

"Yes," Ms. Smith said, "He has been taken into custody by Child Services."

Shocked, Anna inquired, "Robert's parents?"

"That's all the information I can divulge at this time," Ms. Smith said.

Thinking of Robert's well-being, Anna asked, "What will become of the boy?"

"The only living family members outside of his parents are his grandmother and an aunt on his mother's side," Ms. Smith replied.

"One of them will surely take him into their home," Anna said.

Ms. Smith went on to tell Anna that although she hoped that either Robert's grandmother or aunt would take him in, the grandmother was in poor health and was, in fact, in a long-term care facility, while the aunt refused to have anything to do with him. While she regretted her sister's death, she had no place in her life for another child.

Anna was clearly worried about what would become of the young boy. Unless a long lost relative came forward and offered to take him in, Robert would become a ward of the state and put into foster care.

Ms. Smith gave Anna her card before entering the house to pick up a few things for her new client, Robert.

A cloud of sorrow settled over Anna as she blindly made her way back home. No stranger to sadness, she mourned for the young boy who deserved none of the dark events that were raining down upon him. When she arrived home, she went into the living room and leaned back in the sofa.

When she turned on the local news, she was shocked to see a clip of Robert's father being led into the county jail. The reporter said he was being charged with the brutal murder of his wife. Staring blindly into space, Anna experienced a feeling of helplessness taking over her soul. The tears that rolled down her cheeks were for her and Robert.

Many hours passed as Anna sat numbly on the sofa. When she finally glanced out the window, she realized that night had fallen. She hadn't eaten all day, but she didn't have an appetite. Slowly, she made her way up the stairs and crawled into bed. As she lay in bed searching for sleep, she could not help but wonder what Robert was feeling as he attempted to sleep in a strange place.

Questions raced through Robert's head like a ticker tape. *Why did my father kill my mother? Was it because of his drinking? Was it something I did wrong? Will my aunt come to get me from this horrible place?* It was bad enough being in a strange place, but to make matters worse, one of the older boys in the home had punched him in the face, for no good reason. Gently rubbing his bruised eye, he hoped the same thing would not happen the following day.

His terrible thoughts, along with the low whimpers of faceless children, made for a sleepless night. Those who shared the large, cold dormitory with Robert were experiencing the same doubts and fears. Most of them had no one in their lives to give them hope, and as the hours passed by, Robert felt the same way.

❧ ❧ ❧ ❧

Anna recalled her time as a teacher and the young students who ended up in the social services system, but who eventually returned to their families. What she remembered about the children did not sit well with her. Many of them took on new character traits that she suspected were coping skills, in order to deal with what they had experienced. Some became violent and acted out toward other students. Others found solace within themselves, becoming loners. They felt safe as long as they did not interact with other students. Anna was determined not to let young Robert fall victim to the system. Come hell or high water, she planned to rescue the boy. He deserved a fair chance in life, and she would do everything possible to make that happen.

chapter ·············
·············· four

P eeking at the clock, Anna saw that it was four thirty
in the morning. Saving her Robert was the mission
at hand today, so she decided to get out of bed. She
usually started her day with green tea and raisin toast, and
this day would be no different. While waiting for the water
to boil and the toast to pop up, she began gathering the
tools she would need for the day's activities. She snatched a
blank tablet of paper, along with two ink pens. After placing
the items on the dining room table, she went into the parlor
and grabbed the telephone directory from the bookcase.
As she put the phone book on the table, the whistling of
the teapot, followed by the toaster popping up, startled her.
Steam rose in the air as she poured the scalding water over
the waiting tea bag.

As Anna blew on the cup of hot tea, unusual memories
from the past crept into her mind. During her postgraduate
studies at the University of Pittsburgh, she had a philoso-
phy professor that she would never forget. At the time, she
did not agree with all of his philosophical views, but she did
respect him. She especially did not see eye to eye with him
on his beliefs on destiny, and she recalled one discussion, in
particular, they had in his office, as if it was yesterday.

"Professor Silva, can I have a word with you?"

"Sure Anna," he said, "what's on your mind?"

"You gave me the impression in your lecture that we have no control over affecting destiny in ours or anyone else's life," she said.

"What I said was that fate will not be controlled by people," he replied.

Pressing him, Anna said, "Isn't that in essence the same thing?"

"No," he said. "As much as you don't want to believe it, your fate will not have anything to do with planning in your life. Our destinies will blindside us every time."

Anna continued with her questions. "If that's true, why should I be an educator? Why are you a professor?"

Professor Silva said, "I am an educator because I love to pass along information, nothing more, and nothing less. I am of the opinion that academia plays a small part in one's destiny. It's more important that a person be spiritually fit to ready themselves for fate."

Anna sat sipping her tea and eating her toast. Thoughts of the discussion with her former professor made her wonder if Robert was part of her destiny. What had begun as casual interactions between the old woman and the young boy were escalating into something much more heartfelt. The term blindsided immediately rushed into her mind. Anna had spent decades painstakingly molding an existence of mediocrity. That was about to be completely blown out of the water. She felt levels of emotional stimulation that far surpassed anything she had encountered in prior decades of living. Wanting a second cup of tea, she made her way to the kitchen. Anna figured this day would command at least two cups of her favorite green tea. On her way back to the dining room, she opened the bottom door of the armoire and took out an old manila folder labeled "Important Legal

Documents". After gently wiping the dust off, she placed it on the table with the other items she had gathered. Anna decided to contact the law firm her family had used for years. She then retrieved the business card Robert's caseworker, Clair Smith, had given her. There was no doubt in Anna's mind that she would be contacting Ms. Smith later that day. She sat at the table and began formulating a plan in her head to have Robert released from the clutches of social services. Her fear that the boy would get lost in the system far outweighed the personal fears she had of taking on the system. Saving Robert was all that mattered, and failure was not an option!

An array of noises echoing through the large dormitory awakened Robert. Strange voices unfamiliar to him bounced off the cold graffiti-ridden concrete block walls. At first, he was confused and had no idea where he was. When the cobwebs cleared, the real horror of the situation hit him hard. The fact that his mother was dead was difficult to believe, but then realizing his father was in jail for murdering her made it all inconceivable. Hopelessness and despair were closing in on him. He bent forward, resting his head in his hands, and started to cry.

Suddenly, another youngster approached him and said, "Hey, kid, don't you know there's no crying in Big Mama's place."

Shaken and afraid, Robert said, "I'm sorry, I don't know what I'm doing here."

"Either you're a bad kid, or nobody wants you," the other kid said casually.

Robert said, "My mother was killed yesterday."

The stranger replied, "It's a tough break about your mom. My old lady is back in jail for turning tricks and shooting heroin."

Robert had no idea what he was talking about, so he simply said, "Sorry."

His newfound friend said, "That's okay, I'm used to it. This is the third time I have been in this shithole. By the way, my name is Joe."

Feeling a little more comfortable, Robert introduced himself. "I'm Robert."

"Okay Robert, the first thing you need to do is straighten up your bunk before Big Mama comes around," Joe instructed. "Once you do that, we'll go to the chow hall for breakfast."

"Who's Big Mama?" Robert asked.

Joe smiled. "She's that big fat black woman who runs this dorm. You don't want to get on her bad side, because she can be a real bitch."

Curious, Robert asked, "What's a trick?"

Joe laughed. "You're not from the city, are you?"

"No, I'm from Highland Park," Robert said, rather timidly.

His new streetwise friend said, "Tighten up your bed and I'll school you while we eat breakfast."

Anna had prepared ahead of time for her visit to the attorney's office. The outfit she chose, placed neatly across her bed, was meant to give a no nonsense impression. The gray wool pantsuit with vest and matching jacket were very professional, while the cotton white blouse kept the outfit understated. Black leather pumps with a low heel worked well with the suit, and the antique gold butterfly brooch that her grandmother had left her many years earlier was the perfect accessory. Anna felt confident that her outfit would project her inner strength, while the brooch would lend a hint of femininity.

As she brushed back her silver hair, the old woman staring back at her in the mirror caught her off guard for a moment. Anna refused to accept the reflection as a true measure of her age as she applied a small amount of makeup to her face. What she was about to do would take all her courage and faith in herself.

Anna knew she would face many obstacles in her mission to save Robert, but driving her forward was the thought of how lost and scared he must be feeling. Not only did the young boy lose his mother to a senseless murder, she did so at the hands of her own husband, Robert's father. Now he was parentless. With his father in prison, Robert found himself caught up in the legal system that is social services. His grandmother was unable to care for him, and his aunt wanted nothing to do with another child. Anna felt she had no choice but to put her own fears aside and do whatever it took to bring Robert home with her.

The law offices of Levin and Stein were familiar to the Wilson family. When Anna's parents passed away, the firm handled the trust funds for her and her siblings. Now, more than ever, she needed the guidance of someone she could trust, and she was banking on Saul Levin to be that man.

She hoped that he would be able to guide her through the inner workings of the social services system in order to get the one thing that was most important to her: Robert.

The sound of a woman paging Robert on a loud speaker interrupted the boys' breakfast. When he started to jump up from the table, his newfound companion, Joe, placed his hand on his shoulder.

"Cool it, kid," Joe said. "It'll wait till you're done eating. Everything is hurry up and wait around here."

Excited about his possible release, though, Robert said, "Somebody's here to get me out of here!"

"Suit yourself, kid," Joe said, "but it's just one of those lame bitches from social services to do your intake paperwork."

As Robert walked quickly toward the front desk, the sounds of random screams and swearing came from some of the other kids who were still eating. Suddenly, a piece of banana came out of nowhere, striking him on the side of the head. He looked around in fear as laughter rang out all around him.

As Robert approached the front desk, he came face to face with an enormous black woman. Everything about Big Mama was intimidating, from her large three hundred pound frame, to her loud, deep voice, to the three-foot stick she carried. Everything about her terrified him.

"Wilson, why in the hell are you making me come after your boney little ass?" Big Mama barked.

Cowering in front of her, Robert said, "I'm sorry."

"You sure are sorry," she said. "Now get up front and wait for the woman from social services to call you in the office."

"Yes ma'am," Robert said, shaking.

Robert stood next to the front desk, trembling from fear. He was not sure who he was more afraid of, Big Mama or the other kids. It was very difficult to hold back the tears, but he did not dare cry. When his father would come home after drinking, his mother would tell him not to cry because it would just make his father angry. The fear and hopelessness he felt in the air reminded him of the bad times at his house. For a brief moment, when Robert saw the social worker approaching, he thought she might be able to get him out of this place, and it gave him hope.

"Are you Robert Tate?" the social worker asked while looking down at her folder.

"Yes," Robert said, with a bit of trepidation in his voice.

Looking at the small body standing before her, the social worker said, "Hello, my name is Clair. I'll be handling your case."

"I want to go home!" Robert blurted out.

"Come into the office with me and have a seat," Clair said in a calm voice.

Upset, Robert cried out, "I don't want to be in this place!"

"If you settle down, I'll try and explain to you what's going to happen," Clair said, trying to allay any fears the young boy had. "Do you think you can do that for me?"

Robert finally calmed down enough for Clair to try to explain the situation. She reassured him that she was doing everything possible to find him a home, but with his father in prison, his grandmother in a nursing home, and his

Aunt Jean unwilling to take him in, she had no idea who might be able to foster him. The thought of staying in the group home for even one more day frightened Robert.

After determining that Robert wasn't on any prescription medications that he might need—she couldn't find any at his family residence—she again assured the young boy that she would come back and visit as soon as she had new information about his case.

Anna was anxious as she rode the elevator to the seventh floor of the law firm. There was no fooling herself when it came to how hard this battle was going to be, but she was ready for what lay ahead.

When Anna exited the elevator, a beautiful young woman wearing a perpetual smile greeted her and immediately offered her a beverage. Eager to get down to business, Anna politely said, "No thank you," and proceeded to introduce herself. " "My name is Anna Wilson, and I'm here to see Saul Levin."

The receptionist told Anna to have a seat, and then let Attorney Levin know that his client was here.

Anna was happy to be off her feet, as her old joints were rather stiff these days, but she felt more alive than she had in years. The thought of what she was about to do gave her new life, and it made her smile to herself.

Saul interrupted her thoughts. "It's so nice to see you again, Anna."

Anna stood up to shake his hand and smiled. "It's been a long time, Saul."

Walking down the wide corridor to Saul's office, she hoped he was as skilled an attorney as she remembered him to be. She was just a young woman when they first met, but she recalled how smoothly he and his law firm handled their trust funds when their parents died.

"So," Saul said, "what is this urgent matter that you needed to see me about today?"

Anna told him the dark tale surrounding the incident involving Robert. She told a terrible story of a drunken husband who brutally murdered his wife while their young son looked on in fear. She told him that social services came to take the young boy because no one in his extended family had enough compassion to take him.

Saul listened intently. He could tell that Anna cared very much about the boy's welfare.

"That's a terribly sad situation, Anna, but what does it have to do with you?"

"I want to hire you to help me get legal custody of the ten-year-old boy."

Surprised by her request, he said, "Let me see if I understand this correctly. You want me to help you take on the responsibility of a young minor, who is not even a blood relative?"

Anna nodded. "That accurately sums it up."

Confused, the attorney said, "Why would you want to get involved in something like this, Anna?"

Refusing to back down, she said, "My motives are irrelevant. Are you willing to help me or not?"

Saul hesitated for a few moments, and then said, "All right, I'll give it to you straight. I respect your tenacity, but there is no family court judge in Pittsburgh who will grant you custody of the boy. The two biggest factors that come into play are your age and you are not a family member. Besides, you should be out socializing with others your age, enjoying your golden years."

Anna was visibly upset by what Saul said, but she refused to argue her point. Instead, she simply stood up and said, "Obviously, you can't help me, so I need to find someone who will."

The ride down the elevator gave Anna the opportunity to purge her mind of the negativity Saul Jr. tried to feed her. Looking at her reflection in the elevator door, she saw a smile forming on her face. When she stepped outside the doors, she decided that Saul's unwillingness to help would not deter her.

Anna took a deep breath as she stepped outside and looked up and down the busy street. A number of law offices lined both sides of the street, so she began working her way down the block, making random cold calls.

It didn't matter that the first two firms were unable to help her; she was determined to find someone who would take on her case.

Just as Anna was about to stop at a local diner for a bite to eat and a cup of tea, the window of a small law office caught her eye. The worn black lettering on the window read **Jack Porter, Attorne at Law**; the "y" was missing. Figuring she had nothing to lose, Anna ventured inside. Several mismatched chairs rested against the wall, along with a desk. A partially full coffee cup containing a plastic stir sat next to an ashtray with several cigarette butts in it. She was startled when a middle-aged man appeared from the back of the office. His suit was far from impressive, his tie was partially undone, and he was overdue for a haircut. Standing around six feet tall, with black hair, she thought he was handsome in a rugged sort of way. Anna secretly hoped that he was one of Mr. Porter's clients.

"Hello, my name is Jack Porter," he said casually. "I hope you haven't been waiting too long. My receptionist had an emergency at home."

"Nice to meet you. I'm Anna Wilson." Anna continued, "Mr. Porter, do you have time to discuss a legal matter with me?"

Laughing at his empty reception area, Jack said, "As you can see, I'm very busy—but I'll fit you in. I was just on my way to have a little lunch. Have you eaten yet?"

"No," Anna said, "but I was thinking about that very thing before I came here."

"Now, there we have it," he said. "I have a lunch date with a classy woman as well as a potential client at the same time! Let me grab my briefcase and we'll be on our way."

Anna's initial feelings about Jack Porter were not very positive, but that was starting to change. In her mind, his flirty personality was a defense mechanism for disguising some insecurity; it was either that or he was just outgoing. She settled on the latter. She found the carefree attitude he displayed refreshing. Her main concern was his ability as a lawyer. She liked that he gave off a positive energy.

"There's a small diner a couple doors down that I frequent," Jack said. "The food is always good. We can grab a booth and talk while we eat. Does that sound acceptable to you?"

"I hope they have tea," Anna said.

Jack smiled and said, "I can't guarantee it, but we'll soon find out!"

Feeling a little weak from the morning's activities and lack of food, Anna was relieved that they were incorporating lunch with their casual meeting. The aroma floating in the air as they closed in on the eatery was enticing. When they entered the restaurant, two servers greeted Jack by name. Anna had the impression that he was familiar with one of them socially. The diner's décor reminded her of the inside of a modern rail car.

As Jack escorted her to a corner booth, Anna spotted a box of Lipton tea bags next to the coffee machine. When they sat down, Jack grabbed two of the laminated menus from the chrome caddy in the middle of the table and handed one to Anna. He then pulled out a legal pad and pen from his briefcase.

"Anna … may I call you Anna?" he said.

She enjoyed his direct approach. "Actually, I would prefer it."

"Good," he said, "let's order lunch and then get down to business."

After the waitress took their orders—Jack got his usual, a meatloaf sandwich and mashed potatoes, and Anna settled on corned beef on rye, fries, and coleslaw—Jack said, "So, Anna, how can I be of service to you?"

Getting directly to the point, Anna said, "There is a young boy named Robert that is currently being held in social services. I want him released into my care."

"Okay, I want you to tell me all the background information about the situation. Remember, the devil is in the details, so don't leave anything out.", Jack said.

"It is only fair to tell you that I have already spoken with three different law firms before I came to you," Anna said. "Know this, Mr. Porter; I will do whatever it takes to rescue that boy from the system."

"I admire your determination, Anna. You're going to need every ounce of it before this ordeal is over."

After having eaten their lunch, mostly in silence, Anna said, "Well, Jack, are you the one I'm looking for?"

He tried to lighten the mood a little bit and said, "I've always been partial to mature women."

Anna smiled and said, "My guess is that you're partial to *all* women. Can we knock off the friendly banter and get to the matter at hand? Can you help me?"

He paused for a moment. "This is a complicated case, on several different levels, but the answer to your question is yes, I think I can help you."

The waitress came by the table again and Jack ordered a slice of strawberry pie and another cup of coffee.

After writing down a few notes, Jack said, "I'll require a one thousand dollar retainer, cash or check."

"How quickly can we see a judge?" Anna asked, happy that he was willing to take the case.

"If things go our way, we won't need to go before a judge. I'm sure that less creative attorneys than me have already told you that your chances of winning this case are very slim, and that even if you could win, it would be a long, drawn out process."

"What do you have in mind, Jack?"

Jack explained to Anna that he would visit Robert's father at the Allegheny County Jail to try to persuade him to sign over legal guardianship to her, as it would be in Robert's, and his, best interest to do so. It would be a hard sell, as he might not want to give up custody of his only son, despite the fact that he was in jail for murdering the boy's mother. He reassured Anna that even if Mr. Tate refused to sign over legal guardianship, he had other options up his sleeve, but pursuing those avenues could prove to be expensive.

Anna listened carefully to everything Jack said about moving forward with the case. She was not one to back down easily, especially when it came to Robert. Where the young boy was concerned, she refused to put a price tag on his well-being.

"Should I accompany you to the jail?" Anna asked.

"Not just yet," Jack said, "but there is one more thing. I'm going to put a visitation clause in the guardianship papers, stating that Mr. Tate will have visitation rights when released from prison. Robert will be at least twenty-five years old by that time, but it will give him the impression that we are making concessions."

Anna agreed to Jack's suggestion. For all she knew, Robert's father might not want anything to do with him by that point.

Time seemed to fly by on the ride home from her meeting with Jack. Anna knew it would be foolish to be overly optimistic about the journey she was about to take, but she felt good about her chances. Jack Porter was a little rough around the edges, to say the least, but he projected confidence in his abilities, and that made her feel better. She knew the matter could not be in better hands.

While Anna trusted that Jack was the man to handle her case, she couldn't shake the feeling that underneath the surface, there was more to Jack Porter than meets the eye, and she hoped she'd have the courage to ask him about it once the ink was dry on the papers.

Upon entering the large house, Anna went upstairs to change into something more comfortable. Even though the house was filled with plenty of furniture and other fine things, it still felt empty to her, and the real possibility that Robert might move in changed everything.

After changing her clothes, Anna sat down on the bench in front of the dresser and looked into the mirror. Tears began to roll down her checks. In the eyes of most, she had a very fulfilling life. She had been a loyal daughter, she was an accomplished educator, and she had more money than she could spend in two lifetimes. It was all becoming more pointless as the years crept upon her. Anna desperately wanted to enjoy what life had given her, but that was not possible alone, and she suddenly came to the realization that God was not going to let such a thing happen.

Robert spent almost every moment of his time watching the front door, hoping that someone would come to his rescue. The other kids had not been treating him very well, and in the gym this day, a gang of boys singled him out for a beating. The result was a black eye and a bloody nose.

"What in the hell happened to you, kid?" Joe said.

"I got beat up in the gym," Robert said, the fear in his voice evident.

"Why?" Joe asked.

With tears pouring down his cheeks, Robert screamed, "I don't know why! I don't know what I did!"

Joe tried to comfort his friend, and put his arm around him. "Stick with me while I'm here, and I'll look out for you."

"What do mean, while you're here?" Robert asked, not understanding the implication.

"I might be going to a foster home this week," Joe said.

"What's a foster home?" Robert asked.

"It's a house where people get paid to let kids like us stay there."

Curious, Robert asked, "Is it better than this place?"

"Some are, some aren't," Joe said. "The last family they placed me with was cool at first, and then they started knocking me around. The fat bitch wife used to beat me with a sawed off broom handle. Luckily, one of the teachers at school noticed the marks on me, so they pulled me out. Besides, I wasn't crazy that there were five other kids like me staying there."

"I hope somebody comes to get me," Robert said sullenly.

Anna tried to busy herself with chores to get her mind off things. Each time she completed a task, she looked over at the telephone, followed by a glance at the clock. Once every piece of furniture in the dining room was thoroughly polished, she made her way into the parlor. Just as she set down the bottle of furniture polish on the coffee table, the phone rang. Before the second ring, she snatched up the receiver with nervous anticipation. In as calm a voice as possible, she said, "Hello?"

"Hi Anna, this is Jack Porter calling."

"Well, how did it go?" she asked cautiously.

"I've got good news and I've got bad news."

Anna was getting frustrated. "Come on, Mr. Porter. Just tell me the news."

"The bad news is, I spent a lot of your money."

Anna's frustration was growing. "Damn it, Jack." "The good news is, I have a cab on its way over to pick you up. The guardianship papers are signed and in order. I called Clair Smith, and she will meet us down at social services. The young man will be spending the night at your house."

Anna's emotions were boiling over. "I don't know what to say, Jack."

Chuckling, Jack said, "Don't worry about it. We'll discuss the details later."

Anna quickly collected her coat and slipped on the first pair of shoes she found. She seemed to be a ball of nerves, first fumbling with the door keys, and then forgetting her purse in the house. She had to laugh at herself as she waited on the porch, vigilantly watching for the arrival of the cab. Robert's release brought great joy to her heart. After all, an exciting new chapter of her life was about to begin.

chapter ....
.... five

J ack Porter sat on a park bench in front of the large building housing social services, waiting for his client. He had a hard time removing the grin from his face as he watched the relentless pigeons searching for scraps of food on the ground. When at the top of his game, he was one of the best trial lawyers in the city. By all outward appearances, he had it all: cars, a beautiful house outside the city, money, and a drop-dead gorgeous wife. During a high profile criminal proceeding, there were allegations made about witness tampering. He won the case, but after investigation by the Pennsylvania Bar Association, he lost his license to practice law for three years. Soon after, the well ran dry and his trophy wife divorced him and took everything she could. Once the creditors were finished with him, he wasn't even left with a decent vehicle. He survived his expulsion by doing research work for several large law firms in the city. Even after the restrictions on his license were lifted, none of the major firms would hire him. Jack was on a mission to climb that legal mountain again.

A smile formed on his face when he spotted Anna exiting the taxi. Joking, he said "It's about time you showed up!"

Anna couldn't contain her excitement. "You did it Jack!"

"How does it feel, Anna?"

She thought about it for a moment, and said, "It's like being homesick for a place I've never been."

"C'mon, Clair Smith is inside waiting for us. We best get in there before they accidently give your young man to someone else."

Anna smiled and said, "We need to work on your sense of humor, Jack Porter."

As the elevator climbed to the third floor, each of them stood there quietly, smiling to themselves. Both were starting life anew, and things were looking damn good.

When they reached the third floor, Jack hit the stop button to prevent the door from opening. He wanted to let Anna know that there was still much to discuss in this matter, but he wanted to give her and Robert a chance to settle in first. They agreed on a near future lunch date.

Anna's heart was pounding as Jack led her through the double doors to the facility where Robert was staying. She was scared to death and elated at the same time. There were so many things she should have done before coming to get Robert, like which bedroom would he sleep in? Perhaps Elizabeth's old room would suit him. She would have to deal with these things later, though.

As Jack started to introduce Anna to Clair, the two women acknowledged their first meeting in front of Robert's house when this whole ordeal began. Clair let Anna know that all the paperwork was in order, and that she would be contacting her periodically to ensure that the transition was going smoothly. She let Anna know that she was doing a good thing at a dark time in this young boy's life.

Eager to get things going, Clair led Jack and Anna down the hall to the room where Robert was waiting.

Anna could not believe her eyes as she looked around the huge room. Beds were stacked up like an army barracks. Countless numbers of young faces stared in her direction with dead eyes. When she spotted Robert, her anxiety turned to anger.

As soon as Robert saw Anna, he screamed, "Miss Wilson!"

As he ran toward her, she said, "What happened to your face?"

"I got beat up," he said, hanging his head a bit.

Anna's anger over the condition of the place would not permit her to thank anyone that was part of the center. Turning to Robert she said, "Let's go; I'm taking you home."

Overwhelmed, he said, "You're really taking me home?"

"Yes," she said as tears trickled down her cheek, "I'm taking you home,"

Anna offered to share a cab with Jack, but he declined the offer, as he knew that she and Robert needed time alone.

Excited to be heading home with Anna, Robert couldn't help but wonder if the rescue by Ms. Wilson would be short-lived. How long would she shelter him from the terrible reality he faced? He didn't dare ask the question for fear of the answer, and he quickly turned his thoughts to happier times and how much he was looking forward to being in his new home.

When the unlikely duo arrived home and made their way into the house, Anna found herself in a bit of a quandary. On the way home, Robert had said he wanted pizza for dinner. Since it had been at least a decade since she had ordered, or eaten, pizza, she gave the young boy the task of calling and placing the order. They also got formalities out of the way. Anna instructed him to call her Anna, while he asked her to call him Robby. Although she liked the strength the name Robert implied, she would do as he asked.

With the order placed—Robby settled on Papa Joe's pizza—Anna led Robby upstairs to his new room. She had to laugh as the young boy half dragged and half carried the black trash bag containing his clothes up the steps. Clair Smith, the social worker, had made sure to pick up his things at his house. Using both hands, he would climb a half a dozen or so steps, and then set it down to get a better grip. Anna slowly followed, wanting desperately to assist him, but she did not dare. The term *threshold of young manhood* came to mind. Once he was at the landing upstairs, he nonchalantly pushed the bag aside so Anna could get by. She then walked in the direction of the room where Elizabeth slept when they were children.

"Robby, this is your room now," Anna said. "It might seem a little feminine, but we can decorate it the way you want."

"This room is so big!" he said, clearly impressed. "I really like it!"

Anna had reassured him that they could decorate the room however he liked, and for now, he was able to push the horrible events that recently happened from his mind. He had visions of his Indy 500 racing posters decorating the walls and his Spiderman curtains on the windows. He imagined a shadow box mounted on the wall containing rows of shiny new Matchbox cars. Maybe even a collection of GI Joe action figures would be in his future.

For her part, Anna could not wipe the grin off her face as the aroma of freshly baked pizza filled the kitchen. Life had returned to the old house in the form of a ten-year-old.

On the ride back to his office, Jack had a great deal of time to reflect on what transpired that day. During his career in law, he seldom experienced the satisfaction he felt today. Family law had never been his preference in the past, mainly because it is not as lucrative as other areas of the profession. One of the reasons he took on Anna's case was because he needed the cash. The fact that he was able to help her was an added bonus.

As his taxi pulled up in front of the office, he spotted Marge's old Chevy straddling two parking spaces along the sidewalk. What Marge lacked in personality, she more than made up for in looks. She was five feet six inches tall, with a lean, but curvy, build, shoulder-length red hair, and gem-like green eyes.

When Jack walked into the office, he tossed three crisp hundred-dollar bills on the desk. Surprised, Marge said, "What's this Jack?"

He smiled and said, "It's the back pay I owe you."

Laughing, she said, "Actually, you're still a little short, but I'm not complaining. I'm half afraid to ask where you got the cash."

"Red, it was a beautiful thing," he said, boasting about his new client. "An elderly woman came in off the street with a domestic case. She wanted legal guardianship of a young boy who was in social services and wanted it done today. The kicker is that the boy's biological father is in the Allegheny County Jail for murdering the kid's mother. I kicked ass on the case and made it happen. There will also be more work for us in the future."

Marge smiled. "Good, now you can buy a decent suit."

Anna was enjoying the way the old house had come to life again, but she admitted to herself that having a young boy around would take some getting used to. She marveled at how Robby had gobbled up three large slices of pizza so quickly, and she had sat and watched TV with him, something she hadn't done in a long time. Anna preferred reading or listening to music, and she was of the opinion that games and puzzles were much more beneficial to the young mind than television. But there would be plenty of time for shaping Robert's mind. For now, she would simply enjoy spending time with him.

The sound of a man preaching about eternal salvation woke her up on the sofa. Robby was leaning against her, sound asleep, as the TV screen lit up the dark room. Watching him sleeping so soundly made her realize just how small and fragile he was.

After checking the doors and turning out the lights, Anna coaxed Robert up to bed. As she sat in front of the mirror brushing her long silver hair, she reflected on the eventful day that was about to end. When she crawled under the warmth of the comforter, it was clear it could in no way match the warmth in her heart.

chapter six

J ack arrived at the coffee shop around seven forty in the morning, which was at least an hour earlier than usual. He wanted to get into the office so he could get the ball rolling on the Tate murder case. There was no doubt in his mind that he could handle it, but the fact that he represented Anna in the custody case put a new twist on the situation. Conflict of interest needed to be a consideration. Jack needed to find someone respected in the legal community who would not break the bank with his fees. Several people were on the list, and all were good candidates. He finished his second cup of coffee and most of his cheese Danish before heading over to the office.

When he got back, a notice tucked between the door and the frame greeted him, informing him that the rent on the office was late. Once situated at his desk, he took out the file containing the notes he had taken while meeting with James Tate at Allegheny County Jail. Jack read the newspaper accounts about the brutal murder of Robert's mother. They were bad enough, but they could not begin to touch the cold reality of the incident. The Post-Gazette photos included one that showed Robert with blood all over the front of his pajamas.

The sound of the front door opening diverted Jack's attention.

"Jack, what are you doing here so early?" Marge asked, startled to find him in the office so early.

"I'm going over the Tate file," he said. "We need to hire that dirt bag an attorney as soon as possible."

"I'll set up a file for the case first thing," Marge said.

"Marge, how about getting Jake Rollins on the phone for me. Also, pay the office rent today before they kick us out."

"Is there any money in the bank?" she asked.

Jack smiled. "Of course there is."

As he sorted through the paperwork on his desk, Jack felt confident that Jake Rollins was one of the better criminal defense attorneys in the city. He had known him since his high-roller days. Rollins operated a small firm by choice, which impressed Jack. He also had the integrity not to overcharge Anna for his services. Mr. Tate would get the job done well, and Anna would fulfill her obligation to him. Jack figured the case would never go to trial. The amount of graphic evidence the police had would bury Tate in any courtroom in the country. Jack figured Rollins would charge between ten and fifteen thousand for a plea-bargain case. In the unlikely event that it did go to trial, the price tag would be double.

Marge interrupted Jack's thoughts when she came over to his desk and pointed at the phone. "Mr. Rollins is on line two."

Picking up the telephone he said, "How are you, Jake?"

"Good. What's up?" Jake replied.

Jack then filled Jake in on the case, and the two set up a meeting for later that morning.

❧ ❧ ❧ ❧

Anna woke up at five forty-five with an intruder in her bed. Apparently, sometime during the night, Robert decided he would feel more secure in her bed. She smiled and covered him with a blanket before crawling out of bed. She did not intend to wake him up any time soon, especially given everything he had just gone through.

The pleasant thoughts of him crawling into her bed lingered for most of the morning. While sipping her tea, she grabbed a note pad and started jotting down a list of things she had to do, like going to the grocery store and taking Robert clothes shopping.

Heading up the stairs to check on Robert, she heard noises coming from his room. Anna stood in the hallway with a smile on her face and watched as Robert neatly folded his clothes and stacked them in the dresser drawers.

"Good morning," she said, coming into the room. "Did you sleep well?"

"Yes, Anna," Robert said.

"Are you hungry?" she asked. "How about we go downstairs and get you some breakfast, and then I'd like to take you shopping at Kaufmann's for some new clothes, and maybe we can get some items to decorate your room. We can stop at the grocery store to stock up on your favorite foods as well."

Excited by the day ahead, Robert said, "That sounds great, Anna!"

When the cab reached its destination, Jack grabbed the folders off the seat and handed the driver his fare. Jake's office was not exactly a top floor office, but it was very nice.

Once in the office, Jack and Jake exchanged pleasantries and some small talk about their respective lives, and then they got down to business. Jack told Jake about the Tate murder, how Anna got custody of Robert, and how the case should proceed, with Jake handling the murder case. Jack would handle the financial aspect of the matter.

Handing over the five thousand dollar retainer check to Jake, Jack smirked and said, "Don't deposit this until tomorrow."

Anna and Robert made their way through Kaufmann's, stopping occasionally to look at the numerous displays. Robert, not used to shopping in department stores, ran around excitedly, staring at the mannequins dressed in the latest fashions.

When they got off the escalator and headed to the boys' department, Robert made a beeline for the designer t-shirts and the colorful brand name sneakers. Anna quickly guided him to the more conventional, and affordable, clothes. Together, they compromised on styles and colors, and in the end, Robert got several pairs of pants and four shirts.

Robert was pleased when the torture of trying on clothes was over. He accepted it as a minor inconvenience, because they were heading for the cool stuff next. Just about every kind of toy, collectable, electronic game, and poster were on display. It was hard to take it all in.

"Wow, look at all this stuff!" he said.

Anna smiled and said, "It looks like a boy's paradise."

"What am I allowed to buy?" he asked.

"I'll tell you what; you pick out the items you're interested, in and we will decide together whether or not to purchase them. Does that sound fair?" Anna said.

When the pair finished their shopping, they rewarded themselves with a relaxing lunch. Robert went on and on about how he was going to fix his room as he devoured his cheeseburger, and Anna just sat there quietly, enjoying his excitement. When there was a lull in the conversation, Anna noticed that Robert's demeanor changed.

"Where did my mom go after she died?" Robert asked, pensively.

Anna put her arm around him and said, "I'm sure she went to a better place."

"I know her soul went to heaven," he said, "but what happened to her body when they took it out of the house?"

Taken by surprise, Anna said, "That's a good question. I promise you I will work on finding out as soon as we get home."

"Anna, I'm glad you let me live with you," Robert said, rather shyly.

A soft smile formed on her lips. "I'm glad too, Robby."

Some of the excitement of the shopping trip had worn off during their ride home. Anna and Robert were a little preoccupied with the discussion they had at lunch. With all that was happening, it completely slipped her mind to check on his mother's funeral arrangements. She never would have forgiven herself if Robert's mother ended up in a pauper's grave. When they got home, she would be sure to contact Jack to see what the legalities were. One thing was certain; she would do whatever it took to ensure that Robert got the closure he needed so that he could move on with his life.

The grocery store proved to be another adventure for Anna and her young charge. Racing up and down the aisles with the cart, Robert had fun picking out some unhealthy snacks, which Anna approved, but she also made sure there were plenty of healthy purchases too.

Once home, they had the tedious task of carrying all their packages into the house, from Kaufmann's *and* the grocery store.

While Anna took a short break from putting the groceries away, Robert hustled his bags up to his room. With Robert no doubt sorting through his new items, she remembered that she needed to call Jack Porter about the funeral arrangements. When she found his business card in her wallet, she dialed his number.

"Hello, this is the office of Jack Porter, Attorney at Law," Marge, the receptionist, said.

"Hello, this is Anna Wilson. Is Jack in?"

"I'm sorry, he won't be back from court until three o'clock. Would you like to leave a message?" Marge replied.

"Please ask him to call Anna Wilson as soon as he gets back in the office. I have a very important matter to discuss with him," Anna said.

"I will make sure he gets the message."

Anna was aware that giving the boy's mother a proper burial was going to add additional stress to the situation, but it was something she needed to take care of.

Remembering that she still had groceries to put away, Anna walked over to the bottom of the staircase to call Robert down to help, but instead, she sat on the bottom step and just listened. The crumbling sound of bags echoed from Robert's room. Resting her head gently against the stair rail, she smiled, imagining the joy he was experiencing from the new things she had bought for him.

Without prompting, Robert came running down the stairs clutching a stack of empty bags.

"Do you want me to put the groceries away now?" he asked excitedly.

Anna smiled. "Let's work on it together."

Jack had a damn good day. The court appearance went much better than expected, and he got Jake Rollins to take the James Tate murder case. He felt as though his career was back on track again.

Marge was a little skeptical of Jack's newfound positive attitude. Putting her feelings aside, though, she grabbed her notepad containing the day's messages and followed him back to his desk. She listened to him boast like a peacock some more before saying, "When you're ready to get off your high horse, we have some matters to discuss." She told him he needed to call Anna Wilson as soon as possible.

Not quite ready to give up the glow in which he was basking, Jack looked around the office at the things that needed to be changed. Every time he walked in the front door, he thought about changing the decal on the front window—the word Attorney looks better when spelled right. His desk was old and beat up, with a piece of cardboard wedged beneath one of the legs to keep it level. Marge's desk was in much the same condition. The chairs in the waiting room were old too. Jack then looked down at his suit and shoes; they wouldn't do either.

Jack's reverie was interrupted when he heard Marge say, "Jack, Anna Wilson is on line two."

"Anna, what can I do for you?" he said.

Anna told Jack her ideas for planning Mrs. Tate's funeral and asked him to come by the house to further discuss the matter, along with some other things on her mind.

When the cab driver left Jack on the sidewalk in front of the beautiful old stone house, he noticed that it wasn't in an area that boasted of big money, but it sure had old money written all over it. Jack was impressed, but not surprised, by how well the place was maintained. The sound of the front door opening shifted his attention. Anna came partially out of the door and smiled. "Mr. Porter, would you like to come in?"

Once inside, Anna invited Jack to join Robby and her for dinner—hot dogs and macaroni and cheese were on the menu. With a young boy in the house, their family dinners were quite simple.

As the three of them sat around the table enjoying their meager meal, Jack was as impressed with the inside of the house as he was the exterior. He could not get over the beauty of the woodwork.

Robby went on and on about the cool things he got for his new room, and he made Jack promise that he would come upstairs to see everything before he left.

What Jack noticed most was the happiness in Anna's eyes. He found it very difficult to imagine her all alone in the big house. Robby belonged here with her, and it was obvious to him that they belonged together.

When the trio finished their meal, Robby dragged Jack upstairs to show off his new things, and Anna made herself a cup of tea and put on a fresh pot of coffee for Jack. She had always been a good judge of people, and she was certain Jack was a good man.

Over coffee, Jack told Anna his latest news. He hired Jake Rollins to defend Mr. Tate on the murder charges, and that he agreed to a price of around fifteen thousand dollars to handle the case, barring there were no complications. He assured her that Jake was a good man and a fine attorney.

This news made Anna happy, because the faster this whole matter was behind them, the better things would be for Robby. She also told Jack that she wanted him to arrange for Robby's mother to have a proper burial, including a private viewing for Robby. It was important for the young boy to see his mom one more time so that he could have some closure. Anna took care of everything, even down to the engraving on the headstone—Beloved Mother. She arranged to put forty thousand dollars in his bank account to cover the funeral and any other expenses he might incur while representing her interests. In return, she expected regular progress reports, along with documentation showing exactly how he was spending her money.

When Anna dropped the expense account bomb on him, Jack had a difficult time containing himself. The first thought that came into his head was to jump up on the dining room table and dance. Instead, he sat there smiling. A client like Anna Wilson didn't come along very often.

Jack explained to Anna that the only other matter concerning Robert's father was the liquidation of his estate, which consisted of the house and its contents. He informed her that he thought it would be in her best interest to wait until the criminal proceeding was further along before putting those wheels in motion.

Anna conveyed her thanks to Jack and said, "It appears that I'm in good hands, Mr. Porter."

As he headed toward the door, Jack said, "If anything else comes up, I'm only a phone call away."

"You can count on it young man," Anna said.

chapter seven

When Jack sat down for breakfast, he picked up the newspaper sitting on the next table. Most of the articles he looked at reminded him of why he did not read the paper anymore. It seemed like the same thing every day. All that changed were the names and faces. Just as he was ready to set the paper back on the table, an article on the James Tate case caught his eye: Thirty-nine-year-old James Tate, a resident of Highland Park, is suspected of the brutal slaying of his thirty-five-year-old wife, Jennifer. A ten-year-old unnamed minor is in the custody of social services. Criminal defense attorney Jake Rollins is representing Tate at his arraignment on Friday morning at nine a.m. The district attorney's office will not confirm or deny the rumors that they would be seeking the death penalty. Tate is currently in custody at the Allegheny County Jail without bond.

When Jack finished breakfast, he decided to take the newspaper to the office to show Marge. She was busy on the phone when Jack came in the door. Holding her finger up, she motioned for him to wait by her desk. Confused, he let his briefcase drop to the floor and waited. As soon as the receiver hit the phone, Marge lit into him.

"What the hell is going on, Jack?" she said.

"Nothing, Red. Why do you ask?"

"Well, forty thousand dollars mysteriously showed up in the bank account this morning. I double checked, and it's accurate."

"I'll explain it to you after I get settled. By the way, why would you check our bank account balance?" he asked.

"Jack, I check it every morning so we don't overdraw the account. There are a lot of things I do here that you don't know about."

Jack explained his meeting with Anna Wilson to Marge. To say she was shocked at his good fortune would have been an understatement. She knew Jack worked hard, but his hefty forty-thousand-dollar payday would sure make doing his job a lot easier. It made her job somewhat easier, too, because his stress often became her stress, and knowing where his next paycheck was coming from just lightened the load.

While Jack was meeting with a client, Marge got busy contacting the city morgue to inform them that the funeral home would be picking up Jennifer Tate's body within twenty-four hours, and then calling several funeral homes in the Highland Park area for prices. When she found one that suited their needs, she set up a meeting to handle the arrangements.

Jake Rollins was no stranger to the harsh sights and sounds of the county jail, but he never got used to the sound of the mechanical doors opening and the guards staring at him with disdain because he was a criminal defense attorney. Chills went down his spine each time he heard the echoing sounds of inmates screaming obscenities at one another. He thought to himself, *This is my world*.

When Jake got to the door, he said to the guard, "Jake Rollins to see James Tate."

"Sign in and take a seat in room number three," the guard said rather indifferently. "You know the drill, counselor."

The seasoned defense attorney looked around the small ten-by-ten room while waiting for the guard to deliver Tate. A few minutes later, the door opened, and in walked his new client.

Standing, Jake extended his hand. "Hello, Mr. Tate, my name is Jake Rollins, and I've been hired by Jack Porter to represent you."

Not extending a hand back, Tate asked, "Are you a good lawyer?"

The two men sat down at the table, and Jake said, "I've been practicing criminal law for over ten years. I rarely lose a case, because I know when to go to trial and when not to. So, yes, when my clients listen to me, I'm a damn good lawyer."

"The article in the newspaper said they were going to seek the death penalty," Tate said, fidgeting in his seat.

"Don't concern yourself about that. The district attorney's office is posturing because this is a high profile case. Public opinion is a powerful beast. Now, tell me everything that happened that night … and, Mr. Tate, it's very important that you be straight with me."

Tate nodded his head.

During their meeting, James Tate admitted to back handing his wife on several occasions for nagging him. According to James, she was always giving me him crap for having a few beers or because he wasn't bringing home enough money. The attorney explained the arraignment process to his client and told him to plead not guilty, but that because of the seriousness of the charges, the judge most likely would deny bail. He also informed his client that after the dust settled a bit, he would negotiate a plea bargain with the prosecutor, promising to get the death penalty off the table.

After they concluded their meeting, James Tate extended his hand to his attorney this time, grateful for his efforts at sparing his life.

Decorating a boy's room was new to Anna, but she was looking forward to spending this time with Robby and helping him to make the room his own. Given the devastating loss he suffered recently, he needed to feel secure and loved, and that was Anna's sole intent.

Armed with a step stool and a roll of double-sided tape, Anna and Robby hung the posters he had picked out. Next, Anna removed the tags from Robby's new clothing and put everything neatly in its proper place. Robby carefully posed his new action figures on top of the dressers, and the case containing the Matchbox cars found a home on the floor inside the closet, next to his new shoes.

As Robby's room was just about finished, Anna thought it would be a good time to sit Robby down to discuss his mom's upcoming viewing and funeral. She hesitated a moment, as she didn't want to dampen the mood, but this was important, and it was something she knew Robby had to face.

"Robby, have you ever been to a funeral?"

"Yes, when my uncle died my mom and dad took me to see his body. They called it a viewing," he said.

"That's correct, and your mom's viewing will be in a couple of days."

"Then what happens?" he asked, putting his head down.

"The day after the viewing, she will be buried at Willow Grove Cemetery. It's not far from here, so you can visit her grave whenever you like," Anna said, hoping this would give the boy some solace.

"Can we send flowers to the funeral home?" he asked.

"We sure can," Anna said.

Anna wrapped her arms around Robby and held him close. She didn't believe that any child should have to go through such pain and loss, but she found peace in knowing that she would be with him, every step of the way.

While preparing dinner, Marge, Jack's secretary, called Anna to share the arrangements for Mrs. Tate's viewing and funeral and to check on how things were going with Robert. Having her support, as well as Jacks, meant a great deal to Anna, and she planned to thank them again in person at the viewing.

After dinner, Anna and Robby retired to the living room. Robby's eyes lit up when he saw all the books that lined the built-in shelves. Anna's collection, which she started when she was just a little bit older than he was, included fine literary works that dated hundreds of years old.

Anna further stirred Robby's imagination with titles like *Treasure Island, The Old Man and the Sea,* and *White Fang.* In her mind, recreational reading was the best way for a child to learn, and seeing the excitement in Robby's eyes gave her more pleasure than she could have imagined.

"Anna, did you ever write a book?" Robby asked.

"No, but I think I will when this is all over," she said.

"Will I be in it?" he asked excitedly.

"Count on it, young man."

Scanning the shelves, Anna found the book that piqued Robby's interest the most: *Treasure Island.* As she dusted it off and handed him the leather-bound volume, she thought to herself, *what boy wouldn't love reading about pirates and buried treasure and swashbucklers?*

Robby took hold of the book with both hands, as though it were a fragile egg, and gently stroked the brown leather cover. He opened the book with care and peeled back the title page to reveal a colorful picture of swashbucklers in ornamental attire. In the foreground, Long John Silver rested on his peg leg while supporting a parrot on his left shoulder. Robby's eyes sparkled as he leafed through the first few pages of the book, and he knew in that moment that he and Anna would share many adventures together.

Jake Rollins arrived at the courthouse about twenty minutes early. Sporting a fine blue pinstriped suit and a silk paisley tie, he sat on the marble bench outside the courtroom and took in the sights in the halls of the courthouse. Rays of sunlight streamed down the towering walls from the windows above. The term "halls of justice" always came to mind when he entered the courthouse.

Arraignment hearings were merely a formality, and today's should be no different. Dan Williams was prosecuting the Tate case, which suited Jake just fine. He was hoping he would have had time to feel him out on the plea bargain matter before the hearing began, but he had dealt with Dan in the past and knew him to be a reasonable man. One thing that would not be up for consideration today was bail. Despite his reasonableness, Dan Wilson would request remand of Tate, and the judge most likely would grant it. Still, Jake would instruct his client to enter a plea of not guilty.

In the courtroom, both attorneys settled in at their respective tables. While they busied themselves shuffling through their legal paperwork, anticipating the arrival of Judge Edward Brown, two deputies were removing the shackles and handcuffs from James Tate before escorting him into the courtroom.

Jake greeted Tate with a handshake as he approached the defendant's table, and then proceeded to tell him what was about to happen. The court reporter sat patiently in her chair, waiting for the judge to arrive, and several newspaper reporters had gathered in the gallery. As the door to the judge's chamber opened, the bailiff announced, "All rise for the honorable Judge Edward Brown."

Brown had been a circuit judge for more than twenty years. Tall, with a slender build, he had a full head of silver hair. Defense and prosecuting attorneys alike respected him for his fairness.

"What is our first case?" Judge Brown asked.

"The Commonwealth of Pennsylvania verses James Tate," the bailiff said. "The charge is first degree murder."

"Mr. Tate, how do you plead?" asked the judge.

As instructed, Tate replied, "Not guilty, your Honor."

"Mr. Smith, does the prosecution have any thoughts on bail?"

"Your Honor, the defendant is accused of stabbing his wife ten times in front of their ten-year-old son," said Attorney Williams. "I ask that you remand him to the Allegheny County Jail without bond."

The judge looked at the defense attorney "Mr. Rollins, I'm sure you have something to say."

"Your Honor, my client has no prior criminal record. He owns a home in Highland Park and has had the same job for thirteen years. I am sure that he is not a flight risk."

"Nice try, Mr. Rollins, but I'm siding with the prosecution on this one. Bail is denied."

With that, the sheriff removed Tate from the courtroom, and Dan Williams motioned for Jake Rollins to meet him in the hallway. Everything went exactly the way Jake Rollins expected. He knew before he even walked into the proceeding that the judge was going to deny bail, but it was his job to try; however, he was a little surprised when Dan Williams suggested that they meet the following week to discuss the case. For now, his client would have to get used to living behind bars.

❧ ☙ ❧ ☙

Robby couldn't help but notice his father's picture staring back at him from the front page of the newspaper on the dining room table. He picked it up and took it to his room. The article recapped his father's arraignment on first-degree murder charges for the brutal stabbing of his mother. He ripped the article out and threw the newspaper on the floor. Suddenly, the reality of the situation came rushing into his mind: the memory of his father's evil voice screaming obscenities at his mother, her blood splashed everywhere as she lay dying on the floor, and the helplessness he felt when trying in vain to save her life.

Dinner was almost ready when Anna called Robert to the table. When he didn't answer, she went upstairs to his room. Her concern turned into surprise when she saw him balled up on the floor, sobbing. Pieces of torn newspaper were scattered on the floor. Anna sat down next to him and gently took him into her arms. They sat quietly for a long time before Robby spoke.

"I tried to save her! I tried to save my mom. I really did!" he screamed.

Anna tried to comfort him, and said, "It wasn't your fault, Robby."

"There was so much blood everywhere! I was so scared he was going to kill me too."

"Anyone would have been scared," Anna said, trying to calm him. "You were very brave to try to help your mother. Most people couldn't have done that."

He barked back in anger, "I hate my father! I hope he dies!"

Anna hugged Robby tightly and kissed him on the cheek. The thought of telling him not to hate his father entered her mind, but she thought better of it. Her hope was that he would find a way to work through the venomous hatred he was experiencing. While holding him close, she whispered to him, "I will always be here for you. No one will ever hurt you like this again."

chapter ....
·············· eight

Marge arrived at the office a little earlier than usual. The bag she put on the shelf above the coat rack contained black high heels and a new pair of stockings; she was anticipating the trip to the funeral home after work. She had arranged for her sister to watch her son when he got home from school, and she posted the usual to-do list on the refrigerator. Even though her ten-year-old son was a good boy, she was ever vigilant to make sure he remained that way.

When Jack entered the office, Marge could not believe her eyes. He was wearing a sharp grey suit, wing tip shoes, and was sporting a new a haircut that cost more than a dollar.

Jack saw the surprised look on Marge's face and said, "What are you looking at Red?"

She smiled and said, "Damn, Jack, you really clean up good!"

"You know me; anything to please a client," he said.

Anna glanced at the clock next to her bed. It was eight a.m. Her first thought was to check on Robert, especially after the emotional evening he had, but just as she was putting on her housecoat, she heard a clanging sound in the hallway. When she opened the door, she was startled to find Robby holding a breakfast tray. He had gone to great lengths to make sure everything looked perfect, right down to the linen napkin and a silk flower taken from one of the vases in the living room. She was overwhelmed with emotion by the boy's kind gesture.

Anna sat on the edge of the bed as Robby placed the tray next to her. The tea was quite strong, and the toast was saturated with butter. A few bites were all she could bare. Even though the morning meal wasn't the most appetizing of breakfasts, the emotional significance behind it was one of the sweetest experiences she ever had. At that precise moment, she realized that Robby's hunger for love could only be matched by her desire to give it.

Anna sat in front of the mirror, fixing her hair. She decided on a small flower barrette to complement her flowing hair. The string of pearls draped around her neck enhanced the black dress she wore. She was not one to put on a lot of makeup, but this day she made an exception. Everything needed to be perfect, and she was determined to make sure that happened. This was Robert's moment, a moment in time he would always remember. The final time he would spend with his mother's earthly body.

Robert appeared at Anna's door. "How do I look, Anna?"

"You look very handsome, young man."

"Do you know how to fix a tie?" he asked.

"I sure do. When I was a young girl, I would watch my dad do his ties in the mirror. Eventually, he let me tie them for him. After I fix your tie, we will comb your hair."

After the two finished dressing and grooming, they went downstairs to wait for Jack and Marge to arrive. Anna could not help but notice that Robby inserted a shiny penny in each one of his new shoes. That in itself was a precious moment for her.

❧ ❧ ❧ ❧

Jack and Marge finished the day's business and headed out to dinner at Poli's before going to Anna's house. The restaurant was on the way to Highland Park, and it had a reputation for serving great food. Secretly, Marge was just happy to go somewhere that did not feature a "happy meal" on the menu. It was strange for Jack and Marge to be interacting after work socially. Visiting the funeral home was not exactly a social affair, but it felt like one, as they were both sharply dressed, *and* they were going to share a meal together. More important, he was the one picking up the check. In her mind, that qualified as a social affair.

In Jack's eyes, he and Marge were a team. It was obvious they complemented one another. Jack masked his feelings for her with superficial layers of humor and sarcasm. He knew there were not many women out there that would be as loyal as Marge. She stuck with him during the hard times, and he would never forget it.

As they pulled into Highland Park, Jack gave Marge Anna's house number.

Jack pointed, and said, "It's that big stone house across from the park."

"Damn, Jack, this is a beautiful house."

"Years ago, this area used to be for rich folks only. When Anna was a young girl, all of Highland Park was inhabited by the wealthy."

Curious, she asked, "What does it look like inside?"

"Well, my dear, you're about to find out."

Robby was in the midst of fussing about wearing the restricting suit for such a long period when the doorbell rang. The visitors at the door were exactly the sort of diversion the young man needed.

Anna was in the kitchen putting the final touches on a pineapple upside down cake. When she gave Robby the go ahead to answer the door, he raced through the dining room. Anna finished up in the kitchen and followed close behind.

As Jack and Marge entered the house, Anna said, "Hello, it is so nice to finally me you. You look very nice."

"Robby is quite the little gentleman in his suit," Marge said, smiling.

Looking at Marge with a bit of surprise on her face, Anna said, "How did you convince Jack to clean up his act? He looks so handsome."

"I would love to take credit for it," Marge said, "but I think you had more to do with it than me."

While the two women exchanged more small talk, it was decided that they would all gather back at the house later that evening for cake and coffee.

With the few minutes left before they needed to leave for the viewing, Anna took Marge on a quick tour of the house, while Jack went upstairs to visit Robby's room.

In the few short days since he last saw the room, it was taking on the boy's personality quite nicely. He listened attentively as Robby told him all about *Treasure Island*; it reminded him that he was once a child, too.

As Anna and Marge finished the house tour, Anna hollered up the stairs to the boys that it was time to leave for the funeral home. She then turned to Marge and said, Please forgive me for prying, but do you and Jack see each other socially?"

"No, not really," Marge replied.

Anna smiled. "I watch you together, and I think that will change in the future."

The ride to McCabe Funeral Home was rather subdued. Robby was thinking about letting his mother go; Anna was anticipating the young man's emotional needs; Jack was thinking about Anna and the boy; and Marge was digesting the comments Anna made back at the house.

As Anna, Robby, Jack, and Marge entered the front door, the smell of freshly cut flowers was everywhere. Robby remained close to Anna as he looked around. Jennifer Tate's name was above the entrance to the room, and a perfectly groomed man in a black suit was standing next to a sign-in book. Small remembrance cards were in a holder next to the book. Robby and Anna signed in first, followed by Marge and then Jack.

When they entered the large room, Anna escorted Robby to a seat in the first row. She noticed three beautiful sprays of flowers and one smaller bouquet. She placed her arm around the young boy as he looked toward his mother's coffin. When he stood up, he reached for Anna's hand. She walked most of the way over with him, and when he released her hand, she let him go on alone. Without hesitation, he approached the beautiful coffin with his mother's body. Looking at his mom, he reached into a nearby flower arrangement and pulled out a single daisy, and then gently placed it in his mother's hair.

Tears began rolling down Anna's face as she watched the courageous young man facing his fears. He softly touched his mother's hand, kissed her on the cheek, and returned to Anna's side. "Don't cry, Anna," he said, "she's in heaven now. No one can hurt her anymore."

After Anna and the boy sat down, Jack and Marge went up to pay their respects. Marge noticed bouquets from Jack's office, Robby (Anna sent them in his name), and Robby's school, and a bouquet from the Atkins's family. But who was the Atkins's family?

It turned out that Mrs. Atkins was one of Anna's neighbors, who came to pay her respects. One of Robby's teachers, Mrs. Simon, was also there. Robby took both women by the hands over to meet Anna.

"Anna, this is Mrs. Atkins, my friend Ronnie's mom."

"Hello, I'm Anna Wilson."

"And this is Mrs. Simon, my teacher at school."

"It's nice to meet you," Anna said.

Excitedly, Robby said, "Anna was a school teacher too!"

"I want to thank you ladies for coming," Anna said, "and also for the beautiful flowers you sent. This is a very difficult time for Robby, and he needs all the support he can get."

"When I heard about the tragedy in his family, I took up a collection for the flowers. Most of the faculty and some of the students pitched in," Mrs. Simon said.

"This is Jack and Marge." Robby continued with his introductions. "They are our new friends from the city. Jack is our attorney. He fixed it so I can live with Anna."

Jack turned on the charm and said, "It's nice to meet you, ladies. Actually, I have a couple other clients too. Marge does most of the work and I take most of the credit."

While everyone participated in light conversation, Anna was able to breathe a sigh of relief. Much of the tension that had been building up to this point had dissipated. Things were going well at the funeral home, and Robert was proving to be the strong young man she knew he was. The unexpected appearance of his teacher and his friend's mother meant a great deal to him. It demonstrated that people cared about him.

Robby couldn't wait to shed himself of the constricting suit and tie he wore to the funeral home. While he was proud of how he looked for his mom, he was still a boy at heart, and casual wear would always rule the day. Next on his mind was pineapple upside down cake!

As Anna, Jack, and Marge made small talk over cake and coffee, Robby was happily gobbling up his second piece of dessert. While the conversation was light at first, it soon turned more serious.

"It was nice that your friend Ronnie's mom came to see you," Marge said to Robby.

"Yeah, Ronnie's my friend. We go to school together."

"Everything was so beautiful at the funeral home," Anna said.

"Yes, they did an excellent job," Jack remarked.

"The school went out of their way to extend their condolences. You do not see that very often,"

It had been a long day for everyone, and tomorrow would not be any easier. After Marge helped to clear the table, she and Anna chatted briefly, and then everyone said their goodbyes. As Anna stood in the doorway with her arm around Robby, they watched Jack and Marge drive away. She realized that the viewing at the funeral home was the apex of the situation for Robby and he handled it very well for a young boy.

Not many words were spoken when Anna and Robby went upstairs for the night. He even declined her offer to read to him. She simply kissed him on the forehead and retired to her room.

It had been a long day for both of them, physically and emotionally, and Anna welcomed the warm embrace of her bed. Despite her weariness this night, she knew she would never trade the current turmoil in her life for the loneliness she had before. One more day and the bulk of emotional distress would lessen. For now, the warmth of her soft comforter was all she wanted. Sweet slumber promised to lighten the load.

The irritating sound of the alarm clock brought Anna to life at six a.m. sharp. As she put on her robe, the pleasurable thought of a cup of tea came to mind. She looked in on Robby before making her way quietly down the stairs.

As Anna put the bread in the toaster and filled the kettle with water, Robby came bounding down the steps. She smiled as he plopped down at the table, wiping the sleep from his tired eyes. She greeted him with a smile and took his breakfast order: pancakes.

While Robby set the table, Anna mixed the pancake batter and started pouring the mixture onto the griddle. Before long, stacks of perfectly golden cakes adorned their plates.

Anna didn't care that she'd already eaten her toast. It was important for her to share this time with Robby.

Marge was hugging a cup of coffee across the table from Joel while he concentrated on eating a bowl of Sugar Bears cereal. During breakfast, the back of the cereal box was his preferred reading. Sliding the box out of the way, she gave him specific instructions for the day. Trish would be there soon to keep an eye on him. Even though he would be in school most of the day, Marge wanted somebody there to meet him at the school bus when he got home. He liked it when his Aunt Trish was there, because her idea of babysitting was controlled chaos. She made sure he remained safe, but other than that, she was just an adult presence. They had a symbiotic understanding: she did not tell Marge what he did and he did not tell his mom what she neglected to do.

Trish was a little early, which surprised Marge—her sister was always running late. With her sister now in charge, Marge threw kisses and behavioral warnings Joel's way as she headed out the door.

The sound of the doorbell signaled to Anna that Jack and Marge had arrived. She knew this day was going to be difficult for Robby, so she didn't mind when he raced down the stairs and immediately started telling Jack about his cool Matchbox cars.

After discussing where they might eat after the funeral, Anna let everyone know that they should be going. She wanted to give Robby time to say a proper goodbye to his mom before going to the cemetery. The chill in the air made its presence known as the group walked across the parking lot. A hearse was under the canopy waiting to usher Jennifer Tate to her final resting place. Behind it sat a clean and shiny black limousine with a magnetic placard on the hood. Anna ushered Robby through the door, followed by Jack and Marge. Once seated in the viewing room, the director whispered something in her ear. She excused herself and followed him out to the hallway. After a brief discussion, she motioned for Jack to join them. A couple minutes of conversation went by before Jack returned to his seat. Marge watched the entire interaction, hoping she had not missed anything in the planning.

Jack looked at Marge and said, "Thanks Red."

"What are you talking about Jack?"

"You neglected to tell me that I am a pallbearer."

"The funeral home only had three people on hand, and I was trying to keep the expense down. Besides, I knew you wouldn't mind."

"In the future, let me know ahead of time."

"Jack, I hope we don't have to do this again for a long time."

Jack grinned and said, "I agree, Red."

When Anna finished talking to the funeral director, she sat back down next to Robby and held his hand. She explained to him that his mom's body would be placed in the back of the hearse, and that they would follow behind in the big limousine. Marge and Jack would follow behind in a separate car. The caravan would then drive to the cemetery, where Pastor Williams would say a few words over his mother. When it was all over, they were going to take Jack and Marge to a nice restaurant to show their appreciation.

Robby nodded in understanding.

Anna said, "If you want to show your final respects, now would be the time to do so."

The young boy sat quietly for a few moments, and then said, "Anna, I will tell her goodbye, but that's not my mom in that box. She lives in heaven with God now."

After the final viewing, everyone waited in the hallway for the funeral director's instructions on what to do next. When the police car had arrived, it took the lead car position and waited for the signal to leave. Like grammar school children, everyone blindly followed the directions of the man in black. Once everyone was in their designated vehicles, the funeral director placed magnetic flags on each car. The lights on top of the cruiser began to rotate as it slowly drove onto the street. The slow, solemn four-mile drive to Willow Grove Cemetery had begun.

Anna gazed out the back window as the caravan moved along its course. Charcoal-colored clouds filtered out most of the sun's rays. The quilted ceiling above coincided with the rows of trees that long ago dropped their leaves. She would make certain Robby had everything life had to offer. Anna would enjoy her remaining years living vicariously through him.

Robby looked out the window as the funeral procession drove along the last quarter mile of the ride. When the limousine drove onto a side road, he noticed stone columns on each side of the blacktop road, with ornamental iron arches attached.

Mother Nature had stripped the perfectly pruned trees of their leaves. Off in the distance, grounds keepers were raking up dead leaves.

Two beautiful granite mausoleums with names on the front caught Robby's eye. Curious, he asked, "Anna, what are those stone buildings?"

"They are called mausoleums."

"What's that for?"

"Some people don't want to be buried in the ground, so they have those stone structures built with shelves inside."

"What are the shelves for?" These structures seemed to intrigue Robby.

"For their loved ones, when they pass away. They are usually constructed for an entire family."

When the hearse reached the burial site, everything was in order. A beautiful deep red carpet lined the ground leading from the road to the grave. A brass cradle was mounted over the opening in the ground. Everything went in slow motion as the driver opened the back door. When Anna saw that Robby wasn't moving, she and took hold of his hand. She could feel it trembling as she led him from the car. His mother's final resting place was before him, and he was afraid. At this moment, he feared everything about death and life.

Anna and Robby walked hand in hand to the closest point near the grave. It was not long before Marge and Pastor Williams made their way down to the final resting place as well. Jack and the other pallbearers then brought the casket from the back of the hearse.

The good pastor held a bible tight against his chest as they placed the coffin over the grave. When Robby reached out and touched the box containing his mother's body for the last time, he began to weep. He rested his head against Anna and took hold of her arm. It was hard for her to bear the boy's tears, but she realized he needed to let the pain out. If he had remained void of emotion through the entire affair, it would have given her cause for concern.

Pastor Williams called for a moment of reflection for Jennifer Tate, loving mother of Robert Tate. The silence was deafening as he delivered a brief prayer. The pastor opened his Bible to Psalm 23. All were attentive as he started to read, "The Lord is my shepherd, I shall not want …"

After the final prayer, the funeral director thanked Anna and assured her that everything went well. What he was really doing was thanking her for all the cash she sent his way. The representative from Willow Grove then approached Anna to inform her that the headstone would be in place in a week to ten days.

As Marge drove slowly through the cemetery, Robby asked Anna about the headstone for his mother's grave.

"Did the man say my mother's grave stone would be there in a week?" put her around him and said, "Yes, he said a week to ten days."

Looking out the window he said, "Tell me again what it looks like."

"There are beautiful Angels carved along the top. In the center, it has Jennifer Tate with the date she was born and the date she died. On the lower part, it has Loving Mother carved in flowing script."

"She would really like that," Robby said.

As they drove out of the cemetery, Anna brought up the subject of going out to eat. Robby suggested McDonalds, but Anna let him know that she wanted to take everyone to a nice restaurant. Jack then recommended Klein's. All that Robby cared about was that they served steak. They did, so Klein's it was!

While Marge was driving to the restaurant, each of them was lost in their own thoughts. Anna and Robby were embarking on a glorious new adventure in life. In the young boy's mind, he was pleased that his mother had such a beautiful burial. In his heart, he missed her terribly and longed to have her back.

Klein's was one of the most popular eating establishments in the city. They boasted of serving the best steaks in Pittsburgh, and their prices reflected it. When they walked to the front entrance, a smartly dressed attendant greeted them and opened the doors. The lighting inside was soft, but not excessively dim. The bar off to the left was busier than one would expect for the time of day. Anna instructed the host to seat them at one of the large tables away from the bar. Once seated, the wine steward approached the table with samples of their finest wines. Anna looked around the table to see if anyone was interested, but there were no takers. Next, a pleasant young man showed up with pitchers of ice-cold water and baskets of freshly baked bread. Once the crystal goblets were full and the baskets placed, he disappeared as quickly as he had arrived. Robby couldn't understand why two people had come to the table and seemingly forgot the menus. Everyone laughed, as Robby clearly wasn't used to dining in such a fine restaurant. Much of the day's tension melted away with the joyous outburst. Anna did not want Robby to be embarrassed so she explained the service procedures to him.

When the waiter arrived, he went around the table jotting down everyone's selection. It was not long before the aroma of sizzling steaks wafted through the air. Everyone at the table smiled as the elegant meals arrived. The waiter had all bases covered when it came to condiments. He made it a point to put the bottle of Heinz Ketchup within Robert's reach, and he smiled at the boy and assured him that he would bring his ice cream sundae when he was ready.

It was hard for Anna to remember the last time she went out to a nice restaurant. Other than necessary errands, she barely left the house. In recent years, trips to the grocery store had turned into phone-in deliveries. The recent trip she made to the city to handle the situation with Robby was the first time she had been there in almost ten years. When they went to Kaufmann's to purchase the boy's clothing, the store had completely changed from the last time she was there. The cocoon of solitude she created for herself would soon be in the past. School activities, swimming lessons, sports, and homework sessions would now take up a great deal of her time.

Everyone agreed that lunch was a huge success. Robert was the only member of the party to have desert. He was also the only member of the party to get ketchup on his good shirt. When he tried to get the remainder of his ice cream sundae put in a carryout container, everyone chuckled.

Anna paid the two hundred twenty dollar check with her Visa card, and gave the server a very generous tip of forty dollars. Extravagance was never Anna's way, but she felt the situation warranted it.

One of the character traits she inherited from her father was practicality. It helped him to become a wealthy business owner, and it aided her in becoming a good person. Frivolous living could best describe her siblings. They both had the attitude that the family money was their birthright. Her father's dream included his children running the factories he built. Anna went her own way by becoming a schoolteacher. When Elizabeth dropped out of college in her sophomore year, she took a position in the office at Wilson Tool and Die. She became disillusioned because she had to start at an entry-level position. She lasted less than six months at the job. Nathan learned early how to con his parents. Higher education was another tool for him to get what he wanted. He carried just enough courses to receive monthly checks from the family. He attended college in Cleveland Ohio for a couple of years without graduating. Chills ran down Anna's spine when she remembered one of his visits home. While drinking, he bragged to her in private that he got away with the murder of Carolyn Johnson. Even though Anna chose not to work for the family business, her father was proud of her personal accomplishments.

chapter
nine

There were many factors involved in the plea bargain process, and oftentimes, the hype preceding such a process is much more involved than the process itself.

Dan Williams extended his hand as Jake Rollins entered his office. "Good morning, Jake."

"Dan, I appreciate you seeing me so quickly. It would be good for everyone involved to put this case behind us."

The two attorneys exchanged some informal talk before Jake said, "What can you do for me on the Tate case, Dan?"

Shuffling some papers on his desk, Dan said, "We both know this doesn't meet the criteria of a death penalty case. I am thinking twenty-five to life."

"Come on, Dan," Jake said, a little irritated, "the guy was in a blackout and doesn't even remember most of it. He also has no priors in his jacket."

"Yeah, Jake, but he stabbed his wife ten times. Do you know what a jury will do with that?"

Jake tried to counter, and said, "Okay, Dan, how about fifteen?"

"Jake, you know I can't go down to fifteen. My best number is twenty to life, and that is a gift," Dan offered. "He will be out in about seventeen years, which is a hell of a lot better than we can say for his wife."

Jake Rollins paused for a moment, pondering the offer. "I'll see if I can sell it to my client."

Smiling and leaning back in his chair, Dan said, "You'll sell it to him, Jake, because you know it's a good offer. By the way, the offer has a shelf life of one day, so get back to me by the end of business today."

Jake grabbed his brief case and stood to shake the prosecutor's hand. "Thanks, Dan."

As Jake left the courthouse, he felt good about the way the negotiation went. The way he saw it, both of them got exactly what they wanted. Dan Williams was putting a murderer behind bars and increasing his conviction rate, and Jake Rollins was getting a nice payday without busting his ass. James Tate was cheating the hangman with no death sentence. The average person is under the impression that the judicial system is all about grandiose jury trials. The trial process is a small part of the way things operate. The real wheels of justice turn behind the scenes.

Robby and Anna had a very pleasant weekend. The emotional tension of the funeral was behind them, and the young boy was becoming more comfortable in his new environment. With his time off from school for the funeral—he would be going back to school in another week—Robby insisted that they take a stroll in the park each day. He enjoyed his time with Anna, and with his mom gone, he counted on her more than ever. He also had a lot on his mind.

Continuing on their walk, Anna and Robby enjoyed nature's beauty. Robby suddenly stopped and looked up at Anna. "Are you my mother now?"

Taking hold of Robby's hands, Anna bent down to his level and said, "Oh, sweetheart, I can never replace your mother, but I know that we will develop a very special bond between us, and I give you my word … I'll always be here for you."

While Anna was cooking, Robby took the opportunity to do some exploring around the house. The large garage out back looked like a good place to start.

Robby jumped up and down, attempting to look inside the double doors with a row of windows stretched across the front, but he was not tall enough. Not ready to give up, he made his way over to the door on the left side of the garage. At first, he could not turn the handle, but his continued effort broke it free. He looked around to make sure no one was watching before going inside. After searching along the wall, he was able to locate a light switch. The burst of light revealed a wonderland of old treasures inside the old, dusty building. Cobwebs hung from the corners of the ceiling and clung to the legs of a large table saw. A thick layer of dust coated the numerous power tools lined up on the twelve-foot workbench. His attention shifted to a large covered vehicle on the other side of the workshop. All he could see was a silhouette of a car and tires sticking out from under the cover. He looked around to make sure he was alone and then went over to look under the cover. As he pulled back the fabric to sneak a peek, the entire cover slid off and fell to the floor. Robby's eyes lit up as he gazed at the 1939 pearl white four-door Cadillac convertible, with large whitewall ties and lots of chrome. It looked like it had just come out of the showroom. Years of dust could not take away from the timeless beauty of the automobile.

Robby realized that he had spent far too much time admiring the antique car, and attempted to put the cover back on it before it became obvious that he had removed it. Each time he tried to put the cover back in place, it slipped off. Frustrated, he dragged a milk crate over to the car and stood on it while pulling the cover back onto the car. As he did so, he heard a familiar voice in the garage.

"Do you need help with that, young man?" Anna asked.

Startled, Robby said, "Anna! I just wanted to see what was in here."

"In the future, I want you to ask me first. How did you get in here? I thought the garage was locked."

Defending his actions, Robby declared, "The door was open, I promise."

"Okay, Robby, let's cover up the old girl together."

While they pulled the cover over the antique car, Robby asked, "Why don't you drive it? I saw pictures of cars like this in a magazine. This is the coolest thing I've ever seen."

Anna did not want to stir up memories of the past, so, instead, she just said, "It's time for dinner."

While Anna busied herself preparing dinner, Robby raced to the table. It seems his day of adventure made him quite hungry. He did his best to stay away from the subject of the car, but he couldn't help but picture himself driving down the road with the windows down and the wind in his hair. People would turn their heads as the sunlight glistened off the pearl white finish. Riding in that classic car would take coolness to a completely new level.

Anna noticed that Robby seemed to be daydreaming at the table, thinking about the car, no doubt, and she said, "The car is beautiful, isn't it, Robby?"

Excited that she didn't seem upset about the subject any longer, he said, "It sure is! I've never seen a car like that up close!"

"My father purchased the LaSalle when I was teaching English at Erie High School. He enjoyed fine automobiles for as long as I can remember, but this car was special to him. Health issues forced him to turn over the reins of his company to one of his subordinates. Even with a damaged heart, he spent a great deal of time in his car. Every weekend, without fail, while teaching in Erie, I moved back down to spend time with my parents. But after my father died of a heart attack, my mother had a stroke six months later. I moved back home and cared for her until she passed away."

"I'm sorry Anna," Robby said.

Anna smiled. "Don't be; they had a good life."

It was half past three when Jake Rollins arrived at the Allegheny County Jail. After signing in, the guard led him back to an available interview room. Soon after, the clanging of the steel door signaled the arrival of his client.

"How are you, Mr. Tate?" Jake asked, reaching out to shake his client's hand.

I've been better," Tate said.

"Hopefully, the news I have for you will lift your spirits. After meeting with the prosecuting attorney this morning, I was able to get you a good plea agreement. As you know, they were originally going to pursue the death penalty. We went back and forth and finally agreed on twenty years."

"How much time will I have to serve?" Tate asked.

"Sixteen or seventeen years," Jake said.

Tate paused for a minute, and then said, "Is that the best you can do?"

"Mr. Tate, you stabbed your wife to death in front of your son. Considering they wanted the death penalty, yes, I would say that's the best anyone can do for you."

After shuffling in his chair a bit, Tate finally resigned himself to the fact. "All right, Mr. Rollins, I'll accept the deal.

Robby went up to his room to play when they finished with the evening meal. Anna opted to enjoy a cup of tea while sitting quietly on the sofa. Looking toward the ceiling, she could hear the creaking sounds of the floors as Robby raced around. Even though she enjoyed time with him, she needed a little down time for herself. She felt positive about things in general, but was exhausted. It was as though all the recent events were landing on her shoulders at the same time. Leaning back against the plush cushion, she rested her eyes. Finding the perfect twilight state of mind, she drifted somewhere between reality and a dream state, but the solitude was interrupted when thoughts of money matters came into her head. Throughout her life, she made it a point not to be dependent on the family assets. Unlike her brother and sister, she had a career that met her modest needs. Destiny left her as the last one standing in the family. She dreamed of doing something good with the family's wealth before she moved on to the next world. Sure, she donated money each year to several worthwhile organizations, but she wanted to do so much more. With the introduction of Robert into her life, the dream could still happen.

The sounds of little feet running down the steps brought Anna back to total consciousness. Robert went directly into the kitchen and poured himself a glass of fruit juice. He went into the living room to see what Anna was doing.

"Can we watch television together before bed?" he asked.

Happy to share time with the youngster, she replied, "Sure; that sounds like fun."

Once Robby settled in next to Anna with a bowl of snacks, he started flipping through the television stations. He came to a halt when the *Simpsons* flashed on the screen. The excited expression on his face told Anna it was his choice. Robert laughed and jumped around as he the crazy antics. She had never heard of the *Simpsons* show, but most television was foreign to her. Initially, she thought it might be harmless because it was animated. Deciding to give it a chance, she sat back and watched with Robby. One of the first scenes showed the father, Homer, chasing his son, Bart, with a hammer. Apparently, Bart put dog crap on the front step so Homer would step in it. Bart is not very bright, so he compensates for it by taking on the role of a practical joker. The next scene introduces Lisa, who is the daughter in the family. She is very intelligent and creative, which subjects her to constant ridicule. Marge is the ultra-understanding wife and mother who juggles all their personalities. The baby crawling around with a pacifier in her mouth seems to be the only sane member of the dysfunctional family.

Anna was not very happy about Robby's choice of television show. It was hard for her to believe that parents let their children watch such crap. Once things settled down and they got into a more normal routine, she was going to do her best to veer him away from shows like the *Simpsons*.

During a commercial break, Anna said, "How long have you been watching this show, Robby?"

He laughed and said, "Since I was a kid."

"That's a long time," she said sarcastically.

"Yes, isn't it funny?"

"It's definitely different," Anna said.

When the show resumed, Robby's focus was on Homer's outlandish shenanigans. Anna wanted to rest her eyes, so she leaned back and tuned out the television. Staying close to Robby was important to her, so going up to bed would have to wait. She was well aware of the fact that there were many things to learn about him. She wanted him to respect her, but not to think of her as a heavy-handed authoritarian. In many ways, he awoke the child within her, making the seventy-year age difference between them irrelevant.

Anna awakened to her all too familiar aches and pains and the sound of static dancing across the television screen. She felt Robby pressed against her side, sound asleep. She turned off the television, and coaxed the young boy up the stairs and helped him into bed.

From the time Marge got up in the morning until she crawled into bed at night, it seemed like she was constantly busy. At home, she fixed breakfast, dressed her son for school, did the housework, and got herself ready to leave for the office. Usually the drive into the city included concerns about how well the car was running. While at work, she handled all the details that made Jack's cases happen. Even though he was a talented attorney, none of it would work without Marge's organizational skills. As she reached over to turn off the alarm clock, she noticed snowflakes floating in the air.

Cursing the unexpected weather, Marge said, "Damn, it's snowing!"

"What's wrong, Mom?"

Realizing she needed to leave early, she said, "Joel, I want you to hurry up and get ready for school. I'll make breakfast while you get dressed."

Joel saw an opportunity to miss school and said, "Maybe I should stay home today?"

She barked back, "You are not staying home from school!"

She had been through the drill many times before. Joel gave her a hard time and she gave it right back. While hurrying to get dressed, she remembered to call her sister, to ask her to come over a little early. With the snow coming down, she wanted to make sure that Trish got there before traffic got too crazy.

Marge didn't need to wear makeup—she was pretty without it—but the little she did use was going to have to wait until she arrived at the office. As she drove out of the parking lot and onto the street, she pumped her brakes to see how slippery the roads were. She also noticed that her gas gauge was a little below a quarter tank, so she added getting gas to her mental list of things to do.

Traffic was moving slowly, and every now and then Marge hit an icy spot. She was short on patience, and gas, this morning as she maneuvered down the side streets, and just hoped she'd make it to work on time. When she made the turn down Fifth Avenue, she peeked at the clock on her dashboard. Realizing she would make it with ten minutes to spare, she let out a sigh of relief. Normally, it would not have been a big deal if she was a few minutes late, but Jack had a meeting at the jail with a potential client this morning, so he most likely would not be in the office until around nine thirty.

Anna had been up for more than an hour. After her morning tea and toast, she finished her daily chores downstairs. Even though she was not a big fan of the cold weather, she loved the snow. In between her household duties, she opened the front door to view the magical white blanket Mother Nature had delivered. It was not long before Robby came running down the steps to inform Anna that it had snowed. He stood side by side with her at the front door to view the winter wonderland.

"Can I go outside and play?" Robby asked, excited.

"Yes, if we can find a hat and gloves for you to wear."

"Great! I'll go get ready."

"Young man, you'll eat breakfast first!" she called after him.

When Robby finished his breakfast, he hurried up the stairs to change into his play clothes, and then hurried back downstairs. He wasn't happy with the hat Anna placed on his head—it was the Elmer Fudd type, with earflaps—but she promised she would buy him a new one the next time they went shopping. He opted not to wear the gloves.

Eager to get outside and play, Robby headed out the door, with Anna right behind him. A light snow was falling, and a group of birds was huddled together on the electrical line, attempting to find warmth. The accumulation was minimal, but it covered the ground.

Robby ran ahead as they neared the edge of the park. Gleefully, he scooped up a handful of the freshly fallen powder and made a snowball. After tossing it at nothing in particular, he lay down on an undisturbed area of snow and made a snow angel. Anna looked on with joy in her heart, as he reminded her of a fun-filled part of the past. When Robby invited her to make a snow angel, she considered it, but declined.

Neither the freezing cold nor his wet hands could dampen Robby's youthful enthusiasm.

As she watched Robby playing on the slide, Anna's heart skipped a beat when he slipped on one of the ladder rungs leading to the top of the slide. Not to be deterred, Robby got right back up off the ground and made his way to the top. After a couple cold trips down the icy slide, it lost its appeal.

Robby looked over at Anna and saw her bending down to scoop up some snow. She formed a snowball and threw it at him. Laughing, he came running over to her side. She gently placed her hands on his red cheeks and smiled. Standing next to each other, Anna and Robby laughed together as they threw snowballs toward the trees.

When their wintery outing was over, the chilled pair hurried back to the house to change clothes. While Robert was upstairs, Anna prepared two cups of hot cocoa to take the chill off, and then she called the school and left a message to set up a meeting with Robby's teacher, Mrs. Simon. She got a good feeling about the woman when she met her at the funeral home. Anna was anxious to speak with her, because she recalled from her days as a teacher that children could be cruel, and she wanted to make sure that Robby's return to school would not be met with such unpleasantness.

Robert's cheeks were still red as he wrapped his hands around the steaming cup of cocoa. Anna had a great time with him outdoors earlier, and she loved seeing the smile on his face, especially given the heartache he had recently suffered.

As Anna and Robby enjoyed sipping their cocoa, Mrs. Simons returned Anna's call, and the two women set up a meeting for later that afternoon. She was happy to learn in their brief conversation that she was eager to see Robby back at school.

Robby was anxious to know the outcome of the call and what his teacher had to say about him. He asked if he could go to the meeting with Anna, but trying to show his independence, he said, "This time I want to go with you, but you can leave me by myself if you ever need to. My mother used to leave me without a sitter all the time."

"Please humor an old woman, because I plan on keeping you close to me for the time being," Anna said, smiling.

❧ ☙ ❧ ☙

The cab ride to the school was loaded with anticipation along with periods of anxiety. Robby was excited about getting back to school. Even though he complained about certain aspects of school, he missed his friends. Anna realized all too well how important it was for him to return to at least one normal part of his life, and spending time with young people his age was a very important part of his social development. The anxiety she was experiencing originated from fear that other children might say hurtful things to him in light of his situation. It's not every child whose father murders their mother. It would break her heart to have him come home from school in tears. It was obvious to her that emotional ties between them were growing stronger each day.

Robby was excited as the taxi drove into the school parking lot. Seeing how he felt helped to ease Anna's worries. He immediately took hold of Anna's hand, pulling her towards the entrance of the school.

"C'mon, I'll show you around," Robby said.

Robby took Anna on the grand tour, showing her the auditorium, the gym, and the cafeteria where they eat lunch.

"Sometimes there are bake sales for raising money for stuff," he said, "and the baseball field and playground are behind the building."

As they walked into the school's main office, a woman with a look on her face that said she was glad the day was almost over greeted them. "Can I help you?"

"My name is Anna Wilson, and I'm here to see Mrs. Simon."

The weary woman said, "Is she expecting you?"

"Yes, we have a three o'clock appointment."

"Please have a seat, and I'll let her know you're here."

Anna and Robby took a seat along the glass wall next to the doors. While Anna was looking at the setup behind the counter, Robby turned around on his chair to see the kids walking in the hallway. Anna looked on as he waved at several of his classmates. The enthusiasm she saw in his demeanor made her realize that he was ready to return to school.

"Anna, those are some friends from my class!" he said excitedly.

"I see that," she said.

"It will be great to see them again!" Robby said.

"Don't worry, you will be back in school soon," Anna said.

With talk of Robby returning to school, Anna felt a little sense of jealousy. She silently scolded herself for such a ridiculous emotion. The time she had been spending with Robby was very precious to her. She told herself that school was going to be another part of life they could share. Homework would be a daily activity in their lives, along with discussions about the difficulties of his day. A smile found her face as she realized that school would be something else they could enjoy together.

Mrs. Simons came into the office, smiling, and said, "Hello, Robby and Anna, it's nice to see you. How does it feel to be back at school?"

"Great! I saw Bill, Tommy, and a couple other guys in the hall."

"Robby," Mrs. Wilson addressed him, "would you please wait in the outer office for a little while so Anna and I can talk?"

As the two women sat down and got comfortable, Anna said, "Let me get right to the point. What are your plans to help Robby when he's not home with me?"

"As his teacher, I will have the most contact with him, which makes me the barometer of Robert's emotional state. If I notice any unusual changes in his personality, I will call to inform you."

When Anna and Mrs. Simon finished their meeting, Robby was eager to continue the tour of the school. Mrs. Simon set off to work on her lesson plans and reassured Anna that she'd be sure to watch over Robby.

Robby was concerned that he wasn't allowed to be in the meeting with Anna and his teacher, but Anna put his concerns to rest, telling him that he didn't miss anything; it was just a couple of women chit-chatting. Besides, she knew he'd be eager to look for some of his friends while they met.

"It should make you happy that you're coming back to school on Thursday," Anna said to Robby.

Concerned that she would be lonely without him, Robby said, "Don't worry, Anna, we can hang out together after school."

Marge was busy in the office all day. She spent most of her time on the phone talking to potential clients. That was a good thing, because it meant that Jack was going to be busy interviewing new clients, which, in turn, meant more income. She had visions of a larger office, new equipment, and a healthier paycheck. Jack's drive to succeed was fueled by his need to redeem himself in the legal community. Marge had no illusions of grandeur; her goal was to provide a better life for her and her son.

It was close to four o'clock when Jack returned to the office. He'd had a damn good day for himself. Marge was on the telephone, so he put his briefcase on the desk and waited for her to finish with the call.

"How was your day, Red?" he asked as she hung up the phone.

"It was busy as hell here, Jack!"

"That's good, isn't it?" he asked.

"Of course it is. I filled up your schedule for the rest of the week!"

"Great! I had a good day myself. Hey, Red, let's go out to dinner after work."

"Sorry, Jack, I have to get home to Joel."

Jack was clearly disappointed. "Maybe another time, then."

"Jack …"

"Yes, Red?"

"Would you like to come to my place for dinner? That is, if you don't mind Joel joining us."

Pleased by the offer, he said, "It sounds like fun."

It would be accurate to say that Marge was blindsided by Jack's invitation to dinner. Initially, She tried to convince herself it was only a gesture of kindness for a job well done. She was not sure if the attraction to him was because of his tough exterior or the fact that he was an attorney. One thing was certain; she secretly wanted to be with him on more than a professional level. Just the fact that he was willing to come to her place to spend time with Joel increased her respect for him.

The phone rang for the thirtieth time that day. She figured it was another distressed criminal or a member of their family searching for an all-powerful attorney.

"Jack Porter, Attorney at Law, how can I help you?"

"Marge, it's Trish."

Marge was surprised that her sister was calling.

"Did something happen to Joel?" she asked, concern filling her voice.

"Relax, nothing's wrong. I just need you to stop at the grocery store on your way home. You're out of milk, bread, and almost everything else."

Relieved that nothing was wrong, Marge said, "Can you do me a huge favor, Sis?"

"It depends."

"Take Joel and pick up a few things at the store. I'll give you the money when I get home."

"Okay, but you'll owe me big time!" Trish said, joking.

Marge laughed. "Thanks, I have to go. I have another call."

Thoughts of French fries, chicken fingers, and pudding pops filled Marge's head. For a minute, she second-guessed herself for extending the dinner invitation to Jack, and then she tried to focus on her work. Impressing Jack was near the bottom of her list of things to do. At this time in her life, paying the bills, maintaining her car, and taking care of Joel was her number one job. She sure as hell was not going to tiptoe around him like a nervous young girl. She was not even sure if she had the emotional fortitude to participate in a relationship. Nonetheless, she was looking forward to Jack coming over.

꙾ ꙾ ꙾ ꙾

Once they got into the cab, Robby gave Anna a not too subtle reminder about the hat and gloves he needed. He also informed her that he needed school supplies before Thursday; Anna learned that he needed a backpack, too. Robby's store of choice was Kmart!

When they entered the store, Robert instinctively latched onto a shopping cart the same way he did when he would shop with his mother. Eager to shop, he said, "Come with me, Anna. I'll show you where everything is."

Seeing the excitement in his eyes, she said, "You lead the way, young man."

"Do you like soft pretzels, Anna?"

"Sure, they're good."

"They have the biggest pretzels in the world here!"

"Well, then, we better buy a couple after we're finished shopping."

Robby stayed several steps ahead of Anna as he raced around the store. He was moving so quickly that Anna had to walk in front of the shopping cart to force him to slow down. It was obvious the youngster was very familiar with the layout of store. Anna noticed the section where the hats and gloves were located. Robert's idea was to check out the backpacks and school supplies first, but she put a kink in his plan and made him first pick out his new hat and gloves. Although Anna wasn't too thrilled with Robby's selections, she let him have his way. His goal was getting to the backpacks.

Robby's eyes lit up as they arrived at the long table of backpacks. Anna enjoyed watching Robby search for the perfect one. She could tell he was not going to finish his mission until he located the coolest one in the bunch. Just when it looked like he was going to choose the one with Captain America on it, he changed his mind and went for Batman instead.

As they headed toward the door with their new purchases in tow, Robby said, "Can we please have a pretzel, Anna?"

Remembering her earlier conversation with Robby about how much he loved the large pretzels, Anna gave in to his request. They both decided on the giant pretzels with cheese; Anna got mustard with hers, too.

As the duo sat at a small table enjoying their treat together, Anna thought to herself, *Robby was right; these pretzels are very tasty!*

chapter
ten

The ride to Marge's apartment for dinner was full of unexpected surprises. When she stopped to buy gas, Jack instinctively got out of the car and pumped it. She could not remember the last time a man even offered to perform such a service. At work, she found it necessary to be a no nonsense kind of woman. She found her tough demeanor melting away during the drive to her home. In the past, thoughts about her and Jack becoming more than work associates were pushed to the back of her mind. Of course, she knew he was easy to look at, and he would be a successful attorney again, but she did not need any emotional turmoil in her already complicated life. Her life had become one of survival, with little time for enjoyment.

From the first time he met her, Jack thought Marge was one of the most beautiful women he had ever laid eyes on. He wanted to sleep with her from the start, until he realized how indispensable she was at the office. He wanted to be closer to her, but not close enough to burn down what they had accomplished. Jack forced himself to engage in small talk to keep it impersonal, not wanting to pry into her personal life. Whatever she offered would be sufficient, at least for now.

"Jack, I apologize ahead of time for not offering you a better dinner. I'm not used to having guests on the spur of the moment."

"It's my fault for not thinking about Joel being alone. I have an idea that might make everyone happy."

"What idea is that?"

"How about we stop and pick up a couple pizzas on the way to your place? Kids love pizza. Hell, everyone loves pizza! It will save you the hassle of cooking, and it will get me in good with your son."

"Are you sure, Jack? Don't forget, I'm the woman who knows how much money you have."

"It's definitely cheaper than taking you out for dinner. Besides, it will be fun. Did you know I've been looking forward to meeting Joel for a long time?"

"No, Jack, I didn't know. We'll see if you still feel that way after tonight."

"Come on, Red, he's just a kid."

Marge smiled. "He's actually a good boy. Sure, there's the normal stuff, like wanting to stay up later than he should, and there's always the homework battle, but I love him to death."

"Who watches him when you're not at home?"

"That would be my younger sister, Trish. We don't always see eye to eye when it comes to lifestyle matters, but she does a great job with Joel."

They decided on Palermo's Pizza Shop near Marge's apartment. She had ordered pies from them in the past and was pleased with the quality. As they sat at the small round table waiting for the two large pepperoni and mushroom pizzas to be cooked, Jack began talking about his time in college. He explained that most of his meals were from places very similar to this.

"I kid you not; my college roommate and I ate pizza at least five days a week. My family did not have the kind of money to give me an allowance every month. My only source of income was working part-time jobs."

"When I got out of high school, my dreams weren't as ambitious as yours," Marge said. "Going to beautician school was all I wanted to do, but it wasn't in the cards for me."

"Why, what stopped you?"

"Well, my father had left a couple years earlier with some woman he met at the local bar. My younger sister, Trish, needed supervision, and my mother did, too, sadly. The meager income I brought in waiting tables at a local restaurant helped us get by. Once Trish was old enough to take care of herself, I latched onto the first man that was willing to save me from my life. Unfortunately, that was Joel's father, and you already know how that story ended."

When the pizza was ready, Jack held it on his lap as they drove to Marge's apartment. They smiled at one another as the unmistakable aroma of the freshly cooked pizza floated through the car. Even though he had difficulties in his life, they paled in comparison to what she had experienced. Jack felt terrible when he realized there was a time in his past when he would have thought of her as trailer trash. The respect he felt for her before had suddenly increased tenfold.

It was the eve of Robby's return to school. Anna would miss the time she had been spending with him, but it was time for him to return to a regular life, with people his own age. The first day would be the real test, and Anna was a little nervous. No longer could she be his protector day in and day out. Trials and tribulations were lurking behind the walls of the school, things Robert would have to face on his own. When she was an educator, she tried in vain to stop the cruelty of the mean-spirited students. The problem was always the playground or the lunchroom, where there was much less supervision. No matter what she tried to do, there would be children who would poke fun at Robert about his father killing his mother. She knew in her head that she had to let things run their course, but her heart was telling her to protect him at all cost.

While preparing lunch, Anna remembered that she needed to iron Robby's new clothes for the following day. When there was no sign of Robby downstairs, she went up to see if he was in his room. Sure enough, he was sitting on the bed, loading the new school supplies into his backpack.

"Are you ready to go back to school?" Anna asked.

"I'm going to be in trouble, Anna," Robby said, sounding worried.

"What gives you that idea, Robby?"

"My school books are at the old house, and we can't get them."

Placing her arm around him, Anna said, "Your teacher will understand. If we have to pay for new ones, we will. Do you want me to walk you to the bus stop in the morning?"

"Anna, I'm too old for that!" Robby said proudly.

"Forgive me. I wouldn't want to cause you any social issues at school."

As Robby was eating his lunch, he informed Anna that his new bus stop was only a block away. If she was worried that somebody might get him, she could watch out the front window.

When lunch was over and the kitchen cleaned, Anna decided to give Robby a real treat. About once a month, she would go out to the garage and start her father's classic car. Even though the title to the vintage Cadillac was in her name—it had been for many years—she still referred to it as her father's car.

Anna grabbed the keys from the rack on the wall and summoned the youngster. "Robby, will you come with me to the garage? I need a little help."

"Sure, what do you need help with?"

"You'll see soon enough."

"Can I look at the car while we are out there?"

Anna smiled. "As a matter of fact, you can."

Together, they lifted the old overhead garage door, and then removed the cover from the antique car. Robby didn't hesitate to jump into the car when Anna asked if he wanted to climb inside. He smiled ear to ear once he was behind the wheel. Everything inside the old automobile seemed so huge to him. Not able to see over the large pearl-colored steering wheel, Robby pushed himself up using his hands against the white leather seats. He looked down the long, sleek hood of the vintage car, all the way to the sparkling chrome hood ornament in amazement.

Anna walked around to the passenger side and climbed in the car with him. "Fine automobiles are a lot like people. Cars need cared for to stay in good condition. At least once a month, I come out to start the engine," she explained.

"Are you going to start it up today?" he asked, excited at the prospect.

"No, you are. That is, if you're interested."

Robby couldn't believe his good fortune, and exclaimed, "Heck yeah!"

Before handing over the keys, Anna explained the procedure to Robby. His feet dangled over the seat, forcing him to stretch his toes to touch the floor. With one hand fixed on each side of the steering wheel, he grinned from ear to ear in anticipation. When Anna handed Robby the set of keys, his excitement heightened. As he fumbled with the key, Anna reached over to help him guide it into the ignition.

"Now, take your right foot and push on the gas pedal one time. Don't do it any more than once or you'll flood the carburetor."

Robert looked over at Anna and said, "I'm too short to reach the gas pedal."

"That's okay, I'll help you. Believe me, Robby, you won't be too short much longer."

"What do I do now?" he asked, anxious to start the car.

"Turn the key, and as soon as you hear the engine start, release it."

At once, the spark of the ignition sent the roaring sounds of the motor echoing through the garage. The initial look of terror on Robby's face startled her, but her worries were quickly soothed when he started laughing. It was obvious to Anna that he had never had so much fun in his young life. The truth of the matter was that she enjoyed it almost as much as he did.

On the night of the pizza party at Marge's place, something very subtle happened between her and Jack. She saw a different side of him as he interacted with her son, Joel. It had been a long time since she had a man around who was not drunk and abusive. Marge saw something in her son's eyes when he interacted with Jack that gave her hope. Not hope for her and Jack as a couple, but hope that Joel would be able to experience male bonding that would not involve fear. Deep down, she hoped for a relationship with Jack, but she knew things could not change at the office. Business as usual would be her goal.

Marge looked forward to a busy day. Not only would it get her mind off personal feelings that did not belong in the office, it was a sign of increased business. Jack and Marge both deserved a break in their lives.

"Good morning, Red," Jack said as he entered the office. "You're here bright and early."

"Jack, I'm here early every day."

"Trust me, I know that, Red. By the way, I really enjoyed the pizza at your place last night. That is the first time I have not eaten alone or with strangers for a long time. I hope Joel didn't mind the intrusion."

"No, I think he liked an adult male presence around for a change."

"It was a good time," Jack said, smiling.

Marge changed the subject. "We have a busy day ahead of us. You have three appointments this morning with potential clients. At two o'clock, you have a preliminary hearing at the courthouse. When you finish there, you have to go see another potential client at the county jail."

"I really love the sound of that," Jack said.

"It's like that all week. We also need to meet with Anna Wilson soon to go over her expenditures. I think it would be respectful to go to her house to do it."

"Good idea. Go ahead and set it up."

"There's one more thing, Jack. We might need to do it on a Saturday. Anna told me she wants us to come to her house for lunch. I was thinking of taking Joel with us, if that's okay with you?"

"Whatever it takes!" Jack said.

Between phone calls, Marge worked on laying out the schedules for the rest of the month. She had to coordinate Jack's court appearances, jail visitations, and appointments at the office. Her main job responsibility was keeping him in the right place at the right time.

Marge took a break from her paperwork and called Anna to set up a meeting to go over her account. The two women chatted a little about business, as well as a little about pleasure, agreeing to have lunch on Saturday at Anna's. It would be a good opportunity for Robby and Joel to meet, and in the process, hopefully the two young boys would become friends.

Anna peeked out the window and watched as Robby's school bus drove away. As it disappeared down the street, she felt emptiness inside. Suddenly, the house seemed much larger than before. The noises associated with Robby's presence were no longer there. Loneliness had found her, and she was not fond of the way it felt.

Anna sat on the sofa wondering what she would do next. Dust particles danced in the rays of sunlight that shot across the room through the seams in the curtains. Several long minutes passed, and along with it, the self-pity she was experiencing.

Robby's room was her first stop on the second floor. After straightening his bed, she noticed several Matchbox cars under the bed. When she retrieved the tiny vehicles, she also found a couple of the new actions figures they had purchased. The nagging pain in her lower back reminded her that she needed to talk to Robby about his messy room when he got home from school.

Anna thought about baking a chocolate cake, but did not think it would be enough of a treat when Robby got home from school. She wanted to mark the occasion in a very special way. While trying to come up with the perfect treat, she pushed the curtain aside and looked out the window toward the garage. She immediately realized what would please him most. She would pick Robby up after school in style, in her father's Cadillac, for all of his friends to see, and then they would go to Winky's and enjoy a burger, fries, and a soft ice cream cone for dinner.

Smartly dressed in a light gray skirt and top, Anna complemented her outfit with a gray wide-brimmed hat with sheer ties hanging from each side. Snatching the keys off the hook in the kitchen, she headed to the garage. The old wooden overhead door was heavy as usual, but Anna refused to let a couple of strained muscles interfere with Robby's surprise. She ran her fingers along the beautiful pearl finish of the antique automobile as she walked to the driver's side door. As she took hold of the chrome door handle, she smiled, knowing how much joy this day would bring Robby, and because of all the pleasant memories the classic car brought to mind.

After checking the rearview and side mirrors, she put the key into the ignition. She pushed the gas pedal down once and turned the key. The old Cadillac fired up immediately, and the sound of the engine echoed through the garage. Once she was safely out of the garage, she turned down the driveway toward the street. It had been nearly a year since she had ventured out in the old vehicle.

Traffic was light as Anna motored down Highland Park Drive toward the elementary school at twenty-five miles per hour. Along the way, people drove by, many of them sending her a smile or a thumbs up.

When the empty yellow school buses came into sight, Anna knew her destination was not far away. She slowly drove into the school entrance, stopping in front of the building. Other than a group of bus drivers milling around outside the empty buses, the parking lot was vacant. Several teachers positioned themselves outside, anticipating the mass exodus of children. Suddenly, the sound of the final bell ringing changed everything. It was not long before screams of joy preceded the race to the buses.

Several minutes passed by before Robby came running out the front doors. Thinking Anna was going to pick him up in a taxi, he had the surprise of his life. She waved at him as he looked on in disbelief. When she saw the big smile on his face, she felt much better about his first day back at school. There were groups of children all around, marveling at the beautiful automobile.

Anna smiled as Robby approached the car and said, "Hello, Robby. Would you like a ride home?"

Excited, he said, "Would I ever! I cannot believe you picked me up from school in this car!"

"Well, I thought we would celebrate your first day back at school in style." She told him of their dinner plans. "Now, put your backpack in the car and let's go!"

Safely on the road now, Anna said, "So, how was your first day back at school?"

"Good," Robby said. "It was nice to see my friends again. A lot of them heard what happened and felt bad for me. I told them not to worry because I have a new home now. My teachers were very nice, but acted funny around me."

"It sounds like you had a pretty good day."

"Anna, were you okay while I was at school?" Robby asked, concerned.

Anna smiled at Robby and gave him a wink. "It was tough, but I managed."

The trip to Winky's proved to be as much fun as Anna hoped it would be for Robby and her. They both enjoyed cheeseburgers, fries, and Cokes, and they topped off their dinners with vanilla ice cream cones.

Eager to hear more about Robby's first day back at school, Anna said, "Well, Robby, are you going to tell me more about your first day back at school?"

"School went really well today. The guidance counselor even called me out of class to make sure everything was okay. When she asked me to come out into the hall, I was afraid."

"Did you think you were in trouble?"

"No, I thought something happened to you."

"With everything that's occurred, that's an understandable reaction," Anna said.

"A lot of kids asked me where I had been," Robby said.

"What did you say to them?"

"I told them I had family problems."

"Well, that was a very good answer," Anna said reassuringly.

"Pete and Jimmy knew what really happened from their parents. They asked me if I was afraid when my dad killed my mother."

"How did you respond to what they said?"

"I thought about it for a really long time, and then I said I wasn't scared. Neither one of them said anything, but they knew it wasn't true."

Anna did not see any good coming from analyzing his last statement. In her eyes, Robert was doing an extraordinary job at dealing with the situation life had handed him. The fact that he was relaying the important information from school made her feel good inside. She was a firm believer that people are a lot like volcanoes: the dangerous part is what you do not see. Her goal was to keep an atmosphere of free communication going between the two of them. She was also well aware of the fact that raising a child would involve a lot more than band-aiding scrapes and helping him with his homework.

"So, Robby, would you say being back in school was a good experience?" Anna inquired.

"Oh, yeah, it was good. Well, except for the homework."

Anna smiled. "I'm happy things went well, and if you need help with your homework, I will be there for you."

"Do you know what the best part of my day was?"

"No … what?" she asked, curious.

"It was you picking me up at school."

Anna's face lit up at his comment, and she felt utter joy inside. "It was my pleasure, young man."

"Anna?"

"Yes?"

"Can I drive home?"

Anna laughed aloud. "No!"

The ride home was a time of reflection for Robby. When he wasn't waving at passersby, he daydreamed about his first day back at school. Prior to returning to school, his mind conjured up monsters chasing him down the halls, but there were no ominous creatures lurking about. Thoughts of children teasing him never became a reality. Existing friends remained loyal, and many others paid more attention to him than ever before. As he looked over at the wonderful woman who was driving, he finally understood the meaning of a blessing.

Several blocks from the house, a police car drove up behind them with his lights flashing. Anna was sure she had not broken any traffic laws, but Robby was afraid they were going to be in trouble. He flipped around in the seat and looked on as the police officer walked toward the Cadillac.

Concerned, Robby asked, "Anna, why did he pull us over?"

"I don't know," she said, equally concerned.

"He's checking out the car now," Robby said, still watching the officer.

"Shush, try to sit there quietly."

As the police officer approached the driver's side window, he said, "Good afternoon, ma'am. Can I see your license and registration, please?"

"Sure, what seems to be the problem, officer?"

"This is one beautiful antique car," he said.

She proudly replied, "Thank you, it was my father's."

The police officer walked slowly around the vehicle, looking at every detail. Robert leaned over and asked Anna if they were going to jail. For the life of her, she could not think of a reason for him to pull her over. She was not exceeding the speed limit, was safely driving within her lane, and she did not run any stop signs. Finally, she decided to confront the curious law enforcement officer and find out what was on his mind.

"Excuse me, sir, why did you pull us over?"

"Forgive me, ma'am, I'm a bit of a car buff, and I couldn't pass up the opportunity to admire a vehicle as beautiful as this. I am currently working on a total restoration of a nineteen forty-nine Buick. It will never be the same caliber as your antique Cadillac, but when I'm finished with it, she'll be a real beauty."

"I know you didn't pull us over so you could look at my car," Anna said, frustrated.

"Obviously, you don't drive her very often," he said.

"That's right."

"Well, Miss Wilson, today you forgot to put the license plate on your car."

Clearly understanding now that he had a good reason to pull her over, Anna said, apologetically, "I'm sorry, officer! That's what happens when you get older."

The officer chuckled and said, "Don't worry about it. Just try to remember in the future to keep the license plate on the car."

"I assure you, I will, and thank you for being so understanding."

With that little ordeal over, Anna couldn't wait to get home and retire the car to the garage once more.

chapter ∙∙∙∙∙∙∙∙∙∙∙∙
∙∙∙∙∙∙∙∙∙∙∙∙∙∙∙∙∙ eleven

Once Robert's clothes were ready for school and he had taken a bath, Anna was ready to relax. She scrutinized the homework assignments he brought home, but not to the point that she was performing the work. Mistakes were part of the learning process, and she had to let him make his share of them.

Anna agreed to let Robby read a few more pages of *Treasure Island* before turning out the light, as she didn't want to be a tough taskmaster while he was still recovering emotionally. She needed to earn his trust in many different ways, and trust took a great deal of time. She took one last look at the light streaming out from Robert's bedroom door, and then slowly made her way down the stairs. When the last cup of tea for the day was finished brewing, she placed a couple sugar cookies on a plate and went into the living room. After putting the tea and cookies on a small glass table in front of the couch, she turned on the lamp she liked to use for reading. She thought about reading, but decided against it. Instead, she enjoyed the solitude the evening brought. Convinced the worst was behind them, she tried to keep her mind in the present and to look forward to the future.

The warmth Anna was experiencing inside had nothing to do with the tea she was sipping. Before Robert came into her life, the large stone structure in which she lived resembled a tomb more than a home. The small boy sleeping upstairs was quickly bringing new energy into her life—and into the house. The dwelling they shared was absorbing his laughter, soaking up his tears, and breathing in the love he expressed.

Before heading back upstairs, Anna cleaned up the kitchen, and then made sure the doors were locked and the lights were all turned off. When she spotted the light sneaking out from under Robby's door, she smiled. She opened the door quietly, expecting to see action figures spread out all over the bed, but she was pleasantly surprised to see that he was sound asleep, with *Treasure Island* open across his chest. She gently picked up the book and placed it on top of the dresser. Careful not to wake him, she coaxed him under the covers and tucked him in for the night. She kissed him lightly on his forehead, turned off the light, and retired to bed.

Anna found herself awake at four thirty, with no chance of returning to sleep. As she waited for the teapot to whistle, she sat at the dining room table, thinking about Jack and Marge's visit the next day. Marge was bringing her son, Joel, and she knew Robby would enjoy meeting him.

Aside from business, Anna enjoyed socializing with Jack and Marge. She trusted Jack implicitly, and wanted to do everything to help further his career. She could never repay him for bringing Robby into her life.

When Anna was young, she enjoyed helping her mother plan dinner parties. The guests were usually members of upper management from her father's company. The dinners were generally very formal and the menu fancy. She recalled fondly how her mother would sometimes let her wear one of her best dresses and walk around to all the guests with a tray of tea sandwiches and various finger foods. Entertaining was never a big part of her life, but she possessed the skills to do it. She wanted make sure the quaint get together on Saturday was special. At first, she thought about hosting a small dinner party, but after further thought, she decided that although Saturday was partially a business meeting, it was also a social event.

New beginnings for everyone called for a festive atmosphere. The best way to accomplish that was to cook out. There was a beautiful stone barbeque pit in the backyard that her father had constructed when she was a young girl. It rarely found use in the past because her mother disliked the lingering smoke and the smell of food cooking on the grill. But Anna, as well as the old house, longed for the sound of children playing in the yard and people interacting, and a good old-fashioned cookout was just the ticket! After all, who doesn't like hotdogs, hamburgers, potato salad, and juicy watermelon?

chapter ....
.... twelve

Robby had a little more spring in his step as he prepared to leave for school. The weekend was almost here, and he was looking forward to Saturday's festivities. He was no stranger to the fact that Jack and Marge were instrumental in helping him move in with Anna. Even though he continued to grieve the loss of his parents, living with Anna was the best thing that could have happened to him. Besides, Marge's son, Joel, was coming over, which meant that he could possibly make a new friend.

When he finished his breakfast, Robby snatched his backpack from the chair and made a beeline for the front door. Heading out the door, he yelled, "Goodbye, Anna, I'll see you after school!"

"Wait a minute, Robby, I think you forgot something."

Quickly checking his pockets, he realized that he had forgotten to grab his lunch money from the table. He smiled and said, "Boy, I would have been starving today without this."

"Put it in your pocket so you don't lose it."

"Yes, ma'am!"

"Slow down, and have a good day." She followed him over to the front door and kissed him on the forehead goodbye.

Anna smiled as she peeked out the window and watched him walk down the sidewalk with two of his friends toward the bus stop. When he disappeared from sight, a strange sense of emptiness fell over her. With Robert in her life, she truly understood the meaning of the word precious, because that is exactly what he was to her. When they shared time together, she could feel a life-giving force flowing from inside him. Every smile on his face and each inquisitive question about everything and anything empowered her with a youthful feeling.

Horns were honking and impatient people were racing around the grocery store parking lot, making Anna feel uneasy. When she located an area where there were several empty parking spaces, she carefully guided the huge car into its spot. The thought occurred to her that, perhaps, she should buy a new vehicle and let the old Caddy enjoy its well-deserved retirement in the garage. She smiled to herself as she imagined Robby's excitement at running around a car dealership. One thing was certain, he would surely have more to say about the purchase than she would!

Anna filled her cart and headed to the checkout. Greeting her as she took her place in line was a rack of gossip magazines. There was one shopper ahead of her, but Anna could tell that the young cashier wanted to be anywhere but behind the register. The cashier tortured several pieces of chewing gum as she rung up the customer ahead of her, as Anna took notice of the young man tossing the items into the brown paper bags at the end of the checkout isle. He seemed to be enamored with the cashier. Flattered by the attention of the younger boy, the cashier randomly dropped items on the floor and smiled when he retrieved them. Anna diverted her attentions from the flirtatious show and began placing her groceries onto the checkout belt, carefully grouping the items in the order she wanted them bagged, to help make the bagger's job easier. After all, the young man's attentions were on much more important things, like setting himself up for a broken heart.

Anna was pleasantly surprised when someone approached her and offered to assist her to her car with her cart full of groceries. Introducing himself as the assistant store manager, Gabe Cohen, Anna gladly accepted his help. When he finished loading her car, Anna reached into her purse and tried to reward him for his efforts, but he politely declined the offer and pushed the empty cart back to the store. Anna thought to herself, *I guess chivalry is not dead after all!*

chapter ·············
··········· thirteen

A s the sun came up, Anna's age was rearing its ugly head, but she continued to rush around the kitchen. Much like a juggler at the circus, she had a casserole in the oven and several pans sizzling on top of the stove. Condiments and spices were scattered around the countertop, with a wooden cutting board in the center of it all. Sweating from the heat of the stove and the spent energy, Anna sat down for a cup of tea. She spotted a sleepy little figure standing at the entrance of the kitchen. Robert rubbed his eyes as he tried to make sense out of the disarray in the kitchen.

Anna was surprised to see him, and asked, "Why are you up so early this morning? Did you forget that it's Saturday?"

"No, I just thought you might need some help."

Anna appreciated Robby's offer, but set out to make him some breakfast first. He was curious as to why she was hosting a party, and she explained to him that the most important reason was to celebrate that he was in her life, and second, she said it was a way to bring their new friends together.

❧ ❧ ❧ ❧

The side dishes were in the refrigerator chilling, and the burgers were on a tray ready for the grill. While cleaning up the mess in the kitchen, Anna went over a mental list to make sure she did not forget anything. All that remained was getting Robert and her ready before their guests arrived. Of course, Robert gave her a little trouble when he realized she expected him to wear appropriate attire.

"Why do I have to wear good clothes today? I thought we were having a picnic." "It is a picnic, but think of it as a fancy kind of picnic."

Changing the subject, Robby asked, "Do you think Marge's son will like me?" She laughed and said, "Of course! You are a likable guy."

When Robby finished donning the equivalent of his school clothes, he sat in his room and tried to figure out which of his toys he would display for Joel. Considering that his mother died at the hands of his father, he was still a little leery about meeting new people. He felt a special kinship toward Marge and Jack because of all that they had done for him and Anna.

While waiting for their guests to arrive, Anna sat on the sofa while going over the legal matters she wanted to discuss with Jack that were on her mind. Sitting in the chair across from her, Robby was being very quiet. Silence was an unusual companion when they were together, but on this day, it found its way between them. Anna was on the brink of making decisions that would change several people's lives in a big way. She had become very fond of Jack and Marge, believing they were deserving of a break. Even though Robby would be financially secure for the remainder of his life, she had the responsibility of molding him into the kind of man that would be deserving of it.

Robby's reasons for being quiet were much more emotional. Thinking of Marge and her son unearthed memories of when he and his mother would go places together.

Following several long minutes of silence, Robby deserted the comic books on the chair and went to the window to watch for their guests. When he saw Marge's aging car turning into the driveway, he immediately felt a new sense of enthusiasm.

"They're here!" Robby announced, excited. "Jack and Marge are finally here!"

"Okay, let's greet them at the door."

"Her son looks younger than me," Robby said.

"What is the difference if he is a couple years younger than you?"

"I just wondered." He paused for a minute. "Can I go out just in case they need some help?"

"Let's both go outside to greet them."

Marge exited the driver's side and then opened the back door for Joel. The door, which was in dire need of oil, screeched as it opened. Jack crawled out of the passenger side gently cradling a bakery box, secured tightly with string. He was dressed casually, taking advantage of the fact that he did not have to be in court or meet with a prospective client.

Robby ran up to the car and offered an enthusiastic "hello" to Jack and Marge. Joel stood slightly behind Marge, clutching her arm in a protective manner as she prompted him to introduce himself. Anna bent over with a smile on her face, attempting to make him feel comfortable.

"This handsome young man must be Joel," Anna said. "I have heard so much about you."

"Say hello to Anna, Joel."

"Let's go in the house and see if some Toll House cookies will help him feel at home."

While the boys went to Robby's room to play, the adults went out back to converse over drinks. Anna and Marge had a glass of Rosé, while Jack had a tall glass of iced tea. Anna could not remember the last time she had guests over to enjoy the beautiful courtyard.

"I hope you don't mind me asking, but how is Robby doing since the incident?" Marge asked.

"He is doing surprisingly well, considering the traumatic experience he went through. School is going well, and he continues to play with his friends from the neighborhood."

"He is very fortunate to have you in his life," Marge said.

Anna smiled. "I believe I am the lucky one."

Anna recruited Jack to place the charcoal in the fire pit and put the aluminum foil over the grill. Her motivation was to entice Marge into a girl talk session. Anna wanted to know about Marge and Jack's relationship outside of work without appearing to be a busy body.

"Have you been busy at the office?"

"Yes, we have been very busy. Over the past few months, we've brought in quite a few new clients."

"I'm not surprised. Jack is a very capable attorney."

"He is also a great guy, but don't tell him I said so."

Anna smiled. "Do you two get a chance to go out now and then?"

"Do you mean socially?"

"Of course, I mean socially."

"We do go to out to eat from time to time, but I'm not sure what that says."

"I'm not one to meddle," Anna said, "but it's obvious to me that he has feelings for you. It may take a little encouragement on your part. Nothing would make me happier than to see you two as a couple before I leave this world."

"Thanks, Anna; I'll remember what you said."

While Jack finished preparing the grill, Marge went upstairs to check on the boys. As she neared the top of the stairs, she heard the sweet sound of the youngsters playing. Joel's unbridled laughter always warmed her heart, but the sound of him making a new friend intensified the experience. The boys had more in common than they realized. Their circumstances were different, but they both had lost their fathers. Parenting alone was often a perplexing affair for her, but most times, she was pleased with her performance. Not wanting Joel to know she was checking on him, Marge quietly slipped back down the stairs.

Marge could hear Anna laughing when she made her way outside. There stood Jack, wearing an apron and a chef's hat that he had found in the kitchen. Her feelings for him ran deep, and something inside her came alive when he was in a playful mood. As if on cue, the boys came running outside as the hot dogs and burgers began sizzling on the grill. They went straight for the basket of potato chips on the table.

"Is it time to eat yet?" Robby asked. "I'm starving!"

"Yeah, I'm starving too," Joel chimed in.

"They'll be done in a few minutes. You can't rush perfection," Jack said, teasing.

Anna enjoyed the show as she sipped her glass of wine. The warmth she felt inside had more to do with the company than with the Rosé. She could not recall the last time the old house enjoyed such lighthearted laughter. Congeniality flowed in the air as Chef Jack delivered the culinary delights to the table. The boys sat impatiently at the table as Marge generously spooned the various side dishes onto their plates. Hot dogs topped with mustard and relish were by far the biggest hit for the youngsters. Jack and Marge interacted with playful humor as he removed the towering hat from his head and placed it on hers. Anna was convinced that God had placed the people surrounding her into her life. At last, the ever-looming loneliness in the old stone house seemed to be lifting. Even though Anna wanted the festivities to go on forever, she had matters of great importance on her mind. Decisions would be made that would change the future of everyone in attendance. Looking around at their faces, she realized they were the only family she had remaining in this world.

"Now that we've finished dinner, would you like me to take the cake outside Anna?" Marge asked.

"No, dear, I want to have a little meeting with you and Jack first."

Smiling, she asked, "Are we in trouble?"

"Of course not. I hope everyone involved will be pleased with what I have to say. Will you tell the boys we'll call them when it's time for cake?"

"Sure, they will be happy to go back to playing."

Marge seemed to be much more curious about the mysterious meeting than Jack was. Whispering, she said, "What is this all about?"

Taking the situation in stride, Jack said, "I have no idea, but my guess would be that she wants to thank us for our help."

"I get the impression it's something bigger than that."

They didn't need to speculate any further, as Anna was approaching the table with a glass of wine in hand.

"I know the two of you are a little curious about the reason for this meeting, so I will get directly to the point. In recent days, I have made some very important decisions concerning Robby and me. As you are aware, Jack, my family has had an attorney for as long as I can remember, but you have proven yourself to me in so many areas that I would be pleased if you took over that role. If you decide to take on this responsibility, which would make an old woman very happy, we will discuss the details later. Either way, I am dismissing the current firm who is handling my interests."

Jack inquired, "Do you mind if I ask you a question?"

"Of course not. If you decide to do this, I want your eyes to be wide open."

"What prompted your decision to let go of the current firm that is handing your legal matters?"

"There were several reasons, but one stood out above all others. When I approached them about the situation with Robert, they treated me like a crazy old woman, and we both know that only half of that statement is true. There was a time when they would come to my home if we needed to discuss any legal matters or when I needed to sign important papers. Several years ago, the son took over, and all of that changed."

"So that is how our paths crossed."

"The Lord works in mysterious ways, Jack."

"I agree, Anna, and this is definitely a great opportunity for us, but I do have some concerns."

"Well, put them out on the table, Jack. After all, that's why the three of us are having this discussion."

Even though Marge did not say anything, her mind was going a thousand miles an hour. She had been with Jack from the very beginning of his resurrection back into the law game. There were too many weeks when she was not even sure he would be able to pay her. She tolerated the fact that their work environment resembled a back street pawnshop instead of a professional law office. She tolerated it because of her belief in Jack Porter. She had visions of a proper office, in a more fitting location, with large wooden desks and leather chairs. Marge even dared to imagine that she would have an assistant to delegate some of her responsibilities to. Everything from an automobile that she did not have to cross her fingers each time she turned the key to a better place to live raced through her mind.

Jack sat staring into space as he tried to digest the proposal that Anna had just dropped in his lap. He was painfully aware that he could barely manage the client load he had now, but with the added resources, they could handle additional clients. Strangely enough, his biggest concern was disappointing Anna. Jack decided to voice his concerns to Anna.

"What will happen if legal matters arise that are not in my area of expertise?"

"I've already thought about that, and while your practice is growing, I have no objection to you retaining other law firms that you trust. It goes without saying that you will be ultimately accountable."

"Anna, saying *thank you* does not even come close to how I feel about this. I hope I am as talented as you seem to think I am."

"There is no doubt in my mind that you and Marge have a bright future ahead of you. Marge, do you feel comfortable with this arrangement?"

Marge replied quickly, "Umm, yes, very much."

"Good, we will go over the particulars next week, if that is acceptable to you, Mr. Porter?" Anna said in a teasing manner.

"That will be fine, Miss Wilson," Jack teased back.

What Anna needed to discuss next was most important to her. Robert's well-being and his future had become paramount to her. With each new day, she felt her age getting the best of her, and although Robert had pumped new vitality into her life, the fact that she could pass on at any time was inescapable. Marge had her own problems as a single mother, and Jack was struggling with his law practice, but that was all about to change.

"The last matter I have to discuss with you is the most important of all," Anna said.

Jack and Marge looked at each other in disbelief, considering the news she had already dropped on them.

Anna sent Marge into the house to refresh their drinks so that she could have a few minutes with Jack to get his thoughts on his relationship with Marge.

"So, Jack, what do you think of Marge?"

"I'm not sure I understand the question, Anna."

Smiling, she said, "I think you understand perfectly. She obviously thinks a lot of you, and I'm curious if you feel the same way."

"That's a personal question, isn't it?"

"Yes, it is, but old people are permitted to ask personal questions."

He laughed and said, "Then, yes, I like Red, I mean Marge, a lot."

"Good, Jack, because I'd hate to see you let her get away."

When Marge returned with their drinks, the chat between Jack and Anna came to an abrupt end. She apologized for taking longer than expected, but she went upstairs to look in on the boys.

Taking her glass of wine, Anna took a sip, and then said, "As you both know, I've never had any children of my own until Robert came into my life. Dark as the circumstances may have been, he will always be the light in this old house. Lack of money will never be an issue for him, but my goal is to give him so much more when I am gone. Nobody enjoys talking about death, but in this case, I strongly feel that arrangements need to be in place. Marge, I would like you to be Robert's Godmother. You are a good person of sound moral fiber, and your dedication to Joel is obvious to me. Jack, I want you to be his Godfather and play an active role in his life when I die. There is no doubt in my mind that you two could give him the tools necessary to become the kind of man I know he can be."

A heavy silence hung in the air for several long minutes, and it was uncomfortably obvious that the wheels were turning in everyone's heads. Jack was the first to break the silence.

"Are all your picnics this exciting, Anna?"

The sounds of laughter echoed through the backyard.

Marge hesitated a bit, but then voiced her financial concerns. "Anna, I would take Robby in without hesitation, but I can barely get by as it is."

"Jack will be drawing up the papers next week to set aside funds for his caretaker to manage in the event of my death."

"Of course, Anna, I will do it. I just hope I can live up to your expectations."

"You already have, dear. I've been watching you with Joel, and it's obvious to me that you are doing a fine job."

"Thank you, that means a great deal coming from you."

"One more thing, Marge; please don't mention this to Joel. Robert has enough on his mind without worrying about another change in his young life."

"I understand."

Anna felt relieved that she had her affairs in order. It gave her great peace of mind knowing that Jack would be handling all of her business matters and that Robby would be well taken care of.

The evening had been a big success, and Anna was pleased to have entertained in her home once again. The adults enjoyed some grownup time together, and Robby made a new friend in Joel. But she was tired, and she counted her blessings that Marge had cleaned up the kitchen and picnic area, as the day's activities had physically and mentally drained her.

Anna found Robby on the sofa in the parlor, kicking off his shoes. Taking a seat beside him, she said, "Did you and Joel have a good time today?"

"He's a little younger than me, but he is a good kid."

"How did he like your play things?"

With excitement in his voice, he said, "Oh man, he couldn't believe all the great stuff I have! I hope you don't mind, but I told him that he could have some of my trucks when I get older."

"Of course not; that would be a very nice thing to do."

The conversation was minimal on the ride home from Anna's, except for Joel excitedly asking when he could visit Robby again. For Jack and Marge, it felt as though they were in the midst of a Mexican standoff and neither one of them wanted to make the first move. Finally, Marge blurted out, "So, what does it feel like to be a Godfather, Jack?"

Jack was quiet for a minute, but he could not hold back the laughter, and said, "I'll tell you what, Marge, that old woman sure knew how to surprise the hell out of us."

"I'm still not sure what it all means," Marge said. "The Godparent thing is for Robert's well-being, which I understand, but the family, what is the family attorney stuff about?"

"It means a lot more money for both of us!"

"Are you serious, Jack?"

"We are about to see a big change in our lives, Marge."

She smiled and said, "If that's true, Jack, it couldn't happen to two better people."

"I agree, Red."

Anna let Robby talk her into joining him for another slice of cake and a glass of milk before going up to his room. While they were sitting at the dining room table indulging in the extra dessert, Anna had thought about asking him more about his day with Joel, but Robby finished his cake in record time, so she merely smiled and excused him so that he could go to his room and play. As she cut the moist cake into bite size pieces and placed them in her mouth, the sweet taste she experienced reminded her of the successful day she had. Anna knew God was working in her life, now more than ever.

chapter · · · · · · · · · · ·
· · · · · · · · · · · · fourteen

Monday morning brought relaxation teamed with reflection for Anna. Robby was back in school, which afforded her quiet time in the house. Beams of sunlight found their way through the partially drawn curtains, warming her face. Softness danced in the air, reminding her of what she had accomplished over the weekend. The term "ties that bind" came to mind, lending her a strange sense of security. Loose ends were not part of her character, and she had just tied up some major ones in her life. Anna's attitude toward death was the same as in life. Everything must be in order.

Anna's thoughts drifted to purchasing a new automobile. The vintage Cadillac was entirely too large for her to maneuver around in traffic, and it surely did not deserve the accidental bumps it was taking. Yes, it was time for the old girl to retire to the safety of the garage. She would receive the well-deserved waxing from time to time and the occasional drive around the block, so onlookers could appreciate her beauty. She was an old classic that had seen her time come and go. Anna understood that concept all too well. No matter how hard she tried to understand the changing world around her, it remained confusing. Jack's current position in life was partially of his own doing, but she knew there was a great deal of good in him. The term scrapper came to mind when she thought of him. Anna respected anyone who had the courage to rise above a difficult situation.

As Anna viewed the advertisements for new automobiles in the newspaper, Robby arrived home from school. She sensed by his lack of enthusiasm that something was troubling him. The usual announcement of his arrival home followed by a beeline to the refrigerator was not there. Initially, Anna did not want to pry, hoping he would open up to her.

Casually, she asked, "How was school today?"

"All right, I guess." Robby sounded a little dejected.

"It sounds like you have a lot of homework."

"No, I just have to study for a history test tomorrow."

"How about I prepare you a little snack before dinner?" Anna said, trying to cheer him up.

"Na, I think I will go up to my room."

"Okay, I will call you when it's time to eat."

Realizing it was time to figure out what they were going to have for the evening meal, Anna put down the newspaper and headed for the kitchen. Upon opening the refrigerator, she decided they would finish the leftover food from Saturday's cookout. After setting the table, she decided to go up to go up to Robby's room and get his opinion concerning dinner. Besides, it would be the perfect excuse for her to delve into what was troubling him.

The trip up the stairs was becoming slower and slower, which Anna saw as a telltale sign of aging. When she reached the top, she gently knocked on Robby's bedroom door. As she entered the room, Robby was lying on the bed with the history book on his chest.

"Is it time to eat?" he asked.

"No, I'm not even sure what we're having yet. Do you have any ideas?"

"It doesn't matter to me," he said.

Robby didn't seem his usual upbeat self, so Anna said, "You know, Robby, a problem shared is a problem cut in half."

"What does that mean?"

"It means that it is always better to talk about the things that bother us."

Anna stood there for what seemed to be a long moment, but the boy remained quiet. After kissing him gently on the fore head, she slowly turned to walk out of the room. Before she could tell him that she was always there for him, tears began to roll from his eyes.

"My friend Billy's grandma died last week. He told me today when he came back to school."

"I'm sorry to hear that," Anna said. "What happened to her?"

"She had a really bad heart attack," he said, crying hard now.

"It's always terrible to lose someone we love," Anna said, trying to soothe him.

"Please don't die, Anna! My mother died and left me all alone, and I do not want you to do the same! They will take me back to that terrible place to live!"

In a stern voice, Anna said, "Listen to me very carefully, young man. I might be old, but I am still in good health. My plan is to watch you become the kind of man I know you can be. No matter what happens, you will never have to return to that terrible place. I have made sure that you will always be cared for."

"Will you go to the doctor to make sure your heart is not broken?"

"Don't worry, Robby. My heart is fine, but I'll go for a checkup, if it will put your mind at ease."

Anna sat down next to Robby and wiped the tears from his eyes. She placed her arms around him, holding his head against her chest. He, in turn, put his small arms around her, clutching her body close to him. Even though the situation was emotionally upsetting, she enjoyed the warmth they were sharing. In a strange way, she saw a positive twist to the emotional encounter with Robby. The sudden death of Billy's grandmother was merely the vehicle used to bring to the surface the underlying concern he had about Anna's health. He had never mentioned the abandonment issues concerning his mother's death and his father's imprisonment, but she was sure they were festering inside him. She knew just how cruel a young person's vivid imagination could be during the alone time in their life.

Anna gently straightened Robby's hair and said, "I have a great idea!"

"What?" Robby asked. His interest was piqued now.

"How about we go out to eat, and then go to the automobile dealership to look for a new car?"

"Can I have the old one?" he asked, jumping up from the bed.

"Not just yet, young man."

chapter
fifteen

Anna smiled when she entered Robby's room to wake him for school. To her surprise, he was finished straightening the bed and was on his way to the bathroom to get a shower. She suspected that his chipper attitude had something to do with their outing the night before. Secretly, she hoped that their talk had the biggest impact, but she was confident that the trip to the car dealership really made the difference.

Over breakfast, Robby asked, "Why didn't we buy another big car?"

"Now we will have a full size car in the garage and a smaller car for everyday use. We can take the Caddy out for a stroll every now and then."

"I've never heard of a Mercedes Benz before, and it seems kind of noisy," Robby said.

"Like I explained to you at the dealership, they are a very well-built German motor car, and the louder running engine is because they run on diesel fuel instead of gasoline."

"Okay, but I think I should stay home from school today, just in case you need my help when they deliver it."

"Nice try, young man," Anna said, laughing, "but I will do my best to handle the transaction on my own."

Once Robby was off to school and Anna completed her morning chores, she relaxed on the sofa with a cup of tea. It would be several hours before the dealership dropped off the new car, which gave her an opportunity to rest her eyes. Before long, she found herself seated on the swing that was in the park. When she was a girl, the small playground situated in the park was one of her favorite places to be alone. The golden rays of the sun felt warm and comforting against her skin, but dark clouds were quickly moving in. She walked over to the sliding board and viewed her reflection on the shiny metal base. A young girl that she had not seen for many years stared back at her. Dreaming about her youth, she began to play on all the pieces of equipment around her. First, she climbed the ladder and slid down the sliding board. Next, she ran to the monkey bars, making her way across the ladder, hand over hand.

As the ominous clouds overhead attempted to block out the sun, she noticed a faceless figure lurking near the woods. Initially, its presence did not interfere with the fun she was having, but, suddenly, the dark cast from the sky began to overtake the sun. From the corner of her eye, she could see the strange figure that was standing by the woods begin to move in her direction. Afraid and suddenly cold, she started walking toward home. Feeling the presence behind her, she walked faster through the grass. When she looked down at the grass, fear engulfed her when she saw it was slithering up around her body. In desperation, she attempted to scream out for help, but nothing would come out! Once she reached the street, the sight of Robby standing in the front yard calling her name riddled her with fear. Finally, she was able to cry out, "Run, Robert, run! It's right behind me!"

The banging on the front door startled Anna from her nightmare, and she wiped the sleep from her eyes and hurried to the door. Greeting her on the front porch was a smiling young man in a dark suit, clutching a brown leather brief case. Anna though he was a salesperson peddling encyclopedias.

"Hi, my name is Mark, and I'm a representative from Mervis Motors. I'm here to deliver your new Mercedes motor car."

"Of course you are. Come inside and have a seat."

"I was starting to think you weren't home," he said. "I knocked on the door several times."

Anna apologized, and said, "Please forgive me, Mark. I must have dozed off while I was waiting for you."

"Don't worry about it, Miss Wilson. The important thing is that we get you acquainted with your new Mercedes."

"Would you care for a cup of tea, Mark? I'm having one."

Smiling, he said, "Yes, that would be nice."

"How long have you been employed at the dealership, Mark?"

"Not quite a year. After I graduated from Carnegie Mellon University, my father put me to work in the office. The plan is for me to learn every aspect of the business so that I can take the reins if he ever decides to retire."

"It sounds like you have a very good plan."

While drinking their tea, Mark went over the paperwork with Anna. Looking at him, she quickly realized that Mark's youthful looks were deceiving. Though young in years, he obviously knew his job very well. His organizational skills were exceeded only by the articulate manner in which he spoke. He slowly went over all the manuals and service schedules, making sure she clearly understood what was involved in owning a Mercedes. When the two of them went for a drive around Highland Park, Mark instructed her on the proper operation of the car's many features.

"Young man, this is the first vehicle I have ever owned that came with a first aid kit!" surprised.

"Miss Wilson, these vehicles sell themselves."

"That may be true, but do not sell yourself short. You are very good at what you do, and some day you will be the successful owner of the best Mercedes dealership in the city. If I have any questions, you will be the one I contact."

Pleased with her new purchase, Anna stood on the front porch admiring the cream-colored car in the driveway. Suddenly, the urge came over her to visit with the old Cadillac resting quietly in the garage. Even though she felt a little silly, she felt driven by the same feelings she experienced herself when witnessing the changes in her life. Memories of times gone by flooded her mind. The old car was one of the fondest vestiges of the good times she enjoyed with her father. On more occasions than she could remember, she would lend a hand as her father detailed the car inside and out. Anna recalled that the smells of the cleaners and polishes made her feel as though she was a part of something important in her father's life. Gently running her fingers down the sculptured sides of the old automobile, she thought that, not unlike her, it was time for the old girl to rest.

Anna was enjoying driving the shiny new Mercedes down the nearly empty streets this afternoon on its maiden voyage. Adjusting to the sights and sounds of the newly acquired vehicle were challenging, to say the least. Wanting desperately to impress Robby with her driving skills, Anna motored around the park and the back streets where they lived. For the most part, other drivers were tolerant, but several cars felt it necessary to beep and display unkind gestures. On more than one occasion, she drew on the resources that Mark had provided her earlier.

While waiting her turn at a four-way stop, Anna smiled thinking Robby was right about the noise the car made! Glancing at the clock embedded in the fine leather dashboard, Anna realized it was later than she thought. Robby would be getting out of school soon, and she wanted to be there waiting for him. She hoped to impress him with the new driving skills she had acquired.

Anna heard the joyful screams of the children escaping the confines of school as she drove into the school parking lot, and it brought a smile to her face. Like sheepherders, several teachers tried to restore some semblance of order as the youngsters rushed for their assigned buses. The whole scene reminded her of her time as a teacher. To Anna, it was like a Norman Rockwell depiction of life in the schoolyard.

As she exited the car to search for Robby, Anna spotted him racing toward her, his backpack flopping about.

"Is everything okay, Anna?" he asked, concerned.

"Of course it is. I just thought you might enjoy me picking you up from school in our new car."

"When did they drop it off?"

"A nice young man by the name of Mark came by with it earlier today, and I am happy to report that he gave me quite an education on the vehicle."

"Does it drive as nice as the old Caddy?"

"Buckle up, young man, and you can be the judge of that!"

Robert began studying all the new gadgets and knobs before they even drove out of the parking lot. Removing the operating manual from the glove box, he said, "Why is part of this written in a foreign language?"

"It is written in German and English because this motor car, as they like to call them, was manufactured in Germany."

"This is so cool! Wait till I tell my friends we bought a car that was made in Germany!" Robby could hardly contain his excitement.

Anna smiled. "I am glad it meets with your approval, Robby."

"When I told my friends at school we were buying a new Mercedes, they said we must be rich. Are we rich, Anna?"

"Riches come in many different ways. The fact they we have each other in our lives makes us very rich indeed. Monetary riches need not concern you, Robby. As I told you before, you will always be taken care of."

"We are pretty darn lucky to have each other."

chapter
sixteen

After Robert was off to school, Anna carried the fireproof metal box downstairs and placed it on the dining room table. What she was about to do made her feel really good inside. Legal matters usually were tedious and boring, but not the ones she was transacting today. Originally, Jack and Marge were going to come to her house to meet, but Anna decided to go to the office instead. Besides, she wanted to show off her new Mercedes, and she thought it was important to demonstrate her ability to be independent. She strategically planned the eleven o'clock appointment so that she could coax the pair into having lunch with her when they finished with her legal matters.

As she sorted through the legal and financial documents, thoughts of her father came to mind. When she was about Robby's age, it gave her comfort to watch her father study his investments. Many of the early stocks he had speculated on were now Blue Chips in her portfolio. Saul Levin, God rest his soul, was a trusted friend of her father's for many years. She remembered that her father treated him more like a friend than a business associate. Now that Saul Sr. was dead and gone, things were different at Levin and Stein. Anna would not tolerate someone who did not take her seriously. That was exactly what Saul Jr. did. Because of his actions, or lack thereof, Jack and Marge had come into her life.

With her paperwork in order and placed neatly in her leather satchel, Anna headed upstairs to get dressed. Passing by Robby's room, she noticed several of his prized comic books lying on the floor. She picked them up, and then sat down on his bed to enjoy his aura. The vitality she experienced in his space was beyond description. Everything from his toys to the posters he had hanging on the wall radiated his energy. She felt as though every event in her life was preparing her for this very moment. Even though Anna avoided initiating discussion about the death of his mother, she could not help but wonder how much it weighed on his mind. Robert had not inquired about his father, which Anna could understand. One day at a time was the prescription she followed when it came to Robert. This day was promising to be a glorious one indeed, and she refused to let life's pitfalls interfere with it. The wealth the family had bestowed upon her would finally be able to take on a life of its own by influencing those closest to her.

After a luxuriating bath, Anna marveled at the many beautiful dresses hanging in her bedroom closet. Many years had passed since she had worn some of them. Some were out of style, but Anna paid little attention to the rules and regulations concerning fashion. She finally settled on a loosely flowing floral, and to match its easy-going style, she decided to wear her hair down, complementing the upbeat mood of the day's activities.

As Marge leaned against the office door to fish the key out of her purse, she realized it was already open. At first, she thought she may have forgotten to lock it the night before,

– *Gerald Miller* –

but she clearly remembered locking it. Then the thought crossed her mind that it might be an intruder. Standing outside, she pushed the door open about a third of the way and screamed as loud as she could, "The cops are on the way, and I have a gun!"

A familiar voice declared, "Please don't shoot, lady! I give up."

"Is that you, Jack?" she said, relaxing a bit.

"Guilty as charged," he said, rather nonchalantly.

Partially in shock that Jack was in the office early, Marge walked in and dropped her purse on her desk. When she saw the dozen long-stemmed red roses in a vase on the center of her desk, her heart began to melt.

"They are beautiful, Jack!"

"Read the card," he said proudly.

The card read, "You are the flower in my life, Red. Love Jack."

Touched by the card and its sentiment, Marge said, "I don't know what to say, except that I am so surprised. You have no idea how long it has been since somebody gave me flowers. Oh my God, Jack, I love them!"

"I really enjoyed what we shared together yesterday and wanted to let you know how special you are to me."

Marge tried unsuccessfully to hide the tears as she put her arms around Jack and kissed him on the cheek. Unfortunately, the sound of the telephone ringing ended their sentimental interaction. With a tissue in one hand and the phone receiver in the other, Marge embarked on her day.

The proudly displayed red roses put a perpetual smile on her face that promised to last throughout the day. For Jack to put forth the effort to arrive at the office early and

– 166 –

bring her flowers was huge in Marge's mind. Secretly, she was excited for Anna to see the flowers when she arrived for their meeting.

Jack usually hid his emotions well, but he was thoroughly enjoying this moment. Rocking back and forth in his chair, he smiled as he reviewed the day's to-do list.

Lunch hour traffic was mounting as Anna drove toward Pittsburgh. She felt much more at ease behind the wheel of the Mercedes versus the considerably larger Cadillac. The size of the vehicle mattered little when it came to the speed of her driving, though. She thought other drivers were admiring her new car when they were honking their horns, but when she saw the hand gestures as they passed her, she realized that was not the case. She was determined not to let a few rude motorists ruin the glorious life-changing event that was about to unfold.

Suddenly realizing that she had driven past Jack's office, Anna faced the difficult task of turning around on the busy street. After giving it considerable thought, she decided she needed the exercise and parked about a block away. The social condition of the area reminded her that Jack needed to move his practice to a better location. Several women wearing flashy outfits admired her Mercedes Anna walked away. Halfway down the block, a man who needed a lesson in personal hygiene asked her if she had any spare change. She did not think it prudent to open her purse, so she moved along quietly. Normally, she was not a big fan of the city, but on this occasion, the hustle and bustle did not seem to bother her.

When Anna reached Jack's office, she looked at her reflection in the large window facing the street. After straightening herself out, she shook her head in disapproval because the window was overdue for a good cleaning. She secretly hoped that Jack would employ a cleaning service with the additional income he would soon be generating.

The sight of Marge's smile as she walked into the reception area warmed Anna's heart. When she saw the beautiful roses on Marge's desk, she found it difficult to contain her curiosity. The gears were obviously turning in Anna's mind as she looked at Marge's blushing face.

"Well, are you going to tell me who sent you the flowers?" Anna asked, smiling.

Just as she asked the question, Jack appeared from his office in the back. Anna knew that Jack gave her the roses. She did not want to seem pushy, so she did not pursue the subject any further. By all outward appearances, Jack and Marge were moving forward in their personal life together just as she hoped.

Jack had a few things to finish up before they went to lunch, giving Anna a chance to show off her new car to Marge. If she was lucky, Marge might give her a few tidbits of information about her and Jack.

"Marge, come outside with me. I have something to show you," Anna said."

When they reached the sidewalk, Marge had a confused look on her face. "Where is your car, Anna?"

"It's parked just down the street."

The old Cadillac was nowhere in sight, and Marge wondered if it had been stolen.

"Anna, are you sure this is where you parked?"

"Yes, dear, you are standing beside it."

"Anna, you bought a new Mercedes!" she exclaimed.

"Robby and I picked it out, and they delivered it a couple days ago. I am trying to become accustomed to all the new gadgets, but it will take time. Robby thinks the conversions from German to English are fascinating."

"Did you trade in the Caddy?"

"I couldn't do that. She is now retired to the occasional Sunday drive and a lifetime of pampering."

Marge suggested that Anna move her new car down the block and park it in front of Jack's office. Not keen about making the trip around the block during lunch hour traffic, Anna asked Marge if she would like to take it for a drive. A little reluctant at first, Marge finally caved in to her curiosity. When they drove up in front of the office, Jack was standing on the sidewalk shaking his head.

Opening the door for Anna, he said, "It is a beautiful car, Anna."

Anna smiled. "Doesn't Marge look good behind the wheel?"

Everyone smiled.

The quiet restaurant provided the appropriate atmosphere for Anna to share her plans with Jack and Marge. As they waited for their food, Anna explained her wishes in detail. While she had mentioned these matters once before, briefly, she had not gone into great detail. Today, though, she made everything clear. Effective immediately, she was going to dismiss Levin and Stein, the law firm she had empowered to oversee her financial holdings. Those responsibilities would immediately shift to Jack's office and any future associates in his employ. Any fees Jack would charge Anna would include, but not exceed, the going rates in Pittsburgh for said services. At last count, Anna's net worth was a little over sixteen million dollars.

Jack quickly jotted down notes on a pad as Anna dictated to him. The one thing that stuck out in his mind—aside from the sixteen million dollars—was that Anna was a very sharp woman. She knew exactly what she wanted, and she knew the price she was willing to pay for it.

Anna continued to lay out explicit instructions for Jack. She expected him to keep her abreast of things with monthly reports, given in her home when possible. In a timely manner, she expected him to secure a more appropriate office to meet his needs. If he required financial assistance to do so, she would help him in that regard.

When she finished laying out the bulk of her plans, she said, "I hope this will be an acceptable business relationship for all involved. When we finish our lunch, we need to discuss some matters that are both personal and legal."

Jack agreed to all of the terms Anna put before him. He would have been crazy not to. Anna was giving him the opportunity to move uptown with his own law firm. Not only was he returning to the part of town where he started, he was going back on his own terms.

Anna and Marge enjoyed a celebratory glass of wine, while Jack toasted with a glass of sweet tea. Everyone was very upbeat during lunch. Jack and Marge enthusiastically participated in small talk, but both were anticipating the post-lunch discussion. Thoughts bounced around Marge's mind about the many changes that were in the wind. She pictured herself wearing nicer clothes and, more important, wearing the title of office manager. Marge and Jack both would finally be able to work out of an office in which they could be proud. She wouldn't have to worry anymore about her car breaking down every other day, and most important, her son, Joel, would have a better quality of life.

When Anna moved on to the subject of Robby's future guardians, there was a serious tone in her voice. It was very important to Anna that Robby be properly taken care of. It was obvious that Marge was a good mother to Joel, and Jack's actions had shown her he was a moral man.

"As we discussed at my home," Anna began, "my intent is for the two of you to be Robert's legal guardians when I pass on. Along with the business documents, we will sign the necessary papers to make it legally binding. I realize the financial burden will be great, so Jack, you will need to set up a trust fund for that express purpose. Furthermore, you will have the option of moving into my home to raise the boys; the house would then become yours. If you decide against moving in, the house will go to the estate. This is a very big responsibility that I am asking, so I want you to be certain."

Marge was the first one to reply, "Anna, you know how I feel about Robby, and the boys get along very well together. If you are using the old house as an incentive, it is not necessary, but we would be proud to live there. So, of course, my answer is yes."

Jack remained silent for several moments, and then said, "Since our last conversation at your home, I have given the request a great deal of thought. Anna, you have been the architect of my resurrection as an attorney, and I will be forever indebted to you. My experience raising a child is lacking, to say the least. All I can guarantee you is that I will do my best to help him grow into the kind of young man that would make you proud. Yes, I will be his legal guardian."

A warm smile found its way to Anna's lips, and she said, "If matters of the heart unfold the way I expect, you two will be sharing the old house together."

Marge leaned across Jack's desk, and said, "What the hell just happened, Jack?"

Smiling, he said, "Red, we just came into a shit load of money!"

"Does this mean that we are looking for a new office?"

Jack laughed. "No, Red, new *offices*!"

The phone started ringing, and Marge headed out front. She hesitated when Jack asked, "Will you have dinner with me tonight?"

It was impossible for her to conceal the joy she was feeling, and she said, gleefully, "You bet, Mr. Porter!"

Anna was looking forward to relaxing a bit before Robby got home from school. She placed her hat and purse on the table, and then lay back on the sofa. Just as her eyes began to feel heavy, the ringing of the telephone interrupted her rest. It was Robby's principal. At first, Anna was terrified, because she was concerned that something happened to him.

"Did something happen to Robert?" she said, her heart was pounding.

"No, he's fine Miss Wilson, but I do need you come to the school over a disciplinary problem."

Confused, she asked, "Are you sure we are talking about the same young man?"

"Yes, ma'am, I'm sure."

With a tentative tone in her voice, she said, "I will be there shortly."

Thoughts raced through Anna's mind as she walked toward the main entrance of the school building. Concern turned into guarded disbelief the closer she came to the principal's office. Under her breath, she said, "Robert is a well behaved young man. If he is in trouble, there must be some sort of misunderstanding." Then she remembered that even well behaved children are capable of some sort of mischief.

While Anna waited for Principal Brown in the reception area, the bell sounded, signaling the change of classes. Children of all shapes and sizes raced through the halls, chattering loudly, and some of them stopped to peer through the glass panels separating the office from the halls, staring at her. The thought went through her mind that some things never changed. She wanted to smile at the children, but her seriousness of the situation prevented her from doing so. After all, she was in the principal's office.

A tall middle-aged woman appeared from one of the offices in the back. Her smile seemed forced when she said, "I take it you are Mrs. Wilson?"

Anna immediately corrected her. "No, it's Miss Wilson."

"Forgive me; you must be Robert's legal guardian."

Anna was becoming increasingly frustrated with Principal Brown, partly because the woman reminded her of every domineering school official she had ever known. Refusing to answer the question, Anna said, "Where is Robert?"

Principal Brown hesitated, then said, "He is waiting for us in my office. Would you like to know what he has done?"

Glaring, Anna said, "No, I will ask him when we arrive at your office."

Robby was sitting alone when Anna and the principal got to her office. He immediately jumped out of the chair and wrapped his arms around Anna's waist. The bright smile on his face seemed to light up the otherwise dreary office.

"I knew you would come!" he said.

Anna hugged him back, and then said quietly, "Okay, Robby, let's have a seat and get all this worked out."

Principal Brown got down to business immediately. "Robert, would you like to tell Anna why you are here?"

When Robby lifted his head to speak, Anna saw bruises on his face. Before he could explain, Anna interjected. "What happened to my Robby's face?"

"He got into a fist fight during recess," Principal Brown said. "The reason I called you in is because he refuses to tell me why they were fighting."

Anna asked Robby for an explanation, but he didn't respond.

"I know Robert has been through a difficult time with the loss of his parents, so I see no reason to punish him. My thought is that you can best handle this at home," Principal Brown said.

Anna thanked Principal Brown, and then she took hold of Robert's hand and said, "Let's go, Robby."

The walk to the car held a thick silence in the air. Anna desperately wanted to hold the troubled young man during his time of need, but it was not time to show affection. As they drove out of the parking lot toward home, she gave him as much space as he needed. She knew he was not a violent boy by nature, which meant that he had good reason for the altercation. Condoning schoolyard fights was not her way, but she secretly thought it was a good arena for youngsters to learn how to stand up for themselves. She believed that whether they won or lost, the playground was where youngsters began to fall into the pecking order of life.

Anna stopped the car in front of the house and looked over at Robert. Forcing a smile on her face, she said, "Would you like to go to Winky's for dinner?"

The down in the dumps expression on Robby's face gradually began to soften. Through his pouting, he said, "Can I get a double cheeseburger?"

Anna smiled and said, "Sure, as long as you're buying."

When she caught him smiling out of the corner of her eye, she knew the suggestion to go out to eat was the right decision. Anna learned through Robby that there was something magical about sizzling hamburgers, greasy French fries, and chocolate milkshakes.

Anna and Robby enjoyed their fast-food meal amidst the noisy atmosphere. When all that remained were the remnants of Anna's soft drink and Robby's milkshake, he finally started to open up. "David Humphrey started the fight! When he pushed me, I had to hit him back. Principal Brown got mad at me because I told her I was not sorry."

Anna desperately wanted to smile and pat him on the back for standing up for what he believed in, but she realized the important thing was to find out the root of the confrontation. Anna was careful not to push for additional details as Robby stared out the window into the parking lot. It was very important to her that he trusted her and was not afraid to share his problems. Finally, she saw his eyes begin to well up and several tears rolled down his cheeks. Looking down at the table, he blurted out, "David said my dad is a drunk and a murderer. He said it in front of all my friends."

Anna moved over next to Robby as the tears began to flow. She put her arms around him, and he began sobbing on her shoulder.

"Why did my dad kill my mother? I miss her so much!" he cried out.

All Anna could say was, "Of course you do, dear, of course you do."

Anna knew there were going to be further discussions on this matter, but not in a fast-food restaurant.

Anna reached into her purse and dug out a couple tissues for Robby to wipe his tears. Running her fingers through his hair in a loving manner, she smiled. In a teasing manner, she said, "Can I have the rest of your milkshake?"

A gentle smile found Robby's face before he piped up, joking, "No way! I am drinking it all!"

He then picked up the partially consumed drink and offered to share it with Anna, but she smiled and said, "No, thank you, I have all I need."

On the short drive home, Anna's heart ached for Robby, as she knew the day would come when he would face situations like this. The years made her all too familiar with the cruelties of the world. Unfortunately, children often took the brunt of those cruelties. Sadly, they mimicked what their parents professed behind closed doors, thinking it must be the gospel truth.

When they got home, Robby went to his room to do his homework. Anna understood him wanting to retreat the safety of his room, but she felt sad for him just the same. He needed to have space to digest all that had happened to him earlier in the day. What hurt Robby most of all was the fact they he knew that David Humphrey was telling the truth. He was growing to love Anna in a different way than he loved his parents. The softness he felt from her made him feel secure and safe.

Robby remained uncharacteristically quiet through most of dinner. Anna tried very hard to give him the opportunity to open up, but to no avail. Finally, as he was playing with the food on his plate, Anna said, "Robby, I want you to talk to me about what is on your mind."

Looking down at the table, he said, "I guess I'm having a really bad day."

"Well, I don't see it that way, Robby."

Raising his eyes to meet hers, he said, "How can you say that, Anna? I got in a fight at school, and now everyone knows what my dad did. Principal Brown will probably punish me and you will most likely ground me. How can you see it any other way but bad?"

"This is the way I see it. You stood up for what you believed in, which is the most important thing. David Humphrey will think twice before teasing you in the future, and I will talk to Principal Brown about waiving any further punishment." Anna became very quiet for a moment, and then continued, "Robby, I will never punish you for standing up for yourself!"

Anna cleaned the kitchen after dinner and went upstairs to change into her nightclothes. She looked in on Robby, pleased to see him lying on his bed and reading a book. As she turned to leave the room, Robby said, "I have a question Anna."

"What might that be?" she said, smiling.

"I was thinking about what you said downstairs, that you would never punish me for doing what I believe in. What if you don't agree with what I believe in?"

Anna stood in the doorway and thought about the question for a few minutes, and then said softly, "Then you would have to be willing to accept the consequences for doing what you think is right. Robby, you will learn that not everything is black and white. The grey areas are what make life interesting.

Pondering what she had said, he asked, "What are consequences?"

She smiled and said, "Well, knowing you would get in trouble at school for fighting but doing it anyway was the willingness to face a consequence."

"I understand, but I will have to wait until I am older to understand what the grey areas are."

chapter
seventeen

With the ink dry on the legal papers, Jack was officially Anna's attorney of record. The firm that represented the family's interests from the time she was a child called her more in the week following the transition than they had in several years. Almost immediately, the search for Jack's new office space was underway. Their workload was exhausting, as they put in a full day at the office and viewed potential new offices in the evening. Marge had visions of walls of glass and double doors with brass handles. Jack was leaning toward the natural wood look with towering ceilings. Finally, a real estate agent located the perfect offices in one of the best locations in town. It was an entire third floor of a building, with four main offices. Glass walls with ten-foot-high double doors with brass handles surrounded the reception area. The spacious rooms came decorated with deeply polished wood and marble floors throughout. Glass windows stretching from floor to ceiling overlooked the bustling city below.

Anna found herself in the sitting room enjoying some much valued alone time. Robby was outside playing with several of his friends from the neighborhood. Glancing over at the bookshelf, she decided to look at one of her old favorites.

Gently embracing an old volume of *The Grapes of Wrath*, she kicked her shoes off and sat back in the comfort of her favorite chair. She smiled at the memory of how she was introduced to the Pulitzer Prize winning novel. A fan of Steinbeck, her English teacher, Mr. Williams, was pleased to include it on the list of required reading. He placed great emphasis on the reality of the plot and stressed to the students the importance of remembering it. Oftentimes, he would refer to the students in the class as young people of privilege. Anna thought he was an educator with passion, but some students whispered that he was a Communist behind his back.

As she flipped through the yellowing pages of the aging book, Anna remembered something her father once said to both her and Elizabeth. As the two sat silently at the dinner table, waiting to be dismissed, their father looked at them with sadness in his eyes and said, "With privilege comes responsibility, girls. Don't ever forget it." Not certain what he was referring to, they quietly waited for him to leave the room. When they looked to their mother with questioning eyes, she said, "Your father was forced to lay off twenty-five people from one of the factories today, and he is very sad about it." Elizabeth was concerned that it would affect how much money they would have, but their mother assured them both that their quality of life would not change.

Anna's thoughts drifted back to the present when Robby burst through the front door with one of his friends.

"Anna, we are dying of thirst! Can we have something to drink, please?"

She smiled and placed the book on the table. Robby beckoned her again a little louder, "Anna!"

When she walked into the hallway she said, "I heard you the first time, young man. If you and your friend come with me into the kitchen, I'll make you a glass of iced tea."

Robert looked at Anna with a quizzical smile and said, "Don't you remember Billy? He has been over here before with me."

She quickly apologized for needing her memory jogged and rephrased the question. "Would you and Billy like to come with me into the kitchen for iced tea and a plate of cookies?"

The smiles on the boys' faces answered her question.

While the boys were enjoying their afternoon snack, Anna excused herself and went back to the sofa to relax. She heard the sound of their talking drifting down the hall and into the living room. Initially, she felt guilty for eavesdropping, but the volume of their conversation made it difficult not to. Billy could not believe that the two of them were living in such a large house.

"Why do you live in such a large house with just you and Anna?" Billy asked.

Not sure how to reply, Robby said, "This house has been in Anna's family for hundreds of years."

Anna nearly laughed aloud when she heard Robby exaggerate the pedigree of the house.

"My room is twice as big as the one I had in the other house," Robby continued.

"What is it like living with such an old lady?" Billy said. "Is she mean to you?"

"No way, man! She is one of the nicest women I have ever known. When no one wanted me, she took me in."

Sinking into the sofa, Anna took a tissue from the coffee table and wiped the tears from her eyes, thinking about Robby's kind words. To pass the time while the boys were playing upstairs, she continued reading her book. After about an hour or so, she heard the boys running down the steps. Robby asked Anna if he and Billy could have a sleepover the following night, because it wasn't a school night. He promised they wouldn't be any trouble and that they would go to bed on time. Anna agreed on the condition that Billy's mother call her, giving her permission. The boys could hardly contain their excitement as they headed out the front door to Billy's house, to get his mom's approval.

Anna tried to continue reading, but her thoughts drifted to two young boys planning a sleepover. On some level, she was more excited than they were. It gave her a great deal of hope, seeing that Robby was embarking on some sort of normalcy in his life. While she wouldn't reveal to him how elated she felt about the sleepover and, more important, the positive changes in his life, she was elated nonetheless. Excited for Robby, Anna started planning for the boys' big night: snacks, a pizza, and a movie should do the trick!

The aroma of a roasting chicken in the oven wafted through the house, while steaming potatoes were cooking on the stovetop. As Anna set the table in the dining room, she smiled as she placed the bottle of Heinz Ketchup closest to Robby's plate. Since he moved in, it had become a regular staple during mealtimes. Condiments were not looked upon favorably when she was growing up. Her mother was of the opinion that it was an insult to the food preparer to pollute the taste with items such as ketchup. As finished placing the silverware next to the plates, the doorbell startled her. She could hear her rapidly beating heart throbbing in her head.

The woman at the door appeared to be in her late thirties, wearing tan shorts, a summer blouse with a flower print, and white tennis shoes. Anna spotted gardening gloves partially exposed in front pocket and figured she was someone from the neighborhood. Anna got the impression that she had been recently working in the garden. She immediately trusted the kindness she saw in the stranger's eyes. Relieved that it was not official business, Anna asked, "Can I help you?"

In a soft but confident voice, the young woman said, "Please forgive the intrusion. My name is Helen Thomas. Billy is my son."

When Anna realized who she was, she said, "Where are my manners? Please, come in, dear. As you obviously know, I'm Robert's guardian, Anna Wilson."

As Helen waited in the parlor for Anna, she marveled at the beauty of the finely crafted old house. Anna returned with a serving tray that held chilled glasses of amber tea, a crystal bowl of sugar, and fresh lemon wedges.

"Thank you, but you shouldn't have gone to so much trouble," Helen said.

Anna smiled as she placed a glass on a coaster next to Helen. "Nonsense, it's not often that I get the opportunity to entertain these days."

As the young woman squeezed a wedge of lemon into her glass of tea, she said, "Your home is beautiful."

"Thank you. It's been in our family for a great many years."

The two women continued with small talk and cordial niceties for nearly twenty minutes. When Anna finished giving Helen a grand tour of the house, the two women ended up on the back porch. Anna placed her hand gently on Helen's shoulder and said, "Helen, you obviously have more on your mind than a tour of my old house. You're not going to offend me by being frank, so what's on your mind."

Helen laughed nervously. "I'm not going to apologize for being concerned about Billy's well-being, but as a mother, I worry. Of course Billy can spend the night, now that I've met you."

"That is very commendable, and considering the circumstances, it is completely understandable."

"The boys have been friends for many years, and Robby has stayed over more times than I can remember. I thought it was a little strange that he never asked Billy to stay at his house."

"One of the darker things I've learned in this life is that the secrets kept behind closed doors can ultimately destroy people."

The conversation lightened as the two women discussed their successes and failures in the area of gardening. Anna smiled and said, "According to my flowers, the rabbits are having a great year."

Helen smiled and said, "I couldn't agree more. It's been very frustrating for me also." Her tone more serious now, Helen inquired, "How did you and Robby come to know one another? If it's none of my business, please feel free to point that out."

Anna saw the young woman as understandably curious, which did not bother her at all. "Initially, Robby and I became acquainted when he started delivering my newspaper. Being the industrious young man that he is, he asked if I had any chores for him to help earn money for a Halloween costume. It is strange, because he seemed very small as he stood nervously on the porch soliciting odd jobs. From that point on, he raked leaves and took care of small jobs around here."

"So you two became close?"

Anna took a drink of the tea before replying. "Friendly, but not too close, because I always knew he was someone else's child. The same feeling I had when reaching out to troubled students when I was a teacher. It was important that I employ a certain amount of detachment in order to save my own emotional well-being, especially since I do not have any children of my own. Even though the circumstances surrounding Robby's arrival into my life were grim, I feel blessed to have the opportunity to have him.

Anna felt very comfortable with Helen and enjoyed the opportunity to interact with one of the women from the neighborhood. She was not antisocial, but found it tedious to involve herself in meaningless chitchat with people in general. Other than a smile and a wave, she stayed to herself. The fact that Helen took the initiative to come to Anna's home to investigate the surroundings before giving Billy permission to sleep over impressed her. She also liked the way the young woman carried herself in unfamiliar surroundings. Helen was not afraid to say what was on her mind, but not in a threatening manner. The way she saw it, confidence in oneself was a reflection of a person's inner strength.

"My husband and I were shocked when we heard what happened to Robby's mother. The situation occurred so quickly that it was hard to wrap our minds around it."

"My heart ached when I was made aware of Robby's situation in all of it. We don't talk about it much, but I'm sure it was stressful for him to live in a home with such problems."

Helen added, "Even though he never mentioned his father's drinking, Robby seemed to spend a great deal of time playing at our house. The important thing is that he has you now."

Anna smiled and said, "Most important, we have each other."

Finishing her glass of tea and setting it on the tray, Helen said, "Thank you for having me in your home. I would really like to get together again very soon. Good luck with the boys' tomorrow night!" to the door, Anna said, "Maybe we can get to together next week for lunch while the boys are in school?"

"I'll call you tomorrow to set it up," Helen said.

As Marge and Jack feverously juggled casework and made the necessary preparations to make the transition into the new office, the stress level was high. Marge's organizational skills shined, and Jack had no choice but to follow her direction. Employing movers and contacting office supply stores were just a few items on Marge's lengthy to-do list. The hours were grueling, but they still found time to enjoy a nice meal when the workday was done. Hiring the additional personnel needed was a job-specific responsibility.

Marge had the final say on all clerical positions, and Jack would make the decisions on the legal staff. Marge set up the interviews from the local universities for paralegals while Jack evaluated their potential. Drawing on his legal contacts from the past, he spoke with a recruiter for possible candidates to head up the new financial department. The perfect person for the job would need to have a lucrative following. Pedigree was not as important to Jack as performance. The only way to keep the cash flowing was to have an active client list.

Even though there was not a great deal of time for romance, Jack and Marge grew closer each day. The long hours they worked together reinforced the fact that fate had brought them together. Jack was spending more time with Marge and her son, Joel, outside of the office. It seemed to Marge that she was on the brink of realizing a dream. Free time was not something she was afforded very often, but when she was able to sneak away, it was spent shopping for a new car. On Sunday afternoons, she would take Joel out for some fast food, and then drive across town to view apartments in a better area of the city. Most of her adult life was trying to scrape a living for her and her son.

Once the office was set up and the new additions to the team were hired, Marge had plans of organizing a small party as a way of thanking Anna for all she had done. Marge was very excited that she was having the invitations personalized and printed up professionally. It was going to be a cozy affair, with about a dozen or so people in attendance. There would be wine, soft drinks, and various cheeses, along with other finger foods to eat. She was also ordering a beautiful cake from the bakery, which would have a single candle marking the first year of the firm. The guest list would include the newly hired employees, Anna, and selected family members.

The topic of discussion throughout most of the evening on Thursday was the sleepover the following day. It was Anna and Robby's first sleepover. Excitement was in the air, and Anna had no idea how the youngster was going to make it through school the next day. She did her best at being patient with him as he nervously questioned whether there were enough snacks for them to eat. Anna assured him that she was going to the grocery store to secure enough treats while he was at school. She chuckled to herself, wondering if Robby would ever be able to get to sleep. When they turned in for the night, she ended up being the one who had difficulty sleeping. The excitement in the air was a reminder that she never had any school friends who were close enough to spend the night at her house. Before finding sweet slumber, she concluded that she would enjoy it almost as much as the boys would.

At breakfast the next morning, Anna was surprised to see that Robby was up early, with very little coaxing on her part. Breakfast included a barrage of questions concerning the preparation for the evening's festivities. Robby assured Anna that it was customary to stay up late and consume snacks not normally allowed, and Anna assured Robby that there would be plenty of those "not normally allowed" treats.

Robby drained the remaining milk in his cereal bowl and announced he was leaving a little early, eager to get his day started. Before racing out the door, he kissed Anna on the cheek and said, "Thanks, Anna, you're the best!"

As Anna sat down at the dining room table to plan her day, the phone rang. She continued to have a tinge of fear if the telephone rang when Robby was not home. It angered her to no end that she could not control such an unfounded emotion, and she hoped time would rectify that feeling. She smiled when she heard Helen's voice on the other end.

"How about having lunch with me today?" Helen asked.

Without hesitation, Anna said, "Sure, that would be nice."

The two women made plans for Helen to pick Anna up around noon. As Anna hung up the phone, she smiled to herself. "What a peculiar woman. I think I'm going to enjoy her company."

Anna wasn't used to socializing much, but she found it difficult *not* to be excited about having a friend in the neighborhood. She jotted down the name Palermo's Pizza on a sheet of paper with the telephone number. As she finished writing down a small list of grocery items, she placed it on the table and continued with her chores. Before going up the stairs, she shook her head and walked back to the kitchen. Against her better judgment, she added potato chips, soda pop, and chocolate bars to the shopping list.

Before leaving for the market, Anna made some final preparations for the boys sleepover. She was careful not to refer to it as a slumber party, because Robby informed her the prior evening that slumber parties were for girls. After placing an additional comforter and pillow on his bed, she grabbed her keys and handbag and walked out the door. Pleased that her driving abilities were progressing, she confidently made her way down the street. It was her goal to master all the various functions of the gadgets inside her Mercedes Benz. She smiled to herself, recalling the time Robby was looking at the owner's manual and said, "Anna, you are going to have to learn a foreign language to drive this car!" It gave her a great deal of joy that she was accumulating memories with the little man who found his way into her life.

The reasoning escaped her, but Anna decided to drive by Helen's house on her way to the grocery store. Intrigued by her forward personality, she thought she might get a better understanding of the kind of person she was by seeing where she lived. The red brick ranch-style house was a modest size, but typical for the area. Anna immediately noticed the well cared for lawn and the well-maintained gardens. Peering inside the open two-car garage, she could see lawn and garden tools, as well as various children's outdoor toys dangling neatly from the walls. While admiring the hummingbird painted on the cedar mailbox, Anna was startled as Helen came out of the garage carrying a flat of assorted flowers. "So, you decided to do a little spying of your own?" Helen said, grinning.

Embarrassed, Anna said, "No, I was just on my to the grocery store and thought I would drive by your house."

"Isn't the market in the other direction?"

"Indeed it is," Anna said, caught in a fib.

Helen put the flowers down on the driveway and removed the colorful gardening gloves she was wearing. She told Anna to park her car in the driveway and invited her inside. As Anna was getting out of her car, a small miniature Collie mix darted around the house, barking franticly. Helen promptly scolded the dog, and when Anna realized he was no danger, she exited the car, and Toby cautiously solicited her for attention.

As the two women headed toward the house, Anna commented on Helen's beautiful gardens. Helen proceeded to give Anna the grand tour, pointing out the evergreens and flowerbeds strategically located around the house. Anna had made the mistake of petting Toby's long coat, which encouraged him to follow her everywhere they went.

Helen led Anna across the concrete patio and through the French doors, into the kitchen. She apologized for the dishes in the sink, and then offered Anna a cup of tea, which she declined. Anna reminded Helen that she needed to get to the grocery store.

Laughing, Helen said, "Let me guess, you are buying snacks that you normally don't keep in the house for the sleepover tonight?"

"I'm kind of new at this sort of thing," Anna said.

"Just think of it as a night of controlled chaos," Helen said.

Helen took Anna by surprise when she leaned in and gave her a hug and a smile in the driveway before seeing her off to the grocery store.

Fortunately, the grocery store was not busy, so Anna was able to get what she needed rather quickly, with the help of the kind store clerk who assisted her. Scores of treats lined the shelves in every shape and size. She settled on a package of Hershey bars with nuts; the way she figured it, at least the nuts were healthy. She also bought a bag of potato chips and something else that caught her eye: a bag of Dove bars. She would stash these away at home for her later enjoyment.

❦ ❦ ❦ ❦

Marge worked feverishly, trying to organize the mountain of files littering her desk. When she looked out the windows of her new office, enjoying the view of the city, it was a reminder of why she was working so hard. As she was hoping for an excuse to take a break, Jack walked through the doors.

"What's going on, Red?"

"Somewhere under all those files is a beautiful desk!" she said, the frustration in her voice obvious as she pointed to her desk.

"Where is that cute little paralegal you hired?" Jack asked.

As Marge plopped down in the leather chair she said, "She can't start until Monday."

In his devil-may-care attitude, Jack said, "I don't have to be back in court until one o'clock. Would you like to go to lunch with me?"

Eager for a break, Marge grabbed her purse and locked up.

❦ ❦ ❦ ❦

Anna laughed as she was putting the groceries away, because she wasn't used to stocking her shelves with chocolate bars and potato chips. She decided the top shelf in the kitchen cabinet would be best to keep them out of Robby's easy reach. She periodically peeked at the kitchen clock, as it was almost time to get dressed for the lunch date with Helen. She thought about calling Helen to see what type of attire would be appropriate, as she didn't know where they were dining, but instead she decided on a casual pair of pale blue slacks and a white blouse.

As Anna was double-checking that everything was set for Robby's sleepover the doorbell signaled the arrival of her lunch date. She was relieved to see that Helen had dressed casually too. The two women laughed as Anna filled Helen in on her adventure at the grocery store, shopping to satisfy the boys' snack requests, and Helen suggested to Anna that she put away all her expensive knickknacks!

Ready to head out the door, Helen suggested they go to the River's Edge for lunch. "We can sit outside, enjoy a cocktail, and tell intimate tales about ourselves."

Anna liked Helen. She seemed to have the ability of making everything she said sound very important, but with a lighthearted spin. She did not fit the stereotype of the typical homemaker.

Before Anna got into Helen's late model green Ford Suburban, she noticed the books Helen was clearing off the front seat: a combination of gardening and art history. She knew that Helen was an avid gardener, but the art history books stirred her interest. Anna assumed the books were from the Carnegie Library, but art history is not usually a subject for the casual reader.

After clearing the front seat, Helen said, "All right, girl, hop on into my chariot!"

The step up was a little higher than Anna was accustomed to, but she managed to make her way in without assistance.

On the way to the restaurant, Helen said, "So, Anna, what do you think of my green machine?"

Anna looked around at the remains of various projects scattered about the vehicle, and surmised that Helen used it much like a pickup truck. Careful not to offend her new friend, she said, "It's very large. Most likely it comes in handy when working around the house."

"It was a compromise," Helen said.

Puzzled, Anna said, "I'm not sure I understand."

"When I told my husband, Joe, that I wanted a pickup truck, he said absolutely not. 'No wife of mine will drive around in a truck!' We met in the middle, and now I have my Suburban. It's great for picking up house project material and hauling just about anything."

Anna looked out the window at the sparkling current of the Allegheny River as they neared the restaurant. The two women agreed to eat outside on the deck overlooking the water, as it was such a beautiful day, and they could watch the sunlight dance on the water.

The young female server brought both women hefty glasses of the house white wine they had ordered, and then took their lunch orders. Helen settled on a Monty Cristo, and Anna chose a Rueben. Anna had never eaten here before, and she liked the restaurant's light and airy atmosphere. Helen, on the other hand, frequented the restaurant about once a month, as she noted, "Billy loves the nautical décor and thinks the food is great."

As the volume of wine decreased in their glasses, the effect became evident in the conversation.

"I'm really enjoying this," Anna said in between laughing.

"Can I ask you a question?" Helen said.

Obviously feeling the effects of her drink, Anna said, "Ask away!"

"Why did you decide to take on the responsibility of a ten-year-old boy? Don't get me wrong, Robby has always been special to me, but that's a lot to take on for anybody."

"You mean for a woman my age," Anna interjected.

Helen laughed and said, "Hell, none of us are getting any younger. I guess that's part of it, but if I offended you, I offer my sincerest—"

Just then, two large plates of food appeared on the table in front of them. Helen took the opportunity to order two more glasses of wine for them.

Picking up where they left off, Anna said, "As I mentioned before, Robby and I became quite friendly when he took on small jobs around my house to make extra money. There were even situations when I manufactured chores for him to do because I enjoyed spending time with him. When I learned the news about the murder, I did some investigating to see what had become of him. Unfortunately, the members of his extended family had no place for him in their lives, which angered me to no end. Robby was placed in social services, alone and very afraid. Details aside, a legal battle commenced, important people got involved, and I became his legal guardian. And let me clarify something for you, Helen. I have enjoyed the benefits that money has afforded me my entire life, but until recently, it has brought me more problems than happiness."

Helen felt a sadness come over her as Anna told the story, not because of Robby's plight, but for Anna, as she was a person who seemed to have everything except love.

The two women sat quietly for several uncomfortable moments, and then Helen said, "Wow! You know how to tell one hell of a story!"

Anna looked at her very seriously, and then both women began laughing uncontrollably. The conversation lightened as they enjoyed their lunch. Periodically, the server would approach their table to see if they needed anything else, but Helen would say, "Good wine, good food, and good friendship. What more could we ask for?"

Continuing their light conversation, Anna said, "I'm having a pizza delivered for the boys' dinner. I also picked up some candy bars and potato chips for a snack."

Helen said, "You're a quick study, Anna, but there is one more very important thing. Whatever you do, try not to be part of their activities. The safest thing to do is monitor them from a distance. Remember, they are ten years old now, which means they are still children, but they want to be treated as young men."

Anna appreciated the advice.

As Anna and Helen exited the restaurant, Helen asked, "Are you up for a short walk, lady?"

A walk was the furthest thing from Anna's mind, but she gave in to her new friend's request. Besides, the effects of the wine had given her added energy.

Helen led the way down a wooden walkway that snaked around the building and ended on a large patio next to a dock. The two women sat down on one of the concrete benches facing the water. Pleasure boats of various sizes bobbed up and down in the water. Neither woman said a word as the river splashed against the shore. Helen picked up several pebbles from the ground and tossed them into the water. Anna wasn't sure if it was the effects of the wine, but she suddenly remembered how much she loved the river. As they listened to the creaking sounds of the boats rocking back and forth, Anna recalled more pleasant thoughts of her childhood.

Helen was obviously feeling the effects of the wine, too, as her mood was quite playful. She hinted to Anna that she was going to ask her husband to take her out to dinner, since Billy would be at the sleepover, and that she'd use her feminine whiles to woo him.

The women laughed as they made their way to the car. It gave Anna a warm feeling inside as she listened to Helen talk about her relationship with her husband. Robby was in need of good influences, and it was clear to Anna that family values played an important part of Helen's family.

The sound of small footsteps racing across the foyer signaled Robby's arrival home from school. Not only was it Friday, which is a huge event in itself, but he was hosting his first sleepover ever. After dropping his backpack on the floor near the steps, he ran past the living room in search of Anna. She smiled as he doubled back.

"Did you remember to buy the stuff for tonight?" Robby asked excitedly.

Trying unsuccessfully to be serious, Anna said, "Of course I did, Robby. I decided to order pizza for dinner, and Billy will be coming over early to join us. His mother and I spoke about it earlier, and she thought it was a fine idea."

Robby hugged Anna and thanked her before racing up the steps to his room.

It was nearly five-forty-five when Robby spotted Helen and Billy pulling into the driveway. Excited, Robby ran to the front door. "They're here, Anna!"

Anna walked away from the partially set table to greet their guests. Billy had his arms wrapped around a tightly bound sleeping bag, while Helen carried several board games.

"Special delivery!" Helen announced.

Everyone laughed as she handed the games over to Robby. When the boys disappeared upstairs, Anna invited Helen to stay for a slice of pizza, but Helen smiled and reminded Anna that she had to get ready for her date with Joe. As Helen was leaving, she told Anna to be sure to call if she needed anything.

As Helen was leaving, the pizza arrived. She settled the bill and sent the young man off with a "Have a nice weekend, and keep the change" before heading into the house. She was barely inside before the boys came running, enticed by the aroma of the pizza. Nothing generates excitement like two hungry youngsters and a large piping hot pizza. With a couple of slices on their plates, the boys sat in the dining room and dug into the pizza immediately. Anna could not believe her eyes as she watched the boys guzzling their soda while strands of cheese dangled from their mouths. What surprised her even more was the fact that she was joining in on the fun.

When the boys had eaten their fill of pizza, Anna cleared the table and put the leftovers in the refrigerator. Anna assured Robby that she some surprise treats for them later, and sent them off to play. Anna snatched a book off the shelf in the living room as the boys raced up the stairs to play one of Billy's board games. Her plan was to enjoy the evening, reading on the porch, with one ear on the boys.

The warm evening air felt soothing against Anna's face as she relaxed on the rocking chair. She placed the old book on the small table next to her and listened for any alarming noises coming from the house. When all was quiet, she picked up the book she had chosen and laughed when she glanced at the cover. The irony of the title she chose, *Lord of the Flies*, was not lost on her. Immersed in her book, the sound of the boys' laughter echoing through the house made its way out to the porch from time to time. She resisted the urge to check on the boys and, instead, remained steadfast to her commitment to stay in the shadows.

It wasn't long before Robert and Billy made their way to the porch. "We want something to munch on while we watch TV."

"I'll be in soon to get you boys a bowl of potato chips and a couple cans of soda pop."

As Anna walked into the kitchen, she could hear the theme from *Star Trek* coming from the living room. The sound of the boys cheering for the crew of the Enterprise brought laughter to her heart.

During a commercial, Robert and Billy raced into the kitchen and announced rather loudly, "We are starving to death, Anna!"

Billy added, "We really are Miss Wilson!"

Anna smiled and handed Billy a large bowl of potato chips, and she gave each of the boys a soda before they ran off to enjoy more outer space adventures of *Star Trek*. She almost forgot the Hershey bars, but Robby came back and snatched them from her hand faster than the speed of light as the boys took their loot into the living room.

Alone in the kitchen, Anna cleaned up the minor mess, placing the remaining chocolate bars on a top shelf, but not before setting one aside for herself. She desperately wanted to go into the living room with the two youngsters, but she knew it would be wrong in so many ways, so she decided to retire to her bedroom with a good book. Careful not to disturb the wannabe space travelers, she put *Lord of the Flies* back on the shelf and decided on *Jane Eyre* instead. The boys didn't even seem to notice her until she told them she was heading to her room to read.

Briefly turning away from Captain Kirk's exploits of the universe, Robby said, "Is it all right if we sleep down here?"

"Sure. I placed two comforters in your room for you to use."

Anna locked the doors and slowly climbed the stairs to her room, holding the volume of *Jane Eyre* against her chest. Thoughts about the way things had changed so drastically in her life went through her mind. It was not long ago that loneliness and memories were her only friends. She smiled as she realized she was hosting the first sleepover the house had ever known. Once Anna changed into her nightgown, she crawled into bed with her book in hand. She had read all the volumes as a young girl and found them very enjoyable. Though she could obviously not relate to all the trials and tribulations Jane Eyre had experienced, she liked to think she could closely associate herself with the young woman's morality.

Anna awoke with a start, her heart pounding. She saw the book lying beside her on the bed, but she couldn't remember how it got there. It was nearly two in the morning. When the fuzziness cleared from her head, she went downstairs to check on Robby and Billy. The sound of an old black and white horror movie was a lot louder than it should have been. She marched into the living room, intent on scolding them for having the volume up so loud, but what she saw melted her heart. The boys were sound asleep under a makeshift tent they had constructed using a sheet from Robby's bed. Smiling, she turned off the television, covered them up, and retired back to her room. It had been a good night.

chapter ·········· eighteen

Marge stormed into Jack's office, trying to sound stern when she said, "Don't you dare forget about the staff meeting this afternoon! It's our first one, and I want everything to go perfectly!" Then she smiled as she walked around the desk and sat on his lap. She placed her moist lips against his, kissing him long and hard. Whispering in his ear, she said, "Can you believe it, Jack, we have a staff?"

With a devilish smile on his face, Jack said, "If you don't get off my lap, we are going to have a staff to deal with right now."

As Marge straightened her clothes and exited the office she said, "Make sure you are on time, mister!"

Marge was very pleased that all the new members of the firm showed up early for the meeting. She placed high hopes on her new office assistant, Mary Thomas. She was a plain looking young woman, just out of college, who was sharp as a tack. The legal assistant they hired was a woman by the name of Kathy Duncan. She was very ambitious, and Jack used that trait to steal her away from another firm. Rounding out the team was a young attorney Jack hired to head up the financial department. Patrick Borne was only out of law school for four years, but in the short time he worked for Walker and Brown, he had generated close to fifty million dollars in client assets. Unfortunately, for Walker and Brown, they never made him partner. At least half of his clients agreed to follow him to Jack's firm as long as he continued to handle their money. Jack agreed to make him a full partner once he reached certain goals. More important, he trusted him with Anna's assets.

Not one to get nervous, Marge found her knees a little wobbly as she stared down the long wood grain table in the conference room. Professionally printed folders embossed with the firm's logo sat perfectly aligned at every setting. Real drinking glasses sparkled on fancy napkins next to the folders. Sweating pitchers of ice water rested on mats across the center of the table, with bowls of beautifully colored fresh fruit beside them. Just as Marge stole a couple grapes from a bowl, her new assistant, Mary, came in the door.

"I thought I might see if you needed help while the others are waiting in the lobby," she said softly.

"I think everything is ready, but there is one thing," Marge said.

"Sure, anything you need."

"How do I look?"

"You look very professional."

Putting her arm around Mary, Marge said, "I think we are going to get along just fine."

Jack snooped around the conference room before the meeting started. He asked Marge about the agenda, as well as the role he was to play. Marge informed him that it was mainly to welcome everyone, introduce the new people, and to let everyone know how she expected the office to run, and Jack's role was to keep getting the bad guys off.

As he exited the meeting room in his sharp three-piece suit, he winked at Marge and said, "Everything looks great, Red. I'll make sure the rest of the staff is here on time."

Marge and Mary attended to some last minute details, making sure that everything was perfectly set up for the meeting. As the new staff members entered the conference room, Marge greeted them with a handshake and a smile. Mary directed them to their seats, where a beautifully monogrammed ink pen and name card awaited them. Marge took the seat at the head of the table, with her new assistant, Mary, directly to her left. Jack's legal assistant, Kathy Duncan, had the chair to the center of the table, to Marge's right. Patrick Borne had the chair directly across from Kathy Duncan. Jack's chair was directly across from Marge's at the far end of the table. Although the seating chart seemed random, Marge was establishing a pecking order from the very start.

Marge stood up and welcomed everyone with a smile. She looked smart in her new grey suit, appearing to be tailor made to fit her lean, curvy body. The contrast between her red hair and the exposed collar of her white blouse accentuated the beauty of the outfit.

After everyone finished introducing themselves, Marge informed the team that they could be casual in the office, as a casual atmosphere helps to relieve stress, but in front of clients, the attorneys were to be addressed as Mr. Porter and Mr. Borne. She emphasized that they must work as a team, and that she, Mary, and Kathy would be in charge of the daily operations.

"Jack is the head of the firm right now," Marge continued, "but we are confident that it won't be long before the sign over the office will be Porter and Borne. Our goal is that we will fill the remaining seats at this table with sharp, aggressive members in the future."

When the meeting was over, Marge said, "I have one additional announcement to make that will affect all of us. Jack and I have agreed to pay the staff a monetary bonus each quarter, based on performance. When the details are ironed out, you will receive a copy of the guidelines." As the room emptied out, Marge whispered in Jack's ear, "How do you think the meeting went?"

"Very well, Red."

As Anna was nursing her second cup of tea, the phone rang. It was nearly nine thirty in the morning, and the boys were still sound asleep under the makeshift tent they constructed in the living room. Helen's upbeat voice greeted Anna.

"Well, I guess you survived the sleepover, girl."

"Everything went well, but they are still sleeping."

Helen laughed. "That's because they were up all night!"

"I suspected as much. What time shall I wake them?"

"That's your decision, but I suggest you have them clean up the mess they made."

"I think that is a fine idea."

"My hubby and I are going out for breakfast, if that is okay with you. I'll give you a call when we get back."

"Enjoy your meal. I'll talk to you later."

The solitude of the morning was short-lived, as Anna heard the sound of the boys stirring in the living room. She first heard Billy asking, "Are we going to get in trouble for building this tent?" and then Robby responding with, "No,

Anna is a very nice woman and she is never mean to me."
Billy's question made her smile, but Robby's reply warmed
her heart. Not wanting to be guilty of any further eavesdropping, Anna walked down the hall to the scene of the
crime.

"It appears you gentlemen had yourselves a good time
last night."

The youngsters looked at each other and smiled. "We
sure did!"

"Good, while you two are putting the living room back
together, I'll prepare your breakfast. Would pancakes be to
your liking?"

In unison, both boys said, "Yes!"

Anna enjoyed cooking, but did not see the use of it
when she was living alone. It was always her belief that
cooking was for others to enjoy, and now that Robby was
living with her, she found that joy again. Anna watched
the boys devour their stacks of golden brown pancakes
and frosty glasses of milk with a smile on her face. She was
looking forward to hearing about some of their adventures
from the previous night.

"So, are you two going to tell me what sort of fun things
you did last night?" Anna said.

"Anna, it was great! We built a tent in the living room
to sleep under, and we watched the late movie on *Chiller
Theater*," Robby said excitedly.

Billy was just as enthusiastic with his reply. "The snacks
were great, Miss Wilson, and we hardly made any mess at
all!"

Anna smiled and said, "I'm glad you boys had such a
good time. I missed all the fun reading a book in my room."

Rejuvenated by the hearty breakfast, Robby asked, "Can we go up to my room and play until Billy's mother calls?"

With a nod of her head, the boys disappeared from the kitchen and ran up the steps. Although they didn't divulge too much, Anna was grateful that the boys shared some of their evening with her and that they were enjoying themselves.

Robby was always full of energy until Sunday evenings. Sundays were always a little different because they were the eve of another school week. Children everywhere were doing their last minute homework and mentally preparing themselves for another week of school. But it was Saturday, which meant the sky was the limit.

As Anna finished clearing the table, the doorbell rang. Helen's smiling face greeted Anna when she opened the door.

"It appears you survived the sleepover in one piece," Helen said.

Smiling, Anna said, "They were both perfect little gentlemen."

Anna invited Helen in for a cup of tea, but she couldn't stay. She was there to pick up Billy and get back home, because a contractor was coming over to give her an estimate on remodeling the kitchen. As they headed out the door, Helen gave Anna a quick hug and thanked her for her hospitality.

Robby spent most of the remaining morning in his room. Anna sensed that he was sad because Billy had gone home. She was going to do some chores around the house, but decided to pay him a visit instead. When she entered his room, he was lying on the bed with a comic book resting next to him.

"Did you and Billy have a good time last night?"

His reply was short and unenthusiastic. "Yeah, it was nice."

"Why do you seem down in the dumps?"

When he didn't reply, she decided to give him time alone.

As Anna turned to leave his room, she heard a slight whimper. She turned around and saw him crying, with his arms resting against his face. She immediately rushed to his side and sat on the bed. In a soft, loving voice, she said, "Please tell me what's troubling you, Robby."

A long silence hung in the air, and then he said, "Are you going to die soon?"

Stunned by the question, she said, "I sure hope not, but why would you ask such a strange question?"

Wiping the tears from his eyes, he said, "When Billy and I were talking last night, he told me that his grandmother was as old as you when she died of a heart attack."

Before answering his serious question, Anna thought carefully about what she was going to say. She put her arm around him and said, "You and I both have experienced more loss than most people do in a lifetime, but now we have each other. I assure you that I will not leave this world anytime soon. I also promise you that when that day comes, you will always be taken care of."

Anna held Robby in her arms until the emotional upheaval passed. To lighten the mood, she offered to take him to the sporting goods store so that he could pick out a new sleeping bag. She had noticed that Billy had one, and thought Robby might like one too. Anna was happy to see the twinkle in Robby's eyes reappear. After they both finished their chores, it was off to the store they went!

Saturdays at Dick's Sporting Goods were always crowded, and today proved no different. Robby's excitement grew when he saw the sign for camping gear. She learned that Robby had been here once before with his father, but from what the young boy said, it wasn't a pleasant experience, so she didn't pursue it.

Anna had driven by the sporting goods store on many occasions, and she always found it difficult to believe that an establishment could sell enough baseballs and basketballs to stay in business. As they entered the large double doors into the brightly lit store, Anna could not believe her eyes. Colorful displays and equipment for every sport imaginable greeted them.

"Wow! Look at all of the cool stuff!" Robby shouted.

After looking at the various sleeping bags available, Robby finally decided on one that was good to thirty below zero, claiming it was just like the ones they use at the North Pole. While he wouldn't be traveling to the North Pole anytime soon, he wanted to be more than prepared for the cold winters.

Robby couldn't wait to call Billy and tell him about his new sleeping bag. He couldn't thank Anna enough, and he promised that he would do any chores she wanted to show his appreciation. For Anna, though, the happiness in his eyes was all the thanks she needed. She knew Robby well enough to realize that the happiness he was experiencing was only in part because she purchased the sleeping bag he wanted. The truth was that he would now feel more like the other children. He was no longer plagued with the fear that his father would come home drunk. Even though he missed his mother greatly, he felt relieved that she no longer had to be the brunt of his father's emotional and physical attacks.

As they pulled into the driveway at home, Robby got a sad look on his face. Not sure, what to make of it, Anna asked what was wrong. It was a Saturday when his dad took him shopping at Dick's for his gym shorts, because it was his day off from work.

"My dad was always sick from drinking on Friday night, which put him in a really bad mood. He rushed me around the store so that he could stop at the liquor store on the way home. When I could not find the right size shorts, he told me I was stupid like my mother. He then made fun of me when I started crying and threatened to slap me. That was my trip to Dick's Sporting Goods with my dad."

Anna pulled his head against her chest as a tear rolled down her cheek. Holding him closely she said, "No one will ever mistreat you again, Robby."

The lingering pain she saw in his young eyes was a reminder that it would take time for positive changes in his life. Inside his small body dwelled a child, full of hope and joy. Inside the same boy was also a dark place, where the terrible events of the past were fighting for release. She understood this state of being all too well from her own sordid past. Unfortunately, for Anna, there was no one to usher her through the deep crevices of the memories etched in her mind. She wanted so much more for Robby.

After Robby's tears had dried, he returned his focus to his new sleeping bag, resting on the back seat. The bulky bundle of goose down was almost more than he could handle. Of course, he refused to let Anna help him carry it. After nearly dropping it as he walked up the steps, Anna rushed ahead of him to open the door. He started up the stairs toward his bedroom, but decided to put it on the floor in the living room. When Anna saw it resting on the floor, he commented, "There is more room in here for me to open it up." She smiled and said, "It makes perfect sense to me young man."

Robby couldn't wait to show off his new sleeping bag to Billy, so Anna seized the opportunity to visit with Helen. As they arrived at the house, Helen was weeding one of the flowerbeds in the front yard. She was happy for the distraction, because Joe went golfing and she didn't really feel like playing in the dirt today. As the two boys scampered off, the two women retired to the patio for some conversation and wine. Anna enjoyed a glass of wine now and then, but in Helen's company, it was more *now* than then.

When Anna brought up the subject of Joe's golf game, Helen ran with it.

"He goes with several of his friends to the country club every Saturday without fail. They drink beer and tell tall tales about their past."

Anna said, "It must be nice for him to unwind after a stressful work week."

"I don't begrudge him the time with his friends, but it does piss me off that he thinks staying home with Billy is alone time for me."

Trying to lighten the conversation, Anna said, "I can attest to the fact that monitoring the comings and goings of a ten-year-old boy is certainly not alone time."

With a faraway look in her eyes, Helen said, "Do you know what really makes me angry?" Not expecting an answer, she continued, "Joe is a good enough husband and father, but he takes on little to no responsibility when it comes to the duties of raising Billy or the day-to-day issues at home."

Anna decided to change the subject to something less irritating to Helen and commented on the freshly planted bed of Impatiens next to the patio.

"Yes, they are nice," Helen began, "but it's a crying shame that my creativity is limited to this block of land where our house rests. When I was in college, I had grand plans for my future. I was going to be one of those women who had the courage to make it to the top. Not a babysitter, not a house keeper, but a pioneer in the business world!"

Anna sat quietly, trying to find the right words to say, and said, "Do you want to know something, Helen. I had a similar life as you are describing. I went on to college and worked hard to become an educator, but had no real relationships. There was no man or no children to slow me down, and I accomplished all that I wanted. Then one day, I woke up and looked in the mirror at a lonely old woman who had nothing in her life but memories of days gone by. If Robby had not come into my life, I would still be that sad, lonely woman."

The two women sat silently on the patio. Helen clutched her half full glass of wine with both hands while staring down at the concrete floor. Anna was secretly hoping that she had not said too much. She enjoyed Helen's company, and she did not want to do anything to harm Robby's friendship with Billy. The sound of the boys running from the house interrupted the quiet. With baseball gloves and a ball in tow, the boys positioned themselves approximately twenty yards apart in the backyard and began tossing the ball back and forth. Anna smiled when she heard Robby say, "Yeah, I heard that the sleeping bag I got is the same one the Eskimos use near the North Pole," and Billy reply, "It is the nicest one I've ever seen!" When Billy missed one of the throws, the ball rolled onto the patio near Helen's chair. Billy reached under her chair to snatch it up, but before he could run away, Helen placed her arms around him and kissed him, which prompted him to say, "What's wrong with you, Mom?" After wiping the kiss onto his sleeve, he ran back into the yard to resume the game of catch with Robby.

Over another glass of wine, Anna and Helen's conversation drifted from gardening back to emotional issues. Anna felt a little uncomfortable, as she thought Helen had already said entirely too much. Unexpectedly, Helen blurted out, "I cheated on Joe two years before Billy was born. Do you want to know what Joe's response was?"

Anna was not sure if she was inviting a reply, but said, "What did he say?"

"Of course, he called me every name in the book first, but then told me we needed to have a child. Like a baby was going to fix everything." Then she asked, rhetorically, "Do you know what the strangest aspect of the situation was?" She looked Anna straight in the eye and said, "He never even asked who I was cheating with."

Helen offered Anna another glass of wine, and when she declined, Helen poured it anyway. Anna wanted to get Robby and get out of there, but for some reason, she remained glued to her chair. It was a rare occurrence for Anna to witness human beings baring their souls. Part of Anna wanted to relieve Helen of the sadness she felt; another part of her felt relieved that she was not the only person with dark secrets. Helen continued with her melancholy journey, stating that her husband refused to grant her closure by not asking who the other man was. This went on for another half hour before Anna decided it was time to go home. She drove away from Helen's house with a deeper knowledge of their friendship.

When they arrived home, Anna listened to Robby chatter about catching ball with Billy and how much nicer his new sleeping bag was than his friend's. At one point, she put her finger over his lips and took him into her arms. Holding his head against her chest, she softly said, "You are the most important thing in my life, young man."

Surprised by the sudden emotional outburst, he stood quietly near her. When she released him, he said, "I really like you too, Anna."

She just smiled and sent him on his way.

What affected Anna most about her conversation with Helen was what she said about Billy's conception. She prayed that he'd never find out that he was merely a quick fix for his parents' troubled marriage, and she hoped that Helen would someday realize that she was living many women's dreams.

chapter ....
.... nineteen

Inspired by Helen's gardening skills, Anna got her gloves and wide-brimmed hat from the closet. She had thought about bringing in a landscaper to trim the shrubs, but decided to take on the job herself. It was a glorious day to be outside, and Anna started in the front yard, picking out a small flowerbed next to the front porch, where there was a shaggy looking azalea bush, which had given up its blooms earlier in the season. As she proceeded to give the bush a well-needed trimming, she remembered how relaxing it was to work in the garden.

After brushing off the clippings from the well-groomed shrub, Anna piled the pieces on the grass beside her. She continued the process on the next bed, until a couple of hours had passed. When the heat began to overwhelm her, she sat on the steps to rest. As she removed her hat to wipe the sweat from her forehead, she was finding it difficult to catch her breath. As a sharp pain shot through her chest, fear engulfed her. She desperately tried to stand up, hoping to make it into the house to call for help, but she fell, face down on the sidewalk, nearly unconscious.

Nearly twenty minutes passed before Robby came outside and discovered her limp body lying on the sidewalk. Terrified, he shook her to see if she was okay. Tears rolled down his cheeks as he screamed, "Anna! Anna!" He got no response. When he saw the blood streaming down her forehead, he assumed that she had fallen and banged her head. He raced into the house, called for an ambulance, and screamed for them to hurry. Grabbing a towel from the kitchen, he ran back outside and held the towel over the gash on Anna's head. He cried and rocked back and forth as he held Anna's head in his arms.

A few minutes went by before the sound of the sirens signaled the arrival of the ambulance. Afraid and over-whelmed by the situation, Robby was terrified that they would take him to social services again. When the para-medics pulled him away from Anna and started to examine her, Robby ran back into the house to search for Marge's telephone number. When he couldn't find it, he called Billy's house and talked to Helen. He frantically conveyed the details as he understood them, and begged Helen to come over before they sent him away. Helen assured him that she was on her way and that no one was going to take him away.

Robby was terrified and confused as he watched the paramedics perform their duties. When they wheeled Anna into the ambulance, they informed Robby that he would have to go with them, as there was no one there to care for him. When he tried to explain that Helen was on her way, they told him they could not leave him alone. One of the men gently took hold of his arm and said, "You have to come with us, son. Someone will look after you at the hospital."

In Robert's mind, he heard them say that social services would take care of it when they arrived at the hospital. He tried desperately to run away, but the man was too strong. His thoughts were torn between Anna's injuries and doing everything he could not to return to that terrible place.

Just then Helen pulled into the driveway. She quickly exited her vehicle and marched up to the paramedic who was restraining Robby. "Get your hands off of that boy right now!"

Relieved, Robby raced over to Helen's side. She asked which hospital they were taking Anna to before the ambulance raced away with its siren wailing. As the sound of the siren grew faint, Helen put her arms around the terrified youngster. Once she assured him that she was there for him, she calmly said, "Let's grab Anna's pocketbook, lock up the house, and drive over to the hospital. If she is admitted, you can stay at our house."

As they were gathering Anna's things, Robby said, "We have to find Marge's telephone number! Anna told me that if anything ever happened, I am supposed to call Marge."

"Try to settle down, Robby. We'll call her from the hospital."

Seeing Robby looking so fragile reminded Helen of her own son. Although she wanted to speed to the hospital, she knew she'd had a little too much to drink earlier in the day. If the police pulled her over, it would only add fuel to an already serious situation.

As Helen searched for a pack of gum in her purse, Robby said, "Please, Helen, we need to get to the hospital!"

Realizing that the youngster was right, she quickly shoved two sticks of gum in her mouth and sped off.

They arrived at St. Margaret's emergency department parking lot within fifteen minutes. Before getting out of the car, Helen turned to Robby with a stern look in her eye and said, "You stay with me the entire time. Do you understand?" As they entered the emergency waiting area, Helen took hold of Robby's small hand, keeping him very close to her side.

Robert had never seen anything like the site that was before him. The waiting room was filled with people, some crying; others were clutching clipboards; but all seemed to be staring at him with a sad look in their eyes. A homeless man who had not seen the inside of a bathtub for quite some time smiled at him, revealing his blackened teeth. Helen felt Robby squeeze her hand as they walked up to the information desk. She looked down at him as he watched the menagerie of people behind them. As she gave the nurse at the window the information about Anna, she reached down and turned Robby's head away from the commotion. He overheard the nurse tell Helen to have a seat and someone would be out shortly to talk to her.

Robby was riddled with fear as he sat next to Helen on the uncomfortable plastic chair. Fears about Anna's well-being and concerns about his own future were all racing through his young mind. If he had only gone outside to help her, things would have been different. He prayed, telling God that if he would save her, he would never let her do yard work again. Suddenly, he heard two nurses talking behind them, saying, "This place is a real nuthouse today. There must be a full moon."

Robby nudged Helen in her side and said, "Is a full moon a good thing for Anna?"

"Of course it is," she said, trying to reassure him.

He sat back in his chair and said, "Good."

Just as Robby saw a woman vomiting into a plastic container, a nurse with a clipboard called their names. Helen took hold of his hand and they followed the nurse through a set of large double doors. Once the doors closed behind them, Robby immediately noticed the reduction of the noise level. Medical personnel pushing wheel chairs and various types of equipment he had never seen before passed in the large hallway. Some rushed by, others hesitated and sent him a smile. He was startled when the sound of the speaker overhead summoned a doctor, stat.

"What does stat mean?" Robby asked.

Trying to hide her worry, Helen smiled and said, "It just means they want the doctor to hurry."

Unlike the nurses working at the intake area, the nurse who took them back was very kind and personable. She led them to a much smaller waiting room down the hall. The chairs were comfortable and it was very clean. After asking them a few questions, she informed them that the doctor was with Anna and would be with them shortly. The nurse asked Robby if he wanted a snack, but he courteously declined. As he rifled through a stack of magazines on the table next to him, Helen said, "This is a lot better than being out front." They both chuckled as Robby shook his head in agreement. He found an issue of *Boys' Life* and began flipping through the pages. The distraction was not effective, so he returned the magazine to the stack.

Robby and Helen were growing restless, and walked back and forth, hoping the doctor would soon arrive. Frustrated and full of guilt, Robby cried out, "This is my fault! I should have been outside helping her instead of playing in my room. It's my job to do the chores, and I let her down."

Helen put her hands on Robby's upper arms and said, "Listen to me, Robby, this is not your fault—"

Robby quickly interrupted her before she could finish. "Why didn't she call the garden guy with the truck to do it?"

"When you were at our house today, she told me she wanted to work in her gardens. If she wanted your help, she would have asked you."

Just as they both looked up, a young doctor entered the room, causing them to both go silent.

Flipping through the chart in his hands, the doctor said, "Are you Anna Wilson's family?"

Helen quickly replied, "Yes, we are."

Both Robby's and her heart were pounding as they waited for the doctor to say something. Helen thought he was entirely too young to be a doctor and hoped he knew what he was doing.

The young physician said, "Miss Wilson has been stabilized, but she has had a great deal of damage to her heart."

Robert shouted, "No she doesn't! She fell and hit her head!"

"She does have a gash on her forehead, but that must have occurred when she fell," the doctor said. "We admitted her, and I am scheduling further tests with a specialist."

"When can we see her?" Helen asked.

"Once they have her situated in the room, you can spend a few minutes with her."

The doctor excused himself at the sound of his beeper going off. Helen and Robby stood quietly in the room, waiting for the nurse to take them to Anna's side. Helen was very afraid for Anna's well-being, but she did not let her feelings known to Robby.

"Is Anna going to die?" The fear in Robby's voice was evident.

Helen tried to hide her concern. "Listen to me, young man, Anna's a tough old woman, and she will pull through this just fine."

Robby wasn't thoroughly convinced that she was right. Losing his mother had a profound effect on him, but the thought of losing Anna as well was more than he could bear.

Helen could see the fear in Robby's eyes and sensed the heavy burden in his heart. She did her best to comfort him, secretly realizing the gravity of the situation.

While they waited, an angelic figure in white entered the room. "Hello, my name is Mary, and I am one of Anna's nurses." She conveyed a pleasant but commanding presence. She relayed to them that Anna was in her room now and that they could spend a short time with her.

"Can we take her home with us?" Robby asked, hopeful.

The nurse bent down to his eye level and placed her hands gently on his upper arms. "I'm sorry, but we have to keep her here for a while so we can help her to get better."

All Robby heard was that they were going to make Anna well again, and that thought alone greatly eased his worries.

Helen had a feeling things were much worse than the nurse let on.

They followed Mary down the hall to Room 3003. Before they stepped inside, Mary conveyed a few instructions. She bent down to Robby's level and said, "Try not to be afraid when you see all the medical stuff hooked up to your Anna. I want you to understand that the equipment is there to help her.

Helen found herself a little overwhelmed when she saw Anna's damaged body lying in bed. Greeted by the steady beeping sounds of a heart monitor, Anna was not the woman Helen had lunch with the prior day. Robby stood motionless next to the bed, with his eyes glued to the saline solution as it dripped from the bag. It was clear that Anna was still feeling the effects of the sedative they administered when she arrived.

Robby moved close to Helen and said, "Is she—?"

Suddenly, Anna startled both of them when she said in a hoarse voice, "I hope you mean sleeping, young man."

His eyes opened wide. "Anna! Why didn't you ask me to help you in the yard?"

"This is not your fault, Robby. I wanted to work in the gardens myself."

Helen intervened and said, "Anna needs to rest right now. You two can work this out when she goes home." Pulling some money out of her purse, she said, "Robby, here is some money. How about going down to the vending machines and buy us a Coke?"

When Robby left the room, Helen said, "Anna, what do you need from home? Don't worry about Robby. He can stay with us for the time being."

Anna smiled and said, "You are a good friend, Helen. I could use some personal items from home, and I would like you to do something very important for me."

"Anything, Anna."

"Please call Jack and Marge for me. Tell them the situation, and they will take it from there."

Helen did her best at making light conversation during their brief visit. Robby remained close to Anna during the entire stay. She was visibly fatigued, which prompted Helen to suggest that it was time for them to leave. Soon after she made the suggestion, the nurse came in to tell them their time was up.

Robby began to cry as he clung to Anna's wrinkled hand. With tears rolling down his cheeks, he cried out, "Please come home, Anna!"

She brought his hand up to her cheek and said, "Don't you worry, I'll be home soon. In the meantime, Helen will take care of you."

"We can come back tomorrow to visit," Helen promised.

Anna stared at the white ceiling as she lay in bed. The random cracks in the plaster reminded her of the wrinkles on her face. She tried to push her long silver hair back in place with little success. Time was finally catching up with her and there was nowhere to run. Thoughts of when she was a young woman full of energy and vitality brought a gentle smile to her face. Robby was her biggest concern. Arrangements were in place for his care, but she wondered how he would handle the loss of another person in his young life. Tears rolled down her cheeks as she prayed for God to give her a little more time, not for herself, but for the troubled young man who had become such a large part of her life.

Fatigued from the emotional stress and the medication, Anna wanted to go to sleep. She fought the idea of slumber in part because of the fear that she would not wake again. The ordeal overtook her and she fell into a deep sleep. Her rest was interrupted all too soon, as she heard the sound of low voices next to her bed. Initially, she thought it was more hospital personnel fussing around the equipment, but to her surprise, it was Jack and Marge. It gave her such a warm feeling inside to see them standing beside the bed. Jack was holding a vase with twelve beautiful red roses.

Anna cleared her throat and said, "I must really be in bad shape for you two to visit me."

Marge smiled and said, "We just had to see you bed-bound for ourselves. I didn't think anything could slow you down."

Anna coughed a few times and asked Marge if she would go to the nurse's station to get her some juice. Once she left the room, Anna motioned for Jack to come closer to her. In a low, serious voice, she said, "Jack, I'm depending on you to carry out my wishes."

"Anna, don't—"

Stopping him mid-sentence, she said, "I'm serious about this!"

"Of course I will, Anna."

She smiled and took hold of his hand and said, "Make sure you do right by Marge."

"You just need to get better. When you get home, you can watch over the rest of us."

Jack and Marge kept their visit short because Anna was obviously weary. When they left, she proudly showed off the beautiful roses to every nurse who visited her room. Marge was not one to shed tears, but once they were out of the hospital room, tears rolled down her cheeks. Usually, Jack was quick to make a sarcastic remark, but, instead, he put his arm around her shoulder to comfort her. He understood her concern and felt very little humor in his heart. Neither Marge nor Jack was big on religion, but they both secretly prayed that God would see fit to give Anna a little more time.

The harder Helen tried to divert Robby's attention away from Anna's condition, the more persistent he was about calling the hospital. He desperately wanted to hear her voice so he knew she was still alive. Finally, Helen gave into his demands and made the call. Once Anna was on the phone, she put Robby on to talk with her.

In a low and raspy voice, Anna said, "Thank you for calling me, young man. Are you listening to Helen?"

Crying, he said, "Please come home. I'll take care of you, I promise."

Anna took several long moments before answering because she did not want Robby to know that she was also crying. Finally, she said, "Don't you worry about me, young man. I will be as good as new before you know it." She went on to say, "I want you to put Helen back on the phone, and I'll see you tomorrow."

When Helen got back on the telephone, Anna asked, "Will you be able to bring him in to see me tomorrow?"

"Of course I will," Helen said. "We will be there the minute visiting hours start."

"I'm tired, Helen, but I'm looking forward to seeing you both."

❧ ❧ ❧ ❧

A thick silence hung in the air as Marge and Jack drove home. Jack finally asked, "Red, do you want me to stay over tonight?"

"Yes, but I just want you to hold me."

Jack smiled and said, "Sure, Red."

She looked at him very seriously and said, "I'm not kidding, Jack; no sex!"

Realizing the seriousness of her resolve, Jack agreed and mentioned nothing further about it. Marge had the utmost respect for Anna. She had changed her life in many ways, out of the goodness of her heart. She had taken Robby in, which was a great deal more than most others would have done. Most of all, she respected her as a strong woman rising above a society that viewed women as second-class citizens. Everything that Joel and Marge had in their lives was a direct result of Anna's kindness.

Jack stared quietly out the window watching the buildings whiz by. He wanted to be more emotional about Anna's condition, but felt he needed to be strong for Marge. When thinking about the first time he met Anna, a slight smile found his lips. The relationship that developed between them took him by surprise. Early on, it was clear to him that she was not the type of woman to lose a battle. He could never repay her for the spark that she ignited within him. The stubbornness she so proudly displayed gave him the incentive to deliver Robert to her care. Anna may have kept to herself, but she was a sharp judge of character. Using this acute ability, she put all her faith in Jack as an attorney and Marge as his partner. She was confident they would be a success in the new practice that she financed. They both had a deep respect for her, and it had nothing to do with the millions of dollars she possessed.

Sleep eluded both Jack and Marge. As they lay quietly, side by side, they realized how much Anna meant to them, and they did not want to lose her. Marge thought of the hope Anna brought their way—it was by far the most important thing—and she made the decision to be by Anna's side every day she was in the hospital. Jack was going over in his mind the privileged information in Anna's last will and testament. He just wanted her to have more time with the people who loved her.

chapter
twenty

A nna sat up in bed awaiting the arrival of the cardiologist. Just before the doctor came in, she whispered, "Thank you for allowing me a little more time, Lord." A young man in his forties, with premature gray hair, entered her room.

While flipping through Anna's chart, he said, "My name is Dr. Peterson. Did you get any rest last night?"

Anna waited until he made eye contact with her, and then said, "I slept well enough, considering."

The doctor then listened to her heart with the stethoscope, slowly moving it around her chest. The concerned look on his face confirmed that her condition was serious.

Before the young physician could say a word, Anna said, "Don't sugar coat it, doctor. I want you to tell me how much time I have left."

The cardiologist took hold of Anna's hand and said, "We are going to run more tests today, but my guess is six months. The main valve in your heart has deteriorated beyond repair. I will give you medication to help with the irregular heartbeat, and that is about all I can do."

After making a few notations in Anna's chart, the doctor told her he would be back later to check on her. She felt surprisingly calm after the doctor left the room. It was as though she knew she was going to a better place when her time was up. Spending more time with Robby was her biggest concern. Six months, one hundred and eighty days, sounded like a long time, but it was a mere blink of an eye in her mind. Even though it would pass quickly, she was very grateful. She would stay in the hospital for the tests the cardiologist scheduled, but no longer than necessary. Her place was home with the young man she adored, and that is where she would be.

Anna was surprised at her appetite, but she realized that she had not eaten in over twenty-four hours. When the aide placed the tray down on her cart, she couldn't wait to open the containers. The hard-boiled eggs and bran muffin were the only items that seemed edible, but the real prize was the cup of tea, albeit a barely warm one. Other than Robby, she missed the old house, a good cup of hot tea, and the taste of a well-prepared meal.

Just as she hit the buzzer to see if she could get another cup of tea, the head nurse appeared in the doorway. Visibly irritated, the large woman, in her perfectly pressed white uniform, said, "Miss Wilson, I'm sorry to bother you, but there is a woman at the desk from Jack Porter Law Offices who claims you requested an urgent consultation with her. I wanted to check with you before I send her away.

Anna smiled when she realized that Marge was there to visit. She instructed the nurse to show her guest to her room, as she had important matters concerning her legal affairs to discuss with her. Several minutes later, Marge's smiling face appeared in the doorway.

Marge attempted to give Anna a sense that she would be fine, and said, "So, when are you going home, lady?"

Anna smiled weakly. "I hope it will be very soon. They are running a few more tests today, but I think it's just to pad the bill."

Marge was not sure what to think, because Anna was under the impression that she was going to leave the hospital so quickly. Not wanting to upset her, Marge was careful to keep the conversation as light as possible.

Anna's emotions were welling up inside, and thoughts about her situation were racing through her mind. The fact that Marge was there for more than just a social visit made everything real: Anna was facing her own mortality. She would be leaving everyone she loved and cared about in six short months or less. When Marge took hold of Anna's cold, trembling hand, she began to weep. She placed her other hand over Marge's and softly said, "My time is nearing its end. The doctor told me I only have six months to live. Initially, I was grateful for any time at all, but now that you are here, I realize that all the time in the world wouldn't be nearly enough."

The two women remained hand in hand without uttering a word. Marge expected to talk about Robby, Jack, and Joel; instead, she got the unexpected bombshell about Anna's pending demise. She completely understood Anna's desire for more time, because her aching heart also wanted Anna to have more time. Anna wanted more time to witness the growth of the charitable seeds she had sown among the people she now held so dear. Most of all, she wanted desperately to see Robby blossom into the kind of young man she knew he could be. Marge wanted her to have the gift of time to prove to Anna that she and Joel were deserving of what she had done for them.

Marge's moment of sadness dissolved when a young, good-looking medical technician entered the room pushing a wheelchair. A smile stretched across his face when he said, "Which one of you beautiful ladies admit to being Anna Wilson?"

Responding to his sense of humor, they both pointed at one another and laughed.

"One of you is going downstairs for some tests, and it doesn't matter to me who it is," he said, still smiling.

Anna motioned for Marge to give her a hug and whispered in her ear, "Please keep what we talked about between us for now."

Marge kissed Anna on the cheek and said, "Of course, I will. I'll be back in later to see you." Tears began to roll down Marge's cheeks and she was filled with sadness as she raced down the hall to the elevator.

The sound of the elevator bell signaled Marge's only way of escape. As the stainless steel doors clamped shut, she overheard the undistinguishable voices of several people around her. Trying to catch her breath, she felt as though the reflective walls were closing in on her. An older man standing next to the panel of floor buttons asked, "What floor do you need? Excuse, me ma'am, what floor do you want?" Finally, it registered in her mind what he was asking, and she told him the lobby. She was very confused about what she was experiencing. Always the type of woman who kept it together in emotional situations, she suddenly felt as though she was falling apart.

As Marge escaped the confines of the elevator, she raced toward the exit doors of the hospital. She ran directly into someone, and just when she ready to apologize, she realized it was Jack. When the shock wore off, she shouted, "What the hell are you doing here? You're due in court this morning." Then she suddenly remembered the promise she had just made to Anna about not telling anybody about the severity of her condition. She made it a point never to lie to Jack, but this time was different.

"The hearing was postponed because Judge Baker is out sick. Are you going to tell me how Anna is doing? What's wrong, Red, you seem a little rattled?"

Choosing her words carefully, Marge said, "I'm sorry, Jack, but I don't do well with this hospital thing. They were taking her down for tests when I left, so maybe we should come back later this evening to visit."

"Okay, Red, I'll see you back at the office when I'm finished at the courthouse."

As Marge walked toward the glass doors, Jack called out to her. "Hey, Red—"

She turned around with a concerned look on her face. "Yeah?"

"Try not to worry. The old girl will make it through this just fine."

She sent a half smile in Jack's direction and walked out of the hospital.

Helen phoned the hospital several times to see if there were any updates about Anna's condition. Before Robby and Billy went out to play, Helen assured Robby she would find out how Anna was doing and when they could visit her. There was no answer in Anna's room, which prompted Helen to call the nurse's station. All they would say was that she was having tests done and they could not be sure how long they would take. When the boys came in the house for lunch, Robby's inquiries about Anna became more persistent. Helen was becoming more and more frustrated with the situation. She wanted to soothe his concerns about the well-being of the only person he had in the world.

As Helen set the boys' lunch on the table, the phone rang. As she ran to grab the phone, Billy cried out, "Mom, we need juice!"

Her frustration getting the better of her, she hollered, "Get the damn juice yourself!"

The boys giggled at one another as Billy got the pitcher of Kool-Aid from the refrigerator. When they heard the slamming of the receiver, they smiled, but their smiles quickly faded when Helen entered the kitchen.

Billy braved the question, "Who was that, Mom?"

Trying to contain herself, she said, "Some jerk trying to sell us encyclopedias."

"I already have a set of encyclopedias," Billy said.

"Yes, I know, Billy," she said, flustered.

When the boys finished eating, Helen coaxed them into going back outside to play. She assured Robby that she would continue trying to contact Anna. As soon as the boys were safely out of site, she went behind the bar and snatched a chilled bottle of wine from the small refrigerator. Not wanting to subject herself to scrutiny, she spilled the remaining coffee from her favorite mug into the sink and replaced it with the sweet elixir of her choice. Realizing it was a little early, she told herself it was due to the added stress she was experiencing. As she sat in the living room sipping her wine, the reality of the situation began to sink in. Unaware of the arrangements Anna had made for Robby's care, she wondered what would happen if Anna died in the hospital. Even though the two of them were friends, Helen did not want the responsibility of raising another child. The sound of the phone ringing interrupted Helen's relaxation time. *Who the hell is it now?* she said to herself. She set the cup down on the table and angrily picked up the receiver. When she heard the soft sound of Anna's voice on the other end of the phone, her attitude completely changed.

"There is a nasty rumor going around my floor that someone has been calling here, giving the nurses a hard time. I told them it couldn't be my friend Helen, because she is much too sweet to do that."

"Guilty as charged," Helen said, as both women laughed. "You are a hard woman to track down. How are you feeling?"

"I'm a little tired, but it's hard to rest in here. The good news is that I should be coming home tomorrow."

Helen let out a sigh of relief and said, "That's fantastic! Do you want me to call Robby in so you can talk to him?"

"If it's okay with you, he can call me later. Right now I want to take a nap."

"You've been through a lot," Helen said. "We will call you later."

Helen celebrated Anna's news in her usual fashion, by kicking back and enjoying two more cups of wine. She was secretly relieved that caring for Robby for an extended period was not going to be necessary. Of course, she thought very highly of Robby, but was very comfortable with her life the way it was. Added responsibility was not something she was looking for. With her head tilted back in her chair, she smiled as the warm glow from the wine drifted over her body. Thoughts floated through her mind of a time when she was a younger woman. She was full of lofty dreams and great aspirations. The sorority she belonged to while at the university voted her the most likely to succeed. While everything seemed to be going as planned, she was blindsided when she met her future husband, Joe. After they were married, she abruptly put her career on hold. Time passed, and before she knew it, she was pregnant with Billy, which cemented her new career as a homemaker.

The sounds of Billy and Robby rushing through the front door abruptly interrupted the glow Helen cherished.

"Mom, can we have some more juice, please?" Billy asked, panting from running into the house.

"Go ahead, boys, just done make a mess," she said, a little slower than usual.

"Mom, do you have another one of those headaches?"

Helen smiled and kissed Billy on the forehead. "Don't worry, buddy, I will be fine."

After polishing off a half glass of juice, Robby said, "Did you talk to Anna yet?"

"Good news, young man; Anna should be coming home tomorrow. She wanted to rest today, but said you can call her later this evening."

The worried look on Robby's face seemed to fade away, but he would not be satisfied until Anna was safely home.

While Jack sat reviewing the paperwork for his next case, he thought about the surprise he had planned for Marge. Reaching into the pocket of his suit coat, he pulled out a small square box covered in black felt. Looking around the sparsely populated gallery of the courtroom for prying eyes, he proceeded to snap open the box to view the coveted treasure. He smiled ear to ear when he saw the sparkling diamond engagement ring he had inspected countless times since the purchase. Initially, his plan was to take her out to one of the finest restaurants in the city and spring the proposal on her. Unfortunately, Anna's sudden illness put a damper on his plans. When he and Marge crossed paths in the hospital lobby earlier in the day, he was on his way to show Anna the ring and to receive her blessing.

Jack continued to think of Marge as he waited for court to convene. He was flattered when the woman sitting behind him tapped him on the shoulder and complimented him on the beautiful marquise-cut diamond and assured him that the recipient was a very lucky woman.

Mary, Marge's assistant, greeted her when she arrived back in the office with a barrage of questions. Although she usually ran a pretty tight ship, today was different. Having just come from visiting Anna, she needed some space and politely asked Mary to give her a few minutes alone in her office.

Mary wasn't happy with Marge's request, as she was swamped with work and needed Marge's help, but it would just have to wait. Kathy, the paralegal, also found herself on the receiving end of Marge's rebuttal, as Marge warned her to give her some space before closing her office door behind her.

Safely in the confines of her office, Marge closed the blinds to keep out prying eyes and dropped her purse on the desk. Swiveling her chair around, she sat staring blankly out the window overlooking the hustle and bustle of the city. So many things were whirling around in her head as she thought about life without Anna. Foremost in her mind was the fact that all who knew Anna were better for it. When Anna initially requested that she and Joel move into her house when she passed, Marge had a difficult time putting the face of reality on such a notion. She thought it was something that people talked about, but it would never happen. Trying to pull herself back to her own reality—running a successful law firm—Marge reopened the blinds and tried to focus on business.

Anna tried with little success to take a sorely needed nap. Grateful for the twenty minutes of sleep she was able get, she sat up in bed awaiting the results of the tests she had done earlier that morning. Against her usual logic, she began bargaining in her mind about the severity of her condition. The first thought she pondered was the possibility that the doctor was wrong and the tests would bring that to light. Then she placed her head in her hands and began to weep.

As Robby and Billy tossed a baseball in the backyard, they talked about school and then more personal matters. Robby was curious about the work Billy's dad did and how long it kept him away from home—usually no more than a week. It made Robby reflect on his own father being in prison. He wondered if his father's incarceration made him look less than other children his own age.

Not meaning any harm, Billy said, "Maybe you can live with us if Anna dies."

"Anna's not going to die!" he screamed. "Even your mom said she was feeling a lot better. Don't you ever say that again, Billy!"

Looking down at the ground, Billy apologized and said, "I'm sorry, Robby. All I meant was that maybe you could live with us if something happened."

Anna immediately sat up in bed when she saw the doctor enter the room. She did everything but cross her fingers, hoping the results of the tests would allow her a little more time; however, the doctor confirmed her worst fears: her heart was too damaged to repair, and according to her doctor, surgery was not a viable option. Knowing she only had about six months to live, she informed the doctor that she was leaving the hospital the following morning, with or without his blessing.

"Leaving tomorrow is fine," the doctor said. "As time goes on, your condition will worsen. In addition to the medication I prescribe, I want you to hire a nurse for home health care." He took hold of her hand and said, "I'm sorry I had to be the bearer of such bad news."

Anna unhooked the heart monitor and walked over to the window overlooking Freeport Road. Cars and trucks raced from one traffic light to another as people hurried down the sidewalks. All that she had accomplished in her life seemed so minimal in comparison to what lay ahead. There was a loving little boy waiting for her, depending on her, who eagerly awaited her arrival home. She had the heartbreaking task of telling him that she would soon abandon him the same way his mother did. As the tight feeling in her chest began to grow, she made her way back to the bed, just as a nurse entered the room. She gave Anna her medication and hooked her back up to the heart monitor. Anna let the young nurse knew that she was leaving in the morning and to be sure everything was in order for her release.

It was nearly five o'clock before Jack finished up at the courthouse. The afternoon was like most others: a series of plea bargains, recesses, and continuances. The engagement ring was burning a hole in his pocket. It was much like a romantic beacon beckoning to find its rightful home. Strangely enough, he seemed more concerned about Anna's approval than Marge's possible rejection. The way he had it figured, Marge would not dare turn him down as long as Anna was in his corner. Once Jack made it through the crowd of people exiting the courthouse, he headed straight for the hospital. The streets and sidewalks were crowded with people who had just finished their workday. Jack was feeling smug because he knew he was having a much better day than most.

Peeking in Anna's doorway, Jack saw Anna lying on her back with her forearm resting over her eyes. The beeping of the heart monitor reminded him of the severity of her condition. She seemed so small and fragile in the hospital bed. He had come to know her as a larger than life figure who was not overbearing, but made things happen.

Jack knocked gently on Anna's door. She took him by surprise when she said, "Well, young man, are you coming in or not?"

Anna climbed out of bed and put on her robe so that she could properly accept her visitor. The sight of her eyes brightening put Jack at ease as he sat on the chair next to her bed. The two friends made small talk about the food in the hospital, how business was at the office, and, of course, how much Anna missed Robby.

Finally, Jack reached into his pocket and said, "I have something very important to show you."

When Jack opened the small black box, Anna gasped in surprise and placed her hand over her mouth. Jack smiled with delight when Anna took the ring in her hand for closer inspection.

"Jack, this ring is gorgeous! You chose well, my boy."

"That means so much to me, coming from you, Anna."

Excited by the news, Anna said, "So, when do you plan on tying the knot?"

Jack laughed. "She hasn't even agreed to marry me yet."

Anna gently placed her hand over Jack's and said, "Trust me, you two were meant to be together." She followed with, "If she turns you down, I'll marry you."

Once the excitement wore off about the question of matrimony, Jack adopted a serious tone and asked Anna about her health issues.

Anna tried to make light of the situation and said, "We were having such a good time, Jack; why did you have to bring that up?"

Smiling, Jack said, "Come on, Anna, we are in the hospital."

Taking hold of his hand, Anna said, "Have you talked to Marge today?"

He looked at her quizzically and said, "Yes, we ran into each other this morning, in the lobby downstairs. She told me not to come up because you were having tests done. Then she headed back to the office and I went to the courthouse. Why are you asking me if I talked to Marge?"

"I talked to her about the state of my health and swore her to secrecy. It appears she kept her promise by not telling you. It's very important that I tell Robby in my own way."

Jack was confused by all the talk of secrecy. "What is this all about?"

A gentle smile formed on Anna's lips. "Unfortunately, the end of my time is near, Jack. I've been informed by one of the best witch doctors in the city that I have about six months to live."

He moved closer to her, and, in a soft but firm voice, said, "We'll find different specialists that might be able to help."

Anna placed the palms of her hands against the sides of Jack's face and looked into his eyes. "Listen to me, young man. I am not going to waste a single day in an exercise of futility chasing more life. I plan on enjoying everyone I love until my time here is finished."

They sat very close for a long time without saying a word. Jack desperately wanted to take her fragile body in an embrace, but was afraid he might damage her. Jack and Marge both owed Anna more than they could ever repay.

When Anna saw Jack's eyes welling up with tears, she smiled in a comforting manner and said, "Come on, Jack, you're not rid of me yet."

They both laughed as Jack wiped the tears from his eyes.

They were both surprised when Marge appeared in the doorway. Trying to keep the mood upbeat, she said, "So, what's my man doing in your room, Anna?"

Anna laughed and said, "I guess we're busted."

Marge looked at Jack and said, "I thought we were coming down together?"

"I'm sorry, Red; I thought you would be busy at the office."

"Let's not squabble," Anna teased. "The important thing is that you're both here."

Marge walked by Jack to kiss Anna on the cheek. When she turned around, he was on one knee, displaying the elegant engagement ring. At first, she started to say, "What are you—" Then she realized what it was when he declared, "I love you more than life itself, Red! Will you marry me?"

Marge stood breathless for a few moments, staring at the ring, but her excitement got the better of her, and she said enthusiastically, "Yes! Yes! Yes!"

Jack slid the ring on her finger, and then wrapped Marge in his arms and kissed her passionately.

Anna opened her arms and called them over to her bed. Following a loving embrace, she said, "How would you like to grant a dying old woman's request?"

They looked at each other and then back at Anna. "Anything, Anna … anything at all."

Taking hold of their hands, Anna said, "How would you like to get married in the old house? She might not be as grand as she once was, but it is still a beautiful home. If we move some furniture and utilize the large courtyard in the back, there will be plenty of space."

"Anna, you are one of the most determined women I've ever known," Jack said, smiling. "You definitely know how to get your way."

Marge poked him in the side with her elbow in a scolding manner. "Anna, we would be honored to have the wedding at your house."

"Please consider adopting Robby and making him part of your new family. I will not be around much longer, and it's important to me that he be taken care of," Anna said in a heartfelt manner.

Not expecting an answer immediately, Anna kissed them both on the cheek and sent them on their way, but not before instructing Jack to take his beautiful fiancé out for a nice celebration dinner.

Anna lay back in bed and digested all that had happened. She needed to call Helen to arrange for a ride home in the morning, and she needed to talk to Robby. She shook her head and smiled thinking about Jack's shifty move on Marge. He put her on the spot by proposing marriage in front of her, which impressed her greatly. It warmed her heart that Robby would be part of a complete family and not displaced from his home. He and Joel got along well together, and both of them had more than their share of life's problems. Anna was blindsided by the sadness she felt, thinking about her own life. Even though she could not have been more joyful about Marge and Jack's upcoming marriage, it was a sad reminder that she never had the sweet luxury of sharing life with a partner. Reminding herself that self-pity did not become her, Anna closed her eyes, hoping for rest.

Anna didn't know how long she had napped when she was awakened by the sight of a heavyset black woman pushing the medication cart into her room.

"How are we doing today, Miss Wilson? My name is Ruby, and I will be your nurse until midnight. I see you hardly touched your dinner, but between us girls, I cannot blame you. Just let me take your vitals and give you your meds so I can let you be."

As the nurse cheerfully went about her duties, she hummed a song that caught Anna's interest: "Amazing Grace."

In between humming, Ruby said, "I only work when the hospital is shorthanded. That is how I keep my license up to date. My youngest boy is still in college, so a little extra money never hurts. Some of the other nurses think I talk too much, but I'm a firm believer in interacting with the patients."

Anna was thoroughly enjoying herself as she watched Ruby completing her duties and chatting away. At one point, the heavyset nurse leaned down and whispered in Anna's ear, "I probably do talk too much, but it helps me enjoy my work. The Lord knows we have to enjoy our calling in life."

When the nurse was almost finished with her routine, Anna said, "Ruby, would you be interested in taking a job in home health care at my home in Highland Park?"

"Do you mean caring for you, ma'am?"

"I'm the one."

Ruby thought about Anna's proposal, and said, "Don't you want to check my references, because I have plenty?"

"There is no need for me to check your references. Here is my address and phone number. I am being released in the morning, so, if possible, I would like you to come over the day after tomorrow."

Ruby extended her chubby hand and they shook on it.

Anna wondered if Robby and the old house would feel the same magic from Ruby that she did. The fact that she was black had no bearing on her decision; Anna could tell Ruby was a woman of great moral character. Despite the Equal Rights Amendment having been signed into law many years earlier, racial prejudice was still alive and well in the United States. Many people were under the impression that racism was confined to the South, but it continued to flourish in the streets of Pittsburgh and other large cities. She could only imagine the obstacles that Ruby may have encountered during her journey to become a nurse. Putting at least one of her sons through college demonstrated that she wanted a better life for her children. Anna found Ruby to be a very interesting woman, the kind of woman whose company she would enjoy. In her mind, she could picture Ruby humming songs and telling stories that she would enjoy during the declining days of her life.

Anna remembered that she needed to give Helen a call regarding the arrangements for the next day. She was also looking forward to speaking with Robby. When Helen answered the phone sounding overly rambunctious, Anna surmised it was the result of at least a few glasses of wine. Nonetheless, she was happy to talk to her friend. She informed Helen that there was no need to bring Robby by for a visit that evening, as she was coming home in the morning. Her only request was that Helen be there around ten a.m. to pick her up. She then asked Helen to please put Robby on the phone.

Anna was relieved that she reached Helen before she drove to the hospital with Robby. She knew when Helen had too much to drink, and she was afraid tonight was one of those nights. Her heart melted, though, when the little man in her life said, "Anna, I miss you so much. I want you to come home."

As tears rolled down her cheeks, she said, "Yes, young man, I want to come home too."

Before she could continue, Robby said, "I want to come in to see you tonight. Helen said she would drive me."

"There is no need for that," Anna said, "because I'm coming home in the morning."

"Really?" Robby said excitedly.

Anna laughed. "Really."

Robby, pleased that Anna was coming home, said, "Can I skip school tomorrow? You might need my help when you get home."

"That's a fine idea. I'll see you in the morning."

chapter
....twenty-one

Doctor Peterson walked into Anna's room with a young nurse at his side. Before he could speak, Anna said, "I didn't expect to see you again before I left the hospital."

He gently placed his hand over hers and said, "Well, I was in your neck of the woods, so I thought I'd stop by to go over a couple of things personally."

The doctor gave Anna a list of home health care professionals and went over her medications with her. He instructed her to schedule her follow-up appointments and to call him if she had any complications. He said that with good care, it could extend her quality of life, and that's what Anna chose to focus on, as time was no longer the wasted luxury it once was.

When Anna had finished eating the less than palatable breakfast they served, the nurse administered her medications, disconnected the heart monitor, and offered to help her take a shower. Respectfully declining the offer, Anna carried her fresh clothing into the bathroom to take a shower. As she was brushing her partially wet hair, she heard familiar voices in the room. She only got the door partially open when Robby rushed her with open arms, shouting, "Anna! Anna! You are finally coming home."

Anna hugged him and said, "I missed you too!"

"I know we are early, but Robby was hounding me all morning for us to leave."

"Thank you so much for everything you've done. You are a good friend," Anna said.

"Think nothing of it, girl. The important thing is to get you back home."

Anna was enjoying the affection Robby was demonstrating as he held her hand firmly as they headed for the lobby. She dreaded telling him about the severity of her condition. A tinge of sadness briefly overshadowed the joy she felt from the reunion with the most important person in her life.

Anna placed her arm around Robby as he clung to her with both hands. In a soft, tender voice, she asked, "Do you want to stop for lunch on the way home?"

Looking up at her he said, "Sure; that would be great."

"I'll ask Helen if she would like to join us."

The trio decided on going to a restaurant called Hoffstot's for lunch. It was Anna's suggestion, mostly because of its close proximity to her house. More than anything, she couldn't wait to return home. She also wanted to thank Helen for her kindness in taking care of Robby.

While Robby's attention was on the restaurant's aquarium, Helen asked Anna about her health, and Anna, in turn, explained her current condition. While she told Helen about her tests and medications, she did not tell her how much time she had left. It was more important for her to talk to Robby about it before anyone else knew.

Anna diverted the conversation to Helen's husband, Joe. Helen explained that he was in St. Louis all week on business, so having the boys provided good company.

When their lunch arrived, Robby quickly pulled himself away from the exotic fish swimming around the aquarium. As he was chomping down on a crisp French fry, he tugged Anna's arm and said, "Anna, can we get one of these fish tanks at home?"

"We will talk about it when we get home," Anna said, "but you have to understand, there is a lot of responsibility involved. Now eat your lunch and we will discuss it later."

About halfway through his hamburger, Robby said, "Did you have an aquarium when you were young?"

"Yes I did, but my brother flushed all my fish down the toilet," Anna said.

Robby was a little shocked by her reply, and went back to eating his lunch, while Helen burst out laughing.

Anna was relieved that the restaurant was not too far from the house, as she was getting tired and was anxious to get home. She could tell when Joe was out of town by the amount of wine Helen consumed, so when they got out to the parking lot, she asked Helen if she wanted her to drive, doing her best not to be confrontational. Helen, however, was rather offended, even though Anna tried to explain to her that she offered to drive because she thought she was tired. Anna was simply relieved when they arrived home and she once again felt the presence of the old house around her again. The special relationship she shared with the house was uniquely warm. Anna and the old place had seen family members come and go throughout the years. The sturdy stone structure had remained strong, serving her family well. Soon, the house would send her to the next world, leaving her most prized possession behind. She expected the old homestead to embrace Robby with the same care as it did her.

As Anna and Robby got comfortable in the sitting room, he turned to her and said, "Anna, can I tell you something about Helen without getting into trouble?"

"You will never get into trouble for speaking your mind," Robby. "Now tell me what's on your mind."

"I don't want to get Helen in trouble, but I think she drinks too much."

Anna, well aware of the situation, encouraged Robby to continue.

"I accidently saw her pouring wine into a coffee cup early in the morning. She's not the same as my dad, but it brought back the bad memories from my house."

She hugged him and explained to him that he did the right thing by bringing it to her attention. "I think it's best if we keep this between us, and I'll see what I can do to help her."

While Robby was playing in his room, Anna sat at the dining room table reviewing the excessive pile of paperwork from the hospital. She made a list of things she needed to do the next day, including filling her prescriptions at the pharmacy, but she soon grew tired. She slowly climbed the stairs to her room, passing Robby's on the way; he was still playing with his toys. Crawling into bed, a warm familiar feeling settled over her. She fluffed the pillow under her head and got comfortable. Sleep was what she desperately wanted.

Anna found herself hovering above Highland Park among the clouds. It was a beautiful spring day and she could see the pink dogwood trees blooming. People were walking their dogs, and a Cocker Spaniel was eagerly chasing a Frisbee. She noticed two youngsters throwing a baseball. As she focused on the pair, it became apparent that it was Robby and Joel. Once they were finished playing catch, she looked on as they walked side by side toward her house. Both boys laughed while poking fun at one another about their ball handling skills. The happiness and closeness they were exhibiting brought great joy to her heart. She drifted over the house, noticing that the front porch and fence had a fresh coat of royal green paint. She wasn't sure if she liked the color, but she was pleased the house was being taken care of. As the boys entered the backyard, Anna noticed her father's antique Cadillac parked in the driveway. Jack was on one side and Marge on the other as they gave the car a bath. Marge screamed in laughter when Jack squirted her with the hose. When Marge ran around the car to retaliate, Jack wrapped his arms around her, greeting her with a kiss. It was clear to Anna that all was as it was supposed to be. The old house had once again found happiness.

Anna faintly heard Robby telling her that some woman named Ruby was on the telephone. Initially, she was disappointed that her wonderful dream was disturbed, but the sound of Ruby's name perked her up.

When she picked up the telephone, she cheerfully said, "Hello, Ruby, it's nice to hear from you."

"I just wanted to confirm our meeting for tomorrow afternoon," Ruby said. "I have your address, and you are directly across the street from Highland Park."

"I'm looking forward to seeing you," Anna said. "Give me a call if you have any problems finding the house."

As she hung up the phone, Robby said, "Who is Ruby?"

Placing her arm on his shoulder, Anna said, "Ruby is a nurse who does home health care."

"We don't need any strangers; I will take care of you!"

Anna hugged him and said, "I know you would do a fine job taking care of me, but you have to go to school."

After standing quietly for a few moments, Robby said, "I hope I like her."

"I'm certain you will. Now, come on, we'll take a ride to the pharmacy and stop to eat on the way home."

Marge was full of anxiety as they rode the elevator to their floor. Everything was unfolding so quickly, she had a difficult time keeping up. She was to marry Jack, which was a dream come true, but she wondered if she was deserving of her good fortune.

Jack kissed Marge before the elevator reached their floor, and said, "You will be the hit of the office today, my dear."

Squeezing his hand, she playfully scolded him. "Stop it, Jack!"

As they entered the office, Jack smelled fresh coffee. Mary was quick to bring them both steaming mugs of the piping hot brew. Just as she was about to walk away, she noticed something sparkling on Marge's finger. As the two women immediately began chatting about how Jack proposed, he made his exit to his office.

Marge spent a few minutes in her office admiring the beautiful ring on her finger, then, one by one, the rest of the staff filtered in to congratulate her. Jack, in the meantime, had gathered up the files he needed for court and slipped quietly out of the office. Marge held back some of the information when telling the employees about their engagement. She did not think it would serve any purpose to tell them that Anna had only six months to live. It also seemed entirely too complicated to explain what was happening with Robby and the house. They would learn the details of the situation soon enough.

Following a restful night's sleep, the sight of Robby standing in Anna's room took her by surprise. "What's wrong, Robby?"

"Nothing, I was just checking to see if you needed any help."

She laughed. "I'm fine, young man. Now, get ready for school and I'll make you some breakfast."

"Maybe I should stay home again with you."

"Nice try, but you are going to school today," Anna said, grinning.

Anna decided that she was going to talk to Robby about her diagnosis that evening. When she reached the bottom of the stairs, she felt a sudden tinge in her chest. It was a reminder that the doctor instructed her to avoid stairs. She took several deep breaths and made her way into the kitchen to take her medication. It was important to her that Robby not be witness to her bad spells.

After she got Robby off to school, she sat down in the sitting room to enjoy her morning cup of tea. Explaining the situation to Robby was not going to be an easy task. So many changes were about to unfold in his young life. She had the responsibility of explaining to him that she was going to die in six months. She would then have to tell him Marge and Jack would be his new parents and Joel his brother. The only constant in his life would be the old house. She knew he would survive it all, but it broke her heart to bring him more sadness and turmoil. The memory of her holding him and promising she would always be there for him plagued her thoughts.

The doorbell rang twice followed by an aggressive barrage of knocking. Anna was relieved when she saw Ruby at the door, dressed in her green scrubs and carrying a dark cloth bag. Not one to waste time, Ruby was ready to hit the ground running. She got Anna settled and checked her vitals, then asked her several questions.

"Where is your oxygen, dear?"

"I didn't think I needed any yet," Anna said.

"I'll call in an order and have it delivered this afternoon."

The large nurse grabbed a pad and pen from her bag. "Are you a coffee drinker?"

"No, but I do enjoy a cup of tea. Why, is there something wrong with drinking tea and coffee?"

"I hope not, because I could use a cup of coffee about now," Ruby said.

Anna put on a pot of coffee and water for tea while Ruby called in the order for oxygen. "Did you have any problem finding my house?" Anna asked.

Ruby smiled and said, "No, some of your inquisitive neighbors were very helpful when I walked over here from the bus stop, except I don't think they're accustomed to seeing black folk around here."

"I guess they're going to have to get used to it."

Both women laughed.

Anna turned serious. "So, you'll help us out here, Ruby?"

"I've been caring for people like you for most of my adult life, and to me it's much more than work. I will take the job, Miss Anna, but I have certain rules. The rules of your house are exactly that, as long as they don't interfere with your health care. I take Sundays off to spend time with my son and attend church services, unless you have an emergency. I need my own room, preferably on the same floor as yours. If you plan to remain on the second floor, we need to have a chairlift installed. If not, we will have to convert one of the rooms downstairs into a bedroom. It makes no matter to me which way we do it. While in your employ, I will do my best to be part of the family. Helping out around the house with meals and such is no problem. I actually prefer it that way. Oh, I almost forgot, I normally charge a thousand dollars per week, but if that's a problem, we can work something out."

Anna refilled their cups, and then said, "Everything sounds good, and a thousand dollars per week is acceptable. The guest room upstairs, which is located next to mine, should be suitable for your needs. Do you know where we can get one of these chairlifts installed?"

"I'll contact the company this afternoon," Ruby said, "and if we are lucky, they will install it tomorrow."

"Good. There is one more thing. Robby is the other half of our small family. He is currently at school, and I'll tell you all about him—"

Ruby interrupted and said, "If you don't mind, ma'am, I'd prefer to get to know him on my own."

Anna smiled. "I think we are going to get along just fine."

Ruby finished her cup of coffee and placed both of their cups in the sink. She smiled at Anna and said, "Let me help you up the stairs so you can change clothes while I make the arrangements for the chairlift and oxygen. Later this afternoon, I will catch the bus back home so I can pick up some clothes and personal things. I don't need much, because I wear scrubs most of the time when I'm on duty."

"Nonsense, Ruby, we will drive you to your house when Robby gets home."

"That's a mighty tempting offer, but I'm not sure you would feel comfortable in my neighborhood."

"It will be a good cultural experience for Robby. Besides, you will be there to protect us."

They both got a good laugh out of Anna's remark, but Ruby knew there was more truth to it than Anna realized.

The more familiar Anna became with Ruby, the more she knew the decision to employ her was the correct one. She would add a new flavor to the household that would enhance the atmosphere when it needed it most. Anna was well aware that difficult times were ahead for her and Robby. She believed that Ruby's strong personality could be a stabilizer in both of their lives on the tough road ahead. She wanted to sit down with Robby and tell him the truth about her medical condition, but decided to wait a day or two now that Ruby was part of the picture.

It was nearly seven o'clock when Jack and Marge finished the day's work. Jack went in her office to massage her shoulders. She leaned back and said, "I'm putty in your hands, counselor."

Whispering in her ear, he said, "Why don't you call Trish to see if Joel can spend the night and she can give him a ride to school in the morning? We can pick up some take-out on the way to the apartment. Then we can get naked and celebrate in style."

Smiling, Marge said, "If you mean relaxing on the couch with pizza and a good movie, I'll telephone Trish and we can be on our way."

While Jack and Marge waited at Palermo's Pizza for their order, they talked like kids about their upcoming wedding.

"I can't believe we're getting married, Jack!" Marge said, sounding giddy.

"What's the matter, Red, are you getting cold feet?" Jack teased.

"Stop it, Jack; you know how I feel about you."

Jack placed his hand on Marge's cheek as thoughts of spending a lifetime with her overshadowed everything else.

As Robby neared the house on his way home from school, he spotted the medical supply truck that had just delivered Anna's oxygen. Unsure of what he might find, he entered the house cautiously. Small containers of oxygen, along with various other medical supplies, were stacked in the hallway. The sound of Ruby's voice as she came out of the kitchen startled him.

"So, you must be Robby. I've heard a lot about you from Miss Anna."

Robby was quiet for a moment, and then said, "Where is Anna?"

"She's upstairs resting right now. If you are interested in earning yourself a dollar, you can help me put away these medical supplies; that is, after you take your backpack up to your room."

Robby was not sure what to think of this Ruby person, but earning a dollar was right up his alley. He also liked that she set cookies and milk on the kitchen table for his after-school snack.

Ruby found taking on home health care jobs was a double-edged sword. One of the positive aspects was being her own boss, unlike the rigid structure of a hospital setting. The most difficult part of the job was spending long periods with the same patient only to see them die. It was impossible for her not to experience the same loss and grief that the family members did.

Eager to earn the dollar Ruby offered, Robby carried the medical supplies up to the guest room and stacked them neatly in the closet, while Ruby was in charge of the oxygen tanks and the portable cart Anna would use around the house.

"Why are we putting this stuff in here?" Robby asked about the medical supplies.

"I want it stored in the room where I sleep."

Surprised, Robby said, "I didn't know you were sleeping here! Why are you staying here?"

Very calmly, Ruby said, "That's what home health care nurses do."

Visibly skeptical, Robby said, "Are you a real nurse like you see in the hospital?"

Laughing, Ruby said, "Yep, I even have a Pennsylvania state license to prove it. As for the hospital, that is where I met your Anna."

While the two were talking, Anna appeared in the hallway after waking up from her nap. "I see you two are getting acquainted."

"He has been a very big help to me," Ruby said.

"Good. Robby is a big help around here to me, too," Anna said. "Whenever you're ready, Ruby, the three of us can drive over to pick up your things."

"Miss Anna, do you want me to fix something for dinner for when we get back?"

"Ruby, please refer to me as Anna, the Miss is not necessary. I thought it would be nice if we stopped on the way home for something to eat."

Smiling, Ruby said, "As you can see, I don't turn down too many free invites to dinner."

On their way to Ruby's, Robby sat quietly in the backseat staring out the window. Even though he was young, it was clear to him that there was more to Anna's condition than she was letting on. She revealed very little when she arrived home from the hospital, so he assumed that she was going to be fine. Now that Ruby was moving in, he was convinced that Anna's condition was more serious than she reported. He was glad that she had someone to care for her when he was not at home, but Ruby scared him a little. She seemed nice enough to him, but he'd had very little interaction with black people. Not only was she black, but she was big and black. He would never mention his fears to Anna for fear of upsetting her. When they got home, he was going to ask her about the true nature of her illness.

Robby kept his eyes glued to the side window of the car, watching the scenery flash by. As Ruby directed Anna in the direction of Wilkinsburg, Robby was shocked at seeing all the African Americans. He slid over to the middle of the backseat, trying to be as small as possible, but Ruby assured him not to fret; he was in no harm.

While Ruby went into her house to get her things, Robby and Anna waited in the car. Nervous, Robby said, "Anna, are all the people that live down here black?"

"Don't be afraid, Robby; they are no different than we are."

Robby sat back in the seat so Anna would think that her words reassured him, but in reality, he felt no different. Just then, an unshaven old man drinking out of a brown paper bag looked in the front window. Ruby came walking down the sidewalk, and with a mean look on her face, screamed, "Get your nappy headed black ass away from that car before I kick it for you!"

Robby covered his face when he started to laugh, and whispered to himself, "I wouldn't want to mess with her!"

On the drive back to Anna's, Ruby explained that the area in which she lived was not as bad as it appeared. She talked with pride about her three sons, explaining that she raised them on her own, with no male influence, and that none of them ever got into trouble. They attended church, worked hard in school, and always kept a job—the perfect recipe for keeping a young person off the streets.

"Do your sons live in Pittsburgh?" Anna asked.

"My youngest is still attending the University of Pittsburgh, but my older sons both married and have good jobs. One works for Westinghouse in Pittsburgh and the other works for TRW in Atlanta," Ruby said proudly.

"Do you have any grandchildren?"

Ruby's face lit up with joy. "Lord, yes! I've been blessed with two handsome boys and a beautiful little girl."

As Robby listened to the conversation, he began to see Ruby in an entirely different light. Hearing her talk about her family made him realize there was much more to her than meets the eye. It became clear to him that she experienced love, anger, and other feelings, just like everyone else. Sure, she was different in the way she talked and in her mannerisms, but she was still a flesh and blood person.

Jack and Marge enjoyed their coffee and toasted bagels while discussing their upcoming wedding plans. They knew they had to check on Anna's health, though, before moving forward. While they didn't want to wait too long to get married, it was important that they do so before her condition worsened. Jack had a hard time imagining that their dear friend would be gone in such a short time. They discussed adopting Robby and agreed to take on the responsibility.

As the couple was finishing their breakfast, Joel called from his Aunt Trish's house to see if they could stop on the way to school to pick up some money for the school bake sale. While Marge tended to her son's phone call, Jack took his cue and headed into the shower.

On their way to the office, Marge shared her concerns about Joel with Jack. "I hope Joel is okay with all the upcoming changes. I know he will be happy that you and I are getting married, but there are a lot of new things coming his way."

"You worry too much, Red. Joel is a tough kid and can handle a lot more than you give him credit. After all, he is not only getting a great stepfather, he will have a nice house and a live-in playmate."

"You're probably right, Jack, but I worry because he's had a tough life."

Laughing, Jack said, "Red, we have *all* had tough lives, but that is about to change!"

Even though Jack wanted to, he could not reveal the extent of the changes to Marge until the reading of the last will and testament. It was difficult for him not to tell her that they were about to become multimillionaires, but it was important that he adhere to Anna's wishes.

Ruby could see that Anna was visibly fatigued on the drive home from her house, so she suggested they pick up some carryout instead of eating out. This suited Robby just fine, as he was always up for burgers and fries.

Curious, Robby said, "Ruby, where is your car?"

"I don't drive a car, Robby."

Bewildered, he said, "How do you get around without a car?"

"I ride the bus most times. The PAT buses go about anywhere in the city."

'What do you do when it's raining or snowing?"

Ruby laughed at the mundane conversation she was having with the young boy. "Well, that's very simple. I have my trusty umbrella for the rain and my winter clothing for the snow. How about you, young man, have you ever ridden on a city bus?"

Getting a faraway look in his eyes, he said, "When I was just a kid, my mother and I rode the bus downtown to Kaufmann's Department Store so I could see Santa Claus."

With everything that was going on lately, Anna hadn't thought much about Robby's mom and how he felt about losing her. Hearing him talk about his trip to Kaufmann's with her let Anna know that the loss of his mother remained fresh in his young mind. Even though her time in the hospital was a short stay, Anna had missed tucking him in at night and watching him sleep. Now, as he sat at the dining room table eating his burger and fries entirely too fast and chewing with his mouth open, she smiled, enjoying every minute of it.

"Hello, Anna, I called to see how you're doing," Marge said.

"That's very kind of you, dear," Anna said. "I'm feeling pretty fair today."

"Do you mind if Jack and I stop by after work? I'd like to talk to you about the wedding, if you're up to it."

"Nothing would make me happier, dear. I'll see you then."

As Ruby was instructing Anna on how to use the oxygen properly, Robby watched in amazement. Anna informed him that Jack and Marge were stopping later that evening, so he'd better make sure his homework was completed. Anna also informed Ruby that she wanted her to meet her friends, telling her that they were the closest thing to family that she has in this world, and that they were going to be married in this very house. This news excited Ruby, who offered to help with the preparations in any way she could. Anna hoped they would all have an opportunity to lend a hand.

While Ruby unpacked her things in her new living quarters, Anna rested. Robby diligently worked on his homework, but left his door partially open so he did not miss Jack and Marge's arrival. As Anna looked around her bedroom, she spotted the old photo albums on the bottom shelf of the nightstand. In the past, she made it a point not to look at the old photographs because of the painful memories they carried with them. For reasons beyond her understanding, the darker memories associated with them no longer had the same impact on her. A slight smile found her lips as she gently placed the album on the bed. After pulling back her long silver hair, she slowly ran her fingers over the leather cover. On her thirteenth birthday, her father gave her the photo album and a Polaroid camera. The first pages contained pictures she had taken around the house and in the park. She stopped at a photograph that her sister, Elizabeth, snapped of her standing next to the Cadillac with their father. He was not one to smile, but in this photograph, he did. Viewing the pictures of her deceased family members seemed to lose their power over her.

While she was lost in the memories of the past, Robby knocked at her door with his homework in hand.

"I'm finally done with my homework. There are no mistakes, but if you want to check it, that's okay with me."

"I'll take your word for it."

It was obvious to Anna by his body language that the youngster had more on his mind than homework. She let him squirm for a few moments, and then said, "Are you going to tell me what's on your mind?"

Robby shuffled his feet back and forth on the floor several times, and then blurted out, "Are you going to die? I might be just a kid, but I can see what's going on around here."

Anna reached out her arms and embraced him as he started to cry.

"You promised! You promised me you would always be here for me!"

When they dried their tears, Anna had Robby sit next to her on the bed. She held his small hand in hers and placed her arm gently around his shoulders.

"You are an intelligent boy, and I love you very much. I was wrong for not telling you what was going on as soon as I got released from the hospital, but I didn't want to hurt you."

Robby started sobbing again. "What's wrong with you, Anna, and when are you going to die?"

"My old heart is worn out, and the doctors can't fix it. They tell me I'll be around for another six months."

Worried, Robby said, "Who will take of me when you're gone?"

Rocking him back and forth she said, "You will never be forced to leave this house, because it is your home. Once I'm gone, arrangements have been made for you to remain here as part of Jack and Marge's family. I've also left you a great deal of money in a trust fund to make sure all your future monetary needs are met." She paused for a minute, and then said, "Don't ever forget that I love you with all my heart, and I will always be with you, even after I leave this world."

At that moment, Ruby knocked on the door to let them know that Jack and Marge had arrived.

An uncomfortable silence hung in the living room for a few minutes as Marge and Jack went out of their way not to mention Anna's medical condition. Anna broke the silence and said, "You have already met Ruby. I am happy to report that she is exactly what the doctor ordered. Once you become acquainted with her, you'll know what I mean."

"Anna, we already know that you are a good judge of character," Jack said. "After all, you brought me, Marge, and Robby into your life."

That seemed to break the tension, and everyone laughed.

"If there are no objections, I'm going to serve the carrot cake now," Marge said.

Jumping up from his seat, Robby said, "Can I help?"

Smiling, Marge said, "Come on, big guy, let's go serve up some cake."

While Marge brewed a pot of coffee and fixed Anna a cup of tea, Robby placed a stack of plates and forks on the table. Marge smiled as she looked around the kitchen at the beautiful Georgian China and the sculpted silverware. A tinge of guilt found her as she experienced enjoyment over the fact that it would soon be hers. The fine woodwork all around her was a reminder that she and Joel had never lived in a house of their own. Now she would have a house that she could have only imagined.

As she was portioning out the cake, Robby said, "Anna told me I will be living here with you when she dies."

His statement took Marge by surprise. "That's true, but Jack and Joel will be living here also."

"Are you and Jack going to get married?"

Putting her arm around him, Marge said, "Yes, we are getting married very soon, right here in this house."

"I'm sure that will make Anna happy."

When they finished their cake and coffee, the group got down to business: planning Jack and Marge's wedding. Robby armed Anna with paper and pen to write down all the details. Anna didn't want to overstep her bounds, but she had a few suggestions she wanted to share with the couple. Marge welcomed all the help she could get.

"The fifteenth of October sounds like a good date for a wedding," Anna began. "If we are going to use the back courtyard, we want the weather to be favorable. Is that good for you?"

Jack and Marge nodded their approval as Marge poured everyone another cup of coffee and freshened Anna's tea.

"Marge, we will need to look at wedding gowns in a timely manner. If you do not mind, I would like to go with you in a purely advisory role. I would also like the wedding gown to be a gift from me. We should spend part of the day trying on gowns and the rest of the day looking at wedding cakes."

"Anna," Marge interjected, "you are already doing too much for us."

"Nonsense, dear. I have never been married, so helping you with this brings great joy to my life."

Marge hugged Anna and kissed her on the cheek. "Thank you, Anna, I'll call you from work tomorrow so we can set up a day next week to look at gowns and wedding cakes together."

As Anna jotted down a few notes, she said, "I am so excited about this wedding. You young people are bringing so much joy into my life. While attending college, many of my friends had big, beautiful weddings as I sat on the sidelines. Now I will experience a wedding in my home, or should I say, *our* home, from start to finish."

Marge took hold of Anna's hand as tears began to roll down her cheeks. Wiping the tears from her eyes, she said, "As you know, Anna, I was married once before, but it was performed by a justice of the peace. This is such a dream come true for me. Everything you have done for us is more than anyone could ever expect."

Unexpectedly, Robby walked over and grabbed Marge's hand. "Don't be sad, Marge, everything will be okay."

Everyone chuckled as Anna explained to him that the tears were joyful.

Ruby hated to break up the party, but she informed everyone that it was time for Anna's medication and oxygen treatment. Not yet ready to let the excitement of the wedding plans go, Anna had Robby bring her pad and pen up to her room. The day's activities may have left her exhausted, but her damaged heart was swelling with happiness for the upcoming events.

Billy scrambled out of bed at midnight when he heard a loud banging coming from the living room. He was frightened when he saw a plate of food spread out over the floor and his mom lying next to the chair. A broken bottle of wine lay near her feet. He took hold of his mom's arm and screamed frantically as he tried to help her up from the floor. "Mom, please get up!" Looking down at her face, he continued screaming, 'Mom, let me help you back in the chair!" The distinct smell of alcohol on her breath told him why she was lying on the floor unconscious. He knew it was not strange for her to drink a little too much, say she was tired, and then pass out on the couch.

When Helen's blood red eyes popped open, Billy was both relieved and fearful. The woman glaring at him seemed nothing like his mother. It was as though there was a mean, hateful beast living inside her. She abruptly pushed him away, slurring, "What the hell are you doing out of bed?"

With tears rolling down his face, he said, "I'm trying to help you."

As she pulled herself back onto the chair, she said, "Get out of here, I don't need your help. You're one of the reasons I drink."

Billy ran into his bedroom carrying the heart-crushing comments with him. Afraid to leave the light on in his room, he turned it off and crawled under the covers. Thoughts ran through his mind that if he did a better job cleaning his room, or helped around the house more, she would not need to drink. He desperately wanted his dad to come home, and then things would be back to normal.

The sound of his "nice" mom's playful voice woke him in the morning. "Come on, sleepyhead, you're going to be late for school."

At first, Billy wondered if last night was just a bad dream, but when he saw the bruise on his mother's forehead, he knew it was real. While making his way down the hall to the bathroom, he could smell the sweet aroma of pancakes dancing in the air. Pancakes were his favorite breakfast, but he could not understand why she was fixing them for him. After all, she seemed to hate him the night before. Once he was dressed for school, he grabbed his backpack and went through the living room. He was surprised when he saw that all the debris from the prior night's incident had vanished. Placing his backpack on the floor, he sat down to eat his breakfast. His mom proceeded to discuss the plans of her day as he ate, stating that she was going to look in on Anna, pick up a few things at the grocery store, and get the oil changed on the Suburban if they weren't too busy. He quickly finished his pancakes, accepted his mom's kiss on the forehead, and ran out the door.

Billy had an insecure feeling inside as he ran to meet Robby at the bus stop. He wanted desperately to tell his best friend what had happened, but he could not find the strength to do it. What would he think about his mother if he knew the truth? He could not let people think that his mother was a drunk. When his dad returned home, he could not even tell him for fear that it would cause problems at home. He hoped that his dad never found her drunk on the floor the way he had the previous night. Then the thought came to him that maybe she would stop drinking if he helped around the house more.

Ever the taskmaster, Ruby took charge when the company arrived to install Anna's new chairlift, making sure the installers did not damage any of the furniture, and ensuring that none of them wandered into any of the bedrooms. Anna stayed out of the way at the kitchen table with a cup of tea and her notes for the wedding, and Marge called to set up a day to go wedding shopping with Anna. They determined that Marge would work on the guest list and Anna would work on the menu and floral arrangements. Both women couldn't wait to get started on the details.

The teacher led the students down the hall in two orderly lines. Aside from the occasional outburst of laughter, everyone followed directions. When the children reached the double doors leading to the playground, they ran outside screaming. Neither Robby nor Billy was his usual playful self.

"You're not going to believe what I found out last night," Robby said.

Even though Billy was pondering his own experience the night before, he said, "What happened?"

"Anna told me she is going to die soon. Then she told me that I will live with Marge and Jack in our house. She also told me that she is leaving me a bunch of money."

"I'm sorry about Anna, but it's good that you don't have to move. Will you get to keep the old Caddy?" Billy said.

"I don't know, but it sure would be cool. We could ride all over the place in it."

The boys continued walking on the outer edges of the asphalt, oblivious to the mayhem around them. Billy looked down, refusing to make eye contact with Robby. Finally, he said, "If I tell you a secret, a really big secret, do you promise not to tell a soul?"

Curious, Robby said, "I swear to God, I'll take the secret to my grave."

Feeling safe with his best friend, Billy said, "Last night I found my mother drunk on the floor in the family room. She looked evil and said all kinds of mean things to me."

"My dad was exactly the same way," Robby said. "He used to come home at night drunk and hit my mom and me. When I would hear him swearing downstairs, my ass would crawl under the bed."

The boys chuckled because Robby used a swear word.

Billy got a faraway look in his eyes and said, "What can I do to make her stop drinking?"

"I used to scream at my mom for starting arguments with my dad when he came home drunk," Robby said. "It never did any good, but I needed to scream at somebody." He paused for a minute. "You know something, Billy?"

"What?"

"I miss my mom and hope that God told her that I'm sorry for blaming her."

The sounds of electric drills, power saws, and pounding filled the old house, but Anna didn't let it not interfere with the task at hand, which was to call the local printers, caterers, and florists, and maybe, most important, a preacher for the wedding. She called Marge to get her opinion on who she wanted to perform the ceremony, suggesting a preacher from a nondenominational church. With Marge's blessing, Anna assured her that she would make some calls. Marge thanked Anna, telling her that she didn't know what she would do without her.

The wedding plans were coming together nicely, and Anna was overwhelmed with excitement that she could play a small part.

Ruby took a break from policing the installers to grab a cup of coffee and prepare lunch for her and Anna.

"I'm so hungry I could eat a horse," Ruby said.

Anna laughed. "How do you want the horse prepared?"

"Barbeque is the only way to go!" Ruby joked back.

While Ruby prepared tomato soup and grilled cheese sandwiches for their lunch, she inquired about the wedding preparations. Anna explained the progress she had made and invited Ruby to share any suggestions she might have.

As Ruby put lunch on the table, she said, "I'm glad you are enjoying yourself with all this wedding to do, but I'm expecting you not to overdo it."

Smiling, Anna said, "Ruby, with you on the case, I don't see any chance of my overdoing it."

With the chairlift now in place, Ruby directed Anna to practice using it. Anna was very pleased with how easy it was to operate, and loved the fact that it gave her more freedom to travel up and down the steps. No more hanging onto to the handrail and running out of breath after walking up a few steps. The excitement really began when Robby came home from school. As Anna was coming down the stairs on one of her practice runs, Robby said, "It's my turn next!" Anna and Ruby laughed, but Ruby was quick to tell him that the lift was not a toy; however, if Anna agreed, he could take one ride on it. Not one to refuse Robby, Anna gave in to his request. Once Ruby showed him how to operate it, he was on his way!

❧ ☙ ❧ ☙

The drive home from the office started out very quiet. It was obvious to Jack that the plans for the wedding were racing around in Marge's mind. Breaking the silence, Jack said, "Do I have to wear a tie, Red?"

They both started laughing.

"Come on, Jack, this important to me. You had a big wedding when you got married. Please let me enjoy mine. The answer is yes, you will wear a tuxedo and a damn sharp one at that."

"Just so you know, I have decided to ask Stan Logan to be my best man; that is, if it's okay with you."

"Your old mentor Stan is a great choice for best man. I'm sure he will be honored. Tonight I need to sit down with Joel and explain all the upcoming changes in our lives. That means you are going to your place and I'm going home alone."

❧ ☙ ❧ ☙

As Marge changed into her nightclothes, the sound of the front door opening signaled that Joel had arrived home.

"Sis, the little guy really missed you," Trish said.

Marge hugged Joel as he ran up to her and placed his arms around her waist. Kissing him on the head she said, "I missed him too."

Suddenly, Trish cried out, "Oh my God, Marge! When did Jack give you that beautiful rock?"

Marge tried to quiet Trish by placing her index finger over her lips, but it was too late. Joel immediately wanted to know what was going on. Marge saw no use in waiting any longer and decided to share the news with both of them. Sitting at the kitchen table, Marge said, "Jack asked me to marry him, and I agreed. I know in my heart that he will be a loving husband and a good father to you, Joel."

"Mom, you know I like Jack a lot," Joel said.

"We are having the wedding the second week in October at Anna's house."

With a surprised look on her face, Trish said, "Do you realize that's like a month away?"

"The reason we are expediting things is because we just learned that Anna only has six months to live."

Trish and Joel sat quietly after hearing the terrible news, and then Joel asked, concerned, "Mom, what's going to happen to Robby?"

"We are all going to move into Anna's house, and Robby will be part of our family."

"Is the old woman giving you and Jack the house?" Trish said.

"That's right."

Trish was astounded. "I can't believe she's leaving you that huge ass house! Can I move in too?"

"No way!" Marge said.

Once Trish went home, Marge tucked Joel into bed and went to her room to do the same. She felt relieved that she finally had the conversation with her son. After laying her clothes out for the next day, she turned down the blanket and crawled into bed. Just as she was reaching to turn off the lamp, she heard a knock at the door. She sat up in bed and said, "Come on in, buddy." She gently patted the bed beside her and Joel immediately jumped in with her.

"Mom, can I ask you a couple questions about what is going on?"

Placing her hand on Joel's back, Marge said, "Of course you can, buddy."

"When we move, will I have to change schools?"

"Yes, but you and Robby will go to the same school."

"Will Robby be my brother?"

"He will be your stepbrother, and I hope the two of you become very close. Even with Robby in our family, I will continue to love you just the same."

Marge reached over and turned off the lamp as Joel curled up next to her in bed. He had long ago proclaimed that he was too old to sleep with her, but this night was different.

chapter
.... twenty-two

J ack arrived at Stan Logan's office a little before lunch. Stan was meeting with a potential client, leaving Jack at the mercy of the VIP waiting room. He looked over at the fully stocked wet bar with crystal glassware sparkling on the shelves. Soft music floated through the air as he sank into the brown leather chair. The beautiful young receptionist, Lori, who was impeccably dressed, proved to be a great diversion on her own. It did not surprise Jack one bit that his old mentor spent more than the scheduled amount of time with the potential client he was romancing. It was just another way for him to make people feel special. When Jack worked for him many years ago, Stan taught him to allow a cushion between appointments for that very purpose. He understood, and even believed in, the concept, but had not adopted it as his own yet.

Lori entered the room and announced, "Mr. Logan will see you now."

Greeting Jack with a hearty handshake, Stan said, "Is a working lunch okay with you? I'm starving, Jack, and I'll even buy."

Laughing, Jack said, "That's because you can write it off as long as we talk shop."

The men exchanged small talk while walking a couple blocks to the Brown Derby restaurant, and then, in a serious tone, Jack said, "I have something very important to ask you, Stan."

"Is there a problem, kid?"

"No, this is personal. Marge and I are getting married, and I want you to be my best man."

Slapping Jack on the back, Stan said, "I'd be honored to stand for you at your wedding!"

Pleased by the outcome of his request, Jack relaxed with his old friend as they enjoyed their lunch. He told his friend about the role Anna played in his life and about how their paths had intersected.

Stan was proud of Jack, especially since he and Marge were moving up their wedding plans for Anna's benefit. Of course, he couldn't let Jack off the hook so easy, and he teased his friend about the fact that the money was surely a motivating factor. He wasn't surprised, though, when his friend said that he'd give all the money up if it would buy Anna another year of life.

While Anna was resting in her room, Ruby gently knocked at the door. Apologizing for the intrusion, she said, "Miss Anna, there's a woman named Helen here to see you. If you would like, I can tell her to call on you later."

"Thank you, Ruby; I'll be down in a few minutes."

Ruby returned downstairs only to see that Helen had taken the liberty of placing two wine glasses on the dining room table and uncorked a bottle of white wine. Ruby sensed a showdown in the making, because Anna could not drink alcohol while taking medication. She stayed out of the way until Anna arrived downstairs.

Before Helen could say a word, Ruby said, "Ma'am, would you like me to put on some tea water?"

"We don't need any tea water; I brought wine," Helen said.

"It was very kind of you, Helen, but I can't drink any wine. Doctor's orders," Anna said.

Anna and Helen went into the living room, and Ruby went about her chores.

Concerned, Helen said, "What's going on here? You have a full-time nurse, who seems a little bossy, I might add, and a chairlift to help you get up and down the steps."

"Helen, I personally chose Ruby as my nurse because she is not easily swayed when it comes to my health care."

Helen took a long sip of wine, and then said, "Anna, I didn't mean anything when I said she was bossy. My only concern is that you are taken care of properly. Now, are you going to tell me what's going on?"

"I'm sorry, Helen, you are my friend, and I appreciate everything you've done for us. When I was in the hospital, they informed me that I only have six months to live. That's the reason for the nurse, the chairlift, and the special care."

Helen poured herself another glass of wine and tried to avoid what Anna had just said.

"Helen, listen to me! I said I'm going to die!"

With tears rolling down her face, Helen barked, "I heard you, damn it!"

Anna got out of her chair and hugged Helen, attempting to comfort her. Anna could not help but wonder how much of Helen's emotional outburst was due to the wine.

"What will become of Robby? Have you told him what is going on yet? Hell, did you even get a second opinion?"

Anna was becoming increasingly irritated with the situation, and said, Relax, Helen. I'll answer all of your questions. First, I don't need a second opinion about my condition. I trust my doctor, and if he is wrong, I will not die. It is a win, win proposition. As for Robby, he and I have already had a nice talk. He took the news like the tough young man he is. I'm also happy to report that we are having a wedding here on October fifteenth. The newlyweds will be Marge and Jack. Of course, your family is invited. Once I'm gone, they are taking over the house, and Robby will become part of their family."

Helen sipped her wine without uttering a word; then she took hold of Anna's hand and said, "It sounds like you have this all figured out."

"The most important responsibility I have is Robby, and I'm relieved to know that he will be with good people."

"I'm sure he is glad that he won't be uprooted again or have to change schools," Helen said. "Billy will be pleased to know that his best friend will continue to live here."

"Yes, all of those things were concerns of mine."

The atmosphere lightened as Anna started telling Helen about the wedding plans. Helen offered her assistance with the preparations and Anna thanked her. As it was time for Anna's treatment, Helen corked her wine, kissed Anna goodbye, and saw herself out the door. Anna thought about telling Helen she shouldn't drive in her condition, but she did not have the energy for a confrontation.

When Anna awoke from her nap, Ruby was standing next to the bed with a grin on her face.

"That must have been a damn fine dream you were having, Miss Anna. You were smiling ear to ear when you woke up."

Smiling, Anna said, "I think the oxygen treatments agree with me."

Taking Ruby's hand as she slipped out of bed, Anna said, "I am so pleased you decided to become my nurse. You are truly a good woman, and I'm looking forward to spending these last days with you by my side."

"Ma'am, I don't handle warm and fuzzy encounters well, but I like you just fine, Miss Anna."

While the two women were upstairs bonding, Robby arrived home from school and immediately started scouring the refrigerator for a snack. The fact that his best friend, Billy, confided in him about Helen's drinking gave him a deeper sense of camaraderie with his pal. He was very afraid for his friend and hoped that he would not have to live with a similar horror as his. Robby knew that Anna was wise and would know what to do, but he made a promise—not just any promise—he swore to God. The ramifications of breaking such a binding promise could be devastating. One of the older kids in school told him there was a special place in hell for young people who dared commit such an offense.

Robby was eating his oatmeal cookies at the kitchen table and contemplating his dilemma when Anna entered the room, displaying a genuine smile, which brought joy to his heart. She bent down and kissed him on the forehead.

"When did you sneak in, Robby?"

He finished washing down a mouthful of cookies, and then said, "Just a little while ago. How are you feeling today?"

"Don't worry about me, young man; I'm feeling quite well. Tell me about school today."

Unsure whether he should say anything to Anna about his situation, he said, "Maybe we can talk later."

Normally Robby would chatter on about the important matters that went on during the school day, but for reasons beyond Anna's understanding, he chose not to. She was a bit concerned, but she made it a point not to invade his space.

The aroma of dinner cooking in the air helped to allay Billy's concerns about his mother's drinking; however, when he spotted the open wine bottle and the infamous coffee cup on the kitchen counter, he knew better. He was cautious about her state of mind, but when she entered the kitchen, she displayed more affection than usual. Putting her arms around him, she asked, "How was school today, buddy?"

"It was the same old stuff."

"Guess what, buddy? I am preparing your favorite dinner: chicken, mashed potatoes, and corn."

"That sounds great, Mom. I will be in my room doing my homework. Call me when dinner is ready."

Deciding to take a break from his studies, Billy headed to the kitchen for a glass of juice. The aroma of his favorite dinner cooking smelled wonderful, and it gave him a reason to smile, but that dissolved when he overheard his mother talking on the telephone. Billy knew it was wrong to eavesdrop on a conversation, but thought it might have something to do with the current state of affairs. When his mother say, "Damn it, Joe, I'm not drinking again!" it took him by surprise. Realizing his father was on the other end of the line, he pushed himself tightly against the wall in the hallway. He then heard his mom say, "If you are so concerned about what's going on here, then why don't you come home?" She paused for, and then continued, "I just want you to come home, and Billy wants you to come home. I will see you the day after tomorrow. I love you, too."

Billy changed his mind about the juice and went back to his room until dinner was ready. He chose to focus on the good news that his dad would be coming home soon and that everything would be okay, but it didn't take long before he felt uncertain again about his future and the future of his family. It was clear to him that his father was already aware of his mom's drinking, but he wondered if he knew how bad it had become. Then the cold, lonely thought of divorce came to his mind, but the sound of his mom calling his name forced him to carry the thoughts with him to dinner.

Marge was relieved that the workday was almost over. She allowed herself a few minutes to unwind, but it was short lived, as Patrick Borne, the young financial attorney, knocked on her door. Waving him in, she said, "You look like shit, Patrick. Why don't you call it a day?"

Laughing, he said, "I'd love to, but I have a meeting with a wealthy potential client first thing in the morning. Also, I'm a little unclear on how to handle Anna Wilson's account. Jack mentioned she was in poor health. Should I telephone her to discuss the quarterly earnings?

"Thanks for coming to me with this first. Lord knows she does not need any additional stress in her life right now. Bring me the information and I'll make sure she gets it." As he exited the office, Marge said, "We will be disappointed if you don't come to our wedding."

"I wouldn't miss it for the world," he said, smiling.

Sensing that something was troubling Robby, Anna placed her hands on his shoulders, looked him straight in the eyes, and said, "Let's go somewhere tonight and have some real fun."

"It's a school night. We never go anywhere on school nights."

"How would you like to go bowling?" she said, smiling.

"Bowling would be great!" he said, excited that Anna was up to going out.

"I will ask Ruby to come with us, if that's okay with you?"

Robby had no objection to the nurse coming along, as long as Billy could join them. Anna was more than happy to oblige and got Helen's permission.

Ruby, on the other hand, wasn't overly thrilled about the outing, but she wasn't about to let Anna go without her.

As they climbed into the car, Robby instinctively opened the front door on the passenger side to climb in next to Anna. He turned around and Ruby was standing behind him with her large arms crossed.

"I quit riding in the back of the bus a long time ago, young man."

Robby wasn't sure what she meant, but he took the hint and crawled in the backseat. He was not afraid of Ruby, but he was sure that she was serious.

On the way to Bowling World, Billy asked Robby, "Have you ever been bowling before?"

"Yep, when I was just a kid, my mom and dad took me bowling with them. They even let me push the ball down the alley a couple of times."

"My mom and dad don't like to go bowling, so I never went," Billy said. "My mother said it was a pedestrian activity reserved for beer drinkers and hot dog eaters."

"What does that mean?" Robby said.

"I don't know, but it meant we didn't go."

Overhearing the boys' conversation, Anna and Ruby laughed.

The noise level in the bowling alley was almost deafening, with small groups of bowlers were boisterously cheering and bowling pins were flying into the air. As the four of them stepped up to the counter, a man wearing bright colored clothes and smoking a cigarette said, "What can I do for you, folks?"

Robby shouted, "We want to bowl!"

The clerk chuckled and looked to Anna for clarification.

"We all want to bowl and need shoes."

Ruby tried to object, saying she would watch, but Anna insisted she join in on the fun.

Score sheets and shoes in hand, they made their way to alley number three. Anna made herself the designated scorekeeper. After a few practice balls, the game got underway, with Robby knocking down three pins the first frame; Billy impressed everyone by knocking down five; and Ruby ended up dancing in the alley after smashing eight pins down. Anna did her best to throw two slow moving gutter balls, but laughed in delight just the same.

Everyone was having such a great time that there was no room to think about the problems in their lives. Even Ruby was enjoying herself. A couple times, she caught notice of a few negative looks from prejudice-minded individuals, but she shrugged it off. She was no stranger to bigots, recalling when her mother would huddle over her when she was a child as men threw rocks at their home in rural South Carolina. She remembered asking, "Why do those men hate us, Mama?" Her mother would say, "They don't hate us, child, they just hate." At a young age, Ruby was aware of the fact that the white people in her town funneled all their anger into the word "nigger." When her short-lived marriage ended up in Wilkinsburg, she felt free. In her mind, Pittsburgh symbolized freedom and opportunity.

As the boys were enjoying their hot dogs and French fries—drenched in Heinz ketchup—they boasted about their bowling abilities. Laughing, Anna said, "You two better improve your scores when we start again or Ruby will beat us all!"

"No way, Ruby!" the boys cried out in unison.

When Billy noticed several people drinking beer at another table, he was glad his mother stayed home. It was such a relief for him to have a good time without worrying about her overindulging.

Returning to their lane, Anna took her seat at the scoreboard, with Ruby sitting close by. The boys worked on their practice swings, as it was obvious to them that Ruby was a real competitor, so they vowed to bring her down during the second half of play. After all, they could not return to school the next day and admit that a woman got the best of them.

Stepping up to the line, Robby held the ball up with both hands, looking hard and fast at the lead pin facing him at the end of the wooden lane. He tossed the ball down the center of the alley with all the strength he could muster. It slowly lost its momentum and drifted into the gutter. The second ball managed to remain in the alley just long enough to knock over three pins. Even though he aspired for much better results, he screamed in joy when the pins fell to the floor.

Looking in Robby's direction, Billy said, "Let me show you how it's done."

After focusing for what seemed to be a long time, Billy ran to the foul line and threw the ball as hard as he could. Everyone cheered when he knocked down seven pins.

Anna couldn't wait to crawl into bed after their exciting evening bowling. She smiled as Robby, all clean and in his pajamas, came into her room, placed his arms around her, and kissed her goodnight. He thanked her for the special evening they shared together, but seeing the smile on his face was all the thanks she needed. As Anna and Robby snuggled, Ruby came in and informed Anna that it was time for her to get some rest.

Pulling the comforter over her, Anna said, "Thanks for helping us to have an enjoyable time this evening."

"No, ma'am, thank you for the good time I had tonight," Ruby said. "It's been a long time since this old girl had so much fun."

Everyone in Anna's house went to bed with a little more joy in their heart than they had the night before.

Billy was nervous when he got home from bowling, concerned about his mom's drinking. She showed genuine interest about his evening, which helped to calm the anxiety he was feeling. With excitement building in his voice, he told her how much fun he had at the bowling alley and that he hoped to do it again. He did not ask her straight out if she was drinking, but he watched her body language and carefully listened for any deviations in her voice. Convinced that she was not under the influence, he hugged her and gave her a goodnight kiss.

Sensing that something was troubling her son, Helen said, "Is everything all right, Billy? Don't worry, your dad will be home the day after tomorrow and things will be better."

As Billy crawled into bed, the echo of what his mother said—*things will be better*—went through his mind repeatedly. He desperately wanted it to be the truth.

Marge was happy that Jack had accepted her invitation to dinner. It gave him and Joel more time to get acquainted. Joel was excited about their upcoming marriage and the new life they were about to embark upon. He felt comfortable around Jack and, more important, he believed his mother was safe with him.

While Marge put together some heat and serve dinners in the kitchen, Jack and Joel kicked back in front of the television. Jack was surprised when Joel said, "When you and my mom get married, will you be my dad?"

"How would you feel about me being your father?"

Smiling, Joel said, "I would like it just fine if you were my dad, Jack."

The warmth Jack felt inside from Joel's words of affection wiped away all of his earlier concerns of the day.

After Joel was tucked into bed, Jack and Marge decided to call it a night, too. Crawling into bed, Jack said, "I'm so exhausted, Red."

As if she didn't hear him, Marge said, "Do you think Robby and Joel will get along together?"

Jack rolled over and looked at Marge. "Of course they won't, Red, at least not at first. Joel is accustomed to having you to himself, but eventually he will realize how much fun it is to have a brother."

Marge thought about what he said for a minute, and then said, "Damn, Porter, you're starting to sound like an insightful fatherly type."

Jack smiled and took Marge into his arms and held her until they fell fast asleep.

Anna was able to put aside all of her worries while working on the details of the wedding. Robby was already off to school, and Ruby was relaxing in the living room. She had made appointments at two well-known wedding gown shops in the city for Monday morning. She was determined to have Marge find the gown of her choosing. She would also schedule time for them to look at floral arrangements and see what several caterers had to offer. Realizing they were very busy at the office, Anna wanted to figure out a way to give them at least a brief honeymoon. Anna made sure that Ruby was free to accompany them, as she knew that Ruby would want to look out for her. Anna then called Marge to confirm the appointments with her.

Jack had just finished his meeting with a client when Marge strolled into his office. She looked like the cat that just swallowed the canary. "What's on your mind, Red? I can tell you are dying to spill your guts about something."

"I don't know what you are talking about, Porter."

"Come on, Red, spill the beans," he said playfully.

"I just got off the phone with Anna. She called to confirm our time for Monday morning. You know Anna; she made appointments for us to look at wedding gowns, caterers … you name it! You should hear how excited she is, Jack. You would think she is the one getting married."

"Is there a point to all of this?" Jack said, teasing.

"She told me to clear our schedules for at least three days after the wedding." Marge paused. "Don't you get it? She plans on giving us a honeymoon!"

"Well, then, I guess we better change our schedules!"

When Marge returned to her office to catch up on some work, her assistant, Mary Thomas, was waiting for her. They discussed some billing issues and worked together on some other areas of office management.

"How is everything going with the wedding?" Mary said.

Smiling, Marge said, "Mary, everything is going so well. It feels just like a fairy tale come true. I adore Jack and know in my heart that he's the one. On Monday, Anna and I are coming into the city to work on wedding preparations.

I'm going to try on wedding gowns, and we're going to visit some florists and caterers."

Mary looked on in awe as Marge told her fanciful tale. "You are so lucky, Marge. I hope I find a man like Jack someday."

Once Helen got Billy off to school, she started on her daily chores. Even though it was early in the morning, the bottles of wine resting in the liquor cabinet were subtly beckoning her. Never before had she thought about taking a drink in the morning, but her mind told her that today was different. The fact that Joe was due home the following day made her feel trapped. When he came home, it would be necessary to limit the only thing that gave her any relief. The afternoon glasses of wine would need to be at a minimum, and late night drinking would have to stop. She loved Joe, but knew he would never understand the loneliness she felt. The way she saw it, her life was a combination of dark boredom and tedious routine. Drinking provided her with a warm glow that covered all the jagged edges of her world. She told herself day after day that she could take it or leave it, but she always chose to take it.

Helen gave in to the desire to have a small glass of the special elixir that made everything okay. After all, this might be the last day she could drink the way she deserved for quite a while. As she quickly drank the first glass, the thought came to her that Joe might only be home for a short time. She hated herself for having to choose between Joe and drinking. When she realized what she was becoming, it made her feel more alone than ever. After pouring her second glass of wine, tears began to roll down her cheeks. She wept for Billy, who needed her as a mother. She wept for Joe, because she was failing him as a wife. Lastly, she wept for herself, because she felt as though she was falling uncontrollably into the depths of hell.

The sudden ringing of the doorbell brought Helen back to consciousness. The empty bottle of Chablis was lying on its side on the table. She thought about finishing the partial glass, but changed her mind when the doorbell rang again. When she saw Anna standing at the door, she did her best to seem normal. After straightening her hair, she opened the door, not realizing there was a large red mark on her forehead from the kitchen table.

Anna knew immediately that Helen had been drinking, and invited herself in. She started to tell Helen about the girls' day out on Monday, to see if she wanted to join them, but she realized it was a lost cause. In a mixture of anger and concern, Anna said, "What are you doing, Helen? It's only eleven o'clock in the morning!"

With a defiant look on her face, Helen bumped into the hat rack and nearly fell on the floor.

Helen led her over to the sofa and ordered her to sit down.

Concerned that Anna hadn't come out of the house yet, Ruby got out of the car and went inside. As Ruby stood there, towering over Helen, she looked at Anna and stated, "In my expert medical opinion, this woman is drunk on her ass."

Anna wanted to laugh, but the situation was far too serious.

"What do you want to do, ma'am?" Ruby said.

Walking over to the wine shelf, Anna said, "We are going to take these bottles with us for safe keeping. If her husband wants them back when he arrives home, he can have them."

"If he doesn't want them, we can serve them at the wedding!" Ruby said.

Anna laughed and said, "I better keep an eye on you, Ruby."

Once the half dozen bottles of wine were loaded into Anna's car, Anna and Ruby went back inside to check on Helen. As Anna sat down next to Helen on the sofa, Helen began crying, and screamed, "You have no right to take my wine, you old bitch! When you leave, I'll just go to the liquor store and buy more!"

Without prompting from Anna, Ruby reached over and grabbed her keys from the coffee table. After slipping them into her pocket, she bent over and whispered in Anna's ear, "You can't let that boy come home to this."

"Good thinking, Ruby. We will bring him to my house with Robby. I'll figure out something to tell him."

Ruby returned to the car while Anna sat down in the kitchen to write Helen a note: "Helen, you are a dear friend, and that's why I've taken the action I did. Whether you realize it or not, you have a drinking problem. I am sure today was merely a glimpse of what has been occurring in your life. My intent is not to judge you, but to see to it that you receive the help you need. I strongly suggest that you come up with a plan to accomplish this before Joe returns home tomorrow. My belief is that honesty is always the best policy. When you are sincere about treating your illness, I will stand by you every step of the way. Once you sober up, call me, and I will bring Billy and your car keys home.

You will most likely be angry with me, but so be it. God bless you, Helen." Anna took a blanket from Helen's room and gently covered her on the sofa. She kissed her softly on the forehead and said, "Sweetheart, please make the correct decision with this."

Anna felt a sense of melancholy as she got in the car. She looked at the bottles of wine on the floor and the key-chain lying on the console.

As Ruby stared out the passenger window, she thought about all the people she knew who had lost their lives to alcoholism. As Anna pulled into the driveway, Ruby said, "What should I do with these bottles?"

"Please put them on the bottom shelf of the hutch."

"It might not be my place to say, but I know people who turned their lives around by getting involved in Alcoholics Anonymous."

The stressful situation with Helen had taken its toll on Anna, and she said, "That's a good idea, Ruby, but for right now I need to rest."

Ruby dispensed Anna's afternoon medication and gave her an oxygen treatment before she took her nap. While Anna was resting quietly, Ruby recalled her family members who had died of excessive liquor use. She remembered when her uncle Charles would come to visit. He was quick to make a joke, and always had gumdrops for her and the other children. The clear liquid he drank from a mason jar seemed harmless enough, but for some reason, her mother called it the devil's elixir. Uncle Charles never seemed to be able to hang on to gainful employment for long, but he always seemed to have a smile on his face. On more than one occasion, Ruby became angry with her mother for the way she treated her uncle. He would disappear for extended periods, but always found his way back. Ruby repeatedly begged her mother to be nice to him so he would stay. Her mother would sit her down and say, "Child, I love my brother as much as you do, but there is something you don't understand about him. He is the sort of man who will promise you the world with an IOU." Tears would roll down her mother's cheeks as she got a faraway look in her eyes. Smiling, she would wipe away the tears and say, "Before you were born, Charles was dependable and busted his behind working at the saw mill. That all changed when corn liquor got a grip on him." Ruby recalled that it was not long before Uncle Charles died from cirrhosis of the liver.

Anna heard the whistling sound of the teapot coming from the kitchen. As she looked in the mirror to brush her long silver hair, it was clear that the vibrant energy she once possessed was quickly fading away. She did not mourn the passing of time, but longed for more just the same. The woman looking back at her had so much left to give, but, unfortunately, the decision was not hers to make.

Ruby knocked on Anna's door and said, "I fixed you a cup of tea."

Anna smiled. "You don't have to make tea for me, Ruby. That's not part of your job description."

Ruby let out a hearty laugh and said, "Stealing bottles of wine from someone's house isn't part of the job either, but you didn't hear any complaints."

As they sat at the kitchen table enjoying their tea and coffee, a huge grin formed on Ruby's face. "What's so humorous, Ruby?"

Ruby couldn't help but laugh. "Think about it, Miss Anna. So far, we stole wine from Helen's house, and then we took her keys without permission. In a little while, we are going to kidnap her son from school. I hope your Jack Porter is a good lawyer."

They both laughed so hard they cried.

"I can just see us on the front page of the Press. It will show a big black woman in a nurse's uniform and a crazy-haired old lady being led away in handcuffs."

Laughter echoed off the walls as they acted like two young girls.

When the joking died down, Anna turned serious. "Ruby, I can't think of anyone else I'd rather have share in the final days of my life than you."

"I like you too, Miss Anna," Ruby said, a little embarrassed.

At Ruby's suggestion, Anna contacted Alcoholics Anonymous for information about meetings in their area. She was determined to get Helen the help she needed. When an AA representative returned her call, she filled her in on Helen's situation and explained her concern. There was a meeting at St. Mary's church that evening, and Anna assured the representative that she would bring Helen herself.

Anna filled Ruby in on her plans. Ruby was all too happy to help in any way she could, so she agreed to watch Robby and Billy while Anna and Helen were at the meeting.

Anna picked up the boys at the bus stop after school. She told Billy that his mother was not feeling well, so he would be spending the night with Robby. Excited at the opportunity to have another sleepover, the boys were suddenly in a festive mood. When Anna dropped them off at the house,

Billy waited until Robby was out of earshot and said, "Does my mom have another one of those headaches?"

Placing her arms around him, Anna said, "Yes, dear, but I think the headaches will soon be gone."

"I love my mom, Miss Wilson, but she sure has been sick a lot lately."

Touched by what Billy shared with her, Anna drove over to Helen's house with a stronger resolve than ever. She was concerned for Billy's well-being when Helen was drinking. It mattered not whether he was in the house with her or riding in a vehicle; he was in danger.

Anna used Helen's keys to get into the house. She became concerned when she saw that the sofa in the living room was empty. Then she heard the sound of Helen violently vomiting. Rather than rushing to assist her, Anna decided to sit patiently in the living room until Helen was finished taking care of business in the bathroom. A quick prayer found its way into her thoughts as she heard the sound of the toilet flushing.

Helen was shocked to see Anna when she walked into the living room. "Anna, you scared the hell out of me! What are you doing here?"

"Did you read the note I left you on the table?" Anna said.

Helen let out a long breath as she walked over to the sofa, still sick to her stomach. "Yes, I read the note, but it didn't make any sense to me. There is nothing wrong with me except for a touch of the flu."

"Was it the flu bug that made you drunk this morning?" Anna said in an accusatory tone.

Helen didn't say a word; instead, she sat back on the sofa and held her head in pain.

Several minutes passed before Anna sat down next to Helen on the sofa and affectionately embraced her. "Helen, I really care about you and your family, or I wouldn't be here. If you are honest with yourself, you know that your drinking has been escalating. I'm here as your friend to tell you there are people who can help you."

"Sure, I might drink a little too much sometimes, but I can quit any time I want," Helen said defensively. "If you had all the responsibilities I have, you would have a drink now and then yourself. Joe spends so much time out of town on business that it makes it difficult for me. Running the household on my own and taking care of Billy can be very exhausting."

Anna listened as Helen's excuses for drinking continued to mount. She sensed desperation in her voice, as though she was trying not to lose a valued friend. This reassured her that Helen's plight was truly genuine.

"Please, Helen—" Anna interrupted, "I don't need to hear all the reasons why you drink. I'm here to tell you why you are not going to drink."

"What are you talking about, Anna?" Helen said, confused by where this was going.

"I'm referring to your son, your husband, and your very life. Helen, it is all falling apart, and you just do not see it. How many times are you going to get drunk before something terrible happens to Billy?"

When Anna couldn't stand listening to Helen's relentless circle of excuses any longer, she said, "Listen to me carefully, Helen! We can go round and round about this, but the result will be the same. The bottom line is that I refuse to let Billy come back into this house with you like this. As much as I do not want to, I will call social services to make that happen. You also have a husband who loves you very much coming home tomorrow. A situation like this could do irreparable damage to your family."

Helen sat quietly for several minutes before starting to cry. "I don't know why I drink so much! Sometimes I get so lonely being in this big house by myself." Helen sat for several weary minutes, and with no excuses left, she finally gave in. "Okay, Anna, what would you like me to do?"

Anna wiped the tears from Helen's eyes and kissed her on the forehead. "This is what we are going to do, Helen. First, there will be no more drinking today. I want you to take a shower and put on a change of clothes. We are meeting with a woman at St. Mary's church at seven o'clock, and then we are attending a meeting at eight o'clock."

Confused, Helen said, "What kind of meeting?"

"It's an AA meeting, Helen." Before Helen could object, Anna added, "That program helps a lot of people, and, frankly, you are out of options."

"What am I supposed to do with Billy?"

"Don't worry, he's having a sleep over with Robby. I told him you were not feeling well, and he understood. When I go home, I'll need to take a few things for him."

"It sounds like you had this all planned," Helen said, feigning a smile.

"I don't have much time left, my friend, so I must use it wisely."

While Anna waited for Helen to get ready, she called Ruby to check on the boys and to let her know that she was holding up just fine, but she was surprised when she heard, "Hello, thank you for calling the Wilson residence." She was proud of the way her little man answered the telephone.

"What are you boys up to?" Anna said cheerfully.

"We are playing in my room, and Ruby fixed us soup and grilled cheese sandwiches for dinner."

Cutting Robby short, Anna said, "Can you put Ruby on the telephone for me, please?"

Several minutes later, Ruby said, "Miss Anna, is everything okay?"

"I'm holding up just fine, and things are going better than expected."

"Me and the boys are getting on well together. They ate their dinner and are playing upstairs."

"I just wanted to let you know that Helen and I are going to an AA meeting, so I'll be home later tonight. Say a prayer that all goes well."

Helen's mind was racing as they pulled into the parking lot of St. Mary's Church. A well-dressed woman, who appeared to be in her early forties, approached the car. She was very attractive and well groomed, with slightly graying dark brown shoulder-length hair.

"You must be Anna and Helen. I'm Clara, the woman you spoke with on the phone, Anna."

Helen was convinced that the woman was not an alcoholic. By all outward appearances, she had it all together. She figured that Clara must be a recruiter for Alcoholics Anonymous.

Anna and Helen followed Clara into a large room with folding chairs that were set up in a large circle. Clara invited them to have a seat while she brewed the coffee. Anna had a good feeling about Clara, but Helen's emotions were all over the place. One minute she was convinced she was doing the right thing, and the next she just wanted to dash from the building and run away.

Ruby was glad to be relaxing in her room after a long day. She had one ear on the television and another on the boys, who were playing in Robby's room. Raising three sons on her own taught her that the best of children would get into mischief now and then. A knock at her door interrupted her as she was enjoying watching one of her favorite sitcoms. It was Billy, just standing there, on the other side of the door.

"Is there something wrong, child?"

"Ruby, do you know if my mom is okay?" Billy said, staring at the floor.

Ruby saw how upset he was and welcomed him into her room. Putting her arm around him she said, "Don't you fret, child. Your mom is just feeling a little under the weather right now. As a matter of fact, she called to make sure you were okay just a little while ago."

"She really called?" he asked, sounding hopeful.

"Yes, sir, I plum forgot to tell you."

One of Ruby's greatest fears was losing one of her sons to the streets, but vigilance and prayer ensured that it never became a reality. While riding on the bus from work and school, she witnessed the terrible things that happened on the streets of Wilkinsburg. Men who should have been home with their families were spending their paychecks on gambling and chasing women. Young people were giving themselves over to drugs and alcohol. People were killing one another on the streets for the price of a bottle of cheap liquor. She did not hide the horrors of the streets from her sons, but made damn sure that they knew the consequences. Spending quality time with her sons had always been important to Ruby, so she turned that same attention on Billy and Robby. Armed with a large bowl of popcorn, the three of them sat together in the living room and watched the boys' favorite television shows. Surprisingly, Ruby found herself enjoying the adventures of Superman and Maxwell Smart as much as they were.

For some reason, Helen felt very comfortable opening up to Clara and sharing her intimate secrets about the things that happened while she was drinking. The more she shared, the less she feared giving up drinking. She did not completely understand the concept of "one day at a time," but she was willing to try. The way things were going, her entire life was unraveling right before her eyes. Joe was coming home the next day, which left her with another decision: telling him the truth, as Clara suggested; but the decision was hers alone to make. Desperation was Helen's friend, and it was putting her in a position where she needed to take direction from another person.

Clara gave Helen a meeting schedule and told her that if she was willing to give this a try, she would take her hand and show her the way. Helen was moved to tears, because she found it hard to believe that anyone would want to go through all this trouble for her, but Clara explained that in order for her to keep what she has, she must give it away.

~~~~~~

Ruby missed some of her favorite television programs in order to spend time with Robert and Billy. They sat together in the living room watching their favorite shows and munching on a large bowl of popcorn. She thought the goofy antics of Maxwell Smart were hilarious. The boys were excited because it was Friday night and there was no school the next day. She was not certain when Anna would arrive home, but hoped that the old woman was not overdoing it.

Marge was enjoying the evening out, but she was eager to get home to spend some quality time with Joel. Almost every Friday night, the two of them would spend the evening watching movies and eating junk food; the one on one time was very important to both of them. She loved running the office, but it was extremely demanding of her time. The fact that Joel was spending more time with her sister, Trish, secretly troubled her. With the upcoming wedding, she wanted to share the details of the preparation with Joel to make him feel a part of it all. There were many changes about to take place in his young life, and she wanted the transition to be as smooth as possible.

Jack thought Joel was a great kid, and Joel loved Jack's sense of humor, which often times was at Marge's expense. Most times, she took it in stride, but if it was something she did not want Joel to adopt, she made it clear to Jack. Everyone involved in the new union would need to learn their roles over time. Once they finished dinner, Jack asked for the check and whispered in the server's ear to bring a container of chocolate ice cream to go. When she returned, he handed the frozen treat to Joel. Marge shook her head, but Joel thought it was great.

Once Ruby persuaded the boys to go to bed, she put on her flannel nightgown and went back downstairs. She periodically checked the clock—it was almost ten thirty—as her concern for Anna's well-being was growing. Just as she peeked out the window to look for Anna's car, she heard the sound of a key unlocking the front door. Standing in the hall with her arms folded, she said, "Do you know what time it is? You were supposed to take your medication a half hour ago!"

"I apologize," Anna said. "Things took a little longer than we expected."

"You can tell me all about it after you take your medication and your overdue treatment," Ruby scolded.

While Anna was upstairs, Ruby put on a pot of water and reflected about the day's events. While she was fixing Anna a cup of tea, she heard the sound of the chairlift descending to the first floor. Ruby knew it would be best if she turned in for the night, but she was glad to have someone to talk too. When Anna entered the kitchen, Ruby said, "I was just getting ready to bring your tea upstairs."

"My mind is still racing from everything that happened today," Anna said. "But tell me, how did Robby and Billy make out tonight?"

"Me and the boys got along just fine. I watched a little television with them and fixed a big bowl of popcorn."

"Was Billy concerned about Helen?"

"He did ask about her, but I did my best to calm him down."

Anna told Ruby that she had a good feeling about Helen's involvement with AA While it could go either way, she remained hopeful that Helen would get the help she needed. Anna was also excited about going wedding shopping with Marge on Monday, and she was looking forward to Ruby joining them.

Ruby was exhausted from the day she'd had and retired for the night. It seemed like there was never a dull moment since she came into Anna's employ. With all the excitement of the upcoming wedding and her involvement in people's personal problems, she had very little spare time. She was so involved in Anna's affairs that she nearly forgot that her son was picking her up on Sunday for church and then a leisurely afternoon together.

Anna was sitting up in bed with a book opened across her lap. She tried to read herself to sleep, but was having a difficult time clearing the thoughts of the day from her mind. In her assessment, she had a darn good day. The ever-present thought of her upcoming date with death always seemed to find its way into her thoughts. The more things that brought her happiness, the less she was willing to accept death. Entertaining the idea of a gracious demise was something she was not prepared to do. In many ways, she felt that life was deceiving her and death was stealing all that she cherished. Prior to Robby coming into her world, she was living a dull existence with little flavor to speak of. When circumstances brought Robby into her life, colors became vibrant again, flowers took on a new beauty, and the luster of everyday life returned.

❧ ☙ ❧ ☙

Anna was happy to see that Helen was in such good spirits when she stopped by to pick up Billy. She hoped it was a sign of good things to come for her family. After clearing the breakfast dishes, Anna sent Robby to his room to play; Ruby was busy doing laundry. With the weekend upon them, the promise of leisure time and relaxation was in the air. Helen reported that Joe was taking them out to eat and they were going to stop at the park. Anna hoped that it was a glimpse of things to come for her family. Once breakfast was over, Robby went up to his room to play. Ruby loaded Anna's pillbox while working on the laundry. Anna went up to her room and crawled quietly back in bed with a romance novel. She thought it was nice that everyone was enjoying a little solitude.

As the morning slipped away, Ruby went into Anna's room to remind her to take her oxygen treatment, but, instead, she found Anna unconscious on the floor next to the bed. Ruby immediately put the oxygen mask in place before checking her vitals. She called for an ambulance and relayed all the relevant information she had to the dispatcher. Once they assured her that help was on the way, she gathered up the bottles of medication and put them in a bag. Ruby remained perfectly calm until she remembered that Robby was playing in the next room. Before the sound of the ambulance could alert him, she hurried down the hall to his room.

Trying to remain calm, Ruby pushed the door open and said, "Robby, I want you to get dressed. We are going to the hospital with Anna."

"What's wrong with Anna?" Robby cried.

Before Ruby could explain, Robby ran past her and into Anna's bedroom. Seeing Anna lying on the floor overwhelmed him, and he started crying uncontrollably.

"Is she going to die?" he asked frantically.

Taking Robby in her arms, Ruby said, "She is not going to die. We just need to take her to the hospital for some treatment."

Ruby did her best to reassure Robby that Anna would be fine, but the truth was, she was not sure. Ruby calmly held the oxygen mask against Anna's face while praying to herself that the ambulance would get there quickly. Keeping one eye on Anna, Ruby looked over at a frightened Robby, who seemed to be dazed and shaking as he stared at Anna's unconscious body. Forcing a smile, she said, "Robby, I want you to go over to the window and watch for the ambulance." When he did not respond, she repeated her instructions more forcefully. "Robert, go over to the window and watch for the ambulance!"

Minutes seemed like hours as time ticked away. Finally, the piercing sound of the EMS vehicle shattered the silence in the room. Robby's eyes opened wide as he looked in Ruby's direction. She quickly took control of the situation.

"Robby, I want you to go downstairs and open the front door. Tell the EMTs that we are upstairs."

Without saying a word, Robby ran down the stairs and did exactly what Ruby had instructed. Eyes open wide, he pointed up to the second floor. One of the EMT personnel who entered the house bent down and said, "Who needs help, son?"

"She is up in the bedroom. My Anna needs your help upstairs."

Robby stood with his back to the wall, frightened and confused by everything that was going on around him, from the screeching sound of the radio to the metallic rubbing sound of the gurney on the floor. When the two ambulance workers found their way up to Anna's room, he could hear Ruby barking out medical jargon. He then overheard the sound of the radio contacting the hospital for instructions. Even though everything was happening very quickly, Robby felt as though the whole situation was moving in slow motion. In his mind, he was invisible as he watched them carry her down the steps and out the door. The next sound he heard was that of the ambulance siren blaring as it barreled down the street. The touch of Ruby's hand on his shoulder brought him back to the moment.

Ruby led Robby into the sitting room, where they waited for a taxi to take them to the hospital. She put her arms around him and did her best to comfort him by explaining exactly what was going on with Anna. She sensed him settling down when she assured him that his Anna was not going to die. She explained that incidents like this were symptoms of her heart condition, and that they would be by her side during the entire ordeal.

While she gave Robert the job of watching for the arrival of the taxi, Ruby went upstairs to gather a few personal items for Anna. When she came back downstairs, the sound of a beeping horn signaled their ride was waiting. As they started out the door, Robert asked, "Did you bring her book?" Ruby looked at him and declared, "Hurry up, we need to get to the hospital!" The youngster shot up the steps and grabbed her book from the nightstand. Once they were both in the back seat of the taxi, Ruby told the driver in a stern voice, "Take us to the emergency room at

St. Margaret's Hospital." The fact that Ruby brought clothes for Anna and she let Robert retrieve her book, gave him a sense that she might be okay.

Robby had been in the emergency room waiting area once before, but it did nothing to quell the level of anxiety he was feeling. He held on to Ruby's shirttail in desperation as they made their way over to the desk. The nurse who greeted them was an old colleague of Ruby's, which helped to make the process a little easier. In between seeing a man in hand-cuffs accompanied by a police officer to hearing doctors and other medical personnel being paged, Robby listened diligently for their names to be called back to see Anna. Not even the dollar Ruby offered him for the soda machine could move him from his seat; instead, he remained close to her.

After what seemed like a very long time, the nurse at the desk motioned for Ruby to approach. With Robby in tow, she walked up to the desk, hoping her old friend would have some good news. The only part of the conversation that Robby understood was that Anna was stable and they would be keeping her overnight. The rest of their conversation was medical mumbo jumbo to him. All that mattered to him was that Anna would be coming home the following day.

When they sat back down in the waiting room, Ruby put her arm around Robby and said, "Anna is doing fine, but the doctor wants to keep her overnight for observation."

"Can we go see her?" Robby asked, hopeful.

"Yes, but we have to wait here until they admit her."

"Okay. Can I still buy a can of Coke?"

Ruby laughed and gave him the dollar he refused before.

Anna was confused when she regained consciousness in the emergency room. A cute young nurse was by her side, smiling at her. "My name is Sally, and I'll be your attending nurse until we send you upstairs."

"How old are you, dear?"

"I'm twenty-four. How old are you?"

Smiling, Anna said, "A few years older."

The fact that Anna was able to laugh was a good sign.

While the nurse went about her duties, Anna closed her eyes and thanked God for not taking her yet. The doctor had explained to her that she passed out because the oxygen level in her blood was too low. He wanted her to stay overnight so that he could adjust her medication. Even though it had been an unpleasant experience, she was relieved that the hospital stay was only for one night. After all, she had important wedding plans to make on Monday with Marge!

A nurse came through the double doors informing Ruby that Anna was upstairs in room 403. Relieved by the news, she took hold of Robby's hand and they headed for the elevator. Robby's excitement intensified as the elevator neared the fourth floor. He had a barrage of inquiries concerning Anna's condition. When the elevator doors opened, he immediately searched the doors for the number 403. As soon as he spotted the magical number, he pushed open the door and ran to Anna's side. He screeched to a halt when he saw the tube in her arm and heard the heart monitor beeping.

"It's okay, Robby, you can give me a hug," Anna said, reaching for him.

As Robby embraced Anna, Ruby came to the other side of the bed and took hold of her hand.

"Thank you for bringing Robby with you to see me."

"I don't think the boy would have let me come without him," Ruby said, laughing. "You gave us a bit of a scare."

"Ruby, I thought the Lord was coming for me sooner than we expected."

"Anna, we are going to do our best to make sure that doesn't happen. You are going to follow my rules from now on. Robby will be watching you too."

Anna smiled and said, "I guess I'm in trouble now."

Ruby put Anna's overnight bag in the closet, and then looked at her medical chart; the nurse gave her permission after learning that Ruby had worked in the home health care field for many years. The notes indicated that Anna was being discharged in the morning, and Ruby assured her that she and Robby would be back around nine o'clock to take her home by taxi. Unbeknownst to Anna, who had offered Ruby her car to pick her up, Ruby confessed that she never learned how to drive. This information tickled Robby, who teased her about it. She teased right back with "If you want to eat dinner, you will stop poking fun at me."

෴ ෴

With Billy in bed, Helen and Joe were in the living room for what was supposed to be a romantic dinner. The steaks were a perfect medium rare, the broccoli and baked potatoes were prepared just right, but something was wrong. They muddled their way through the tension in the air, pretending to enjoy the rented movie. Helen desperately wanted to tell Joe about everything that was going on in her life, but she could not find the strength to do it.

As Helen cleared their plates and went into the kitchen, it was clear to Joe that she had something heavy on her mind. It was his first day home from a long business trip, and he did not want to ruin their long-awaited reunion.

When Helen returned from the kitchen carrying two small bowls of mixed fruit, Joe blurted out, "Are you having an affair, Helen?"

"No!" she said, defensively. "Why in the hell would you ask me something like that, Joe?"

"I'm sorry, Helen, but you're definitely not yourself. During this last trip, there were nights I called and you didn't answer the phone. That has never happened before, and when we did talk, you seemed very distant."

Before the thought of her cheating on Joe sank in, Helen remembered what Clara told her at the meeting: "Helen, you will never find comfort in a lie." It was clear to her that she could no longer put off telling Joe the truth.

Helen moved closer to Joe on the couch and took hold of his hand. She looked into his eyes and could see his confusion. Before losing her nerve, she said, "Joe, I have a drinking problem." Joe attempted to reply, but Helen continued, "Please let me finish before you say anything. I've been drinking entirely too much on a daily basis for quite a while now. When you are home, I try to keep it under control, but even that was becoming difficult to do. This last period, while you were away was very bad. Thank God, Anna intervened and took me to see some people who want to help. I hope you're okay with this, Joe, because I love you with all my heart and don't want to lose you."

Helen felt as if a great weight had been lifted off her shoulders. She and Joe sat and talked about her issues in a positive manner for the remainder of the evening, and while Joe didn't fully understand how the AA meetings worked, he pledged his support just the same.

Marge was getting so excited about her upcoming day out with Anna to go wedding shopping. Taking a break from watching television with Jack, she called Anna to confirm their outing for Monday morning. The first time she called, there was no answer, so she figured that Anna, Ruby, and Robby may have gone out for dinner. A couple hours later, she tried again with the same results. When she mentioned it to Jack, he told her not to worry. As her concern grew, she decided to call again, and this time Robby answered the telephone.

Realizing it was Marge, Robby blurted out, "Anna's in the hospital! Ruby and I just got home."

Fear took hold of Marge as thoughts of Anna's death ran through her mind. Fear turned to anger as she thought about the unexpected turn of events. Anna was supposed to live for another six months, and the clutches of death were trying to cheat her out of her time.

Ruby motioned for Robby to hand her the phone. "Hello? This is Ruby."

"Hi, Ruby, it's Marge. What happened to Anna? Should Jack and I go down to the hospital? I can take Joel over to Trish's place for the night."

By this time, Jack was standing next to Marge, catching bits and pieces of the telephone conversation.

"Settle down, Marge. They are only keeping Anna in the hospital overnight. The oxygen level in her blood dropped too low and they're adjusting her medication."

"Do you want us to pick her up tomorrow?"

"Thank you, but no. Anna made it clear that she did not want any of us to make a big fuss. I guarantee, the old woman will be right as rain for Monday morning."

Ruby realized that in the midst of everything that was going on, she and Robby had not eaten dinner, and Robby's "I'm starving" only confirmed what she had forgotten. She was hoping that Robby would settle for something simple, like soup and grilled cheese sandwiches, but he requested pizza. Not usually one for ordering in, at least they had a two-dollar coupon for the pizza!

While waiting for their pizza, per Robby's request, Ruby called Anna at the hospital for him.

"Hi, Anna," Robby said, "I just wanted to make sure you're still coming home in the morning?"

"Wild horses couldn't keep me from coming home!" Anna exclaimed. "I promise you, we will be together tomorrow."

Ruby did not see any reason to tell Anna about the telephone call from Marge. There would be plenty of time to inform her about the conversation once she arrived home.

Stuffed from pizza and Coca-Cola, Robby and Anna tried staying awake to watch a movie, but neither of them was able to keep their eyes open. Hours passed before the steady shrill of the test pattern on the television pulled Ruby from her deep sleep. It was half past three. Rather than carrying Robby to bed, Ruby covered him with a blanket and let him sleep on the sofa. As she watched him, she said a special prayer for the Lord to watch over him during the difficult times ahead.

Climbing into bed, Ruby realized that she needed to call her son to cancel their church date in the morning. As she lay in bed, wide awake but feeling utterly exhausted, she thought about ways to improve Anna's quality of care. The problem was that she was accustomed to caring for patients who were either bedridden or rarely left the house. Anna wasn't even close to fitting either level of care. The fact that she remained active was a positive thing, and Ruby knew her well enough now to know that Anna would never limit herself.

Robby awoke with sweat pouring down his face. Alone on the sofa, he felt the same fear he experienced on that fateful night when his mother was killed. The relentless nightmare seemed to pursue him repeatedly. Afraid to be downstairs by himself, he went upstairs and climbed into bed next to Ruby.

Ruby woke up when she felt Robby's little body nuzzling close to her. She gently covered him with the blanket and rested her head back on the pillow. She smiled as she remembered the late nights when her sons crawled into bed with her. Pulling Robby closer, the two of them slept soundly through the night.

Jack walked up behind Marge as she was sitting quietly at the kitchen table drinking her coffee and placed his hands gently on her shoulders. Bending down, he whispered in her ear, "What's really going on with you, Red?"

Marge was silent for a few moments, and then shouted, "Jack, we are getting married in less than a month! I now have the responsibility of managing the personnel in a law firm that I never dreamed we would have." She started crying. "Soon I will have the responsibility of yet another troubled child, and Lord knows, I could do a better job with the one I have. Jack, I do not even feel like I deserve what we have let alone a beautiful house in a nice neighborhood. What in the hell is wrong with me, Jack? Why do I still feel like that little girl who was nothing?"

Jack sat in the chair next to Marge and wiped the tears from her face. Looking deep into her green eyes, he said, "Red, you're not the only one who is scared. I understand and share many of the fears you have. There are so many people depending on us: the employees at the firm, Anna, the clients I deal with every day, and most important, you and Joel." He paused for a moment, then said, "We did nothing wrong to deserve the bad things that happened in our lives. Maybe it's our time to enjoy the good things that are coming our way."

Embarrassed by her emotional outburst, Marge laughed nervously as she did her best to compose herself. Perfect timing, as Joel suddenly appeared from his bedroom, wiping the sleep from his eyes.

"What's for breakfast mom?" he asked, leaning against the wall.

Placing his hand on Joel's back, Jack said, "If it's okay with your mom, we'll go out for some pancakes."

"I guess we better get dressed then!" Marge said.

Breakfast at the International House of Pancakes revealed one thing to Marge: Joel's concern over Robby's place in her heart. She did her best to reassure him that he would *always* be her son, and that Robby would just be a new addition to their family, and like a brother to him. Apparently, her answer satisfied Joel, because he dove into his pancakes a happy camper.

As usual, Ruby was wide-awake at six a.m. She crawled out of bed, trying not to disturb Robby, and smiled as she covered him with the blanket. Dressed for the day, she went downstairs to finish cleaning up from the night before and to call the cab company to confirm the nine a.m. pickup time. Her thoughts drifted to the night before and how her interaction with Robby brought back fond memories of her sons when they were young and it made her smile.

Ruby hated to disturb Robby from his sleep, but it would soon be time to leave, and breakfast was almost on the table. Ruby loved to cook for others, but her youngest son always seemed to be too busy with school and other social activities to come home for meals. Sunday was the only day they spent together, and he always insisted on taking her out to eat. This fine morning she was going to enjoy eating a home-cooked breakfast with the new little man in her life.

Right on time, the cab was waiting out front at nine a.m. Robby was so excited about Anna's return home that he could barely stand it, and all thoughts about her dying seemed far removed from his mind. A part of him truly believed that Anna's stay in the hospital cured her. During the ride to the hospital, he wanted to ask Ruby if Anna was still going to die, but he refrained from asking because he was afraid of what the answer might be.

Anna let the long hot shower wash away her worries for now. She was going home, and that's where she was going to put her focus. As she finished dressing in the fresh change of clothes that Ruby had brought, she heard the sound of her friend's voice down the hall saying, "Now I told you before, boy, slow down!" A few seconds later, Robby bounded into the room and threw his arms around her.

"I'm sorry, ma'am, I told him to slow down, but he didn't mind me," Ruby said.

"It is okay, Ruby, I'm just pleased to see both of you."

As the nurse was escorting Anna to the lobby in a wheelchair, Robby tugged on Ruby's shirt and said, "Will she always have to use a wheelchair now?"

Bending down to his level, Ruby whispered, "No, it's policy to wheel everyone to the front door upon their release. The people in charge don't want folks to fall and get hurt before they get out the door."

"What happens if a person falls when they get outside of the hospital?"

"If that happens, they scoop the person into the wheel-chair again and bring them back inside."

"We better make sure that Anna doesn't fall."

As they exited the hospital and got into the back seat of the taxi, "Robby said proudly, "I told you she wouldn't fall."

Anna enjoyed a few minutes of solitude on her front porch when they got home from the hospital. From the minute the taxi dropped them off in front of the house, she felt that it was inviting her to rejoin the home she had always loved. While she was eager to spend time with Robby, she asked Ruby to give her this time alone. Robby hesitated leaving her side, but Ruby managed to usher him inside without incident.

About fifteen minutes had passed when Robby came running out onto the front porch announcing that it was time for lunch and for Anna to take her medicine and do an oxygen treatment. It was clear to Anna that Ruby and Robby intended to keep a very close eye on her following her recent trip to the hospital.

Over lunch, Anna, Ruby, and Robby centered most of the conversation on the wedding preparations. Anna was excited about going into the city to shop for the perfect wedding gown for Marge. It was also very important to her to spend quality time with the most important women in her life.

Talking about the wedding reminded Ruby that she had neglected to inform Anna about Marge's telephone call.

"Ma'am, I forgot to tell you that Marge called yesterday. When she heard you were in the hospital, she wanted to visit, but I told her you were coming home today. I told her you would telephone her sometime today to confirm tomorrow's outing."

"Why can't I go?" Robby asked.

Ruby laughed.

"First of all," Anna began, "you have school tomorrow. Furthermore, it's an all-girls' shopping trip, which means no boys allowed."

Before taking a much-needed nap, Anna returned Marge's telephone call to confirm their shopping date. After filling Marge in on her trip to the hospital and how she was feeling, the two women chatted about the upcoming wedding preparations.

"Are you ready for our shopping trip tomorrow?" Anna asked.

"I'm so excited, I feel like a young girl again," Marge squealed with delight.

"You *are* a young girl compared to me! Can you meet us here at eight thirty?"

"I'll see you then!"

Excitement was in the air the following morning. Anna and Ruby were up early, while Robby slept in as long as he could. Over their morning tea and coffee, Ruby's and Anna's thoughts turned to matrimony.

"When I got hitched, it was just me, the poor excuse for a man I married, and the pastor and his wife in attendance," Ruby said, laughing. "My wedding gown was one of the two dresses I owned." Shaking her head, she added, "The only wedding gifts I got were a lot of broken promises from the smooth-talking groom."

"As terrible as that sounds, at least you had a wedding!"

Anna and Ruby laughed about the strange sense of humor that life often had. When Marge arrived, Anna joked with Ruby that she'd better not share any of her horror stories with the bride-to-be, or she might rethink things.

Cruising down the road in Anna's Mercedes, with Marge at the wheel, the happy trio was on their way for a girls' day out. Marge fell in love with Anna's car as soon as she hit the road. By the time they hit the main drag, all three women were interacting like old girlfriends. Though they were all from different walks of life, it was strange how well they could relate to each other. Ruby and Marge found it easy to share the struggles involved in being a single mother. Anna was enjoying the friendship and closeness of spending time with her friends. She could not help but see the dark humor in how her mother would have felt about both of her friends. Ironically, Marge and Ruby would have been "those people" in her mother's eyes: Marge, because she had the misfortune of being poor, and Ruby, because she was born black. Anna thought to herself, *Mother, I hope you don't hurt your back when you roll over in your grave.*

First stop of the day for the women was a little shop called Sheer Elegance. Stepping inside the elegant store, Ruby looked at Anna and whispered, "You best have a big piggy bank for this place."

A well-dressed woman wearing a less than sincere smile immediately escorted the women to an area of the store where there was a runway with small tables and chairs around it. As soon as they sat down, a young woman appeared with a tray of fine pastries and champagne glasses filled with mimosas. Anna had the attitude that she belonged wherever she chose to be, but Marge and Ruby felt completely out of their element.

As the fashion show got underway, an attendant diligently kept their glasses full and breakfast treats coming. Marge was ready to note the dresses that caught her eye, but after a number of models crossed the runway, Anna noticed that her notepad was blank.

"Marge, if you don't like any of these dresses, we can go to another shop."

"Anna, these dresses cost too much money. You've already done entirely too much for Jack and me."

Taking hold of her hand, Anna said, "I'm sure you've heard the saying, you can't take it with you. Well, you know I will be gone in a matter of months, and spending money on the ones I love is what I want to do. Please let an old woman enjoy her last days on Earth."

Marge smiled and kissed Anna gently on the cheek. "Then let's find me the nicest bridal gown in this overpriced place!"

After viewing a dozen dresses, Marge narrowed her selection down to two that she really liked. One was a layered princess cut with a long train, chiffon with lace beading, and was more of a traditional gown. The second was an ivory princess wedding dress with beading. It was a light and carefree bridal gown.

While Marge was in the back trying on the first dress, Ruby said, "You know, Miss Anna, that young woman would look beautiful in every dress in this place."

"The Lord knows that's the truth, Ruby."

When Marge emerged from the dressing room wearing the first dress, she looked as though she was moving in slow motion as she twirled on the runway, holding the dress out to the sides. She looked simply beautiful. Modeling the second dress, Marge was beaming as she walked the runway with a certain confidence. Anna and Ruby both agreed that the ivory color looked fantastic with her beautiful red hair. It was no surprise when Marge returned holding the second dress over her arm.

"The first dress would be nice if our wedding was in a large cathedral, but everything about this dress is perfect. As soon as I felt the satin against my skin, I knew it was the one," Marge said, grinning ear to ear.

After the alterations were taken on Marge's dress, she looked at Anna and said, "Now it's your turn, maid of honor."

"What about your sister, or one of the girls at work?" Anna asked, puzzled.

"No, you're the one I want," Marge said, putting her arms around Anna.

Tears ran down Anna's face as they walked her back to try on the dress that complemented Marge's dress. Anna even persuaded Ruby to pick a dress too.

Anna's bill was nearly twelve thousand dollars, but all three ladies were very happy when they left the shop.

Having worked up an appetite at the dress shop, their next stop was a quaint Italian restaurant two blocks down the street. The ladies thoroughly enjoyed rehashing their time at the bridal shop. Anna could not say enough about how proud she was to be Marge's maid of honor.

"No one has ever asked me to play such an important part in their wedding," Anna said.

"I wore a pants suit when I got married the first time," Marge said.

"I've got both of y'all beat," Ruby said. "My wedding dress came from the clothing drive at my old church!"

It was clear to the women that even if you had all the money in the world, it could not guarantee that a person wouldn't be touched by sadness. The important thing was that they were able to laugh when looking back at the difficult times in their lives.

Next up for the trio was wedding cake shopping. Anna knew a great little bakery that promised samples, but before they ventured off, on orders from her nurse—Ruby—it was time for her medication and oxygen treatment; after all, her health came first.

While Ruby was tending to Anna, Marge went into a stationary store nearby. She had so much gratitude for everything that Anna was doing for her, and she wanted to pick up a nice thank-you card as a token of her appreciation.

After looking through stacks of cards, she finally found the perfect one, depicting a young vibrant woman kissing an elderly woman on the cheek. Inside, it read, *Thank you for loving me.*

Tasty Tiers was everything Anna promised it would be. Beautiful cakes and pastries lined the bakery's shelves, and the aroma that filled the store was divine. An impressive cupcake stood nearly three-feet high, covered in a shiny chocolate ganache with multicolored sprinkles, but the most impressive cake, in Anna's estimation, was a four-tier cake with butter icing and multicolored flowers that looked like they had just been plucked from the garden.

A plump middle-age woman greeted them with a joyful smile. "Welcome, ladies, my name is Beth Peters, and I am the proprietor of Tasty Tiers. Which one of you is Anna Wilson?"

Anna raised her hand. "I am! We spoke on the telephone last week. This is my friend Ruby, and this beautiful young woman is the bride to be."

Beth invited them back to her office to review the catalogues showing the various styles of cakes that were available. Ruby and Anna huddled around Marge as she flipped through the pages of culinary delights. The one thing Marge was certain about was that she wanted a tier cake. She came across a beautiful three-tier white cake with almond cream icing, decorated with dozens of beautiful flowers that looked freshly picked. Ruby and Anna agreed with her choice wholeheartedly.

Things were going even better than expected, as Marge seemed to be making her choices rather easily. Their next stop was the caterer. When they arrived at Mancini's Catering, a plump man with gray hair, who appeared to be in his early sixties, greeted them at the door. "You must be Anna Wilson," he said, remembering Anna from her phone call. "I'm Anthony Mancini, the owner."

Shaking his hand, Anna said, "Guilty as charged."

Winking, he said, "Are you the one who's about to be married?"

The women chuckled at his sense of humor. Anna introduced everyone, and then they got down to business. As they walked through a large commercial size kitchen, Anna saw about a dozen employees working hard to finish what appeared to be a large banquet order. She was very impressed by the efficiency of such a sizable operation.

Once in his office, Anthony said, "What is your budget per guest for this joyous event?"

Without hesitating, Anna said, "There is no budget. I want Marge to order whatever she wants."

"No restraints … you're my kind of lady I'll give you ladies some time alone so you can look through some of these menus and talk about it."

"If this grub is half as good as it looks in these pictures, we sure are at the right place," Ruby said.

With a minimal amount of suggestions from Anna, Marge finally decided on the menu. Marge loved shrimp cocktail, so it was definitely going to be the appetizer. Next, she decided that French onion soup would start the meal. When it came to the main entrée, she was torn between the capon and the chicken cordon bleu. She thought the capons made for a nicer presentation, but the chicken dish sounded more high class. When the final dinner menu was complete, it included shrimp cocktail, French onion soup, chicken cordon bleu, baked potatoes, and fancy green beans, along with a small bowl of fresh fruit. Marge also fell in love with the Georgian china with colorful red flowers; it would make for a beautiful place setting. Once all the paperwork was complete, they bid farewell to Anthony.

The final stop of the day was to a unique little shop called Memorable Printing. They had a great reputation in the Pittsburg area for high-quality wedding invitations. The décor of the store resembled something out of the eighteen hundreds. Brass fixtures and dark oak shelving adorned the walls and ceiling. A short man well into his sixties, with wire-rimmed glasses, appeared at the desk.

"How can I assist you lovely ladies today?"

"My name is Anna Wilson. We spoke on the telephone last week."

"Yes, I remember you inquired about wedding invitations. Welcome to my humble stationery shop. My name is Carl Thomas, and I hope I can be of service to you."

With introductions out of the way, the storeowner excused himself and went into the rear of the shop. He reappeared with a stack of leather albums containing sample-wedding invitations. After placing them gently on the table, he softly tugged at Marge's arm, leading her over to the table. Pulling the chair out for her, he said, "I guess you're the beautiful bride to be."

While Marge was looking at the samples, Anna inquired about the origins of a set of antique pens he had on display. Mr. Thomas seemed to be a quiet man by nature, but when it came to the collectables proudly displayed in his shop, he came alive. The antique pens that intrigued Anna had been in his family since the mid-eighteen hundreds.

In the midst of showing off his various printing devices from the past, Marge cried out, "This is the one! Look at this, Anna, its perfect!"

The eager proprietor stopped talking in mid-conversation and promptly joined Marge at the table. When he looked at Marge's choice, he smiled and said, "You have great taste, young lady. It's such an elegant design." The invitations were ivory parchment, with embossed swirling script done in a brilliant gold leaf finish.

"Those are so beautiful, Marge," Anna said.

"I don't know what the big fuss is all about. Just call the invites up and tell them on the phone!" Ruby said, winking.

Four down, one to go! The weary trio was thankful the florist was merely a block away from the stationery store. Ruby kept a close eye on Anna because she was showing signs of fatigue. Determined not to let another hospital incident occur, she made sure that Anna sat down upon entering the store. A young woman greeted them immediately.

"Welcome to Flowers Forever. My name is Violet Anderson, and I am the floral designer and owner of this shop. In case you are wondering, Violet is my real name. My parents are horticulturists and have an interesting sense of humor."

While Marge was with Violet deciding on floral arrangements, Anna took a moment to reflect on how blessed she felt to be a part of Jack and Marge's big day and how deeply she was touched when Marge unexpectedly asked her to be her maid of honor.

Marge was busy looking at photographs of the floral arrangements Violet had put together for clients who owned large houses. She tried to picture the same floral designs in Anna's house, and finally found the perfect choice. It was subtle and consisted of large bouquets of roses. There was no escaping the sheer elegance of the multicolored roses surrounded by the soft, almost magical, sprigs of baby's breath. The floral arrangements would perfectly complement the yellow and white rose bridal bouquet Marge would carry.

The ride out of the city seemed a lot longer than the trip in. Conversation was light because each of the women had a great deal on their minds. Marge felt a little overwhelmed by the day's activities. Everything was happening so fast, and she was having a difficult time processing it all. Ruby kept a close eye on Anna during the ride home as she thought about the bittersweet aspects of her role in Anna and Robby's lives. Early on, she learned that it was impossible not to have some degree of emotional ties with the patients she cared for. It was already becoming clear to her that letting go of Anna was going to be one of the most difficult things she had ever done. She recalled Lester Jacobs, a former patient who was eighty-five years old, with Alzheimer's disease. Once a robust man weighing two hundred twenty-five pounds, he lost nearly forty pounds because he would routinely forget to eat. Not wanting to put him in a nursing facility, his son hired Ruby as a live-in health care nurse. Ruby remembered how the old man had insisted on walking a dog that had died many years earlier, but she would place the leash in his hands and pretend to walk the dog every afternoon. She also set up birthday parties once a week for his deceased wife. The periods of joy and the dark hours of pain he experienced were never easy to take. When he died of a massive stroke, she secretly wept for her loss. She felt so helpless because keeping people alive was completely out of her control. Now, no matter how well she cared for Anna, the Lord was going to take her in His time.

Anna gazed out the passenger side window as they made their way home. She felt herself drifting into a hypnotic state as the telephone poles and oak trees whizzed by. Thinking too deeply was a dangerous place for her to dwell since finding out about her medical condition. She tried very hard to put on a front that she had accepted her pending demise, but deep down, she desperately wanted to live. She treasured this day with Marge and Ruby, but she was tired and needed to rest.

The absence of chatter made it apparent that the day's activities lay heavy on all of them. Anna held onto Ruby's arm for assistance as they entered the house. Marge needed to return to the office for a couple hours, so she would have to be on her way. She placed the car keys on the table and hugged Anna goodbye. "I don't know how I can ever thank you for all that you're doing for us," she whispered in Anna's ear.

"Just be the woman I know you can be," Anna said, clearly tired.

Marge gave Ruby a gentle hug and thanked her for her time.

As the evening was settling down, Ruby led Anna over to the chairlift and said, "I don't want any trouble out of you. You're going up to bed to rest and take an oxygen treatment."

"You'll get no argument from me," Anna said.

While Anna was taking her treatment, Ruby went down to the kitchen to brew a cup of tea. She was becoming painfully aware that she would have to start restricting Anna's activities, because her health was going to get progressively worse as time went by. Nothing could change that fact, but Ruby had a responsibility to moderate the progression with proper treatment. She did not want Anna to end up in the hospital again.

As Ruby walked into the bedroom carrying the steaming cup of tea, Anna lifted the oxygen mask from her face. "Thank you, dear, you must have read my mind."

After insisting that Anna put the oxygen mask back on her face, Ruby went back to the kitchen and returned with her medication and a glass of water. She stood there for a moment, watching Anna sitting on the edge of the bed, enjoying her cup of tea. As she exited Anna's room, Ruby said, "Time for you to take a relaxing nap. Getting enough rest is very important."

Ruby was surprised when Anna asked her to sit and talk with her a little while. Judging by the tone of her voice, Ruby sensed that she was troubled. She walked over to the bed and sat down close to her.

Following a long silence, Anna said, "For a large part of my life, being alone was what I preferred. Now that I have people in my life to love, that part of me has changed."

Ruby put her arm around Anna and said, "At the risk of sounding like a back woods preacher, life is full of mysteries. Either we can drive ourselves crazy trying to figure them out, or we can accept them for what they are. The Lord expects us to accept certain things on faith, and often times they are the very things we want to understand most."

Anna thought about Ruby's words for a minute. "You've spent a lot of time working in the home health care field. Unfortunately, you have worked closely with many patients who were in the final days of their lives. Can you explain to me how they coped with the fear of death?"

Ruby sat close to Anna and took hold of her hand. "Miss Anna, I know you're scared about what you don't know. I'm not going to tell you that it's normal, because there is no norm when it comes to the way folks deal with death. When you said it was unfortunate that I worked with terminal patients, that couldn't be further from the truth. For this old girl, it was a privilege to comfort and console another human being in the final moments of their earthly life."

Anna was obviously weary from the long day. Ruby removed the empty teacup from her hand and placed it on the nightstand. She gently persuaded Anna to lie back in bed and get some well-needed rest. As she was covering her with a blanket, Anna again asked Ruby to stay and talk with her.

"The sound of your voice gives me a sense of security," Anna said.

Ruby chuckled. "No one has ever told old Ruby *that* before! Of course I will sit with you and talk."

As Anna lay back in bed with her eyes closed, Ruby held her hand softly. "A lot of folks are concerned about two things when their time is near, and in my estimation, both are important. First, they want to be right with the people they love. Knowing you the way I do, you already have that covered. Second, they want to be on the up and up with the Lord. Miss Anna, you are the only one that knows if that is true." She caressed Anna's wrinkled hand for a few minutes, then added, "There is one thing in this world you can count on, Miss Anna. This old girl will be by your side when you are called home."

Mary was trying to keep up with the overwhelming work-load in the office all on her own. It was important that she prove to Marge that she was worthy of her respect and of being her assistant. When she saw Marge walk into her office carrying the samples from her shopping trip, she followed briskly behind her to apologize. "I'm a little behind, but I'll stay late to catch up!" she said, excited and out of breath. "There are several messages by your phone, and the one from Stan Logan's office seems important." As she turned to leave Marge's office, she stopped and said, "How was the shopping trip today?"

"Sit down and relax, Mary. You did a great job today."

As the two women enjoyed a break from their workload, Marge filled Mary in on all the details of the shopping trip.

When Robby and Billy got off the school bus, Billy said, "Can I come over to your house to play for a while?"

"Sure, as long as we stay out of Ruby's hair. Are you sure you don't have to go home first?"

"Nah, I'll call from your house."

Knowing his best friend the way he did, Robby got the impression that he was avoiding going home. Confidential conversations he and Anna had about Helen's drinking led him to believe that *that* might be the real reason. Concerned about his friend, Robby approached the subject cautiously. "Is everything all right at home now that your dad's back?"

Billy looked down at the sidewalk and hesitated. Robby expected him to remark about his mother's drinking, but it was something completely different.

Obviously embarrassed, Billy said, "You have to swear to God that you won't tell anybody!"

"I swear."

"My mom and dad have been spending hours in the bedroom almost every day, and I can hear weird noises coming from the room. I'm pretty sure they are having sex."

Robby started laughing. Billy seemed upset at first, but he couldn't refrain from laughing too. Trying to make his friend feel more comfortable, Robby told Billy that when he was with his parents, he could hear them doing it too.

As the boys entered the house, Ruby appeared from the kitchen holding her index finger up to her lips. In a very low, but stern voice, she told them to keep their voices down, as Anna was sleeping. Quietly, they set their backpacks down and took in the aroma of the meatloaf cooking in the oven. Ruby sensed they were hungry, so she fixed them each a sandwich and poured them each a glass of milk. Upon their request, Ruby also called Helen and got her permission for Billy to stay and play a while.

While they were playing with model cars on the bed, Robby wondered how Helen was doing with her drinking problem, and said, "When you told me about the sex today, I thought you were going to say something else."

"I know what you were thinking, and I don't blame you. My mom hasn't been drinking at all, and there's a woman that picks her up and takes her to some kind of meetings. I don't know what the meetings are, but they sure are helping."

Knowing that Billy's mom was doing better made Robby happy.

chapter ············
···· twenty-three

In the weeks prior to the wedding, Anna's health was declining. She had good days, but there were also periods when she could not get out of bed. During the difficult times, Robby would often stand by her bed with fear in his eyes and love in his heart. He began sleeping with his bedroom door wide open, and Ruby could hear him check on Anna in the middle of the night. The diligent health care worker had taken over all the responsibilities of running the household. She was secretly afraid that Anna might not make it to the six months the doctor gave her. Even though she knew there were no guarantees, she desperately wanted Anna to have the six months the doctor offered. Ruby marveled that Anna seemed to be the calmest member of the household. She was now Anna's constant companion, and Robby was always waiting for the other shoe to drop. He had gotten to the point where he was trying to draw on Ruby for emotional strength in a way that he never had done before.

Marge's mind was obviously elsewhere when Jack came into her office unannounced. He attempted to interject some humor when he said, "Aren't you going to give me hell for not knocking?" She feigned her enthusiasm. "Sorry, Jack, I'll give you twice as much next time." In recent days, she had been a frequent visitor to the Wilson house. Disguising the visits as conferences to iron out the details of the wedding, she was really checking on the state of Anna's health.

Ruby used the vast knowledge she acquired over the years and came up with a new approach to Anna's health situation. She instituted a plan when Robby came down for dinner and had offered to take Anna's plate up to her room. "You go upstairs and tell Anna to take an oxygen treatment and then join us for supper."

"But, Ruby, she's too sick to come down."

"Now you mind what I'm telling you, boy, and don't treat her like she's dying," Ruby said determinedly.

Robby's feelings were hurt by Ruby's tone, but he did exactly what he was told.

Ruby's deep voice echoed up the stairs, yelling, "Supper is on the table, and don't forget to wash your hands!"

Robby thought about boycotting dinner, but he was hungry, and Ruby had made her famous fried chicken. When he sat down at the table across from Ruby, the teapot began to whistle. He started to get up to turn off the stove, but she motioned for him to sit back down. Ruby smiled when she heard the sound of the chairlift descending the stairs. She immediately turned the water off and placed a freshly brewed cup of tea at Anna's place setting. All eyes were on Anna as she turned the corner into the kitchen.

"Ruby's fried chicken … this is my favorite," Anna said, smiling.

As Ruby cleared the table after dinner, she brought up the subject of the wedding. Doing so, she noticed an uplifting tone in Anna's voice.

"Maybe we should see if Marge can go down to the dress shop with us to pick up the dresses the day after tomorrow?" Anna said.

"I'm up for another trip to the big city!" Ruby said.

Ruby said nothing as Anna went back upstairs. She secretly hoped that she would have stayed out of bed longer, but she didn't press the issue. When she finished with the dinner cleanup, she walked out of the kitchen and was shocked to see Anna standing there, fully dressed.

"Ruby, would you mind going for a walk with me? I already told Robby we were going, so I hope you will join me."

Ruby was a little surprised by the request, but said, "Lord knows I need the exercise, so sure I'll join you!"

As they were heading out the door, Robby ran down the steps, giggling.

"What's tickled your funny bone?" Ruby said.

"I can't believe you two old ladies are going walking!" Anna pointed up to Robby's bedroom and said, "Young man, you have homework waiting for you in your room."

It was a beautiful fall day, with a cool breeze in the air. Ruby and Anna made their way down the sidewalk parallel to the park, marveling at the brilliant fall blooms and the fiery red leaves of the randomly placed burning bush shrubs.

"Have you lived here all of your life, Anna?" Ruby asked, interrupting their quiet walk.

"My father had the house built shortly after I was born," Anna said with a faraway look in her eye. "There were only two other houses on the street when the construction of ours was completed. I can still remember playing in the fields of wild flowers on both sides of the property. Even though I taught upstate for several years, I always ended up back in the house. It was as though it beckoned me to come home."

"Once I got hitched, we couldn't get out of that backwater town fast enough. I was only back one time, and that was to see to my mama's funeral."

The two women had walked a few blocks when Ruby suggested, "Miss Anna, maybe we should start back."

Smiling, Anna said, "No need to worry, I feel fine."

Laughing, Ruby said, "Heck, I wasn't worried about you!"

They crossed the street and headed back along Highland Park.

"My father was a very busy man, but he always made time to take me for leisurely walks," Anna said. "He tried to make up for the kindness that my mother lacked. She was not a bad person, but she just had a difficult time finding room inside herself for anyone else but her."

When they got home, Robby was there to greet them on the porch. "My homework is done! Can I watch television for a while?"

Pulling him against her waist, Anna said, "That's fine with me, but not for too long."

Ruby signaled to Anna that it was time for her to take her medication and oxygen treatment. As she went upstairs for some well-needed rest, she felt a calm come over her.

When Ruby looked in on Anna later, she found her fast asleep. She turned off the light and went back downstairs to watch television with Robby. She fixed a big bowl of pop-corn for them both to share over an episode of the *Lone Ranger.*

❧ ☙ ❧ ☙

After tucking Robby safely into bed, Ruby tidied up the kitchen before calling it a night. Before going up to her room, she called her son. "How's my boy doing?"

"Is everything okay, Mama? I wasn't expecting you to call."

"Your old mama's just fine. I missed you on Sunday and wanted to hear your voice."

Mother and son enjoyed talking for a while about school and matters of the heart Every time one of her sons said they loved her, it filled Ruby's heart with such joy.

❧ ☙ ❧ ☙

While rushing around to get ready for work, Marge reminded Jack that he had an appointment at the tuxedo shop after work. As she gave Joel the once over and sent him off to school, she informed him that Jack was taking him and Robby to be fitted for a tuxedo. Once she squashed his objections, she kissed him on the cheek and he was on his way. Gulping down a cup of coffee while putting on her makeup, she said, "Don't screw this up, Porter; it's very important to me!"

During the ride to work, Jack said, "Can I ask you why you are forcing the boys to wear tuxes?"

"Anna and I want everything to be perfect. If dressing those boys up like little monkeys is part of being perfect, then that's the way it's going to be," Marge said a little defensively.

Considering how much he loved both women, Jack figured that putting aside his petty complaints was a very small price to pay for a lifetime of happiness.

When waiting for the traffic light to turn green, Marge said, "I forgot to tell you something else about the wedding."

"Red, I'm not wearing a crazy looking hat!" Jack teased.

They both laughed at Jack's remark.

"In place of a gift registry, I'm going to suggest a list of organizations that guests can make a donation to in our name. I think it is a very small gesture of gratitude for everything that we have received in our lives."

Jack was going to ask who came up with the idea, but instead said, "You know what, Red, I think that's a noble idea."

Marge laughed. "I never thought I would hear my name in the same sentence with noble!"

Anna was up early following a good night's rest. As she looked at the notepad on the kitchen table and waited patiently for the teapot to whistle, she realized that she neglected to contact a photographer for the wedding. She made a note to herself. Her quiet solitude was short-lived, as Ruby came into the kitchen and went straight for the coffee machine.

"You're up bright and early this morning," she said.

"Probably because there is still much to do for the wedding," Anna said.

"It is a big event, but I know you will pull it off," Ruby said while preparing breakfast.

As Robby came running down the steps, he blurted out a quick "good morning" to everyone, and then sat down to his oatmeal and cinnamon toast.

After getting Robby off to school, Ruby and Anna took advantage of the quiet and enjoyed a little conversation with their tea and coffee.

"I talked to my youngest last night," Ruby said.

"How's everything going with him?"

"School's fine; he's such a bright young man. His girl-friend is doing well. I just needed to hear his voice. I'm so proud of all three of my sons, and I miss having them underfoot."

"Ruby, I think not having children is one of my biggest regrets."

"Miss Anna, that little boy who just went off to school thinks of you as his mama."

Believing what Ruby said brought joy to Anna's heart.

When they arrived at the office, Marge made it a point to free up some time to call Anna. The big day was closing in, and she found herself thinking more and more about the details. By all outward appearances, everything in her life seemed to be perfect, but she still felt some measure of uncertainty. She could not be sure, but thought it had something to do with the upcoming transition into Anna's home. In the blink of an eye, every member of the new household would be entering uncharted territory. Joel and Robby would become brothers. Enrolling Joel into a different school would be stressful. The transition from apartment living to the responsibilities of a large house was something she knew nothing about. The fears she was experiencing were very real to her. Talking to Anna about such emotionally sensitive matters was out of the question. Offending her abundance of generosity could break both of their hearts. Discussing her feelings with Jack would invite comments that are simplistic at best. She could almost hear him saying, "You'll get over it, Red. Don't look a gift horse in the mouth, Red." Then she looked around the beautiful office, with her name on the door, and said to herself with a smile, *Don't worry, Red, you'll get over it.*

Marge was pleased when Anna answered the telephone on the first ring, "Good morning, Anna, I hope I'm not disturbing you."

"Of course not, dear. Actually, I was going to call you."

"I wanted to remind you that Jack will be taking the boys to be fitted for their tuxedos today after work. If Stan can get away from the office, he will be with them; otherwise, he'll go on another day."

Anna laughed. "I can't wait to see our little men in their cute tuxedos. Do you mind if I hire a photographer?"

"Of course I don't mind, I'm glad you thought of it."

Reviewing her notes,, Anna said, "I just have a couple more things to go over with you. If you don't mind, I'll check into the availability of a local pastor to perform the service. If you have any preferences, let me know. We will need to give him a nice envelope for his services."

"That would be great. Do whatever you think is best."

"I'm sure you and Jack have been fitted for your wedding bands, but you might want to pick up a small gift for the people in the wedding."

Marge wrote herself a note about the wedding bands because she had forgotten all about them. Realizing that none of the storybook wedding could have been possible without Anna's help, she said, "Thank you for everything you've done for us! I love you and wish you had been my mother."

Teary eyed, Anna said, "It gives me great joy to be an important part of your life. Dear, I've come to learn over the years that we are tied together no matter what walk of life we come from or what trials we have endured."

As she hung up the phone, Marge began to cry. She was full of emotion, and she felt guilty about the petty concerns she had earlier. Motivated by her conversation with Anna, she walked straight over to Jack's office. "Do you have a lunch appointment today, Jack?"

"No, I thought we could go to Mario's."

"Think again; we are going to the jewelry store to order our wedding bands and gifts for the people in the wedding. I'm not sure what the gifts will be yet, but they will be elegant."

Jack sensed that Marge needed to get that stuff off her chest, so he gave her some space before adding, "I spoke with Stan Logan this morning and he has a late meeting today. He assured me that he would go to the tuxedo shop tomorrow."

"I need to get back to work, but I'll meet you here at lunchtime."

❧ ❧ ❧ ❧

Once Anna secured the services of a photographer, her attention shifted to hiring a pastor for the wedding. It had been a great many years since she was a member of a church. When her parents were alive, it was mandatory to attend mass at St. John's every Sunday. When Anna went off to college, she made the decision not to attend church any longer.

When Ruby returned to the kitchen, Anna said, "How does a heathen like me go about hiring a man of God to preside over the wedding?"

"Most times, folks would ask the pastor of the church they belong to, but it appears that none of you people go to church."

Laughing, Anna said, "That's a terrible thing to say, Ruby, but it's the truth! Listen, I hate to ask, Ruby, but do you think the pastor from your church would consider performing the ceremony?"

Ruby was both surprised and amused at Anna's request. "You realize he is black," she said.

"I don't have a problem with that."

"I will see if he's available, and you make sure that everyone involved is okay with it," Ruby said. As she walked out of the kitchen she declared, "This is turning into one wild wedding!"

Anna had a lot to think about regarding the big event. She didn't think anyone would object to a man of color performing the ceremony. There was no doubt in her mind that some would hold private prejudices, but that would be a mountain they would have to climb on their own. What bothered Anna the most was what Ruby said about their lack of church attendance. Anna was disappointed in herself for overlooking the fact that Robby needed an opportunity to know the Lord. She had a great deal of both soul searching ahead and decisions to make, with very little time for either.

❧❧❧

As Marge searched for a parking space near the jeweler's, Jack said, "I'm starving. Can't we do this tomorrow?"

"Listen, Jack, we are taking care of this today!" Marge said seriously. "When we're finished, there will plenty of time to eat. It really ticks me off that you're complaining. I haven't asked you to do anything throughout this whole process."

It was evident to Jack that Marge was stressing out over everything that was happening in their lives. "You're, right Red, I'm sorry for acting so childish and will help out any way I can."

Marge remained quiet until she finally found a place to park. As she and Jack strolled toward the jewelry store, Marge turned to Jack and said, "Since you're so willing to help now, I have decided to give two top of the line bicycles to Robby and Joel for participating in the wedding. It would be very helpful if you picked them up and hid them in the garage at Anna's house."

Of course, Jack agreed, but he would have said just about anything to fend off Marge's Irish temper.

Jack smiled as Marge got back into the spirit of things. As she rattled off ideas about gifts for the wedding party, he chuckled to himself that they could not have been a more diverse group of people. Choosing just the right gift for everyone would not be an easy task, but there was no doubt in his mind that Marge would be up to the task. The responsibility connected with the union was slowly starting to sink in. Anna showered Jack and Marge with a great many blessings, but along with them came more responsibility than Jack could ever imagine.

Instantly becoming a father of two young boys had not been part of Jack's long-term plan. Operating a thriving law practice with a new life partner promised to be a challenge in itself. Prior to crossing paths with Anna, he was not one to buy into the notion of fate. The chain of events that unfolded made it difficult for him to deny that some force beyond his understanding was in control of the situation. He tried not to look too deeply into matters not under his power, but during those quiet times, when his soul reached out to his mind, he saw the connections. The ties that bound a lonely old woman to an abandoned boy released the unbreakable chain. Robby soon became the ray of light to lead Anna out of the solitude that was smothering the dwindling years of her life.

Jack was struggling to reestablish his career when Anna wandered into his office for help. In his mind, she was a check that would clear the bank. He had no way of knowing the extent of her wealth or if it would ever benefit him. Marge had noticed something special about her. She was a little more sympathetic because she had a young son at home. Once Jack demonstrated his degree of legal skills, Robby went into Anna's custody. From that point on, Jack and Marge were the recipients of her total trust and gratitude.

When Jack and Anna had found the perfect gold wedding bands, the jeweler showed them possible gifts for the

members of the wedding party. There was only one suggestion that Marge thought was appropriate: a gold Cartier
pen set for Stan Logan.

There was very little about the wedding that was typical
of the usual etiquette of such ceremonies, and the partici-
pants in this one were colorful, to say the least. Anna was
the most difficult to buy for, mainly because she had such
little time left. All the items the jeweler suggested seemed
so frivolous considering all she had done for them. After
scouring the glass showcases for the perfect gift, she finally
discovered exactly what she was looking for. An elegant
gold infinity necklace called out to her. It was heavy enough
to be substantial, but delicate enough to project elegance.
To Marge, the beauty of the piece was secondary to the
symbolic meaning behind it. Anna would wear the infinity
symbol close to her heart for the remaining days in her life
and into the realm of the next world. Its brilliance would be
a constant reminder of the ties that bind her to the people
whose lives she touched the most.

Ruby's gift was proving to be more challenging than
Marge anticipated. The tough black nurse had become a
very important part of Anna's life when she needed her
most. It was important that Marge give her a substantial
gift from the heart. She would not present her with a trin-
ket that would find its way into a dark drawer.

As they concluded their business at the jewelry store,
it was obvious to Marge that Jack was hungry. "Come on,
Porter; there must be a place around here to get a bite to
eat." As they walked to the nearest sandwich shop, Marge
added, "What do you think about my gift ideas?"

"Is this a trick question, Red?"

❧ ❧ ❧ ❧

The emotional ties that Ruby and Anna shared had already surpassed that of a normal relationship between nurse and patient. As each day passed, she became more and more like a member of the family. There would be nothing wrong with the situation if Anna had a chance to recover. Ruby had been down this slippery slope before and it always ended the same. She repeatedly told herself that she was merely doing her job, but deep down inside, she knew she gave so much more. Those she cared for carried a part of her with themselves into the next world. Even though she told herself it was part of the job, the pain that accompanied the ultimate end remained the same. The occasional well-intended greeting cards from the families of the deceased brought back the heart wrenching memories of the past.

Ruby had secretly decided to retire when her time with Anna was over. Initially, thoughts of retirement included spending time with her sons, but she knew that could only be short-lived. They had their own lives, and she never wanted to be a burden to them. She was very proud of her youngest son and his accomplishments thus far in life. It would not be long before he would venture out on his own. Like his brothers before him, he would finish college, start a career, and marry the girl he loved. Once out of the nest, her son would no longer belong to her. The thought of spending her free time volunteering at the church brought joy to her, but as much as she loved the Lord and the church, she knew that too much of a good thing could fuel resentments. The one thing she was sure of was that she would not allow herself to wither up and die, as many people did in the name of retirement.

Ruby went into Anna's bedroom when she noticed her getting dressed for the day. "Are we going somewhere this morning, Miss Anna?"

Without giving away too many details, Anna said, "Yes, I hope you don't mind."

"No, I don't mind at all, just give me a few minutes to get ready."

Anna waited downstairs holding the keys to the car with a mischievous grin on her face. Once Ruby joined her, they got into the car and headed to a destination unknown. After driving several miles, Anna mysteriously turned into a large vacant parking lot of an abandoned strip mall.

At first, Ruby thought Anna had taken leave of her senses, but it was soon apparent what was going on.

As Anna turned to get out of the vehicle, she said, "Switch seats with me!" Ruby tried to object, but Anna pressed on. "We can sit here all day long if that's what it takes."

Knowing that Anna would not buckle on the matter, Ruby got into the driver's seat. "If I smash up this new Mercedes, this old girl's not paying for any of the repairs."

Anna went over the basics with her new pupil and encouraged her to embark on her maiden drive. Once Ruby turned on the ignition, Anna told her to place her foot on the brake and put the transmission in drive. She then explained to her to put her foot on the gas and put pressure on it. Ruby followed her instructions, but gave the car a little too much gas. When the vehicle shot forward across the parking lot, Ruby cried out, "I told you I can't drive!" Anna calmly replied, "Back your foot off of the gas pedal and gently apply the brake." After the car jerked severely when she pushed down on the brake, it came to a stop. With each drive around the parking lot, Ruby became more confident in her abilities. Far from a skilled driver, she was quickly learning the basics. Later that afternoon, they drove down to the Bureau of Motor Vehicles so Ruby could get her learner's permit. Anna could sense Ruby's excitement at having the opportunity to learn how to drive. What started out as a stressful endeavor was quickly turning into an enjoyable outing for two good friends.

With no prompting from Anna, Ruby began studying the instruction book for the written part of the test. She kept her new pursuit a secret from Robby to avoid the endless barrage of inquiries. A small part of her did not want him to find out if she failed to get her driver's license. In the days that followed, Anna would take Ruby out to practice her driving skills. Eventually, they moved from the vacant parking lot to driving on the back streets in the neighborhood. When the day arrived when she drove in traffic and on the main streets, she glowed with pride for a job well done. Occasionally, she would ask Anna to explain certain terminology out of the book, but for the most part, she took on the challenge herself.

Marge and Jack picked up Joel on their way to Anna's house. While the boys were at their tuxedo appointment, Marge wanted to ask Anna for input about the gifts she had purchased for those participating in the wedding.

As Jack gathered up the boys to head out, he promised them ice cream if everything went smoothly. He was not always the most diplomatic person when it came to family matters, but he knew what the priorities of a young boy were.

Robby and Joel were initially a little standoffish toward each other, but Jack paid them no mind and treated them as though they were old friends. Both boys were aware of what was going to happen when Anna passed away, but there were territorial issues on each side that would need to be resolved. When Robby was thrust into a new world following his mother's death and his father's imprisonment, he clung to Anna for security. The old house had become a haven from the ills of the outside world and, more important, his new home. Losing the woman who rescued him was going to be one of the most difficult things he would have to face. When Anna was gone and Ruby had no reason to stay, his emotional stability would be very fragile.

Joel had to deal with a very different situation, but it contained many of the same emotional variables. He enjoyed Jack's presence in his life and appreciated that he treated his mom with respect. Once they were married, he was secretly concerned that Jack would demand more of his mom's already limited time. He loved his mother dearly and made it a point not to complain. Aunt Trish did her best at filling in when he stayed with her, but it was not the same. Trish went out of her way to explain to him that his mother was trying to give him a better life. He'd always said, "I know," but was not sure what she meant by a better life." There were not enough hours in the day for his mom to get involved in many after-school activities. Another concern of his was what effect another child his age was going to have on him. He wondered if the two of them would share her time. Joel's greatest fear was that the new people thrust into his life would not leave any time for his mother.

When the threesome headed for the vehicle, Joel immediately jumped into the front seat of his mother's car. Jack smiled as he witnessed the territorial issue being resolved the old-fashioned way. Once the men in her life were safely on their way to the tuxedo store, Marge joined Anna in the kitchen. While they waited for Ruby to join them, Marge said, "What should I give Ruby for helping with the wedding? I was thinking about a gift certificate."

"No, I think you should buy her a very nice keychain."

Marge was puzzled, because she knew Ruby didn't own a car or drive, but before she could question Anna's suggestion, Ruby returned to the kitchen.

It didn't take long for the three women to start talking about the status of the wedding preparations.
Anna pulled out her notepad and said, "What style of wedding bands did you and Jack agree on?"

"We got plain gold bands. I wish everything would have been that simple."

"Damn, girl, any band would look plain next to the rock you're wearing!" Ruby said. Then, looking over at Anna she said, "Look, her face is almost as red as her hair!"

This made everyone laugh.

"The first order of business is simple," Anna said. "We needed a photographer, so I found one that comes highly recommended and is available on the fifteenth. He is coming over later this week to check out the surroundings. The young man said something about checking the shadows and natural lighting."

When Anna next announced she had located a pastor to perform the ceremony, Marge's eyes lit up with excitement. Ruby looked down at the table and began to chuckle, but she stopped when she felt Anna sending a cross look in her direction.

"It's a challenge to find a man of the cloth to perform a ceremony if you're not a member of the church," Anna began, "but Ruby was kind enough to ask Pastor Charles, who presides over her congregation, if he would be willing to accommodate our needs. I am pleased to report that he agreed to help us out. You and Jack will need to go down to the church with Ruby to meet Pastor Charles a week before the wedding."

Marge was obviously relieved that Anna took care of the arrangements for such an important part of the wedding. The bride-to-be was never a church member, but she liked to think she believed in God.

Ruby's impatience was growing as she waited for Anna to address the elephant in the room. When Anna indicated she was ready to move on to other matters, Ruby interrupted her. "Miss Anna, if you do not tell this child right this minute, I will!"

Marge glanced around the table with a confused look on her face. "What is Ruby talking about, Anna?"

Anna was silent for a few moments, and then said, "I guess Ruby is referring to the fact that Pastor Charles is a black man. I didn't think it would matter, so I didn't mention it." Anna sensed that Ruby was staring her down.

Following what seemed to be a long pause, Marge said, "That's fine with me."

The tension in the kitchen dissolved as Marge turned the discussion to the boys' gifts. "I realize that buying Joel and Robby new bicycles is a bit unconventional, but I'm looking at the situation long term."

Anna smiled and took hold of Marge's hand. "What better way to encourage the boys to become friends than riding side by side on their shiny new bicycles."

"My boys seemed a lot closer after they were scraping around in the dirt," Ruby chimed in.

Marge was pleased that Anna understood her reasoning behind the bikes.

As Marge refilled the coffee cups and brewed Anna another cup of tea, Anna brought up the idea of a honeymoon. "I'm sure you remember my asking if you and Jack could get away from the office for a few days. Well, have you had any success with it yet?"

"I'm happy to report that Jack has been able to clear his calendar, and I have been working with my assistant, Mary, to take the reins while we are away."

"It warms my heart when a plan comes together," Anna said. "I'm certain that the people you hired are capable of handling the duties in the office."

Ruby could not stand the suspense any longer, and said, "Are you going to tell us where you are sending these young people on their honeymoon?"

Grinning from ear to ear, Anna said "Well, I hope you and Jack like Martha's Vineyard, because you're going there for four days. I made reservations at Thorn Croft Inn, which is directly on the beach. I thought it would be a quiet place for you to spend some quality time together."

Marge stood up and wrapped her arms around Anna. As tears welled in her eyes, she said, "Thank you. I love you, Anna."

"I expect you to bring me back some photographs of the rich and famous folks you rub elbows with," Ruby said, injecting some lightheartedness. She added, "Joel can stay here while you're gone. It will give him and Robby a chance to try out those newfangled bicycles you're buying them."

Marge's heart was bursting with joy as she thought about all the things the people around her were doing for her.

❧ ❧ ❧ ❧

While Jack checked in with the sales clerk at the tuxedo shop, Joel and Robby walked around the store giggling at the various outfits on display. Pink frilly shirts, shiny leather shoes, top hats, and tails were among the items they found funny. The boys genuinely seemed to be enjoying each other's company. A few minutes into their adventure, Jack got their attention.

"Boys, come over here by the counter."

As Robby and Joel went over to Jack, they saw three dark brown suits with almond colored shirts dangling from hangers. Resting on the floor next to each tuxedo was a pair of glossy leather shoes with a bow tie draped across them.

"Boys, we have to try these on so this gentleman can make the adjustments needed," Jack said.

"I don't want this color," Joel said. "Can I wear a white one?"

With all the patience he could muster, Jack said, "Listen, Joel … no, listen both of you; these are the monkey suits we have to wear. Marge picked them out and none of us has the power to change it. If you do what the man tells you and there are no problems, we will stop for ice cream on the way home."

They agreed to the conditions, but as soon as Jack went into the fitting room, Robby and Joel started laughing about the monkey suits.

When the minor alterations were set for Jack's outfit, the clerk went through the same process with the boys. Neither one of them had ever put on a tuxedo before, which led to numerous schoolyard remarks. Once the fitting was complete and the youthful shenanigans held to a minimum, they were ready to wrap it up. While finishing the paperwork, the clerk inquired about Stan Logan's appointment. Jack informed him that he would be in the following day. As Jack anticipated, his youthful companions were reminding him about the earlier promise of ice cream before they were out of the store. Attempting to get into the spirit of things, Jack said, "Dairy Delight sounds good to me! I don't know about you guys, but I'm having a banana split."

The boys looked at each other with excitement in their eyes about Jack's choice.

As quickly as the car doors slammed, the boys raced ahead of Jack into the large cone shaped building. Jack laughed as he did his best to catch up with the excited youngsters. Their eyes sparkled while gazing at the various frozen treats pictured on the wall behind the counter. A less than enthusiastic high school student greeted them from behind the register. Jack ordered his banana split, and both boys ordered hot fudge sundaes. Excitement danced in the air as they carefully carried their cold treats to the table. Jack placed a pile of napkins in front of the youngsters and as he slid a spoonful of soft ice cream into his mouth. He instructed them not to make a mess. When a drop of chocolate syrup dripped onto Jack's tie, the boys could not hold back their laughter. Initially, he was embarrassed, as he quickly wiped it with a napkin, but unable to ignore the irony, he laughed right along with them. While enjoying the company of the boys, Jack witnessed the two of them showing signs of a growing friendship. It did not matter to him if he was the catalyst. In time, they would learn that sticking together would be their best chance for success.

As they were closing in on the bottom of the plastic ice cream boats, the boys had questions for Jack.

"Will you and Marge be my parents when Anna dies?" Robby asked.

After spending a few moments thinking about Robby's question, Jack said, "We will take over the role of your parents in many ways, but no one can ever replace them."

Robby and Joel seemed satisfied with Jack's answer.

"Did you know Anna said I could have the old Cadillac?" Robby added.

"If that's what Anna told you, then I'm sure she will leave you the car."

"She also told me I could drive it around the neighborhood until I get my license," Robby said, grinning mischievously.

"That will never happen on my watch, buster!"

Turning serious, Joel said, "Do you believe in spanking?"

"Normally no, but for you two, I'll make an exception," Jack teased.

Hearts were lighter and everyone's sense of humor was on point as they headed back to Anna's. Due to the large amounts of sugar they had consumed, everything said in the car sent the boys into an uncontrollable state of laughter. At first, Jack just shook his head in disbelief, but he soon joined the fun. One of his biggest concerns about the upcoming domestic changes in his life was whether he had what it took to be a good parent. He was not a hundred percent sure that he could be a good husband, but he was confident that Marge would teach him. Obviously, Anna believed in him or she would not be turning Robby's future over to him. Spending the evening with Robby and Joel helped ease his concerns.

Anna interrupted the humorous interaction between Ruby and Marge and said, "Well, young lady, everything is set up for your big day. If you are half as excited as I am, the butterflies must be fluttering in your stomach."

"This is the first real wedding I ever had. Do not tell Jack, but I am very excited about the upcoming day. If it wasn't for you, Anna, none of this would have ever happened."

"Don't sell yourself short, Marge. You and Jack would have eventually accomplished this on your own. Whether you realize it or not, you are destined to do great things in your lives. That much was clear to me from the very first day we met."

"Anna, you talk about accomplishing great things as though it's tangible. How does a person know if they are on the right path to foster greatness in their lives?"

"My belief is that if we search for greatness, it will remain elusive, but when situations present themselves, we must seize the opportunities."

Pondering what Anna said made Marge sad. Even though she did not understand everything Anna said, she believed in her heart that it would someday reveal itself to her. Her sudden state of melancholy was a direct result of anticipating Anna's departure from her world. Anna was the closest thing to a mother figure that she had ever known. The bittersweet outcome of the situation promised to take Anna away while there were so many unanswered questions. Many of the things Anna brought to the table were things that Marge dreamed of all of her life. Once she departed from this earthly world, Marge would have to draw on the limited time they spent together for solace.

⁊ ℘ ⁊ ℘

The sound of boys laughing and carrying on as they came through the front door prompted Ruby to say, "It sounds like the boys have been up to no good!"

"I think you're right Ruby," Marge said," and I'm sure Jack is somehow in the middle of it."

Racing into the kitchen, Robby said, "Anna, can I take Joel out and show him my car?"

"I guess so, but no driving around the neighborhood," Anna said, teasing.

Once the boys were outside, Jack filled the girls in on what Robby had said about the Cadillac.

"Everything he said was true except for the part about driving before he is sixteen," Anna said, laughing.

"Jack, how did the boys do at the tuxedo fitting?" Ruby asked.

"They did great, but I sort of bribed them with a trip to Dairy Delight."

"You're learning fast young man," Ruby said, as they all laughed.

After Jack, Marge, and Joel left, Ruby ushered Robby upstairs to get ready for bed in the midst of his endless chatter about the events of the night. Cleaning up the kitchen a bit, Ruby said, "Let's go, old woman, it's time for your medication and a treatment."

Anna was not experiencing any pain, but she was physically weak and emotionally drained. The big event would unfold in one week, her first-ever wedding ceremony. As important as it was, the inevitable continued to weigh heavily on her mind. Each day seemed to pass so quickly, and she felt a little more of life's precious energies leaving her body. She was beginning to feel a dull but constant fear of the unknown.

Ruby sat down on the bed next to Anna as she rested before falling asleep. Anna wore a smile on her face, but the sadness in her eyes was unmistakable. Years of experience in the health care field taught Ruby that death comes in stages. Anna's stamina was progressively declining. If she spent more than a few hours without oxygen, she became very fatigued. She had seen it time after, time, and she knew that Anna was coming to the realization that the grim reaper would soon be near. When Anna finally fell into a deep sleep, Ruby gently kissed her on the forehead and turned off the light.

Anna found herself drifting among the clouds. The sky was a brilliant blue, with fluffy pure white formations drifting about. At first, she was frightened, but as she floated effortlessly through the animal shaped clouds, her fear subsided. Some took on the shape of rabbits, while others looked like little puppies. The euphoria she experienced was like nothing she had ever imagined. Her heart felt a new freedom, and she did not have a care in the world. As she pushed her arm into the rabbit's furry coat, she realized the appendage was not her own. At that point, she looked down at her body and saw that she was young again. She laughed hysterically and began to do summersaults through the drifting clouds. While enjoying the playful antics, she heard a strong, but kind, voice announce, "Don't let fear be your master! You will come home to your Father soon."

When Anna awakened from the dream, she looked around the dark room until her eyes rested on the rays of the moon peeking through the bedroom window. She ran her fingers over her face to see if she possessed the youth of her dream. The same wrinkles remained and the once chestnut brown hair had lost its color. Disappointed that it was only a dream, she began to weep. Anna wept for her lost youth and the loved ones she was leaving in the wake of her death. She mourned the loss of Robby's smile and watching him grow into the man she knew he would be. When the sadness left her, she closed her eyes, hoping she could return to soaring through the clouds. The hope of returning to the dream did not happen, but sweet slumber found her just the same.

The morning delivered Anna a pleasant sense of serenity. *Don't let fear be your master! You will come home to your Father soon* were the first words that echoed through her mind. She sat up in bed and thought fondly about the details of the dream. When pondering the words she heard, she thought long and hard as to whether they originated from her deceased father or from her spiritual Father. The deep-rooted fears concerning her impending death suddenly lightened. Whether or not the dream was a literal depiction of the afterlife mattered not to her; the important part of it was the peace it brought to her soul.

Ruby was out of bed early, as usual. As she fussed about the kitchen, Robby suddenly appeared in the archway, sleepy eyed. "Are you trying to stop my heart, boy!" She cried.

"I'm sorry, Ruby. When I woke up early, I decided to come down to see what you and Anna were doing."

"Don't disturb Anna. I want to let her get a little extra rest. All this wedding excitement is starting to wear her down."

"I promise not to bother her."

Feeling as though she was a little hard on Robby, Ruby said, "Come sit with me in the kitchen and I'll fix you some breakfast."

Ruby and Robby talked about the upcoming changes in his life while eating breakfast. When she asked him what he thought about living with Jack and Marge, he said, "I like them just fine, and they helped Anna to bring me into her life. I love Anna, and if there was anything I could do to save her life, I would."

"They are good people and will do their best to look out for you. Besides, I think you're going to have a good friend in Joel."

"Do you know what else I wish would happen?" Robby said.

"No, what's that, Robby?"

"I wish you could stay here and take care of me after Anna's gone."

Robby's request touched Ruby's heart, but she remained silent on the matter. Instead, she just told him to go upstairs and get ready for school.

Ruby thought about Robby's request as she brewed a cup of tea to take upstairs for Anna. As she looked at the overall picture of her current life, she had a very lonely home waiting her once her time with Anna was over. Even though she loved her sons and was proud of all that they had accomplished, they had their own lives. Now that they were adults, they could never be the center of her life again. For Ruby, retirement was an abstract joy that seemed much better in thought than in reality. Most likely, she would just move on to another home health care job before she spent her days volunteering at the church. Slippers and afternoon soap operas were not her style. In the back of her mind, she thought about Robby's request and secretly wished that she could stay on once Anna was gone.

Ruby tapped on Anna's bedroom door and was surprised when she heard, "Enter at your own risk!" Ruby smiled as she walked in, carrying the hot cup of tea. Anna was already dressed for the day and had made the bed. She was sitting on the bed with a book of short stories by poet Kahlil Gibran next to her. The outside cover had seen better days, and the pages were yellowing, but the book remained precious to Anna. Once an avid reader, recent events made it difficult for her to keep her mind on a story line. Ruby thought about scolding her for exerting herself while making the bed, but thought better of it when seeing how chipper she was.

When Robby heard Ruby and Anna chatting in the bedroom, he came running in, first asking for lunch money, and then giving Anna a hug. He noticed the small book on the bed and said, "What are you reading?"

"It's a book called *The Prophet*, by a man named Kahlil Gibran. He was an artist, a poet, and an author, who was born in a little country called Lebanon in the late eighteen hundreds.

Robby tried to pronounce the author's name with little success. He looked at the unassuming cover and said, "Why are his books so small?"

"He was the type of man who made powerful statements using few words."

"It sounds like a good book," Robby said. He really didn't understand what Anna meant, but he pretended to.

"Maybe we can read it together tonight," Anna said, like we used to."

"That would be great, Anna," Robby said as he kissed her on the check.

Ruby hated to interrupt their moment, but she reminded Robby that he needed to get to school. She did not know what to think about Gibran, but she knew the love of a young boy and an old woman when she saw it.

The conversation between Jack and Marge during the drive time to the office usually consisted of client related subject matter. As Marge attempted to organize the day ahead in her mind, Jack gave a detailed account of the time spent with the boys. His usual complaints about the traffic and the judicial bullies he had to face all took a backseat to the prior evening's events. Though Marge was pleased that Jack had found new playmates, he was interfering with her concentration. Life and work issues were coming at Marge like a whirlwind. It was extremely important for her to succeed in both areas. She knew they would never have a home life that would resemble the stereotypical household, but a home that fostered happiness would be a job well done.

❧ ❧ ❧ ❧

When Anna entered the kitchen, she noticed the book from the Department of Motor Vehicles on the table. "Have you been studying for the written test?" she said

"Yes, whenever I have some free time," Ruby said.

"Well, are you going to tell me how you're doing with it?" Anna asked, interested in how her friend was doing.

"You sure are a nosey old woman! I am doing well with the studies and have taken the practice test in the back of the book several times. The last time I took it, I only missed one question."

"I feel good this morning," Anna said, "and would appreciate it if you took me for a drive."

Ruby tried to hide her enthusiasm, but she couldn't. "Once I finish the breakfast dishes, I reckon I can chauffer you around."

While Ruby cleaned up the kitchen, Anna went up to her room to pull her hair back. She placed a brightly colored floral scarf over her head and tied it in a loose knot beneath her chin. After retrieving a light jacket from the closet, she picked up her handbag and rode the chairlift downstairs. Ruby had done the kitchen chores in record time and was patiently waiting at the bottom of the steps. She was wearing her signature scrubs, a black jacket that had seen better days, and orthopedic shoes. The unlikely pair ventured out into the cool, but sunny, fall morning to embark upon their drive.

Much like two young girls out for an after-school drive in the family car, Ruby and Anna motored their way around the neighborhood. Laughter filled the car as they chatted about the upcoming wedding. When Ruby felt comfortable behind the wheel, Anna suggested they explore the main roads, saying, "Ruby, I want you to drive us to the Department of Motor Vehicles."

With a surprised look in her eyes, Ruby said, "Miss Anna, I don't think this old girl is ready to take the test yet. Maybe if I practice for a few more days I can pass."

"Nonsense, Ruby. We are going down right now, and you are going to pass with flying colors!"

Under protest, Ruby drove to the testing center as ordered.

The people waiting in line at the DMV were mostly teenagers and several middle-aged women. Ruby could hear chuckling from some of the immature teens, but all it did was strengthen her determination to succeed.

A woman sat down next to Anna with a proud smile on her face. "My little girl is about to get her license. Are you here with your granddaughter?"

"No, I'm here with my nurse, and she is about to get *her* license," Anna said, smiling proudly.

When Ruby finally made it to the end of the line, the woman working at the window reviewed her learner's permit and sent her to a booth to take the written part of the test. As Ruby picked up the paperwork and turned to walk away, the woman said, "You go, girl!" While Ruby worked diligently at answering the questions on the monitor, Anna looked on as nervous parents sat with their fingers crossed. Witnessing the smiles of the young victors and the occasional tears of the temporarily sidelined youngsters reminded Anna she was eighty-four years old. Everything seemed different when she took her driver's test so many years ago, but she still felt the same excitement and anticipation in the air.

Anna's thoughts of the past quickly dissolved when she saw Ruby coming toward her with excitement in her eyes. Before Anna could say a word, Ruby blurted out, "I passed and answered every question correctly! I need the paperwork for the car so I can take the driving part of the test!"

"Everything you need is in the glove compartment," Anna said, grinning ear to ear. "Now relax and go get that driver's license!"

Ruby walked briskly out the door to wait for the instructor to meet her in the car.

Anna's damaged heart had no problem finding room in it for the pride she felt for her beloved caretaker. Twenty minutes or so passed before she saw Ruby walk back through the doors. When she immediately got back in line, Anna tried, unsuccessfully, to read her body language. She watched as Ruby approached the window, and then saw the same woman who had wished her luck award Ruby with a driver's license.

Ruby ran toward Anna waving the all-important piece of paper in the air. Hugging Anna tightly, she cried, "This old girl thanks you from the bottom of her heart!"

As they drove out of the parking lot, Anna said, "Let's go somewhere special for lunch to celebrate, and it will be my treat."

"Thank you, Miss Anna, but this celebration lunch will be on me."

They decided on a small rib and seafood joint called Leroy's Eatery. Ruby told Anna that she used to take her boys there to eat on very special occasions. It wasn't much to look at, but it more than made up for it in the quality of the food.

Situated on the outskirts of the Strip District, the restaurant was an aging wood frame structure that had definitely seen better days. Feeling adventuresome, Anna went into the lunch date with an open mind. Ruby was well aware of the fact that Anna had never been to a place like Leroy's before. It gave her a great deal of satisfaction to introduce Anna to a new and exciting experience.

Ruby pushed open the heavy wooden doors with porthole style windows and entered the restaurant. A middle-aged black server wearing bib overalls whizzed by them carrying a large tray with two plates of steaming ribs, a pile of greens, and a stack of potato planks. Also on the tray were two frosty mugs of beer. A younger woman wearing the same attire appeared clutching two laminated menus in her hand. "Follow me, ladies; someone will be with you directly."

As Anna looked around the restaurant, she could not believe the diversity of the clientele. Small groups of men wearing suits were scattered among people who were obviously from the neighborhood. The nautical décor consisted of thick plank tables with captain's chairs and various brass ship components mounted on the walls.

Anna and Ruby placed their orders and talked about Ruby's big day. Ruby gave a detailed description of the testing experience at the DMV, and confessed that she was afraid of failing when Anna first suggested she take the test without warning. She remained nervous while waiting in line for her turn, but when the woman working at the window gave her words of encouragement, she started to believe that she had a chance to succeed.

As Ruby sat back against the chair and let out a sigh of relief, Anna said, "There was never a doubt in my mind that you would pass. I might be old and sick, but I know how hard you worked for this."

"What you don't know is that the man who gave me the driving test seemed like an old redneck! I was sure he hated black people and would fail me to eliminate one more of us from driving in the city. When he asked me if the Mercedes was mine, I was sure he would fail me."

Anna wasn't sure how to reply, but said, "The important thing is you passed."

Leroy's Eatery was famous for one thing: its finger-licking good ribs, and Leroy's special sauce made them that much sweeter—and messier! The women thoroughly enjoyed their rib-fest lunch, and they used every extra napkin the server provided. When they'd had their fill, Ruby settled the bill, and the two ladies were back on the road again.

The days that followed were busy with matters of the upcoming wedding. Anna performed checks and double checks of every minor detail while sending Ruby on errands in the car. When Ruby saw signs of fatigue in Anna, she would immediately put a stop to her efforts and prescribe rest. Marge handled the arrangements on her end with the same eye for detail that Anna employed. As the big day drew nearer, an evening of introductions and conversation was set up with Pastor Charles at Anna's home. Marge and Jack would announce their commitment to one another, followed by cake and refreshments. Normally, the pastor would have gotten to know them much sooner, but he made allowances because of the extenuating circumstances. Ruby had served the church well and, because of that, he held her in high esteem. Among parishioners, it was common knowledge that Pastor Charles was partial to lemon slice cake. The night before the gathering, Robby hovered around the kitchen as Ruby baked the cake from scratch. Helping her in any way he could, she rewarded him with exclusive rights to the sweet remains in the icing bowl. Ruby assured Robby that he would get a slice of cake the following evening.

Ruby wanted the wedding to go smoothly for Anna's benefit. Excess stress could steal some of the precious days she had remaining. Even though Ruby helped with the preparations for the wedding, her true allegiance was to Anna.

Anna came downstairs carrying the notepad she always seemed to have in her possession. Looking at Ruby she said, "Can you hear it, Ruby?"

Puzzled by the question, Ruby said, "Can I hear what, Miss Anna?"

"The excitement coming from the old house," Anna said, smiling.

"All I hear is the house asking for more chores to be done!"

Ruby was up early on the morning of Pastor Charles' visit to the house. She had polished all the furniture in the living areas and had washed the good china. Crisp white linen napkins and everything needed for a fine tea party were in place.

"I always wondered what people were talking about when they said casual," Anna said as she entered the room.

"I thought it was high time some of this fancy glassware got some use," Ruby said.

"I couldn't agree with you more. I hope Pastor Charles knows how fortunate he is to have you in his flock."

Over tea and coffee, Ruby told Anna about the important role Pastor Charles had played in her life over the years. "Where I come from, the church is much more than a fancy building where folks throw a dollar in the basket and mumble a few prayers. Most of the members of our small congregation are just a paycheck away from the poorhouse. The simple little church is the center of our lives, and the pastor is the guiding force. When we hold a bake sale, it is to raise money to buy groceries for a family who has none." Ruby paused for a moment and then continued. "Miss Anna, I hope the good Lord never lets me forget who gave me school clothes for my boys when they were young. That's the kind of stock Pastor Charles is made of."

Even though Anna considered Ruby a valued friend and companion, there was much about her that remained a mystery. Touched by Ruby's testimony, she said, "Let me help you get ready for tonight."

"Maybe you can sit for a spell to keep me company," Ruby said, concerned about her friend.

Robby dropped his backpack on the floor and headed straight for the kitchen for a snack. On the way, he stopped in the dining room to marvel at the majesty of the perfectly set table, but the sweet aroma of the lemon slice cake filled the air. As he rummaged through the kitchen cabinets in search of a something to eat, Ruby came downstairs after administering Anna's oxygen treatment.

"Don't even think of touching that cake, young man! There will be plenty to go around when the company gets here."

"Why is your friend coming over tonight … the one you baked the cake for?"

"Pastor Charles is my friend, but more important, he is my spiritual advisor," Anna said as she fixed Robby a peanut butter and jelly sandwich. "Tonight's gathering is his way of meeting Marge and Jack before the wedding ceremony."

"Will Marge and Jack be like my parents when they get married?" Robby said with a mouthful of sandwich.

Ruby reminded Robby not to eat with food in his mouth, and then she put her arm around his shoulder. "Folks don't get to pick their parents, but sometimes people who care step in to pick up where birth parents left off."

Robby was still a little confused about the situation, but Ruby made him feel more comfortable with her explanation.

Immediately after dinner, Marge began barking out orders to Jack and Joel, insisting that they both wear a sport coat and tie to Anna's. Jack objected, assuming the meeting with the pastor was a casual meeting, but Marge was quick to let him know just how important this evening was, and she expected him to do as she asked. Joel found the whole thing funny, but since Jack got into trouble for protesting the required attire, he thought it best to keep his complaints to himself. For her part, Marge wore a conservative dress and less than usual makeup.

The dressing dance was much less dramatic at the Wilson house. Ruby made it a point to lay out Robby's entire outfit. Everything from socks to black tie awaited him on the bed. Remembering how young boys liked to complain, she beat him to the punch by assuring him he could take off the coat and tie after the pastor arrived.

Anna understood the importance of the evening to her friend, so she did all she could to comply. She wore a dark gray dress, complemented with a string of white pearls, and simple black leather pumps. She wore her long silver hair pulled back. After a light dusting of face powder and a light spray of Subtle Rose perfume, she was ready for the evening.

Ruby was the last to get dressed for the evening. She put a slight curl in her hair. She rarely wore makeup of any kind, but on this occasion, she highlighted her large brown eyes. The tops of her feet bulged because the old black shoes she wore were a half size too small. She struggled pulling the conservative black dress over her large frame, but eventually succeeded. When she looked in the mirror, she shook her head and laughed about the size of her bottom.

As Ruby hurried down the stairs to answer the door, her thick midsection jiggled in the confines of her tight dress. She greeted Jack, Marge, and Joel, and escorted them into the sitting room while they waited for the pastor. The boys went up to Robby's room to play while the adults discussed the wedding.

The sound of an old Ford Falcon with a broken muffler alerted Ruby that Pastor Charles had arrived. The pastor, in his early sixties, was a rather large man, with silver hair. He was dressed in black, with a large cross hanging around his neck. As he entered the foyer, he embraced Ruby.

"Bless you, Sister Ruby."

The first thing Anna noticed about the clergyman was how kind his features were. He had the gentlest eyes she had ever seen, and his overall demeanor was reassuring. When he walked into the sitting room and introduced himself, it was obvious to Anna that the man of God knew how to work a room.

Jack was more than a little surprised by the fact that Pastor Charles was a black man.

Ruby disappeared into the kitchen to brew the coffee and put the water on for tea. Next, she placed the cake on the kitchen countertop. Anna popped in to see if she could be of help, but Ruby, who commanded the kitchen with the ease of a dancer, assured her that she had everything under control.

There was no seating arrangement at the dining room table, but Pastor Charles requested that Jack and Marge sit on either side of him. Robby and Joel knew their places because of the glasses of milk waiting for them. The adults had coffee, except for Anna, who had her usual cup of tea. As everyone settled in their seats, Ruby sliced up nice-sized pieces of her famous lemon slice cake for each of them.

The sound of small feet racing down the steps signaled that the youngsters knew it was time for a scrumptious slice of cake. As soon as they spotted the two ice-cold glasses of milk, they knew exactly where to sit. The sweet aroma of lemon danced in the air as Ruby portioned it out. Pastor Charles turned to Marge and said, "I would never admit this to the other ladies in the congregation, but Sister Ruby makes the tastiest cake this old boy has ever had."

As Ruby placed a generous slice of cake in front of Robby and Joel, Robby instinctively reached for his fork. Before it could touch the plate, Ruby sent a serious look in his direction, and said, "Don't either one of you touch that cake until we say the blessing!"

Robby was not accustomed to saying prayers over meals, but he set his fork down and sunk back in his chair a bit.

Pastor Charles crossed his large black hands over the table and began to pray, "Lord, I petition you on this very special day to fill our hearts with wisdom, understanding, and most all, love. I pray that the young and old alike in this room accept you into their hearts. I give you all the praise and all the glory, in Jesus Christ's name. Amen."

The moment the good pastor's fork touched the lemon cake, everyone else followed suit.

After taking several bites of cake and a sip of coffee, Pastor Brown turned to Marge and Jack. "So, why do you two young people want to join in holy matrimony?"

The couple hesitated at first, but then Marge said, "I could say that Jack is a great influence on my son, Joel. I could also say he treats my son and me with the respect we deserve. The truth is, I love him for his good qualities and even more for his faults."

"Joining with this woman is everything in life to me," Jack said, looking into Marge's eyes. "When I look into her emerald eyes, I lose all sense of reality and think I will never find my way back. I love this woman more than anyone else in the world and want to spend the rest of my life with her."

Everyone, including the boys, listened intently as Jack spoke.

"Did you two plan that ahead of time?" Pastor Charles asked, impressed by the couple's sincerity.

"No, we couldn't make up anything that good," Jack and Marge said in unison.

"Forgive my sense of humor; I was just fooling with you," Pastor Charles said, laughing heartily. "I say that to all the couples I work with. About fifteen years ago, I sat around a kitchen table in Wilkinsburg with another young couple and three of their parents. They, too, were embarking on the same adventure—matrimony—and they were as jittery as two scared rabbits! When I asked why they wanted to get married, they responded in much the same way you did. As I did with you, I asked them if they planned their response ahead of time. The bride-to-be was cool as a cucumber when she said 'no,' but the young man was sweating, and as he pointed at his fiancée, he said, 'She made me do it, Pastor! She told me what to say if you asked.' I'm happy to report that they are still married, and she continues to be the driving force in the relationship."

They all got a good chuckle out of the pastor's story, and it seemed to break the tension. Ruby cleared the plates from the table and brought out a fresh pot of coffee, while Robby and Joel scurried upstairs to play. Marge stopped the boys about halfway up the steps and told them they could take off their ties and jackets now.

"This is not an interview," Pastor Charles interjected. "I knew I was going to perform the ceremony before I met you. Sister Ruby thinks very highly of all of you, especially Miss Anna, and that is good enough for me. This will be a simple ceremony, but I need to go over a few details with you. And, Ruby, if there is an extra slice of that heavenly cake, I'll be more than happy to take it off your hands."

"I already wrapped it up for you in the kitchen," Ruby said, a little embarrassed by the pastor's flattery.

Anna was not a hundred percent sure, but she thought she noticed some romantic undertones between Ruby and the good pastor.

After Pastor Charles determined that Marge and Jack had their marriage license and wedding rings, he shared an amusing tale about a couple whose best man lost the bride's ring. As the wedding party was in an uproar, a guest who had been a widow for over five years decided it was time to enter the dating community again, so she slipped off her wedding band and gave it to the best man, and the ceremony went on as planned. The story had a happy ending for the widow, too, as she remarried a member of the congregation two years later.

At this point, Jack was secretly hoping that Pastor Charles was not going to tell a story concerning every detail of the wedding. As far as Marge was concerned, the pastor could tell tales all evening long. She was excited about the wedding and spending the rest of her life with Jack. Fortunately, at least for Jack, the pastor was ready to get down to business. He verified all the members participating in the wedding and what part they played in the ceremony.

Anna informed the pastor that the dining room would be cleared of furniture for the wedding and set back up for the reception by the caterers. The pastor pointed out to her that they would need a spot for Sister Williams to set up her portable organ to play the wedding music. In a subtle way, he added that it was customary to give her a little something for her trouble.

When everyone returned to the sitting room, Pastor Charles found himself intrigued by the fine quality of

Anna's home. "Miss Anna, would mind giving me a tour of your beautiful home?"

"I'm not one to shy away from an opportunity to show off the old house," Anna said, surprised by the request.

As the pastor offered his arm to Anna for assistance, she smiled and placed her small wrinkled hand over his forearm. As they made their way through all the rooms on the first floor, memories of her father came to the forefront of her mind. She pointed at the fine woodwork and explained that her father had employed the best woodworkers when constructing the house. The pastor was equally as impressed with the second floor. He commented that Anna must have had a happy childhood in such a home.

"Yes, this was a happy home when I was a young girl."

As they continued down the hall, the sound of the boys laughing caught the pastor's attention. He lifted his hand to knock at the door, but looked at Anna and said, "Do you mind?"

"Of course not," she said, smiling.

Hearing the knock at the door, Robby said, "Come in."

The pastor smiled when he saw the trucks and comic books spread out over the bed. "Whoever said that youth is wasted on the young must have forgotten how much fun it was to be young!" he said, smiling at Anna.

Pastor Charles cleared a spot on the bed and sat down in front of the boys. He engaged them in a story about growing up in his home state of Georgia. At a young age, his grandmother took him and his cousin Raymond in as her own. "The house we were raised up in could fit on the first floor here, with room to spare!" the pastor said, chuckling. "Ray and I became closer than brothers could ever be. We loved everything about Granny's house. I can still remember the sweet smells dancing in the air when she was baking a mess of pies." Lost in the memory, he sat there quietly for a few long moments. Smiling larger than ever, he reached out for the boys' hands and said, "Embrace these times, young princes, for the Lord has very special plans for you."

Curious, Joel said, "Pastor, what special plans?"

The pastor placed his large hands on top of both boys' heads and said, "If you follow the path of truth, the Lord will let you know."

It was clear to Anna that she and the pastor came from very different worlds.

"Did you enjoy the tour of the house, Pastor Charles?" Ruby asked and he and Anna joined the others again.

"Your description of this elegant home was very accurate. I might add that your description of the lovely people involved in this glorious event was also accurate."

The group of friends continued their small talk for a short time longer, but the pastor finally said, "The hour is getting late for this old boy. God willing, I will see you folks on Saturday for the holy union."

Marge cut an extra slice of cake for the pastor and accompanied him to his car.

After hugging Anna and thanking her for such a lovely evening, Marge went upstairs to tell Joel it was time to leave. Everyone gathered in the sitting room for a few more minutes before heading out the door.

Anna took Jack by the arm and said, "Before you go, I need to borrow my attorney for just a few minutes."

Jack followed Anna into the kitchen with a puzzled look on his face.

"Jack, I want you to make a slight change to my will."

"Sure, but we can do that any time."

"Jack, time isn't exactly my ally these days."

Realizing how important this was to Anna, he said, "What would you like me to do?"

"Ruby recently got her driver's license, and I wish to leave my Mercedes Benz and two hundred fifty thousand dollars to her."

Jack assured her it would be done first thing in the morning.

As he turned to walk out of the kitchen, Anna said, "One more thing, Jack. I want you and Marge to consider keeping Ruby on for a while after I'm gone. The decision is yours, but she would be a big help with the house and the boys."

"You're full of surprises tonight, Anna," Jack said, laughing.

Anna just smiled and wished her friends a good night.

As soon as the front door closed, Robby beat Ruby to the punch and said, "I know, I know; it's time for me to go to bed."

While Robby slow stepped it up the stairs, Anna helped Ruby straighten up the first floor.

"I think everything went pretty good," Ruby said.

"Yes, the get-together went very well, Ruby, and your Pastor Charles was a big hit. He seems to have a high opinion of you, and he *definitely* loves your cake!"

Anna's observation brought a huge smile to Ruby's face. "I can still remember when my boys' daddy left us in this city with close to nothing to live on. A much younger Pastor Charles embraced us in his congregation without hesitation." She paused for a moment, then added, "Without his support and that of the congregation, my sons and I might have much different lives."

"Thank you for making me realize that we are all very blessed in this house," Anna said, taking hold of Ruby's arm.

Jack was uncharacteristically quiet on the drive back to the apartment. At first, Joel went on about the good time he had playing with Robby's toys, and then he talked about the nice elementary school he would be attending when they moved in together. Marge was encouraged by the excitement she heard in Joel's voice. With all the major changes unfolding in their lives, the emotional well-being of her young son was one of her biggest concerns. When Joel finished talking, Marge shifted the conversation to the evening with Pastor Charles. She was obviously a fan of his, as she went on and on about the various stories he shared, but she realized that Jack was not himself and tried to engage him in the conversation. Jack let Marge know that Anna had given him more to think about, and he would discuss it with her when they got home.

After Ruby helped Anna prepare for bed, she set her up with her oxygen treatment, and then went into her bedroom and changed into her favorite flannel nightgown. Spending time with the pastor outside the church reminded her that neither one of them were getting any younger. More important, it showed her that they remained on the same path for the

Lord. As a young clergyman from Georgia, Pastor Charles had worldly visions of a radio ministry reaching out to tens of thousands of people. Their journey from the Deep South to the bright lights of Pittsburgh may have been different, but the road delivered them to the same place.

As Marge crawled into bed beside Jack, she couldn't wait to hear what he had to say about his conversation with Anna. "Tell me what's going on, Jack. I've never known you to be as quiet as you were on the ride home from Anna's."

"Do you realize Anna's house will be ours in a short time?" he said. "With running the law firm and the added responsibilities of raising two boys, we will have our plates full."

"If you think I'm going to quit working to become Susie Homemaker, you're wrong, mister," Marge said, confused by what Jack seemed to be implying.

By this time, the couple was wide awake and sitting up in bed.

"Red, one role I could never see you in is Susie Homemaker. Besides, our law firm is as much your dream as mine. Tonight, Anna and I discussed a couple things, one of them being that she wants us to consider keeping Ruby on when she is gone. She could help run the house and would be a positive influence on the boys."

"That's a great idea!" Marge said without hesitation. "I'll go over and talk to her about it. "Now, let's get some sleep, Jack; we have a busy day ahead of us tomorrow."

❧ ☙ ❧ ☙

As Ruby handed Anna her evening medication, she said, "Can I ask you a personal question, Ruby?"

"Sure, Miss Anna. "If I don't like it, I won't answer it."

Anna laughed at her friend's humor. "Why haven't you and Pastor Charles ever become a couple? It's obvious that the two of you have a connection."

Ruby sat next to Anna on the bed, her eyes a bit distant. "There was a time when this old girl wanted exactly that, but when I realized he was already married to the Church, that dream fell away. Besides, whether he was married to me or not, half the women in the congregation would still be trying to bed him. Coming to blows with those sinners would not look good for the pastor's wife. We will always be dear friends, but I'm afraid that's as far as it will go."

"Then what will become of you when I'm gone?"

"What are you up to, Miss Anna?"

"I want you to consider staying on to run the house and take care of the boys when I'm gone."

"It seems to me that Marge and Jack might have a say in that."

"Give it some thought, because they just might ask you."

The following morning started as a typical day for Ruby. She sat in the kitchen having her first cup of coffee while waiting for Anna's tea water to whistle on the stove, and went over her list of errands to run while Robby was at school. She enjoyed the freedom that having her driver's license brought her. Anna's request that she stay on after her death was weighing heavy on her mind. While she loved the work she did in caring for those in hospice, nearing the end of their lives, it can take its toll on a person emotionally, and taking care of Anna's friends might be a nice change.

It was only two more days until the wedding. Ruby had put her thoughts about staying on aside for now, as she and Anna had to take care of last-minute details in the city, including picking up the wedding dresses. They decided that Marge, Jack, and Joel would get ready at Anna's on the morning of the big day. They learned from Jack that Stan Logan had already picked up his tuxedo, and now they were on the way to pick up the boys' suits.

"When we are finished here, would you mind driving over to Jack's office? Anna said. "It has been a long time since I have seen it, and I would like to have a word with Marge."

Ruby was more than happy to drive Anna wherever she wanted to go.

As Ruby and Anna entered the lobby of the building where Jack's offices were located, Ruby said, "You didn't tell me we had to take an elevator. I don't like elevators, never did."

"Ruby, this is Pittsburgh. Almost every building has more than one floor. How did you get around when you worked in the hospital?"

"I didn't say I never used them. I just don't think they are safe."

"Well, I'm going to take my chances," Anna said, grinning.

Ruby had no choice but to follow Anna into the elevator, but, clearly, she wasn't happy about it.

As they got off on the fourth floor, a gold and black sign reading Jack Porter Law Offices greeted them. Ruby had never been here before, and this was only Anna's second visit since she financed its birth.

As they waited in the well-appointed reception area for Marge, Ruby leaned in closer to Anna and whispered, "Why do I think you were responsible for this fancy office?"

"They did all the work; I merely assisted them with the resources to make it happen," Anna shared. "If it wasn't for Jack's hard work and skills as an attorney, I would have never been able to have Robby in my life."

"Miss Anna, you are not one of those people that try to take it with you when you die."

"That's where you're wrong, Ruby," Anna whispered back. "I'm taking it with me the only way I know how."

"Why didn't you tell me you were coming!" Marge said excitedly as she greeted her friends.

"We were in the city and thought it would be nice to stop in. Ruby's never been here before, and I thought she might enjoy seeing what you and Jack have created."

As Marge led them back to her office, she said, "We both know you're the one that made all this possible."

Ruby looked around Marge's large office, astonished by the expensive furniture and the beautiful décor. "Is this office all yours?"

Laughing, Marge said, "That's the same thing I thought when I first saw it."

After the three women finished discussing the final details of the wedding, Marge asked Ruby if she could speak with her in private. Anna had a good idea of what it was about, so she excused herself and went next door to Jack's office while they talked.

Once they were alone, Marge got directly to the point. "The reason I wanted to talk to you was that I want to know if you would be interested in staying on after Anna's gone. As you can imagine, working in this office takes up a great deal of my time, and I do not plan to quit anytime soon. The boys will need structure in their lives, and I can't think of anyone better to give it to them. I'm sure we can come to terms on your salary and the conditions of your employment, but the truth of the matter is that I'd like you to be more like an extended family member instead of an employee."

Ruby was quiet for a few moments, letting Marge's words sink in, and then said, "I *knew* that old woman was up to something!"

Confused, Marge said, "What are you talking about?"

"She brought me down here today because she somehow knew you would ask me to stay."

"Does that mean you won't take the position?"

Placing her hand on Marge's, and looking intently into her eyes, Ruby said, "Of course I will, child. This old girl is tired of looking after folks who are dying. I was fixing to retire after Anna is gone, but looking after the boys will be a good way to end my career. Once the dust settles, you newlyweds will need to sit down with old Ruby so we can lay down the ground rules to the new household."

Marge wrapped her arms around Ruby in a heartfelt hug. "Thank you, Ruby. You have no idea how happy your decision makes me."

When Ruby and Anna got home from Jack's office, Ruby fussed at Anna to go upstairs immediately to do her oxygen treatment and get some rest. It had been a long day, and Anna was clearly fatigued. Once Ruby gave Anna her medication and made sure she was following her orders, she returned to the car to bring in the outfits for the wedding. She smiled when she hung Robby and Joel's pint-sized tuxedos in Robby's bedroom. Needing a little pick-me-up, Ruby then went into the kitchen and made herself a strong cup of coffee. Taking a short nap came to mind, but she decided against it when she looked at the clock. She had several chores to do, and it was nearly time to start dinner. Sipping the rejuvenating mug of coffee, Ruby recalled the day Anna asked her to tend to her at home. Even though Anna had just gotten devastating news from her doctor, she still displayed an impressive amount of grace and confidence. Ruby smiled at her friend's subtle but effective way of getting exactly what she wanted from people.

Robby came in the front door to the sound of Ruby chopping onions on the wooden cutting board and to the aroma of something good cooking in the oven. Steam was billowing from the pot of potatoes tumbling around in the boiling water. Hungry, Robby said, "What's for supper, Ruby?"

"We are having pork roast and mashed potatoes," Ruby said as she continued chopping vegetables. "I won't be done fixing dinner for a couple hours, so if you want a snack to hold you over, you can have a couple peanut butter cookies and a glass of milk."

Robby immediately dropped his backpack to the floor, sat down at the kitchen table, and patiently waited for Ruby to fix his snack.

While chewing the last of his cookie, Robby said, "How's Anna doing?"

"Don't talk until that mouth of yours is empty," Anna scolded. "Anna is tired right now and resting upstairs."

Concerned, Robby said, "Will we know when Anna is going to die?"

Ruby was surprised by Robby's question and stopped what she was doing. She sat down in the chair next him and placed his small hand in hers. "I won't talk to you like you're a little boy, because you're not. Your young eyes have seen more than most, and I'll show you the respect you deserve. It seems like I have been tending to sick folks for most of my life, and death has been a big part of that. Old Ruby has seen folks die a painful death, leaving this world kicking and screaming. Other patients lingered, dying a little bit each day. Then there are the blessed ones who accept death. They go into the next world softly, usually while they sleep. My experience tells me that Anna will be one to go out gentle like."

Ruby assumed that Robby was satisfied with her answer because he indicated that he wanted to head upstairs to change into his play clothes. She had something she wanted to tell him, though. "Can you keep a really big secret?" she asked.

"I'm real good at keeping secrets!" Robby exclaimed.

"Today, Marge asked me to stay on here after Anna is gone. Old Ruby gave it a lot of thought and decided she'd better stick around to keep your little butt out of trouble."

Robby was thrilled with the news and tried, unsuccessfully, to place his small arms around Ruby's waist. Touched by his gesture, Ruby rested her hands on Robby's back as a single tear rolled down her cheek.

Not one to get overly emotional, Ruby quickly wiped her tears and then guided Robby out of the kitchen, saying, "Now, you get on upstairs to change your clothes and get that homework done."

Anna was resting quietly in her room when Ruby opened the door to look in on her.

"I fixed pork roast and mashed potatoes for dinner," Ruby said. "Robby is chomping at the bit to eat, so you better come down."

"Thank you, Ruby, I'll be down in a few minutes."

As Ruby started out of the bedroom, she turned to Anna and said, "I almost forgot to tell you. When Marge and I talked today at the office, I agreed to stay on with the boys. She's got enough smarts to know that she can't look after the boys and work without help."

"That's good news, Ruby. It had completely slipped my mind."

Ruby snickered. "Old woman, nothing slips your mind."

The day before the big event found Marge juggling the duties of her job along with the details of the wedding. Mary, Marge's assistant, was not sure if her boss was more nervous about the wedding or being out of the office for several days. Regardless, Mary listened patiently as her Marge micromanaged each of the days she would be away. Finally, Mary couldn't take it anymore.

"Marge!"

"Did I forget something?" Marge asked, looking frazzled.

"Quit worrying," Mary said, trying to calm her boss. "I will handle every situation exactly the way you trained me."

"I'm sorry, I know you will do just fine," Marge said, hugging Mary.

Jack loosened his tie and kicked back in his chair. It was no accident that he avoided contact with his bride-to-be. He was aware of how wired up she would be, and he did not want to be the focal point of her well-meaning wrath. He smiled to himself as Marge barged into his office to check on the progress he had made on the minimal list of things he had to accomplish before day's end. He immediately took his feet off the desk and assumed a professional posture.

"How's it going Red?" he said, looking a bit mischievous.

"I'll let you know in a few minutes," Marge said, glancing at the notepad she was holding. "Did you find someone to cover for you in court for the cases you couldn't postpone?"

"Yes. I arranged for one of Stan Logan's attorneys to handle things."

"Did you go over everything with your paralegal?" she said, going down the list.

Jack started to say "yes," but changed his mind when he saw Kathy standing outside his door. "There's Kathy now. I was just getting ready to meet with her."

Jack asked his paralegal to give them a minute alone. He put his arms around his bride-to-be and kissed her on the cheek. "I love you, Red. Tomorrow at this time we will be husband and wife. We have so many wonderful things to look forward to together."

"I know I'm being a real pain in the ass," Marge said, with tears rolling down her cheeks, "but I want everything to be perfect."

"Babe, everything is already perfect."

All the members in the Wilson household were awake early Saturday morning. Anna had hired a local moving company to move some of the furniture on the first floor into storage for the day. Once the furniture was loaded in the truck, the movers set up thirty folding chairs in the dining room. As of the prior day, twenty- three people sent RSVPs, and more were expected. Ruby walked around with a cup of coffee in her hand, keeping a close eye on the men working in the house, to make sure they did not damage anything. Robby sat on the steps trying not to miss any of the action.

Anna sat calmly at the kitchen table enjoying her first cup of tea of the day.

Once all the commotion was over, Ruby joined Anna in the kitchen. "Miss Anna, you got to keep a close eye on those workmen while they are in the house."

"They seemed like nice young men to me."

"Yeah, but they will rob you blind if you don't watch them."

Robby interrupted Ruby and Anna when he came bounding into the kitchen declaring that he was starving, so Ruby fixed him some scrambled eggs and toast.

"Why don't you have some breakfast with the boy?" Ruby said to Anna.

Anna graciously declined, flipping open her notepad of information on the wedding.

As Ruby cracked the eggs into the hot iron skillet, Anna began reading aloud the schedule for the morning deliveries.

"When I called yesterday, the florist told me the flowers should be here around nine. The bakery promised the cake delivery by eleven, and the caterers will be here the same time. Two employees will remain here during the entire affair to set up tables and serve the food. Lastly, the photographer will arrive in time to have everything set up by noon."

"You forgot something, Miss Anna," Ruby said as she placed Robby's breakfast on the table.

"What did I forget?" Anna said, surprised that she forgot anything.

"You forgot to add that Miss Anna goes to her room to rest for an hour at ten thirty," Ruby said in a slight scolding tone. "Don't you worry, ma'am; Robert and I will handle anything that comes up while you're sleeping."

Anna shook her head and reluctantly agreed to Ruby's demands.

Marge took control of the situation at her apartment the moment she got out of bed. She brewed the coffee, set Joel's cereal on the table, and went into the bathroom to run a brush through her disheveled hair. Looking in the mirror, she said to herself, "I guess this it, Marge. It's too late to turn back now." When she finished in the bathroom, she went into Joel's room and whispered in his ear that it was time to get up, and then she went into the bedroom to give Jack a shake. When he finally mumbled, "Okay, okay, I'm up," she kissed him on the forehead and returned to the kitchen. As she walked by Joel's bedroom, she directed a stern warning in his direction: "Get your little butt out of bed!"

It was obvious to Marge that the sugar and caffeine were kicking in when Jack and Joel started fooling around. As she got up from the table with coffee mug in hand, she said, "You two figure out who is taking a shower first, but one of you better get in there soon!"

When Marge turned her back, Jack and Joel each pointed at one another to signal they were going first.

"I'll be in Joel's room packing a few things for him while we are away," Marge said.

"Mom," Joel began before she walked away," I still don't see why I can't go with you."

"I already explained this to you. Jack and I are getting married, and it's a special trip for the two of us."

A fluster of activity was going on in the Wilson household this day. Robby was guarding his post downstairs as directed by Ruby, while she was busy getting ready upstairs. Anna was in her room resting, per Nurse Ruby's orders. The bakery delivered the beautiful multi-tiered cake, and the caterer had arrived to set up for the ceremony.

Robby finished taking his shower in record time, as he did not want to miss any of the excitement going on downstairs. The sound of him running down the hallway toward his room alerted Anna that it was her turn to shower and fix her hair.

As Ruby was busy directing the caterers through the front door, the excitement in the air intensified when Jack and Marge arrived with Joel. It was only a matter of minutes before the women would be dressing in their beautiful wedding attire. Jack was in charge of making sure the boys got dressed in their tuxedos. By the time Anna made her way downstairs, everything was ready except for the photographer. The main cast of characters had all arrived for the joyous event about to take place.

Stan Logan and his wife, Katherine, arrived early to assist with any last-minute details. While Stan waited in the foyer for the arrival of Pastor Charles and the photographer, Jack ushered the boys upstairs to get dressed. Ruby brewed a pot of coffee for the Logan's, and then she joined Anna and Marge upstairs to finish dressing.

The photographer arrived first and quickly began setting up his equipment. Pastor Charles and the organist, Sister Williams, were the next to arrive. Sister Williams was a large woman, dressed in a dark blue dress with a bright colored floral design. Stan offered to assist her with carrying the portable organ, but it was obvious that she could handle the job herself.

As the guests began arriving, the excitement continued to build. Mary Thomas, Kathy Duncan, and Patrick Borne arrived together. They placed their beautifully wrapped gifts on the designated table located in the sitting room. Marge's sister, Trish, was the next to arrive, followed closely by Helen and Billy. On cue, the caterers, in their crisp white uniforms, began working their way through the crowd with a variety of tasty finger foods. Twenty guests in all were present for the glorious event.

Pastor Charles went upstairs to escort Marge and Joel to the sitting room to await the start of the ceremony. He gave her a soft hug and told her she looked breathtaking. He instructed Joel to come out with his mother when the wedding march started playing. The sound of Sister Williams playing spiritual tunes hung softly in the air as all the main characters emerged down the stairs. Sprays of brightly colored flowers accented the dining room, converted into a makeshift wedding chapel. The guests sat quietly in anticipation as bridesmaids Anna and Ruby, holding their lovely bouquets of colorful flowers, took their place in front of Pastor Charles. Jack smiled nervously as he stood next to the best man, as young Robby waited for the wedding march to begin. Jack asked Stan several times if he was sure he had the ring in his pocket. Laughing each time, Stan said, "Take a deep breath, friend. In a few minutes, you will be married to the most breathtaking woman in the room."

Pastor Charles pointed in Sister Williams' direction, and a quiet fell over the room. The moment they had all been patently waiting for was about to unfold. When the church organist placed her fingers on the keys, a spark of excitement ignited in everyone's heart.

Marge, dressed in an elegant satin gown, started slowly down the aisle, with Joel walking close beside her. All eyes remained fixed on the beautiful bride as she walked toward the pastor and her groom.

As Marge and Joel reached their places in front of Pastor Charles, Marge's eyes met with Jack's in an emotional moment. Pastor Charles directed the couple to stand next to each other, and got the ceremony underway.

"We are gathered here today to join this son and daughter of the Lord in holy matrimony. I'm pleased to join these two young people into the sacred bond of marriage." The pastor continued with his rendition of the marriage vows until he got to the part about exchanging rings.

As the couple faced each other, Pastor Charles asked Jack, "Do you take this woman as your lawfully wedded partner in life? In sickness and in health, until death do you part?"

Stan handed Jack the gold band, and reminded his friend to slide the ring onto Marge's finger.

Mesmerized for a moment, Jack finally said, "I do!"

As the Pastor repeated the vows to Marge, she motioned for Joel to hand over Jack's wedding band. Placing the ring on his finger, she said, "I do."

Pastor Charles raised his hands in the air and declared, "Praise the Lord! I now pronounce you husband and wife!"

He then granted Jack permission to kiss his new bride. Everyone clapped as the newlyweds exchanged their first married kiss before their friends and loved ones.

As the newly married couple was about to greet their guests with handshakes and embraces, Marge sought out Anna before all others.

"You are the most beautiful bride I've ever seen," Anna said as she embraced her dear friend.

"I love you, Anna," Marge said quietly as tears rolled down her cheeks.

The house was alive with guests mingling about, enjoying the celebration of love they had just witnessed. The caterers intermingled among the guests with beautifully embossed silver trays of champagne.

Anna thanked Sister Williams for her part in the ceremony and handed her an envelope for her services. She then turned her attention to her friend Ruby, who was enjoying a glass of champagne with a fellow member of her church. Without saying a word, Anna smiled and looked at the fluted glass. Ruby just laughed and said, "This old girl is not driving anywhere today, Miss Anna."

Marge worked the room, making sure she spent a little time with each one of the guests.

The caterers transformed the makeshift chapel into an elegant dining room, with tables covered with crisp white linen tablecloths and adorned with beautiful floral arrangements. The wedding party's table was just as beautiful, decorated with vases of roses. The wedding cake rested on a small table to the right of the wedding party, for all to see. Guests enjoyed a nonstop flow of hors d'oeuvres and wine.

Stan Logan stood up and tapped his glass with a spoon as he was about to propose a toast to the couple. He looked down at his wife, Katherine, and then raised his glass. "Jack, I hope you and Marge share the same happiness my bride and I have enjoyed for all these years." Everyone raised their glasses and cheered the happy couple.

Marge stood up next and waited patiently until the room was very quiet. She reached into a silver gift bag and pulled out the box containing Anna's gift. She removed the gold infinity necklace and placed it around Anna's neck. With tears in her eyes, she said, "This gift is a symbol of my never ending love for the woman I consider my mother." The two women enjoyed a long embrace. Next, Marge pulled out Stan Logan's gift. "What can we say besides 'thank you' to the man who played such a big part in my husband's professional career. I'm glad you are in our lives, and we hope you will continue to be for many years to come." He proudly held up the elegant Cartier gold pen set for everyone to see. Marge then took the small square box containing Ruby's gift out of the bag and held it gently against her chest. "This is a small token of our gratitude for everything Ruby has done for Anna and for helping to make our wedding possible." Ruby was beyond touched when she pulled the delicate gold keychain with an angel pendant out of the box.

Marge took a moment to sit down and let the guest interaction resume while the photographer moved about the room snapping photographs.

Jack refused to let his new wife steal all the thunder when it came to handing out the gifts. Earlier, he slipped the caterers a few extra bucks to set up the new bicycles they purchased for Robby and Joel. Just when he noticed the boys were feeling a little slighted, he signaled for the caterer to bring one of the shiny new bikes into the house. He stood up and tapped the glass of ginger ale he was drinking.

"Ladies and gentlemen," Jack said, getting everyone's attention. "It appears we forgot to give Joel and Robby their just reward for the important part they played in the wedding." Just then, the caterer wheeled in a shiny red Murray bicycle from Sears. "There is another one of these babies sitting in the driveway out back." The boys eagerly followed the man out to the driveway.

Anna was delighted to see the guests enjoying the wonderful meal the caterer had prepared. She sat next to Pastor Charles and handed him a thick envelope. He smiled graciously and placed the generous envelope with cash into his pocket. He thanked Anna, and she whispered in his ear, "Maybe you can put in a good word for me with your boss."

"You can count on it, Miss Anna," he said, winking playfully.

Anna had one more envelope to deliver, and that was to Mr. and Mrs. Jack Porter. As soon as she saw an opportunity to talk to them together, she handed Marge a plain white envelope. Marge gasped when she saw the gift from Anna: reservations for four days at one of the finest hotels in Martha's Vineyard, along with a stack of crisp one hundred dollars bills.

Anna walked quietly back to her chair and cherished the moment of showering happiness down on two people she loved.

Everyone involved in servicing the wedding, from the invitations to the caterers, performed as she had hoped. A peace came over her, knowing that Robby would be in

Marge and Jack's care. She hoped that having Joel as a step-brother would lend further stability to his life.

Ruby noticed that Anna looked exhausted and said, "Lets you and me go upstairs for a spell. Ruby will give you your medication and you can take some oxygen while you rest. We'll be back down here in no time."

"Ruby, old girl, you'll get no argument out of me."

Anna sat on the edge of the bed, listening to the people laughing and enjoying themselves below. Once she took her shoes off and lay back on the bed, she thought about how nice the satin dress felt against her skin. Ruby administered her medication and set up her oxygen before sitting down next to her on the bed. The two friends exchanged small talk and discussed how well everything went during the wedding.

Holding the infinity necklace Marge had given her, Anna said, with tears in her eyes, "There is not a better gift she could have bought me."

"Yes, ma'am, now I got my driver's license and a blessed keychain," Ruby said, taking the angel pendant from her pocket. Anna took hold of Ruby's hand and said, "I want you to go back downstairs and enjoy the festivities."

"I can stay up here with you, Miss Anna."

"No, if you stay up here, I'll never be able to take a nap." As her trusted friend and companion stood up to leave the room, Anna added, "Thank you for agreeing to stay on with Robby after I'm gone. That little boy loves you very much."

❧ ❧ ❧

Joel and Robby were chomping at the bit to ride their new bicycles, but they waited while Marge and Jack cut the cake, each feeding the other the first tasty slices. The guests clapped their congratulations for the happy couple.

Ruby caught the tail end of the cake cutting as she walked down the steps. A series of camera flashes captured the newlyweds locking lips for the crowd. Marge looked around the room, hoping to include Anna in the festivities, but when she couldn't find her, she approached Ruby to find out where she was. Ruby assured her that she was resting comfortably in her room and would rejoin the festivities a little later.

As Marge was putting Anna's cake in the refrigerator, she saw Ruby carrying a bulky trash bag out the back door with the car keys in her hand. Opening the door for her, Marge said, "Ruby, you don't have to take the trash out. The people from the catering service will take care of it."

"Ma'am, these are your envelopes and wedding gifts from the table in the sitting room."

"Are you playing a joke on me, Ruby?" Marge said, surprised.

"Old Ruby wouldn't joke about your wedding gifts. I'm locking them up in Anna's car until all these strangers are gone. These folks are probably all honest, but let's not take a chance."

The act of locking the gifts in the car seemed a little excessive to Marge, but she let Ruby do what she thought best.

Anna rested quietly on the bed admiring the beautiful ivory gown she was wearing. Her damaged heart had found more happiness than she had ever imagined possible in one magical day. She had the opportunity to see others' dreams come true and realized a dream of her own in the process. Robby's future was promising to move in the right direction with Jack and Marge taking on the role of his stepparents. Anna made sure the youngster would never need for anything material for the remainder of his life. If she had learned anything during her long life, it was that wealth alone was not the key to happiness.

Once Ruby returned from securing the gifts and envelopes in the Mercedes, she accompanied Pastor Charles and Sister Williams to his dilapidated old vehicle. She thanked them for their participation and assured the pair she would see them in church soon. As she made her way onto the front porch, noticing her reflection in the window brought a smile to her face. Seeing the beautiful ivory dress made her feel very special. It was the most elegant dress she had ever worn. Having the honor of participating in the wedding was a memory she would cherish for the rest of her life.

Anna removed the oxygen mask from her face, hoping to rejoin the festivities downstairs, but instead, she decided to rest a little longer, and lay back down and closed her eyes. She thought about the difficulties she and Robby had endured together, but those thoughts gave way to proud visions of how he would turn out as a man. She felt blessed for having crossed paths with so many good people, like Jack Porter, Marge, and Ruby, just to name a few. As her eyes grew heavy, Anna gave in to the gentle sleep that was calling her. Soon, deep sleep came and covered her like a warm blanket.

The guests began to filter out and extended their congratulations to the newlyweds as they departed. When most of the people were gone, Jack and Marge prepared to leave for Martha's Vineyard. Marge went up to Anna's bedroom to sit with her for a while before leaving on their honeymoon. As she entered her room, a tear rolled down her cheek when she saw that she was sound asleep, holding the infinity pendant tightly in her hand. She was going to let her sleep, but it was very important to her that she thank Anna for sending them on their honeymoon.

"Anna—" Marge said, softly. Wake up, Anna; we are going to be leaving soon."

When there was no response, Marge gently took hold of Anna's arm. She was cold to the touch. Even though she knew that Anna's time was near, she was in denial that it would actually happen. Instead of alerting Ruby right away, Marge sat close to Anna and stroked her hair while talking softly in her ear. A few minutes later, she went to the top of the steps and called Ruby's name. When Ruby reached the top of the stairs, the blank look on Marge's face told Ruby that Anna was with the Lord.

While Ruby was checking for a pulse, Marge said, "What do we do now?"

"Help me take this gown off Anna so that we can change her into her nightclothes," Ruby said softly. "Remove the necklace and put it somewhere safe," she added.

Confused by the requests, Marge started crying, and said, "Who cares about the damn dress or necklace!"

"Settle down, child," Ruby said as she took hold of Marge's hands. "If we send her in an ambulance, the necklace will disappear before she gets to the hospital and the gown will be cut up when they examine her. Now you be strong and help old Ruby out. The old girl would want to be buried in the dress and wearing the necklace you bought for her. We owe her at least that much."

chapter •••••••••••••
•••• twenty-four

Robby stayed close to Marge as they carried Anna's coffin to its final resting place. It was a pleasant surprise when nearly a hundred people showed up at the viewing at the old house. Anna's passing was giving way to the birth of a new generation in the stone house she held so dear.

Ruby thought the overcast day was appropriate for the occasion, and the light drizzle reminded her of the heavens weeping. She interpreted it as tears of loss for this world, but tears of joy for her taking her rightful place next to the Lord. Pastor Charles spoke at the viewing, emphasizing that Anna was the best example of humility he had ever encountered. His final words were, "Sister Anna gave much more than she ever received. Those of us whose lives she touched will carry her in our hearts for the rest of our lives. Her legacy for all those she loved would be that they pass the acts of kindness she so freely bestowed onto others."

A large wake would not have been Anna's style. Jack, Marge, Ruby, and the boys went back to the house for a quiet dinner. For reasons revealed later, Jack asked Stan Logan and his wife to join them. Afterward, they toasted Anna with wine and shared humorous stories about her life.

"I loved that old woman, but she was the only soul I've ever met who could play life like a damn fiddle," Ruby said, a little tipsy. "If that old girl wanted something to happen, it did, and it didn't take her many words to do it!"

"The day I met her, Jack and I were struggling on the outskirts of lawyers' row," Marge shared. "We were her last resort when it came to the custody case with Robby. At first, I thought she was a little crazy. After all, why would this old woman want to raise a ten-year-old child who was not even a relative? We took the case because we needed the money, but from that point on, our lives changed."

Jack and Stan Logan put their briefcases on the table and asked for everyone's attention. Before Stan spoke, Jack announced, "Reading the will on the same day as the wake is a little unorthodox, but this is what Anna requested. It was her wish that matters be disposed of quickly and we move forward with our lives."

"Jack requested that I serve as co-counsel in handling the Last Will and Testament of Anna Wilson," Stan said. "The reason behind this is to avoid any claims of impropriety, since Jack is one of the recipients of her estate. Of course, my services will be billed directly to Mr. Porter, now that he can afford it." Unfortunately, Stan's attempt to inject a bit of humor into the situation was lost because of the sadness weighing heavily on everyone's heart.

Anna's will was not a very complicated affair. She allocated six million dollars to Jack and Marge, along with the deed to the old house. The only stipulation on the transfer of ownership of the house was that it could not change hands until Robby left for college or reached the age of twenty-one. Stan noted that Anna had set up a trust for Robby, whereby he would receive seven million dollars when he reached the age of twenty-five. Jack would oversee the trust. The antique Cadillac would transfer ownership to Robby when he turned sixteen. Anna left her Mercedes Benz, along with two hundred fifty thousand dollars, to Ruby.

Ruby was speechless when Stan handed over the title and the keys to the car. Tears rolled down her cheeks as she held the gold angel keychain Marge had given her in the palm of her hand.

When Stan finished the reading of the will, everyone sat around the table in silence. The echo of Jack and Stan snapping their briefcases shut and placing them on the floor was the only sound they heard. After a few long minutes of reflection, Marge said, "I'll put a pot of coffee on."

Ruby got up from the table and followed Marge into the kitchen. As the hot water dripped into the filter, the two women embraced one another in tears, mourning the loss of their dear friend.

Robby waited until he and Joel went outside to play before he celebrated the gift of the old Cadillac.

While Stan and Jack waited for the coffee to finish brewing, Stan patted Jack on the back and said, "I'm sure you are relieved it's finally over."

"No, Stan, everything Anna put into motion is only just beginning."

WA